You have to think highly of this bush pilot, because he's dirty, he has a ratty airplane ... and he's alive.

-- John McPhee, *Coming Into the Country*

There's a land where the mountains are nameless,
And the rivers all run God knows where;
There are lives that are erring and aimless,
And deaths that just hang by a hair...

-- Robert Service, *Spell of the Yukon*

I've had nightmares like this. More than once. They all end the same way— with me jerking awake in a cold sweat, staring into the night for a long time before sleep comes again. I loved these mountains and these rocks. I just didn't want them to be my final resting place. Not yet anyhow.

-- Johnny Wainwright,
North To Disaster by Jim Craig

OTHER BOOKS BY JIM CRAIG

North to Disaster

Blue Ice Dying in the Rain

An Alaskan Novel

Jim Craig

Bushak Press
Seward, Alaska

Published by Bushak Press
P.O. Box 46, Seward, AK 99664
www.bushakpress.com

This is a work of fiction. Names, characters, places and incidents either are the product of the author's imagination or are used fictitiously, and any resemblance to actual persons, living or dead or events is entirely coincidental. Specifically, Taroka Island is a fictitious place.

Cover design by Cal Sharp, Caligraphics, www.caligraphics.net

ISBN13: 978-0-9617112-3-8
ISBN-10: 0-96171123X
Library of Congress Control Number: 2013906021

If you've ever wanted something (or someone) way more than was good for you, this book is dedicated to you...

CHAPTER
1

They say there's a million ways to make a living. For me there's only one. I fly airplanes. Small airplanes in remote Alaska. Sometimes I even get paid. It isn't much of a living but I get by. Man and machine battling the elements in the final frontier. It's the only life I want to live.

My name's Johnny Wainwright. I'm a bush pilot repo man. When the wind's howling and I'm flying low and almost sideways over white capped freezing water, I curse my fate and wonder why I'm here. But when I'm soaring through a green spruce valley with the sun sparkling off snow topped jagged peaks above me, I know I couldn't do anything else. What can I say? I'm an Alaskan pilot.

It's a job full of dreams and freedom. And there's danger too. Even on a beautiful calm day on a routine flight, a life and death struggle can spring out of nowhere, but most days it's just a job. That's why I carry a phone. Customers.

What makes a damn cell phone ring anyhow? Don't bore me with the science. It's the timing I'm curious about. Some say it's fate, but I don't know. Maybe it is. Maybe it isn't. Even a no account bush pilot can wonder about the forces and events that start the dominos falling.

A few minutes before my phone rang that day in early September, life was normal in Seward, Alaska. If I'd known what that call would bring, I would have flung the damn thing in the ocean.

The late afternoon sun glowed on the lingering snow slopes of Mount Alice. On the edge of town a short walk from where I sat a frigid stream spilled down a cliff draining the high ice and snow above the bay like it has for thousands of years. With a relentless power, the water pounds its way to the sea.

Nothing fateful about that, I guess. Just freeze and melt, freeze and melt in endless repetition. Blame it on the sun if you need something to blame. And gravity too, but that's not fate. That's just the way it is.

I was sitting in the Yukon Bar pondering the meaning of life. I was away from the beer taps where I could see out the front window overlooking Fourth Avenue. A few tourists wandered by enjoying the sunshine. Some glanced up at me through the glass while they took in the sights. I suppose I'm part of the local color. Right where you want to find your resident bush pilot. Lurking in a corner of the Yukon Bar nursing a bad attitude and a bad memory named Brandy. Not the booze, the woman.

I'm sure I looked pretty ordinary sitting there. Scruffy dark beard, sunglasses, blue baseball cap with an airplane logo on the front. Black jacket, black jeans, well worn running shoes even though I hadn't run anywhere in years. Not for fun anyway. You might call me a regular. I liked the Yukon Bar because you can lose yourself in there if you want. Even if you don't want, it's easy to get lost in the Yukon Bar.

Dark shadows were spreading through town. It was getting late, but the shining mountainside in the distance beckoned with an almost painful brilliance. A car drove by once in a while, and one of the local dogs meandered across the street unconcerned. The tourists even seemed to notice that things were winding down.

This time of summer feels like a few minutes before closing time in any store or bar. The staff is still friendly, but you can tell they're tired. They want to go home. They want to quit smiling and saying please and thank you. They don't say it but the locals want to tell the tourists: Go home. Back to all the warmer places you're from. Leave us be. It's been a long summer. Go home so we can deal with the gloom of winter on our own.

Goldie set a cold bottle of fresh brew in front of me on a small white napkin and gave me a look. She knew better than to interrupt and slipped away. Better to let me wallow for a while. I was there to watch the remains of the day. Watch them fade into the night. And to drink beer. There was a twenty dollar bill in front of me because I'd had a flight that morning. One flight. Followed by seven hours of sitting around watching the phone not ring.

Then I noticed Willie push through the front door. He nodded at me and made for the bar sizing up the guy sitting next to his usual spot. He didn't want to be stuck next to anyone boring, broke or needy. Cross eyed George was on a stool nearby, so that was cool. They were pals and started gabbing about something right away. I stayed put and glanced up at the TV screen above the door. Two big sweaty guys were pounding the hell out of each other in some kind of cage. The sound was off and the fighters thrashed away in vicious but silent mayhem while the bar's stereo played a sappy love song.

Goldie came over again, snatched away the twenty and then left to make change. I thought about how many beers I could buy and still have a few bucks left for some kind of meal. I needed one. Yesterday had been a rainy, no fly kind of day, and my dinner had come from a rusty can of mystery soup off a back shelf in my camper.

That was part of my rotten mood. When I worried about money. About the fact that I didn't have any. On days when I wasn't busy, I had too much time to think. Trying to make a living as a scenic flight pilot in one of the rainiest places on the planet. What a dumbass idea.

Rain is a way of life in Seward. On the south central coast of the Gulf of Alaska, rain and fog drift in off the sea on a regular basis, chilling the locals and visitors alike and obscuring the scenery in all directions. But life goes on. The fishing boat crews work in the rain in their yellow slickers and knee high boots. The tour boats come and go loading and unloading tourists with steady efficiency. Straggly haired hitchhikers plod along the highway hunkered inside their ponchos clutching wet cardboard signs. Anchorage, Florida, anywhere but here. Their signs don't really say that, but that's how they look. Some are backpackers but mostly they're seasonal workers. Cannery hands, hotel staff, restaurant help. It was the end of another summer. The jobs were drying up and they were moving on.

Rain doesn't bother the water operations. Even dense fog is no problem for the boats. Besides, fishermen are crazy and could care less about the scenery, but flying is out of the question when there's fog. If I can't see the mountain just north of the airport, I'm grounded. And it's tough to get tourists to go flying unless there's some blue sky around. And I'm not on a salary, I only get paid when I'm flying.

On those days I'm glad for the Yukon's free peanuts in the galvanized bucket just inside the front door. I try not to let the rain discourage me. I just crack open shells, toss back the nuts and wait for the next spell of better weather. Sometimes that strategy works, but only sometimes.

Cross eyed George stumbled out the door just as Mitch Woofley, my friend the lodge operator was walking in. But then his phone rang and Mitch turned a three sixty and left without looking back. Willie drifted over from his station at the Revenue Corner. That's what he calls the first stop inside the front door of a bar. He likes to check on me when things are slow. Slow for Willie means no one else to bullshit with. He paused to stare at the blinking video game on the corner of the wooden counter. I could tell he was deciding whether to throw a few coins in the machine or not. He whined about money even more than I did.

He was wearing one of those visors with fake hair bristling from the top. It sat with a slightly crooked slant on his round head. Bright blue eyes glistened from his ruddy face over a silver gray mustache and mutton chop side burns. His bulging burgundy t-shirt wore a picture of a sockeye salmon. The white lettered caption read: "Hook Me, Beat Me, Cook Me, Eat Me."

"Hey, Willie. Anything dangerous to do around here?" He was a pilot too with his own plane. It was our standard greeting. Alaska pilots are like that. Rough and ready, risk takers living on the edge. Full of life and full of crap.

"Uh...Goldie?" he answered. We both laughed and glanced toward the bar.

"Don't remind me, man," I muttered. He chuckled and sat down beside me.

"How many flights today?" he asked.

"Just the one this morning. Season's almost over." I flipped the page on the Anchorage newspaper and gazed at the headlines. Change from the twenty sat next to an empty ashtray where Goldie had left it.

"You gonna drink that or what?" Willie poked his jaw toward the bottle I hadn't yet lifted.

I could feel his eyes squinting without even looking at him. Willie was a man of action. He couldn't stand to let events unfold at their own pace. He was a man in a hurry. Hard to say why. Like he had some kind of fuse burning inside. Worried that if he slowed down, it might blow.

I glanced at the beer. Large droplets rolled down the side of the brown glass bottle and soaked into the napkin underneath it. I looked outside to see Mount Alice still basking in the evening sun.

Eyeing Willie I reached for the beer. I took my time, enjoying the private chance to torment him a little. I'm generally not in a hurry and resisting his push always felt like the right thing to do.

He watched the bottle on its path from the wet spot on the counter to my mouth with the concentration of a man dying of thirst. His watery blue eyes tracked my movements like a kid on Christmas morning.

I stopped halfway to my mouth and turned to look at him.

"What?"

He didn't answer. His lips parted and his mouth moved like a baby in a high chair waiting for the spoon to deliver. A parishioner on bended knee waiting for the Eucharist.

I finally gave in and set the bottle back on the counter. "Hey, Goldie. Bring my thirsty friend here a beer, will ya? Jesus, Willie. All ya gotta do is ask." He grinned and looked away. Goldie came over with a bottle in one hand. She lifted a bar hook from the back pocket of her jeans, popped the cap and set the bottle in front of Willie with a fluid motion. With a smirk she plucked a five from my stack of bills, then turned and left.

"Now that's the kind of bartender I can respect," Willie grunted. "Fast, quiet and efficient. Reminds me of a gal up at Skinny Dick's."

"Skinny who?" I knew he was setting me up, but I went along for the ride.

"Damn, Johnny. You don't know about Skinny Dick's? It's a bar halfway between Fairbanks and Nenana. Skinny Dick's Halfway Inn."

It was a good thing my mouth was empty. I would have sprayed beer halfway across the bar. I shook my head in admiration for his endless supply of one liners.

He grinned again and tilted his bottle in my direction in thanks.

"No problem," I said, watching Goldie's backside moving away from the corner of my eye. Run silent, run deep. I picked up my bottle and returned Willy's gesture. Ah, Goldie, Goldie, Goldie, I remember when...

Lurid thoughts brought me back to Brandy. "So, uh, Willie, have you heard from ..."

"No," he snapped. He knew where I was headed and cut me off. "You need to forget about her."

I studied his face but it was blank as he drank and ignored me. Brandy was his daughter. She was a Learjet pilot in the lower forty eight. Cleveland, or some damn place. I'd made the mistake of getting too close to her the year before when she was in Seward. It was a long story. I'll never recommend getting involved with a best friend's daughter. Like I said, it was a long story. I took a deep breath and tried to get her petite curves, brunette curls and the smell of her strawberry shampoo out of my head.

It was at that precise moment my cell phone began to vibrate and ring. It was just after six o'clock.

"Oh hell, what now?" The phone was buried in the front pocket of my jeans. I set down the bottle and scrambled to dig it out. The electric impulses next to my loins were unsettling but at the same time titillating.

"Is this Seward Air?" The voice on the other end was distorted and scratchy and I fumbled to position the tiny plastic speaker closer to my ear.

"Yes, sir. This is Johnny Wainwright. How can I help you?"

"Mr. Wainwright, this is Officer David Rankin with the Alaska State troopers here in Seward. Do you all fly to Taroka Island?"

"Out in Prince William Sound? Sure, that's no problem." I reached for the beer bottle with my free hand. "When did you want to go?"

"Right now."

My hand froze in mid air. Reluctantly I set the bottle back on the counter and pushed it out of reach. Booze and flying don't mix. I shook my head at the timing. Another two seconds and I would have had to turn down the flight.

"Right now? It's getting a little late."

"Yeah, I know, but we need to make an arrest out there, and we need to move quick. The department's chopper is in Anchorage for maintenance, so we're kind of in a pinch. Can you get us out there and wait 'til we bring the guy back? Maybe overnight?"

I glanced at the beer and felt the lonely dry spot at the back of my throat. Then I noticed the ten dollar bill and a few ones laying on the counter beside the soggy napkin. I made fifty bucks an hour for charter flights and another fifty for each hour if I have to wait. Sounds good until you realize I average less than an hour a day during a typical rainy summer. That ain't squat.

"Sure, I can do it. It's about a thirty minute flight out there. How soon can you be at the airport?"

"There's going to be two of us. Myself and Officer Daniels. We can be there in about twenty minutes. And it sounds like we'll be bringing one subject back with us. He'll be in handcuffs, of course."

"Okay, no problem. I've taken you guys out to Chenega before for this kind of thing. Taroka's right nearby with a gravel strip. As long as the weather's okay, it should be routine."

He hesitated. "Is the weather alright over there?" He sounded like he hadn't thought about it which was typical. Weather is the last thing on a passenger's mind, but it's the first thing I think about. And weather is what kills more pilots than anything else in Alaska. Actually it's not the weather that kills. It's the pilot making a bad decision in bad weather. Then he winds up killing himself and his passengers.

"I have no idea what it's doing over in Prince William Sound. I'll check on it while you're on the way."

"Sounds good, Mr. Wainwright. See you in a few."

Sliding the phone back in my pocket I told Willie the details as I stood up.

"Kind of late, isn't it?" he asked.

"Yeah, but it's still light for a while, so I'm not worried about it. Moonlight should be good tonight if it gets dark out there, and besides we might be staying overnight."

"You check the weather?" Willie's been flying these mountains all his life. He knows.

"I looked at the Middleton radar before I came down here. One big system way south of here but nothing nearby."

"Out there you gotta worry about fog. It can kill ya quick."

"I know, I know. I've been around here a while now, remember? You don't have to mother hen me so much any more."

"Yeah, but you're still a rookie about a lot of stuff." He changed the subject before I could get pissed. "You taking a gun?"

"A gun? What for?"

"You gotta be prepared for anything. Like bears." He paused. "Or anything really. You just never know out there."

"Hell, I've got two troopers going with me and they'll be armed. You worry too much."

"Yeah? Well, you don't worry enough, ya ask me. Your luck's gonna run out one of these days, Johnny."

"Like you keep telling me. Look, I'd love to hang around for more therapy but I gotta go make some money."

I stood up and scooped the change off the counter and into my pocket. Willie took a long pull on his beer and wiped his mouth with the back of his hand. And he nodded. He understood about money.

"What if the prisoner tries to wreck the plane when you're landing or something?"

It felt strange to have Willie asking me questions about an airplane job. He was the expert, but then I realized that he didn't know about this kind of flying, because his plane was a Piper SuperCub with only one seat in the back. No room for this kind of work.

"The troopers are cool with that. They always handcuff the guy and they tell him right up front, 'Any funny business and we shoot you'."

Willie frowned. "Well, that's comforting. As long as you don't mind bullets and blood splatter in the cockpit."

I felt my eyes go dim. "You don't have to tell me about bullets and airplanes, Willie."

He caught my tone and raised his eyebrows.

"Oh, yeah. Sorry. Guess you learned that during your little adventure on Montague Island last year. Doesn't take much to bring down a small plane, does it?" He didn't wait for an answer. He turned back to his beer. He knew I wouldn't answer.

I was halfway out the door when he called me back. "Hey, man. What about that?" He pointed at the bottle I'd left behind.

"Oh, help yourself, my friend. By all means, but I'm never buying you two beers in one night ever again. That reminds me. You be sober enough to take a phone call when I get out there? I'll have a sat phone. In case I can't get hold of Moose Pass?"

Moose Pass is where my boss lived, thirty miles up the highway. Phil Bartlett's the owner and he has five airplanes altogether, four of them on floats for flying fishermen and hunters into the back country. My job is the wheel plane in Seward. A Cessna 172 with extra horsepower and seats for three plus me. Phil's okay as a boss. At least he usually pays me. As long as we're thirty miles apart we get along fine.

Willie sniffed and pulled back with a frown. "You know better than to file a flight plan with a drunk."

"C'mon, man. Who else am I gonna call?"

"You can always file with the FAA."

"Yeah, I know, but they're way over in Kenai and they never know crap about what's going on over here. I'm not sure they care much either. I'd rather file with somebody that knows me."

"Okay, okay. Gotcha covered," he said with a grin. "Call me when you get out there. You're just going out to Taroka and back, right? No sweat. I'm not drunk yet anyhow. But hurry."

I grinned back at him knowing it wouldn't be long. I also knew he wouldn't wait. He'd probably forget the whole conversation in the next five minutes. I thought for a moment about calling the FAA, but then I left him and the bar behind, my mind going over the details of the flight ahead of me.

I hustled around the corner and jumped in my pickup. The airport was just five minutes away.

CHAPTER
2

The old Toyota pickup had suspension like a kid's red wagon, and it rumbled up the street slamming pot holes like it had some kind of a personal grudge. It had been painted powder blue years ago and left for scrap behind the airport's main hangar. But with a few parts and some elbow grease I had it running fine. I was proud of the abandoned heap that I'd resurrected from the weeds and snow. Something about it felt like hope.

I kept my speed around thirty. The last thing I needed was a speeding ticket. Not to mention the delay. Having the State troopers calling me for flights was a good thing. Good money too. If they knew they could depend on me, they might call more often. Didn't want to screw that up.

I had to brake for a huge motor home that turned in front of me coming from the marina. Slowing to fifteen I groaned but then took a deep breath and settled into the drive. I used the time to call Moose Pass. As expected I got their answering machine, so I was on my own with this flight. I left a brief message and felt glad that no one was there to ask me annoying questions.

Did I have enough gas? Did I have my survival gear? Did I have the sat phone? Did I get their credit card information? Blah, blah, blah. I know, I know. Safety first, I get it. Are you sure about the credit card? I smirked to myself and shook my head. They're already out of the office at six o'clock? Whatever.

The RV finally turned into the Safeway but as I picked up some speed I noticed flashing blue lights a mile ahead. Looked like an accident or something holding up traffic by the bridge over Resurrection River. As I got closer I spotted a city cop I knew, waving cars along. She looked exasperated.

As I got up to her, I rolled down the window. "Hey, Judy, what's happening?"

She grunted at me. "Hey, Johnny. A grizzly sow and two cubs are down in the river over here fishing off a gravel bar, and all the tourists are stopping to take pictures. Even parking on the bridge. It's a freaking mess. Now get the hell out of here, would you?"

She stepped back and jerked her thumb down the road, but with a side wink and a smile, I knew we were cool. Judy was a good friend. Owned a Cessna 170 and flew it once in a while when she wasn't working.

I turned across the railroad tracks and made my way along Airport Way past some tall trees parallel to the runways. It wasn't a busy airport and glancing down toward the bay I couldn't see any activity or other airplanes moving. Small buildings and hangars lined the west side of the field, but no one was around. My office was the first in line - a small A-frame chalet with wide windows and a wooden deck in front. A white sign board leaning against the front rails offered scenic flights over the nearby glaciers.

The company airplane was parked next to the office. She looked ready and willing sitting there on the tarmac in the dim light. The shadow from Mount Marathon was already spreading across the runways, but it was still plenty light out past the orange windsock twitching lazily halfway down the field.

Behind the office my motor home sat next to an empty tie-down space. It used to hold my personal aircraft, a Piper SuperCub like Willie's that I had flown with such pride through the back country of Alaska sharing adventures and scenery. Then one too many adventures of the wrong kind, and it was gone. I frowned at the image. Why had Willie brought it up again at the Yukon? Thanks a lot, pal.

I shook off the memory and started thinking about the gear I'd need for the flight. The usual stuff was already in the plane in a survival kit. Fishing tackle, first aid kit, a couple of granola bars, a signal mirror, mosquito hats. Most of the normal things required by Alaska law for every flight. I kept it to a minimum to keep the weight down. Then I stepped into my camper and grabbed a sleeping bag and a green day pack where I always kept a couple books and a change of underwear.

I always had flotation devices in the plane. They were like suspenders that slid over the shoulders and clipped around the waist. Lightweight but easily tangled. I didn't usually wear one in flight and I tried to ignore the possibility of a splash landing in the sea. Hank McDougal, one of the other company pilots in Moose Pass, liked to call them Coast Guard body retrieval devices. A cheery guy, that damn Hank.

I unlocked the door to the office and walked over to the laptop on my desk. The Middleton Island radar image was still on the screen and it looked the same as it had all day. No significant precipitation was showing anywhere except at the bottom of the screen where just the edge of a dark green shape lurked just out of view. That was the far southern edge of the radar's range. Not close enough to worry me for the next couple of hours anyhow.

I went outside again and after checking to make sure I had enough gas, I walked around the plane, tested the fuel tanks for water and made sure all the necessary parts were still connected. I gave the oversized tires a kick and unhooked the tiedown cables from the wings. A quick peek at the oil dipstick, and I was done. So much for the preflight checklist.

Gravel crunched behind me and I turned to see a white Alaska State Patrol car pull up and park. Two officers in dark blue uniforms emerged and walked toward me. The one in the lead looked to be around thirty years old. Short cropped blond hair, about five ten or so and clean cut, his head was shaped like an ice cube. He reached out and shook my hand with a strong grip.

"You must be Johnny Wainwright," he said.

"I am," I agreed.

"I'm David Rankin. I'm the one who called." He nodded toward the other guy. "And this is my partner, Officer Daniels."

The partner was taller, darker and older with a wiry frame and a thin weather beaten face. He reached toward me slowly like you move toward a mongrel you don't know. He took my hand and stared intently into my eyes. I nodded at him and returned his stare. Something told me to hold his look. He hadn't said a word but I could see questions running through his mind. The slow percolation of a hundred hidden opinions like the part of the iceberg you can't see. I wondered what was below the surface. I dropped my gaze and pulled my hand back. He let go like he was releasing something that smelled bad.

I turned to listen to Rankin who was starting to talk. Daniels stayed behind me, but I could feel him back there studying me.

"We got a call from the island just over an hour ago. Their communications aren't the best, and the signal was breaking up, but our dispatcher said it sounded like a women screaming like she was getting beat up. I think the department's been out there before for this same guy, so it's probably routine."

"Okay," I said. "How big is this guy?" I didn't want to overload the airplane.

"Ah, if it's who I think it is, he's pretty good sized. Two fifty at least." Rankin tilted his head back and watched me as I frowned and mentally calculated the figures. Remembering that we would burn part of the fuel load on our way out there, I shrugged.

"Should be okay." I glanced behind me to get a look at the partner. Something about him made me uneasy, but

Daniels had moved away and stood with his back to us staring down the runway toward the bay. He was much older than Rankin but so far seemed to be letting the younger officer take the lead. His gray hair was shaped into a severe flat top about an inch long. The sides of his head gleamed as though freshly shaved. High and tight as the Marines call it. He wore a black leather equipment belt that held a radio, pepper spray, handcuffs and a handgun. His profile was a craggy mountainside and his face was deeply creased with what could be laugh lines except he didn't seem like the laughing type. His nose had a couple of turns in it, the unmistakable marks of breaks and self repairs.

While Rankin talked his partner stared into the distance in silence. I wasn't sure if he was listening or not.

"We're not expecting any real trouble, but you never know. By the time we get there he'll probably be calmed down. Maybe sleeping if off if he was drunk. That's what it usually is. Depending on what we learn we may have to bring him back with us. He'll probably do some time in the Seward jail, then the judge'll send him home."

"Okay, no problem," I said. "We probably ought to get moving. There's not a lot of light left."

Officer Daniels turned then and his silver gray eyes locked onto me and froze me to the spot. "You ready for this?" he growled at me in a graveled rasp.

My throat went dry. "Uh, whattya mean?" I tried to keep my voice level, but I knew I didn't sound very convincing.

"Are you ready for this?" He repeated, biting off each syllable like he was talking to a suspect that didn't speak English.

I frowned and squinted back at him. "Uh, yeah, I think so. Is there something else I should know?" *What was this guy's problem?*

He ignored my questions, the spoken and the unspoken. "You got a flight plan and current weather?"

His eyes were unblinking and fixed on mine like a rattlesnake in the Mojave. All of sudden I knew what it was like to be an insect pinned on a black felt board.

"Yeah, that's all taken care of." I tried to keep the annoyance out of my voice.

"So what is the weather?"

"I didn't see anything to be concerned about. You want a briefing or something?"

His jaw set and his eyes narrowed to tight slits. His words spat at me like machine gun bullets, and I started to feel like I was sitting in ice water.

"I know the weather information around here ain't jack. Middleton radar is all you've got and it won't show fog. Just because it looks nice here doesn't mean it's okay out there."

I turned then to face him directly, folded my arms and returned his hard edged stare. I'd had enough.

"I'm well aware of all that. Look, Officer Daniels, this flight wasn't my idea. You guys called me. If we get out there and it doesn't look good, we come back. That's all you can do around here. Or we can forget the whole damn thing right now. Your choice."

Daniels wasn't backing down. "I've flown in and out of the bush all around Alaska for a lot of years," he said. "Too many hot shot pilots have killed people flying into bad weather. And even the best have disappeared in Prince William Sound."

I looked at him for a moment and glanced over at Rankin. The younger officer was busy checking equipment on his belt. I bit back on the tightness building in my throat and worked to keep my voice slow and controlled.

"Like I said, officer, we don't have to go. It's your call. We won't know what it's like at the island until we get out there. That's all you can ever do around here. You fly out and you take a look. Believe me, I'm not going to fly into something I can't get out of. You can count on that."

Daniels smirked like he was closing the door on a salesman. He dropped his stare and began to adjust the equipment around his waist. Rankin's head lifted then and they looked at each other. Then they both shrugged and turned toward the plane. As they walked away from me, I gawked after them and wondered what had just happened.

I went to relock the office doors and then followed them to the plane and opened its side door for them. As I walked back to my side I shook my head to myself and thought, 'Why can't it ever just be easy?'

Without another word, I climbed in the Cessna and waited for them to squeeze into the front and back seats. Their equipment belts squeaked and protested the tight quarters. I realized then why their shapes were so bulky. Bullet proof vests.

Daniels got in the back. While Rankin was settling into the seat beside me our eyes met for a second. I thought he looked apologetic. Who knows? Maybe I just wanted him to be. I pointed out the headphones they needed to wear for the intercom. Rankin placed his on his bright blond head, but Daniels only stared out the window and said nothing.

Starting the engine and running through the rest of my preflight checks I mentally went over the weight and balance figures. I had a half load of fuel, light survival gear, two troopers with equipment, probably four hundred pounds between them and myself at one fifty. The total left us room for another two hundred and fifty pounds or so.

The engine rumbled smoothly and the oil pressure was in the green. Pushing in on the throttle we started moving forward. I taxied toward the runway and spoke into the intercom.

"Can you hear me now?"

Rankin adjusted his microphone and said, "Roger that."

I glanced behind me and Daniels was still staring out the side window without putting on the headset. I looked at Rankin and he gave me a slight shake of his head. Like he was saying let it go.

I went over the final safety items with him. I checked that their seat belts were secure and talked about where to find the life vests, survival gear and fire extinguisher. The emergency exits were kind of obvious. I'd climbed in one of them and they'd come in the other.

Everything in the plane checked out. I made a radio call for the takeoff, but no one answered. That was typical. Even on a nice night like this one, the Seward airspace was deserted. All the better, I thought. No one around to get in the way. Before pulling out onto the runway I ran up the engine and checked the mags. It all felt good.

I shoved the throttle full forward and the sudden surge of power started us down the runway. Eager to be back in the air I focused on keeping the white centerline of the runway straight in front of the nose.

It didn't take long. The bird wanted to fly, and in a few moments we lifted off. The ground slipped away underneath us and we sailed out over a grassy meadow and then the beach south of the airport. A hundred feet off the ground the cabin suddenly filled with sunlight as we climbed above the ground shadow. I looked to the left and saw where the shadow was creeping up the side of Mount Alice like a gray tide invading a beach. But we were free of it, soaring into clear Alaskan air. A couple wisps of evening clouds above us glowed pink and orange in the sunset light.

The peaceful waters of Resurrection Bay slid past below us as we climbed toward the ridgeline east of Seward. There were none of the usual white caps thanks to the light winds. Fourth of July Creek passed beneath us mixing its flow of gray silty water into the smooth turquoise mass of the bay. Street lights in town were just visible to our right reminding me that daylight was in its last throes. I glanced at my watch and figured that I'd have enough light to find Taroka, but not much beyond that.

The irony wasn't lost on me. Town was shutting down for the night, and here I was just setting out on a job. And I'd already put in a full day. Not that busy maybe, but staring out the office window and waiting for customers can be exhausting.

I almost started my usual scenic tour spiel but then remembered I didn't have to say a word on this flight. As I leveled out at a thousand feet it was all I could do to avoid my usual announcement: "Seward down there is a town of about three thousand people, a little more in the summer, a little less in the winter."

I liked that about charter flights. I didn't have to describe the sights. Not that I minded, but at the end of a summer I got tired of the sound of my own voice, saying the same things one flight after another. Sure, I could get creative and mix it up, but that takes energy. It was easier to follow a routine. Like the grizzly bears that stood in the creek letting the salmon jump into their jaws rather than chasing them around. In September it was time to earn what you could with minimal effort.

In June I'm a funny guy, Mister Entertainment. It's a kick to mix it up with the tourists, joking about their nervousness and telling tall tales. Rambling on about some extraneous Alaskan history. Most are looking for a good time, a diversion, an eye popping vista, and that's what I give them. Cruising over glaciers, fjords, milky blue water and jagged mountain peaks gives them the thrill of a lifetime. I show them lots of bears and other wildlife too and when we land they're gushing like a bus load of kids in Disneyland.

The troopers looked out the windows in silence. I was glad for the quiet, but uneasy at the same time. I kept glancing at the mountaintops passing below and watched the shadow line creep higher and higher. The pink alpenglow is always a beauty to behold, but it rides with darkness close behind.

We were passing the prison then. Spring Creek Correctional Facility sat in the valley across from Seward, glimmering with a wicked brilliance. Powerful flood lights illuminated razor wire fences around a green grass courtyard. Maximum security prisons are all like that, I guess. Let there be light, the enemy of evil. Banish darkness where the devil plays. Spotlight their unspeakable deeds committed in the black of night. Light 'em up for the man. The man in the tower. The one with the sniper rifle.

Feeling like a privileged soul, unfenced and free, I pulled back on the controls and trimmed the plane for more altitude. As expected the air was smooth. Not a single bump disrupted our steady climb over the ridgeline of mountains. The wide expanse of the Gulf of Alaska filled our world on the right side of the airplane. Rugged mountains and glaciers filled the left. The last of the direct sunbeams lit the highest peaks, but below that the details faded to gray. Directly beneath us the rocky coastline slipped by where placid waves splashed white foam against a black gravel shoreline and sheer granite cliffs.

Rankin and Daniels stared out at the view without a word as if mesmerized by the spectacle. Silence was good. I figured they were enjoying the respite from a busy life fighting crime. Soaking in the quiet beauty of the Alaskan wilderness while leaving the driving to me had to feel good. No headquarters calling in, no surly offenders in their face, no hostile stares from the clueless public. For thirty minutes or so their thoughts were their own.

The murky twilight of the evening made it difficult to see very far into the distance. I could tell we were going to be okay for another hour or so, but a low blur on the horizon to our south had me concerned. I wasn't sure, but it looked like a fog bank. With the south wind it was probably moving north. Towards us.

At three thousand feet I pointed the plane across Day Harbor. Familiar beaches passed below as we crossed Horseshoe Cove and Whidbey Bay. Cruising easily around the high mountain on the west side of Johnstone Bay I spotted lower clouds ahead.

Damn. I silently cursed the unexpected surprise. I was going to have to descend low over the water to get underneath them. And just like that, the prospect of a pleasant evening flight in perfect cloudless skies evaporated. My jaw clamped a little tighter.

Low clouds aren't usually a big deal. Especially when there's no wind. I like to fly low. It gives me a close and intimate sense of being connected to the earth. But not over the ocean. Less than a thousand feet over the water doesn't leave much room to glide to shore if the engine quits. And there were two wide expanses of water between us and Taroka Island. Keeping three thousand feet of altitude would have been comfortable and safe. But the clouds ahead meant not tonight. Comfortable was gone, and safe was becoming a question.

As the airplane settled toward the ocean I tried to remember everything I knew about Taroka. It was a narrow island only about five miles long, a slim finger of forest covered hills nestled in Prince William Sound in a gap between two other islands, Evans and LaTouche. A high mountain on its south end rose a thousand feet in the air and blocked some of the wind and rain that roared in regularly off the Pacific. It had been uninhabited until 1950 when the rich owner sold out and the new owners built a lodge.

The north end of the island was fairly flat and a gravel airstrip had been built to bring in guests and supplies. A road from the airstrip wound through the trees for a couple of miles to a tiny bay where the lodge and other buildings clustered at the edge of the water. I'd been out there a few times in prior years dropping off guests. There was a nice overlook to the dock below where I'd seen fishing boats, yachts and an occasional float plane.

The island and its lodge now were owned by a wealthy family from back east somewhere. Word was their money came from war profiteering. The old man had taken his fortune and purchased the whole island, built a fancy lodge and ran a five star fishing operation every summer for three decades. Then I heard he passed away and although his heirs went through the motions of continuing the business, it had been the old man's dream, not theirs. The passion was gone. I wasn't even sure they were still open.

What was it they'd said about the guy they were after? Nothing really. Just that he was big and probably a drunk. I glanced over at Rankin, but he was just quietly watching the waves below. He looked deep in thought, so I decided not to interrupt. I wanted to know more about the job we were undertaking, but they weren't sharing.

I didn't want to look back at the other guy. Officer Daniels. I could feel him back there. His presence loomed like a final exam I could never pass. He knew more about their mission than I did, so he was one up on me. He knew it, and I knew it, but there was no way I was going to let him know that I knew. If that makes any sense. My job was to fly the plane. Get them there and get them back. The rest was none of my business. My curiosity be damned.

To them I was just a cab driver. Mind your own business. Cops are a closed club. They don't share much with outsiders. My part was to pretend I didn't care. Shut up and drive. I could do that.

I turned my thoughts back to my own mission. With a subtle shrug I built a mental wall between them and me. I'm the pilot here. You guys need me so you can get your job done. You don't want to talk, fine. You don't know how to do what I do, and vice versa. Okay, I'll deliver you to the island and then you're on your own.

First, I needed to find the airstrip and get the plane on the ground in one piece. When they got their guy I needed to get us back to Seward. I glanced around at the growing shadows. With the clouds ahead, the ground was definitely getting dark. I took another nervous glance south at the suspected fog bank on the horizon. Was it getting closer? But first things first. Where the hell was the island?

The clouds ahead were dark gray and covered the Sound for as far as I could see. There was blue sky above, but the dense layer sealed off the terrain completely. It wasn't very thick, maybe only a couple of hundred feet top to bottom. Like a moldy old comforter from grandma's damp basement, it lay on the earth in front of us sullen and unmoving. As I descended toward the water to get underneath the front edge of the cloud layer, I estimated that we'd be about eight hundred feet in the air. Eight hundred feet above the water. The icy cold unforgiving water of the Gulf of Alaska. And that's if I kept the airplane's radio antennas in the cloud.

The sun had dropped behind mountains way behind us and the lower we descended, the darker it got. Sliding underneath the front edge of the cloud bank, we entered a different world. A world of water all around us with the murky shapes of mountains and cliffs emerging from its surface reaching up to the cloud. There was enough light to see the mountains, but that wasn't going to last long. I felt my teeth starting to grind and I made a conscious effort to relax my jaw. It was decision time.

Should I turn around? Tell them it's too dark? I spotted a cruise ship in the distance, its full array of lights sparkling gaily against the water. I could see far enough beyond it to give me a little confidence. I kept going.

The good news was I knew we were close. All I had to do was find a path in between the clouds and rocks. The bad news was nothing looked familiar. I couldn't tell which way to go. The island was out there somewhere less than twenty miles away behind one of the lush green mountain sides that loomed in front of us in the murk.

But everything looks different when the Sound is covered with low cloud. That's a bad thing about flying low. You can see everything close up just fine, but you can't see things far away. Like familiar distant shore lines that you've seen many times before. The ones that guide you in or call you home.

On bright sunny days Prince William Sound glistens and glimmers, its islands and mountain peaks are clear and distinct. Everything you want to see is in plain view. But throw grandma's comforter on top and it's a whole new deal. The peaks thrust up into the overcast and instead of wide open spaces it's all tunnels, burrows and obstacles. A maze of jagged rock cliffs and tree covered ridgelines in all directions.

The last few times I was out here postcard photographers would have wet their pants. The beauty of the Sound is unequaled in the world. But not tonight. I peered into the murk looking for familiar landmarks and saw none. My hands grew damp, and I had to remind myself to relax my shoulders. I didn't want Officer Cranky noticing the tension. He was uptight enough without seeing that his pilot was nervous and lost.

Was I lost? Uh, well, yeah, sort of. I mean, I kind of knew where we were but not exactly. I knew how to get home. That was no problem, but I couldn't very well admit that I didn't know where to find the island. What the hell kind of professional pilot would that make me? I needed to find that airstrip quick and get the damn plane on the ground.

I glanced at the fuel gages. Both tanks held enough to let me explore for an hour if needed and still get home with gas left over. But I didn't want to wander around admitting I didn't know the way. It had taken a long time to establish myself as a dependable pilot in the Alaska back country. The last thing I wanted to do was fail.

Too bad I didn't have a GPS on board. The company shared one between three planes. Normally I never needed it, so they kept it in Moose Pass. There hadn't been time to get it before this flight.

The officers shifted in their seats. Rankin beside me leaned forward slightly and peered into the distance. I could sense him glancing over at me from time to time. Like passengers do when they get nervous. I ignored him and concentrated on looking calm, cool and collected. I adjusted the throttle with my right hand, then dropped my arm on my leg in a relaxed gesture. Giving the appearance that everything was fine. Just another routine trip through paradise. The last thing I needed was their anxious questions distracting me and adding to my own.

I started to realize that I was setting myself up. Pride and determination were powerful forces, and I was letting them cloud my thinking. I needed to make good decisions out here. Decisions based on common sense and safety. The little voice in the back of my head was poking me. An old song came to me: *Should I stay or should I go? If I stay there will be trouble, if I go there will be double.*

I gave myself a quick shake and looked hard at the shorelines that were approaching now on either side. They looked familiar. I was pretty sure that the channel ahead was the water between Evans and Bainbridge Islands. Evans was the island on our right. Taroka was on the other side of Evans, but there was a mountain there tightly capped by the cloud layer. There were some openings along the wall like ridgeline, but I couldn't see well enough through the gaps to tell if the far side was clear. It was a real bad idea to squeak through a cloudy gap hoping the other side was okay. Too many dead pilots had plunged through with false confidence only to find themselves surrounded by impenetrable fog and rock.

I stayed with my best option. I would follow the coastline of Evans Island all the way around the north end until I could see the conditions and hopefully the familiar shape of Taroka Island. The plan was okay as long as the clouds behaved themselves. I studied the gray shape above and craned my neck to look behind us making sure I had a way back to Seward if things closed out ahead. It looked okay. I turned the plane to follow the easily visible line of white frothy waves where they dashed against the rocks on the ragged coastline below us.

"Did you get us lost?" Daniels's gravelly voice cut through the intercom like breaking glass. He had finally pulled on his headset.

"No, we're fine. This is the Prince of Wales Passage we're following. That's Evans Island to the right and Taroka's behind that. I just have to find a way to get over there under these clouds." I was glad he hadn't asked me two minutes before.

He didn't respond. Out of the corner of my eye I noticed Rankin look out where I had pointed. Then he pulled out a notebook and started reading. Like he was preparing for the next step and reviewing his notes.

Light rain began to spot the windshield. It was still twilight behind us, but much darker in front. I didn't like it, but there was no wind and I had room to turn around. I reminded myself that these kinds of clouds were pretty stable in light wind. I'd never seen them change fast enough to trap me. But I would keep my eye on them anyway, just in case. I kept going.

A low place between two high hills came into view on our right. Steep forested walls rose into the clouds, but a saddle dropped away from the gray ceiling to let me see through. I put the plane in a steep bank and turned toward the gap. I had to make a decision quick. If I couldn't detect clear airspace on the opposite side of the pass, I'd need to make another steep turn to get back on my original track. At the last possible moment I spotted the water on the east side of Evans Island and the white rimmed shoreline of Taroka Island less than ten miles away.

I hugged the right side of the saddle and sailed straight through. All of a sudden the huge gravel airstrip called Chenega Bay appeared directly ahead of us and just two hundred feet below. I felt my lungs inflate with a deep breath of relief. Seeing an easy place to land after so much water and so many rocky shorelines and cliffs settled my nerves. The Chenega airstrip was my alternate. If everything turned bad unexpectedly, I could easily get back here. I pressed on for Taroka five hundred feet over the water.

"That's it straight ahead," I announced with all the calm I could muster. Rankin leaned forward and squinted into the gloomy scene ahead.

"Got enough light?" he asked.

"I think so," I answered. "I'll overfly the strip to be sure."

I could feel Daniels in the back seat shift his weight forward. Out of the corner of my eye I saw his dark shape come up close behind me where he could see out ahead.

I jerked my attention back to the destination, pulled back on the throttle and slowed the plane. My hands seemed to move over the controls automatically as I set the flaps and pulled on the carburetor heat. My eyes flicked rapidly over the instruments and the fuel gauges. Everything looked good.

Setting the trim for eighty knots I flew straight and level across LaTouche Passage. I looked all around for other airplanes but the area was deserted. No boats in sight either, no planes and no wind. Nothing moved.

I keyed the radio. "Taroka traffic, Cessna four four nine five zulu, five miles west, inbound."

The words echoed in my headset, but no one answered. I wondered if anyone on Chenega Island was listening. They didn't have a transmitter but a Native council leader over there told me once that they had an old receiver set up in the health clinic and somebody usually monitored air traffic in the area. I hoped so. After all, Willie was the only one who knew I was out here. Besides the troopers. And their dispatcher, I guessed.

Then I could see the strip ahead of us. It was just light enough to make a landing, but the approach was going to be tricky. The near end of the strip started just above water's edge, only a few feet from jagged rocks. The tide was high, and white foam was splashing against the shore. Rotted moss and small driftwood logs were scattered at the top of a small slope of dark gray rocks above the water. The rest of the runway ran uphill toward a steep embankment. A pile of boulders had been left there by the bulldozer that cleared the strip years ago.

I had one chance to make the landing. No room for error. If I set it down too fast or too far down the runway, there wasn't enough room to stop or to take off again. The embankment and the mountainside made sure of that. It was what they called a one way strip.

Tall trees lined the left edge of the runway by the water's edge. Another hillside on the right gave me just enough space to set the plane down between the two obstacles. If I set the wheels down just past the water line nice and slow and got on the brakes in a hurry, we'd be okay.

I looked at my watch. It was after eight. I kept my altitude and lined up the plane so I could fly over the right side of the field and look at the runway surface for problems. It looked rutted but fairly flat. No big rocks in the middle anyhow. No abandoned vehicles, lumber or wandering moose. No airplanes down there either. It would have been nice to see another plane for some confirmation, but like so many remote landings in Alaska I was on my own. A faded windsock hung limply on a wire frame halfway down the strip. No wind to push me off track on landing, but no wind to help slow us down either.

Then I had to bank to the left to keep clear of the approaching mountainside. I took another look down for any surprises on the far end of the landing area. I felt Officer Daniels behind me leaning over to look down too.

I straightened the plane's flight, it was decision time. "How important is this flight?" I asked.

"Why? We need to get in there. Now." Daniels snapped.

"Because it's a little iffy," I answered. "The weather's turning. It's starting to rain and getting dark. I doubt we'll get back out of here tonight."

"We're here, let's land. If we have to stay over, we stay over. Can you do it or not?"

"I'll make that decision when I'm ready, alright?" I snapped back.

Daniels didn't answer. I could tell he didn't like not having the control.

I turned for another pass over the strip. "Help me look for anything down there that looks like a problem," I ordered.

It was silent inside the plane as we repeated the pattern over the island a little lower. The only sound was the drone of the engine as we all stared down and I maneuvered. The rain was picking up but the airstrip surface didn't look wet or muddy yet. I thought about the slight incline of the strip and the condition of my tires and brakes and decided to keep going.

"Anybody see anything to worry about?"

"No," they answered in unison.

"I didn't either. Okay, here we go."

I kept the bank going and swung out over the water again. Out of habit I keyed the mike. "Taroka traffic, ninety five zulu is left downwind, turning base to final." Like talking to ghosts in a graveyard.

Looking down and to my left I searched for my touchdown point, but all I could see were trees. I could only guess at where the exact spot was. I took a deep breath and concentrated on setting up the plane.

I pulled back on the throttle and let the plane start sinking toward the water. I put down all the flaps and trimmed for sixty five knots. Glancing back over my left shoulder, I gave myself an extra wide turn to make sure I had plenty of time on final to get it right the first time. Once I committed to landing I only had this one chance.

With my right hand ready on the throttle, I turned left and then left again. The white foamy waterline was straight ahead. Sinking just a little too low I punched in just a few more RPM to get back on track, then chopped it again. We glided toward the dark spot between the trees and the hillside. I slowed us to sixty. Then I saw the touchdown spot clearly, just past the foam and the rocks. I glanced down the runway to make sure no obstacles had suddenly appeared. From this angle it looked short but doable. The boulders at the far end loomed in the dim light.

My last chance to abort came and went. Then I was committed. As we slid the last fifty feet out of the sky, I took a deep breath, relaxed my shoulders and prepared myself to land.

I noticed Rankin's hands twitching out of the corner of my eye. Apparently he didn't like the look of the rocks and water coming straight at the windshield. I didn't either but I fought off the alarm rising in my throat. If he did something stupid like grabbing to pull back on the controls he'd kill us all. There wouldn't be time to stop him. It had happened before in small planes with dual controls and nervous passengers.

"Everything looks good," I droned with a practiced steady tone. "We'll ride it down just like this."

He looked over at me for just a second and then immediately went back to staring straight ahead. I noticed that his hands stayed on his thighs where they belonged.

Just above the water, I pulled smoothly back on the yoke and flared the plane ten feet off the deck. I could see the embankment waiting up ahead at the end of the gravel. She floated for a split second, then descended further and the stall horn started to squawk. I felt the final sink and saw the rocks pass by on the right and the left. I pulled back even more and all I could see over the nose was the immense pile of rocks at the far end. If there was something on the runway now, I was going to hit it.

For a moment I felt helpless, almost panicked, knowing there was no escape. I set my teeth and gave into it. At this point it's all you can do. You know you're committed and there are no other options. You have to let the landing happen. If you hadn't made good decisions up to this point, you could have a real problem. If you'd done everything right, it would work out. Usually.

I felt the main tires touch the gravel and we settled with a rolling rumble. I pulled off all the power and slid my toes up to the brakes. As we slowed the nose dropped, the front wheel touched down and our weight pushed forward. It was all feel then as I pushed hard against the pedals but not enough to make us slide, I stretched myself as tall as possible and peered into the shadows ahead. The ground crunched underneath as I brought us to a stop.

The boulders looked huge now just thirty yards away. I felt my breath release and a wave of exhilaration rushed over me.

"Whew! Nice job." Rankin bubbled with the euphoria of a doomed man with a new lease on life. Daniels said nothing. I felt him unlatch his seatbelt and the plane moved as he shifted his weight toward the door. With a burst of power I turned the plane around and taxied back to find a parking spot. There was an area just uphill from the center of the strip and I turned us around again to stop clear of the runway. You never know when another plane might come in for a landing.

I pulled the mixture to shut down the engine and flipped all the switches to their OFF positions. The propeller lurched to a stop. Rankin popped open his door, and a cool rush of wet salty air flooded into the cabin. The scent of spruce and seaweed was as thick as a wet dog in an afternoon rain. As the officers climbed out of the plane, I reached for the record book and wrote down the date and 'Seward to Taroka Island.'

I looked up to the instrument panel to locate the Hobbs meter. It's the instrument that records the time the engine has been running. Zero point seven. Forty two minutes.

I wrote it down and did the math in my head. Since I was paid for the time the engine was turning, according to Mister Hobbs, I had just earned thirty five dollars.

I snapped the book shut, stowed the pen away and rotated my head to relax the muscles in my neck. With a deep breath I slid my seat back, unfastened my seatbelt and stepped out to take a look around.

CHAPTER
3

When I came out from under the wing, Daniels and Rankin were standing together by the tail of the plane. The rain was more like a mist. Rankin had his notebook out and was reading his notes out loud while Daniels listened and took out his flashlight. It was a long, heavy duty model that looked like a night stick. When he pointed it at his own face and flicked it on, his features lit up like a demonic Halloween mask. He looked at me with a steely glare, his rigid flattop forming a sharp vee at the top of his face. Shadows carved his hatchet face like a gargoyle, ancient and fierce as death itself.

I stopped in my tracks, but then he snapped off the beam and his face went dark, almost invisible in the dim light. I shuddered and reminded myself that he was on my side. At least I hoped he was. I dug in my pockets for something to do, found a pack of gum and took my time removing a piece from the aluminum foil.

Ignoring me, Daniels slid the flashlight back into his belt. Then he pulled out his handgun. It was black too, and as the light continued to fade around us, he pointed the weapon at the ground, hauled back on the slide and chambered a round. He flipped on the safety and put it back in its holster and looked over at his partner.

Rankin's blond head and fair complexion gleamed in the night. He put away the notebook, and together they pulled on black baseball caps. Rankin's glow disappeared. He went almost as dark as Daniels if not just as deadly, their eyes lost in the shadows. I stepped toward them determined to look casual.

Sure, this is business as usual. Just dropping off a couple of special ops assassins on a mission of murder and mayhem. Hiya fellas. How's tricks?

"Expecting trouble?" I asked glancing at their handguns.

"No, we always check our gear. It's standard procedure for DV cases," Rankin answered.

"DV?"

"Domestic violence," he explained. "The call we got sounded like a family quarrel, but the phone went dead before the dispatcher could get much information."

That reminded me that I needed to give Willie a call. I turned toward the baggage compartment and the satellite phone. I opened the small door in the side of the plane, reached in and popped open the catches on the orange plastic container.

Rankin moved up beside me. "We gonna have enough light to take off when we get back?"

I took a look back toward Seward. I could see across the water for miles under the layer of cloud. There was even a gleam of moonlight on the side of a mountain in the distance.

"Shouldn't be a problem as long as the weather holds like this. It's going to be a lot darker in another hour but as long as I can see the ground and those trees down there we'll be okay."

Rankin looked down the airstrip in both directions as if trying to imagine the takeoff. Daniels had moved away from the plane and was standing motionless looking down the road toward the lodge. His back was to us. I could barely see him, black on black.

"Flying in the dark is no problem," I went on. "As long as there's no fog. How long do you think you'll be?"

Rankin looked at his watch. "Shouldn't take long. We're going to walk to the lodge. It's about a mile away. If we need to bring the guy with us, we'll be back in an hour or so."

"Okay," I answered. "I'll be ready."

Rankin turned toward the rear of the plane again, but then I stopped him. Turning my back away from Daniels, I asked in a low voice. "Uh, everything okay with your partner there? He seems a little edgy."

Rankin hesitated for a moment but then he leaned toward me and with a tight smile said, "Ah, he's okay. Just a nervous flier, I think. Don't worry about it."

I studied his face. He looked apologetic. "And he doesn't like DV cases either. Well, none of us do, but, hey, you know."

He didn't have to say any more. I knew. People are strange, and they get stranger with booze. Not to mention that remote Alaska attracts a special breed of individual. Some that aren't that tightly wired. And then with time and isolation, they sometimes unravel.

"Okay, good luck," I said, instantly regretting it. Rankin turned stiffly and walked off to join Daniels. I didn't know if cops shared the same superstitions with pilots, but a lot of us avoid using that phrase before a flight. Like we don't want any reminders that a lot of what we do depends on luck.

We prefer to think that's it's all science. And good planning, good maintenance and smart decision making. We try to pretend that misfortune is completely preventable. We read the accident reports and the NTSB analyses, and we tell ourselves we wouldn't make the same mistakes. It's said that more than ninety percent of all airplane accidents are pilot error. The rest are mechanical. Supposedly. But we all know that some are unexplainable. Somebody's luck just ran out. That's why a good luck wish can feel like more of a curse.

I waited for a minute watching the troopers move down the road together. Pretty soon all I could see was the white luminous strips of tape on the back of their caps. Bobbing ghostlike in the gloom, the tape lurched and swayed with the movement of their bodies but disconnected somehow, floating like drunken fireflies, dimming and dull.

Within a few moments the darkness swallowed them completely. All that was left was the sound of their heavy shoes scuffling over the gravel surface. Another minute went by and even that was gone.

That's when it hit me. Luminous tape. Long forgotten memories from my Ranger School days crawled back into my mind. It had been a long time ago, but military training in the dead of night never really leaves you. I'd spent too much time following two strips of white tape in the dark to ever forget it. It was a world where everything was black. Grease paint on our faces, electrical tape on our dogtags. White nametags and t-shirts were removed or covered. Chest deep in a Florida swamp, the luminous tape on the back of the guy's hat in front of you was the only thing you could see. It was the only thing keeping you from getting separated from the others and lost.

I was twenty one and I'd never experienced such darkness. Or terror. The swamps were filled with alligators and snakes. I remember being wet and cold and scared for hours and hours. Carrying heavy packs and weapons. Constantly moving, too exhausted to think straight, but never too tired to escape the fear. Or that surreal line of ghostly white strips dancing in the dark. Knowing that if I lost track of them, I could die.

I jerked myself back from the memories and looked around feeling a helpless sinking sensation. The kind you get when you don't know what's going on. When you just have to wait to see what happens next. I strained my ears trying to pick up any sound of the troopers but they were gone.

That's the first thing that always hit me in the wilderness. The quiet. No engine roar, no highway traffic in the distance, no human sounds of any kind. Leaning against the airplane, I let the quiet wash over me and tried to imagine what it would be like to live out here every day.

Free of people and all their maddening racket. So peaceful and still. Then comes the second thing that always hits me in the wilderness. The noise. All the other surrounding sounds began to rise to the surface. It really wasn't quiet at all.

There was a burble of water somewhere close. A small stream trickled from the hillside above me on its way to the bay. An owl called out from the darkness of the trees above the runway, and I heard an answer from its mate in the distance. Insects buzzed nearby, and an occasional mosquito brushed against my face, its high pitched scream just audible before I waved it away. I couldn't hear waves from the shoreline but I could imagine the water lapping against the rocks not far from where I stood. The tick of cooling engine metal was the only reminder of humanity.

Before long there was sound everywhere. Soft, subtle and steady, the rhythm of nightlife in Prince William Sound. The low tone of a foghorn in the distance floated through the evening calm and echoed against the hillsides. When it stopped the sounds all around me continued. Bugs, and birds and water. Suddenly I felt acutely alone standing there in the middle of nowhere. I could have been the last man alive in the universe.

I shook myself out of the reverie and turned to the baggage compartment again. I took the satellite phone out of its orange plastic container and flipped open the cover. It took me a moment to remember how to use the thing. Then I pressed the power button and waited while the screen lit up and went through its start up sequence. When it was finished I dialed Willie's number. I didn't bother calling Moose Pass. I knew I'd just get the answering machine again. I'd fill them in tomorrow.

After four rings, Willie's slurry voice came on. "Y -ello?"

"Hey, man, we made it."

"Who's this?"

"Come on, Willie. Wake up. It's Johnny. I'm out here on Taroka Island. We should be heading back in another hour or so."

"Johnny who?"

"Very funny, butthole."

"Hey, Johnny. How ya doing? Yeah, I'm drunk as a motherfucker. Seeya." The line went dead.

I stared down at the phone in my hand. So much for reaching out and touching someone. Goddamn guy. Just when I could have used a little connection with a human being. Even one like Willie.

I snapped the phone shut and packed it back in its box. I left it on the front seat to remind myself to call him again before we took off. Then I walked around the plane and looked her over for something to do. And to make sure no important parts had fallen off or a tire had gone flat. I glanced at my watch. It was after nine.

I walked toward the water line leaving the plane behind. With nothing to do but kill time I thought I'd look the place over and inspect the runway a little closer. I wanted to know it well when I took off in the dark. And it was getting steadily darker. The clouds seemed thicker and their lumpy gray bulk loomed motionless above me like dirty soap suds clogging a drain. I hadn't seen any rain drops since the landing, but I could feel water in the sky all around me, ready to release at any moment.

The surface of the airstrip looked okay, a mixture of tiny gravel, bare dirt and small rocks scattered randomly along its length. The middle lane of the strip held fewer rocks than the edges, but it didn't have the well traveled appearance of other gravel strips I'd used. I figured this one didn't get many airplanes. It was one way and short and a long way from help, not exactly welcoming features.

I found the place where I'd touched down. Fresh scuff spots marked the gravel about five feet past the grassy edge of the embankment above the water. I'd nailed it.

Down at the edge of the water white foamy waves murmured quietly against the shore. Their ebb and flow was muffled and soft, moving restlessly back and forth against the jagged rocks scattered here and there. I spotted one solitary light in the distance. It was probably the big dock on Evans Island a few miles away across the passage. And way off to the right I could see what must have been a ship of some kind. Lights clustered in a tight knot moved along the horizon. Could have been a cruise ship but probably wasn't. Not enough lights. More likely a tanker or an ocean going barge piled high with containers and pulled by a tug. It was too far away be sure.

With the officers gone, I was alone. More alone than I'd been in a long time. Alone and in the dark. In more ways than one. A wave of emptiness rippled deep in my gut.

I thought about Seward then. And my home at the airport. I craved the feel of my camper and the cozy warm smell of last night's leftovers. The softness of the air mattress bed beckoned from above the driver's compartment. I was tired and wanted nothing more than to kick off my shoes, pull off my clothes and climb into that softness under the down sleeping bag. And, of course, I imagined another warm presence there too. My fantasy lover. Smiling up at me from the dark pillow, her open arms welcoming me home.

But that was just a dream and miles away. Nevertheless, home pulled at me the way it always did. Like a long rubber band tied around one ankle. The further from the safe and familiar, the stronger the pull.

I turned away from the waterline and walked back up the left side of the airstrip scanning the surface for any problems. Something scurried through the brush to my left. I looked that way but saw nothing. A bear? Probably not. The trees on that side of the runway were thick and blocked any view to the north. Dense brush formed a thick dark wall filled with small skittering sounds muffled by the heavy foliage. I glanced over to where the airplane sat and wondered if I could get there before a bear chased me down.

Relax, dummy, it was probably a squirrel. The voice in my head tried to settle me down with little success. I wished I had more of Willie's paranoia. Having a shotgun slung over my shoulder would have felt a lot better. He worried about this kind of stuff all the time, and I usually didn't think about it until it was in my face. And too late.

"*You don't worry enough,*" he'd said. He was probably right. I liked to think of myself as cool, calm and collected. Worrying didn't fit the picture. He'd scoff at that. '*You wanna be cool or alive?*' he'd probably ask. His nervous habits all served to keep him alive, avoiding the careless oversight or dumb ass mistake.

I clapped my hands together a few times to make sure the local wildlife knew I was there. Counting on that old theory that they were more afraid of me than I was of them. As if a theory would protect my butt when my lack of firearms wouldn't. I took a deep breath and moved on.

Halfway up the strip I stopped and turned around for the view I'd have on takeoff. That was the way home. I was uphill then with good visibility over the water below. Moonlight from the west was starting to flood dimly under the clouds lighting up the channel, but I didn't like what I saw.

CHAPTER
4

Fog. The moonlit mountainside I'd spotted earlier was still there but dimmer. In fact, I could see the whole moon low in the sky just above the horizon. Except now it was fuzzy. Fuzzy from the tendrils of fog reaching across it from the south. Creeping silently and steadily northward the low bank of impenetrable gray covered everything in its path.

The moon had become a dull orb shining through a lace curtain, like a small glowing cotton ball. My heart sank at the sight of it. Any fleeting thoughts of flying home or my beckoning warm bed flew away with them. I glanced at my watch. Unless the troopers were back soon, taking off was going to be impossible.

I hunched my shoulders to relieve some tightness and turned back toward the plane. The fog bank I'd seen out over the Gulf was moving a lot faster than I'd thought. As if to confirm my suspicions a gust of wind swept down the hillside rustling the bushes and pushing at me as I walked.

I heard a new sound. A strange metallic squeaking somewhere above me. As I approached the plane I spotted its source. It was the windsock. A tall pole stood just ten yards away. A rusted ring of metal was attached to its top like a basketball hoop but bent vertically. A ragged hunk of faded orange cloth hung from the ring, and it flapped sluggishly in the breeze. With every nudge of wind the rusted metal cried out in decrepit protest. As if it wanted to rust and wither in peace and to slumber through the twilight of its life undisturbed. But no such utopia existed on the remote islands in Prince William Sound. This place wasn't for sissies.

Staring up at the windsock frame creaking in the wind I saw more bad news. Wispy gray threads of cloud were streaming over the ridgeline high above the airstrip. No doubt about it, the fog was rolling in fast and would have us covered within the next fifteen minutes. I looked at my watch again fumbling to find the little button that lit up the dial before I could see the time. They hadn't even been gone a half hour.

I looked down the road toward the lodge. If they came back right then, we might have a chance. Even so I shuddered at the thought of taking off and trying to find my way through thick fog, mountain sides and cliffs. The heavy blanket of the low overcast sealed us in like the top of a coffin. There was no way.

I've had close calls out here before flying in heavy rain. Blinded by cloud and water on the windshield, all you can do is try to keep the rock walls in sight off the wingtip. Sometimes the cliffs are your only visual reference. Lose that and vertigo can take over, spinning you straight into the sea. You can slow the plane down and creep along trying to feel your way home. Bad choice of words. At sixty miles an hour you don't want to feel anything.

Feeling your way in a dark basement is one thing. You bump into something, you stop, adjust your path and move on. In an airplane in the fog, if you feel anything you die. A shot of ice water dashed down my spine. I shook myself trying to erase the image from my head.

Then it started to rain. Wet pellets slapped the airplane's aluminum skin with erratic intensity. It wasn't some little shower that might pass by in an hour or so. It was thick wet air choked with wind, rain and mist right down to the surface. We weren't going anywhere.

I moved under the wing to stay dry and listened to the drumbeat of raindrops pummeling the metal above my head. The random pattern shifted into a steady downpour, and became a loud roar surrounding me in the dark. I sat down on the left tire and inhaled the aroma of damp Goodyear rubber. I looked at the time again and wondered what was happening at the lodge. Where were Rankin and Daniels? Were they aware of the weather? Did they care about spending the night out here? How would that work?

I remembered my sleeping bag in the back of the plane. At least I could curl up in the backseat somewhat comfortably. One of the advantages of being a little guy. I could sleep anywhere.

I used to wish I was taller, but I'd learned to get by on smarts and persistence. And it was good to have friends like Willie. Bar fights weren't my thing, but nobody messed with Willie. He wasn't much taller than me, maybe five foot eight. But get him riled up and the sonofabitch could tear your head off. It seemed like his temper simmered just below the surface under a thin ice veneer of jokes and good old boy stories. But when something cracked its surface, his cold blue eyes went wild. His barrel chest expanded with rage, and hardened fists of cement could crush a guy in a whirlwind of fury.

The breeze began to pick up and blew rain sideways on the back of my neck. I stood up, opened the airplane's door and climbed in. Wind fought me for control of the door before I could get it shut. More gusts rocked the wings and jostled the plane back and forth. It was like the inside of a hollow log in a hail storm, but at least I was dry. I peered through the windshield to look for the light across the water but it was gone. Through the fog and rain I could barely see white caps shimmering just offshore. I took a deep breath and tried to fight off the rising tension in my neck.

Calm down, chucklehead. You're warm and dry. You ain't even dead yet.

I thought about Rainey then, a waitress friend of mine in Seward. I don't know why. Maybe I knew she'd cheer me up. She was my good mood charm. Like a positive mental attitude coach. Ever since she'd read some book about it, she was always pointing out the silver linings in life. Not exactly Pollyanna but close. At least she didn't go around saying "It's all good" like so many people do without thinking. I was sick of that phrase. Sometimes it wasn't all good. Sometimes it just sucked. Like now for instance.

I looked out the window again. Rainey. I had to smile at the irony of her name. She was the brightest ray of sunshine I'd ever met. Her blond hair and flirty smile lifted the spirit of every room she walked into. I wondered what she was doing. Her work day was long over by now. She was probably getting her beauty sleep, as she called it, preparing for another day slinging hash for tourists at the Breeze Inn. Then I remembered she'd left town a few days ago for a new job on a boat somewhere. Missing her washed over me like a dizzy spell. I had to remind myself she was married and not available.

The raindrops continued to roar down without mercy. I shook my head at my reflection in the window. A tired bearded face stared back at me, dark rings under round sunken eyes. I rubbed my face with my hands and tried to relax.

Rainey, Rainey, Rainey. A brief jolt of impending gloom gripped me deep inside. Would I ever see her again? I owed her so much. It was Rainey who had pulled me through a rough time the previous year. A runaway affair of the heart that had almost destroyed me. I'd made such a mistake, such a dumb mistake. I'd let down my guard and fell down a rabbit hole. Head over heels like I hadn't done in a long time. Like I'd been run over by a truck and left on the side of the road watching tail lights disappear in the distance.

Her name was Brandy Fontaine. An amazing person really. Smart, pretty, playful and tough. A Learjet pilot of all things and Willie's daughter. I'd fallen hard. The irony still made my head spin.

When she fled I think I went into shock. Pulled my head inside a shell and tried to turtle my way through the winter with blinders on.

Willie was no help. I'd asked him about her once, and he'd just shrugged. I could tell a brick wall when I walked into one. It was a guy thing, I guess. Willie and I had never been able to talk about Brandy.

Rainey had called me back then at just the right moment. How she knew to do that I'll never know. Cell phones and fate. I tell ya, I'll never get it.

"Hey there, Johnny. Wanna buy a lonely girl a beer?"

Rainey's voice on the phone that night had been exactly the life preserver I'd needed. Rainey and I were safe with each other. We were friends. Never been lovers, never would be, I guess. We both understood that without needing to talk about it.

I was embarrassed to admit how hard I was taking the whole Brandy thing. I wasn't supposed to be that fragile. Wasn't supposed to feel that kind of pain. Wasn't supposed to be that needy. That wasn't the plan. That wasn't the deal. My life was supposed to be orderly and sane. Not mixed up and weird. I don't roll like that. Or do I?

I stared out at the rain again. What the hell was I doing here? What's happened to me? Where was the fame and fortune? Where was the high life? I was supposed to be a renowned Alaskan bush pilot glowing in the success of one amazing adventure after another. But instead, here I was, stuck in the middle of nowhere in the rain and getting all weepy over some woman.

Where were the big bucks? Hell, I was scratching just to make a living any way I could. Where's the honor in that? What was the point? Where was the applause? The crowd of smiling admirers?

I pushed open the door of the cockpit. The air inside was suffocating me. I had to get outside. The swirling thoughts were making me nuts. Where's the remote? Change the channel. Please.

I paced under the left wing for a while. Twisting my neck from side to side I tried to release the tension. Tried to force my mind to think about something else. I couldn't tolerate a lot of whining. Especially my own.

Back and forth I walked and waited for the troopers. I wondered how they would take the news that we couldn't take off. Shouldn't be a big surprise. They knew about Alaska. Weather forced most of the decisions around here.

Just for a second I thought about taking off without them. Make my escape before the fog closed us in completely. Get back to Seward and go to bed. I knew it was a bad idea and I dismissed it immediately, but it was tempting. After all, they hadn't come back on time, and fog like this can close down an area for days. It could be a business decision, staying available for other customers.

But I'd never be able to justify abandoning the troopers. And if kept my job, I'm sure we'd never get any more calls from them. You can't turn your back on government work. Not unless you're independently wealthy or stupid.

I thought about the guy they'd come out after. What was his story? Probably some drunken loser. A guy who beat up his wife and was headed for jail. Pathetic, no doubt, but I didn't really know. Could be something else altogether. I didn't need to worry about his drama. I couldn't even control my own.

The rain started to let up then. The owls sang out to each other from nearby trees, their haunting calls echoing in the night. I thought about the little voles and field mice huddled under the heavy grass nearby. They had to be listening too, their little eyes twitching at the sound. I wouldn't want to be a vole. Knowing you were one of the major menu items for a long list of predators.

I looked at my watch and wondered again what to do. It was after ten and dark. Thick fog had descended on the whole area blocking any help from the moon or stars. I couldn't escape now even if I wanted to. Were the troopers waiting for a break in the rain before they came back to the plane? Or had they settled in for the night at the lodge and were just letting me figure that out for myself? I kicked the tire absentmindedly listening to the dull thump and felt the vibration rattle its way up my leg.

It didn't seem right. Something was wrong. Too much time had gone by. I was getting pissed. Why hadn't they left me any instructions? Officer Daniels was a jerk for sure, but Rankin seemed like a nice guy. I thought he would at least come back to tell me what was going on.

I was usually slow to anger, especially when there might be another explanation. But not knowing made me nervous. I hated that. I'd never make it as a beach bum waiting to see what might wash up on the shore. I had to do something. I needed to go look for answers. I'd been waiting long enough.

The drizzle had quit by then, and the wind had stopped too, but the fog was relentless. Some kind of weather system had moved in, then stalled and shut down for the night. Lights out.

I tried to decide if I was really pissed or not. I wanted to remain professional and not give these guys any attitude, but I was feeling pretty damned inconvenienced. I was cold, damp, hungry and stiff from standing around too long. And these guys were probably cozy and warm up at the lodge.

Whatever, I shrugged again. Hell, just write it off to life in Alaska. Flying the bush wasn't supposed to be easy. It was usually one unexpected surprise after another. Nothing predictable about it. Isn't that why I was up here in the first place? Living the Dream?

I could hear Willie griping at me in one of his big brother speeches. "You came up here to avoid boredom, so why bitch about the hardships? If you don't like it, get the hell out. Go back to some nine to five shit until you rot and die. But just remember, there ain't no adventure in Lazyboy Land."

Thanks, Willie, just what I needed. A bullshit pep talk from a burned out bush pilot. But. He was right.

"Yeah, so what?" I thought to myself. *"So I had to spend the night on an island airstrip trapped by fog and rain. Whatever, dude. Big deal."*

I had to find out what was going on. I stuck a large rock under the front tire and made sure the doors were closed. I looked around with a quick glance to confirm there was no one nearby, but I pulled the keys from the ignition anyhow. Just in case.

Then I started to walk the road to the lodge. I'd never walked it before. My previous trips had all been simple pick ups or drop offs. The guests had always been waiting at the airstrip. But I'd seen the road from the air and it was an easy walk through the trees for a couple of miles to the lodge.

Leaving the open air of the airstrip and moving into the forest, I noticed the strong sweet smell of spruce. The road inclined and inky darkness surrounded me like I was walking into the open mouth of a whale. Silence dropped on me like a net. Only the sound of my footsteps on the soggy trail kept me company as my shoes slip slopped along, the muddy surface sucking at my soles. I could only see about ten yards of the road in front of me. Its brown surface was wide enough for one vehicle with little room to spare on either side. It was slightly crowned with a ditch on each side and assorted pot holes and puddles along the way. The ditch on the right carried a shallow stream of runoff, the remnants of the recent rain shower running down to the sea.

I walked along listening to my own scuffle. The fog had crept in tight and muffled all sound. Except there was no sound. Even the birds and the bugs had gone silent like they were frozen in place and time, watching and waiting. All I could hear was my breath and my heart pounding against my eardrums in the stillness.

A guy in my line of work needs to be vigilant, but I wasn't that concerned. I was only mildly nervous and slightly annoyed. Staying up this late cut into my sleep. I had business waiting for me back in Seward. The good weather there was holding, and a cruise ship was coming in. If I could get back, I might make some good money. I didn't like being tired on busy days. I enjoyed flying and talking with the tourists, but not when I was strung out from too little sleep. Or hung over.

The deeper I moved into the trees, the darker it got. I didn't have a flashlight with me. I almost never carried one. Never have. Probably a leftover from my Army days and special ops training. A flashlight lets others see you from miles away. Way before you have a chance to see them. It's a dead give away. Besides, when I was poking around on a repo job, I made my living in the dark. It was safer to be unseen.

The human eye is an amazing thing. If you just stand still and wait a while, it'll adjust to low light, and you can see plenty. Because of that, complete and total darkness is a rare thing. It's not often when you can't see your hand in front of your face.

I've actually learned to enjoy sneaking around in the dark. Relax into it and you have the upper hand. You need to move carefully and feel your way along with your hands and feet. That way you don't drop into a hole or fall off a cliff. And you avoid sharp sticks in your face.

It's like an art form easing your way along like a deer moving through the forest. Muscles and limbs moving with liquid slowness, gracefully choosing each step with care. Avoiding dry sticks and crispy patches of dried leaves. That way you can hear better too. Humans are very noisy. You can hear them a long way away. Especially when they're don't know you're nearby.

But, like I said, I wasn't that concerned. I wasn't exercising that kind of care. I kept up a steady pace, scuffling along on the dirt and gravel. I didn't need no stinking flashlight. *What, me worry?* It felt good to walk. A lot better than sitting at the airstrip lost in confusion. I just needed to hike down this road, find the troopers and figure out what to do with the rest of the night.

It was colder in the woods, and my fleece jacket felt good zipped up high around my neck. Walking was warming me up too which was a good thing since the wet air and fog were nipping at my hands and cheeks.

Not seeing anything ahead of me, I started wondering if I'd taken the wrong road. What was that old joke? Sure we're lost, but we're making good time.

The road curved now and then and rose and fell with the irregular shape of the island terrain. Once in a while I could see down the slope toward the ocean. Then I could barely make out the sound of water lapping innocently at the shore.

In about a half hour I felt a change. A subtle shift of energy in the air. I guessed that I was getting close to the lodge but it was too dark and foggy to tell for sure. I topped a rise and started down a long slope. I remembered seeing this from the air last summer. Just ahead the woods opened up into a circular driveway, and there was a light.

I almost bumped into something on the left side of the road. It was an ancient pickup with a snow blade on the front. Both of the tires that I could see were flat. The rusted rims dug into the dirt with a look of silent resignation.

A solitary light bulb shining in the distance had to be the front door of the lodge. Fog dulled its reach but it gave off enough illumination to reveal the clearing in front of me. I stopped and looked around listening. Nothing moved.

The circular driveway held two other vehicles, a log cabin barn and a small cabin with a front porch. In the center of the drive a couple of large boulders were surrounded by a soggy morass of mud and beaten down grass. An old split log bench lay on its side, moss covering its broken legs.

I walked toward the light and studied the lodge that loomed above me. It had a wrap around deck and a log railing that led around to the back. I frowned at the sight of it. I couldn't tell if anyone was there or not. Where were the troopers?

All the windows were dark. Only the one light bulb above the door gave any sign of life. I felt the muscles in my face tighten in confusion while I stared at the place. It looked shut down and deserted. At first I'd expected to meet them along the road on the way back, but then I figured I'd find them at the lodge sitting in the kitchen or the dining room talking to someone. I had imagined their faces as they looked at me in surprise and then remembered who I was and why I was there.

But there was no one in sight anywhere around the lodge or inside the windows. I moved to the double door in the dark shadow under the light and found a handwritten sign taped from the inside. Closed for the season.

Had I taken a wrong turn? Or missed some other place along the way where they'd gone? I retraced my trek along the road in my mind, but I couldn't remember any other place they could be that I wouldn't have found along my walk. Then again it was really dark and maybe I'd missed it. Weird.

I looked around more carefully then, using the light to search for signs. There were footprints in the muddy surface in front of the deck, and muddy scuff marks on the deck itself. Small clods of dirt and mud were scattered around an old welcome mat at the door. I picked one up. It still felt damp. Someone had to be around. Whoever had last cleaned off their boots before going inside must be in there. Were they inside and asleep for the night?

I knew I was going to have to do something. I was going to have to make some noise and draw some attention. The polite approach wasn't working out. I hated to impose myself, but I had no choice. This was too strange. I'd brought two Alaska State troopers out to this remote island in Prince William Sound and they'd vanished? If I'd felt alone before, I felt ridiculous now. Like one of those dreams where you find yourself wandering around the halls of a school building looking for the room where you have to take a final exam that you've never studied for. For a class you never attended. And you're in your pajamas.

I knocked on the door and listened to the rattle of its loose wooden frame and flimsy lock disrupting the stillness. After so much time in silence the sounds seemed harsh and out of place. No response. I pressed my face against the dirty window panes and tried to see into the room inside. It looked like a large entry parlor next to a kitchen, but I could barely make out any details.

I knocked again harder and heard a dog bark from deep inside the structure. Okay, I mentally prepared an apology for disturbing whoever I was waking up. Surely whoever was in there would at least listen to my questions. I guess if I lived in a remote place and a stranger knocked on my door with a story about missing troopers, I'd at least listen. Before I shot him.

I shrugged off that thought and tried to reassure myself that I wasn't doing anything wrong. It was the most normal thing in the world to ask for help. Even though it was a weird story, I had to tell it to somebody who might be able to help.

The dog had gone silent. Nothing moved. I glanced around the yard behind me, but the damp and darkness sat out there unchanged. Then I heard a sound. A bump from somewhere inside and above me. Like it was coming from an upstairs bedroom. I heard a door open and someone moving. I pressed my face tighter against the window and noticed a tiny light flickering at the top of the stairway inside. It was a candle and someone up there was holding it while leaning out of a doorway looking down toward me across a wide lobby.

"Hello?" I called up to the shape behind the light.

"We're closed," came a high pitched scratchy voice barely loud enough to hear.

"Hey, I'm really sorry to wake you up, but have you seen a couple of troopers?"

There was a hesitation. "What?" The voice sounded confused.

"Troopers. Alaska State Troopers."

"Cops? No. There's nobody here. Can't you see we're closed?" The voice was Minnie Mouse high and getting shrill. It was a woman's voice, tense and guarded.

"Yeah, I see that. I'm a pilot from Seward. I flew these guys out here a couple of hours ago, and they walked over here to talk to somebody, and they didn't come back. You sure you haven't seen anybody?"

"I said we're CLOSED." The shriek echoed in the lobby. Then the door slammed and I was in the dark again.

CHAPTER
5

What the hell? I stood there for a moment in disbelief.
I looked around the yard again. Did I miss something?
The troopers had to be around here somewhere. I pushed
away from the door and stepped off the deck. I walked
around the muddy drive looking everywhere for another
place they could be. I didn't care who I woke up anymore.
Little Miss Squeaky could take a flying leap. I wanted
answers and I didn't care who got upset about it. I mean,
for crap's sake. What was I supposed to do, stand around in
the dark growing old?

Okay, calm down. There had to be a simple
explanation. The officers would apologize and explain what
happened and where they'd gone. Then we'd talk about the
weather and the fog and make a plan for getting back to
Seward.

There was nothing in the yard but a generator shack,
some decrepit sheds, the barn, a couple more old trucks and

that little cabin which was probably a staff dorm. Its front door was locked, and I could tell it hadn't been open for a long time. The barn's front door stood ajar, and I looked inside to see a dark space filled with old kayaks, paddles and moldy life jackets scattered across the floor.

I walked back to the lodge being careful to stay out of the deeper mud. I stepped back onto the deck and walked around to the back. My footsteps sounded hollow against the rotting wood flooring, and I slowed to be sure it was going to hold my weight. There were more windows along the back of the lodge and another door. But no lights inside or out.

The back side of the building opened out over a cove and a dock down below. All I could see were the stairs headed down to the water. No lights, no people, nothing moved. There were a few boats I could barely see, tied to the old pier.

I almost turned and left, but then I realized that if I didn't look everywhere I'd regret it. I thought about it for another minute but then decided to explore the dock. As I descended the old staircase I tested each step along the way. The boards were loose and soft, and they moved and sagged under my weight.

When I reached the bottom there were rubber tires cut and nailed into the sides of the pier where two fishing boats and a Zodiac bumped against them. The decks were strewn with old fishing poles and gaffes. White plastic buckets and nets lay everywhere. Moss and crusty residue clung to the sides of the fishing vessels from lack of use. They were as deserted as the rest of the place. An old shed full of more fishing gear was decaying in place, its ancient door hanging on one hinge.

At the end of the dock I turned and looked back at the lodge. It was a good sized place, probably eight bedrooms on the second level. And downstairs a kitchen, dining room and a greatroom with big windows facing the water behind me. I turned and looked out to the west imagining the view on a clear day. Sparkling water, mountains and sunsets would make this spot a fantastic setting. On good weather days anyhow. A stone chimney filled the wall on the south end. There were no lights in any of the windows. Looking up I couldn't even see the top of the chimney for the thick layer of fog pressing in from above.

I climbed back up the stairs avoiding the weak and broken spots in the boards. The enormous windows mirrored my dark reflection. I tried to look through them but all the rooms through the glass were black with gloom. I moved back around the other side of the building to get to the front again watching myself in the glass as I walked by. In my dark coat and cap I looked fairly sinister. No wonder the woman upstairs hadn't let me in. My footsteps echoed on the hollow wooden boards of the deck.

Out on the driveway, I thought about knocking again, but with a glance toward the upstairs windows, I dismissed the idea and turned back for the road to the airstrip. At least I could sack out in the airplane and wait for morning. Maybe by then the officers would show up. I stopped and took one last look behind me, but nothing had changed.

I turned and started walking down the dark road through the woods, but something made me stop again. I had the distinct sense that I was being watched. Slowly I knelt down on one knee and pretended to tie my shoe. As I fumbled with the laces, I strained to look out the corner of my eye back toward the lodge. I could have sworn I saw a movement in an upstairs window, but when I turned my head to look at it more directly, it was just as blank as it had been before.

The bugs and other creatures of the night watched me stand up and walk back toward the airstrip. I couldn't see them, but they couldn't have helped noticing the twisted expression on my face or the slight shaking of my head back and forth as I walked in the dark. I'm sure I carried the bewildered look of a man without a clue.

My leg muscles felt tired as I pushed myself up the hill, and in my mind I went back over everything I'd seen. My eyebrows scrunched together until I felt a cramp in my forehead. Confusion enveloped me. Like a pebble in a boot, it wouldn't let me relax. It was way past my bedtime, but there I was marching along in the middle of nowhere.

What had I missed? Had there been a path behind the barn leading somewhere else where the troopers had gone? I hadn't seen one back there, but what other explanation could there be? And why wouldn't that woman have known about them? That was too weird. Something was very wrong.

The troopers were smart men, professionals obviously. If they'd returned to the plane and found me missing, they would have looked around and then decided that I must have gone to the lodge. But I still didn't know how I could have missed them unless there was a path somewhere else that I didn't know about.

I must have turned back and forth three or four times making a muddy circle of confused footprints on the road before I caught myself. How ridiculous was this? A guy could get dizzy and fall on his ass trying to make up his mind.

As if to push me into action, it started to rain. I pulled my cap lower over my eyes, pulled the fleece tighter around my neck and headed for the airplane. She was my ticket out, my backdoor. My escape. And the only dry shelter around. Besides the lodge, that is. And I wasn't going back there. Bad vibes.

Besides, Daniels and Rankin were probably standing there waiting for me. Great, I muttered under my breath. The cranky one, Daniels, was probably going to rip me a new one for leaving. Water was soaking through my hat and dripping down the back of my neck, so I pushed myself to walk faster feeling the moisture seeping into my shoes.

When I got back to the clearing, the airplane sat all alone right where I'd left her. There was no one anywhere around. Tucked tightly against the edge of the soggy airstrip, her white shape glimmered in the foggy darkness as I walked toward her. I studied the glass thinking maybe the officers were waiting inside, but her dark windows stared back at me as expressionless as dead fish on a river bank. Heavy rain drops plunked against her hollow skin, a sodden off key concert in the night.

Holding out hope that they were lying down inside and out of view, I reached the plane and jerked the door handle. It wasn't to be. The cabin was empty. I stood there for a moment staring at nothing, trying to think. At least the familiar sight and smell of the seat cushions, the headphones and the instrument panel comforted me for a second.

I thought again about flying away. Back to where the world made sense. But reality had me trapped. Fog, rain, darkness and a sense of duty held me in place like I was suspended in time. I could always fire up the engine and take off, but I wouldn't even make it across the bay. I shuddered at the image of flying a few feet above the water in a nightmare world seeing nothing through the windshield but fog.

I kicked at a stone next to the tire and stamped my feet on the wet ground. I needed to get warm. Standing under the wing I stared out into the night. Fatigue weighed on me like a hundred pound pack. I thought about using the sat phone to call the trooper's dispatch office, but I didn't have any phone numbers. The idea of struggling with a directory service through the explanations and questions over-whelmed me. Besides what was the point? There had to be a simple solution. They had to be around here somewhere. It began to rain harder.

Finally, I shook my head and gave up. I climbed into the backseat and pulled the sleeping bag out of the luggage compartment. I pulled off my wet shoes and socks and rubbed my feet. The cold flesh felt clammy and numb under my stiff fingers, but it felt good to sit down. I wrapped myself inside the bag and tried to get comfortable. Grimacing at the dampness in my clothes, I threw my soggy hat into the front seat. Then I pulled off my coat and balled it up into a makeshift pillow. I laid down, hunched around into a semi-comfortable position and closed my eyes.

There was a steady pattern of rain drops on the wings, and occasional wind gusts rocked the plane slightly. I listened for any foreign sounds or approaching footsteps, but there was nothing out there but dark. I worked at ignoring the annoying thoughts battling each other in my head. It was time to give in and get some rest. I could feel some warmth beginning to build inside the bag, and I started to relax.

My thoughts kept flashing back to the things I'd seen since the troopers left. And the candle lit apparition squeaking at me from the top of the lodge stairs. I pulled the sleeping bag up tighter around my face and squeezed my eyes shut in a vain attempt to block them out. Maybe it would all make sense in the morning. At least I was doing my job.

What was my job? Always a good question when things got confusing. I was just the cab driver. Fly 'em in and fly 'em back out. In between you just wait. Nothing fancy, no thinking required. Just do your job. When the troopers walked up to the plane and found me sleeping inside, I would be right where I was supposed to be.

I couldn't do anything else. All I could do was get warm and get some rest. Be ready to fly when the weather cleared. I knew that fog like this would surely still be thick in the morning, but what did I know? Maybe I would awake to clear skies and troopers ready to fly back to Seward.

Somewhere inside I knew it wasn't to be. My eyes kept popping open as I studied the back of the seat in front of my face and tried to ignore the little voice telling me something was definitely wrong. I knew it, and the little voice knew it.

I hate it when that happens.

After a while fatigue took over. My eyes closed, my muscles relaxed and I dropped off to enjoy a long rest.

It wasn't to be.

CHAPTER
6

"Wainwright!" It was a shout not far away and my eyes snapped open in the dark.

A knife edged pain gripped the right side of my neck. My head was wedged against the side of the airplane cabin at an odd angle. Like an idiot I'd let myself fall asleep braced against the arm rest in the back seat. All the weight of my head had been leaning against one neck muscle. For a couple of hours at least. And the muscle was complaining. In fact, it was screaming.

I sat up in agony and looked toward the sound. Somebody came rushing toward the plane with his flashlight spraying all directions in the dark. He jerked the pilot side door open.

What the hell? I pushed myself to straighten up, but it was a struggle. I winced with one eye closed from the effort and grabbed at my neck.

It was Daniels, wild eyed and breathing hard.

"Get up, Wainwright!" he rasped. "We got a problem. Can you reach anyone with your radio?"

The fog in my head was as thick as the fog all around us. "I don't know, I can try." I struggled to get out of the sleeping bag, and he moved back to give me room to get out of the back seat. I reached around for my shoes and started to pull on my wet socks. They were cold and jolted me into some clarity.

"What's wrong?" I asked.

Daniels had obviously been running and was gasping to get his breath.

"We got jumped at the lodge. The asshole's got Rankin at gunpoint. I need to get backup out here."

I worked at getting my shoes on not worrying about the laces and tried to think. Moving from the back seat into the pilot's seat I looked at Daniels. He was bent over at the waist with his hands on his knees wheezing and spitting.

I looked at my watch. It was just after midnight. I knew no one was likely to answer on the normal radio frequency, but there was an FAA remote antenna site north of us a ways. Problem was aircraft radios depend on a line of sight connection to send and receive and there was lots of terrain between us and that antenna.

I knew Daniels didn't want to hear any of that, so I flipped on the master switch and pulled on my headphones. Keying the mike I made a call. Nothing came back. I switched the speaker system so that Daniels could hear what I was hearing without a headset. Just static.

I told him about the FAA antenna while I reached for the manual in a side pocket of the cockpit that listed all the frequencies. He straightened up and stared at me signaling with his hand for me to hurry up.

The pressure didn't help any, but I finally found the right page and changed the settings on the radio. Making another call I got the same response. Nothing.

I called again and waited. "They monitor this frequency from Juneau and it might take them a minute to get back to us," I said.

He nodded silently and I watched his eyes flashing like his mind was whirling through his options. The time gave me a chance to consider what was going on. Holy crap. This could be big trouble.

When there still was no response, I called again. "Juneau Radio, Cessna four four five nine zulu, calling from Prince William Sound, mayday, mayday."

Nothing.

"The battery might run down if I keep this up. I could start the engine and try again, but I don't think they're able to pick us up."

"Shit!" he muttered looking off into the dark.

That worried me. What the hell were we going to do? If he was clueless where did that leave me?

Then I remembered the sat phone. I got it out of its box and pressed the power button. Nothing happened.

Oh no. Sure enough the battery was dead.

Daniels was watching me. "You're fucking kidding me, right?"

I looked at him in stunned shock. I couldn't think of anything, so I stayed silent.

"Jesus Christ, we are so screwed." He spun on one heel and walked out from under the wing.

"Hold on, hold on. Daniels, tell me what happened."

"Like I said, the guy jumped Rankin. I was waiting for him with the woman. He said he'd show Rankin the guy's cabin and when they didn't come back I went looking for them. When I got over there the guy yelled out that he'd kill Rankin if I kept coming. I split to get backup."

"Holy shit, is that what you're supposed to do?"

"Hell yes, that's procedure. What the fuck do you know about it?"

"Sorry, sorry. Look, take it easy. I don't know shit about police work. What are you going to do?"

Daniels let out a deep sigh. "Argh, shit, shit. Can you fly us to Chenega?"

I pulled off the headset, stepped out of the plane and moved out from under the wing. I stared down the airstrip toward the water. All I could see was darkness and a wall of fog.

"No, there's no visibility."

He looked at me hard, the gears turning. He looked back and forth from me to the water.

"Are you sure? This is goddamn life and death."

I looked at the fog again and shook my head. "Yes, I'm sure. There's no way. It would be freaking suicide to even try."

He groaned again and walked off. I went back to the plane and made sure I'd turned off the master switch. I never liked having to say no to a flight, but this situation wasn't iffy. Not even close. There was no way I was going to take off.

Daniels had a weapon and it went through my mind that he might be considering forcing me at gunpoint to attempt the flight. What the hell would I do then? It had happened before not far from here. Disgruntled hunters had forced a pilot to fly at gunpoint. He'd lived to tell the story but it wasn't pretty.

Daniels came back to the plane in a few minutes. He looked determined.

"Okay, get ready, we're going back up there. You gotta weapon?"

"What do ya mean?" I asked, suddenly feeling my throat go dry.

"I mean, we're on our own out here, and Rankin's in deep shit. We need to go get him."

"Uh, whattya mean we?" I stuttered. "What can I do?"

"Look, Wainwright, I know you're just a pilot. I get that, but I need you to do more now than just fly a goddamn airplane. Normally I wouldn't ask a civilian to get involved but this is different. Can you help us or not?"

I gulped and stared at him. "Oh man, I don't know. What's your plan?"

"Look, Rankin needs us up there. This guy could kill him if we don't move quick. I'm not sure what's going to happen but I'll keep you at a distance. If I get hit, you've gotta find a way to get out of here and get help. If you stay down here you won't know what's going on, and this creep could come along and take you out too before you knew what was happening."

I swallowed hard. He was right. It was better to go along than stay with the plane and maybe get ambushed.

"Okay," I tried to keep my voice steady but I could feel my knees starting to shake. "But I don't have a weapon."

He frowned. "Oh well," he murmured sarcastically. He shrugged his shoulders and turned his back. "Let's go."

Daniels headed for the trail, and I pushed myself to catch up with him after closing the door to the airplane. He turned to watch me coming.

"Bring the sat phone," he barked. "Maybe we can charge it at the lodge.

I turned and ran back to the plane. When I returned with the phone in its box, he spun on one heel and took off again.

"You said there was a woman at the lodge?" I asked when I caught up to him.

"Yeah, why?" He was hiking fast and it was all I could do to keep up. He only used the flashlight once in a while and my eyes adjusted to the darkness better without it as we made our way along the same road I'd already traveled once by myself.

I was feeling nervous as hell, but knowing he had a gun calmed me down some. Besides, Daniels seemed like a warrior and ready to take on any threat. I took deep breaths to try to stay calm. Then I figured I better let him know everything I knew.

"When you guys didn't come back I walked up there and knocked on the door. She yelled at me that they were closed and wouldn't open up."

He looked at me but kept marching up the old road. After a minute thinking about it, he started talking.

"When we got to the lodge, it was just the two of them," he said. "She told us she didn't know anything about a phone call. The husband said they had a hired hand and that maybe he knew something about it. I stayed with the woman and Rankin went with him to another building down the trail a ways to talk to this other guy."

"She told me she didn't know anything about any cops."

Daniels shook his head. "That lying bitch, I knew there was something going on. It had to be her that made the call."

"I looked around but didn't see the trail you're talking about. That's why I came back here."

He nodded. "It's not easy to see in the dark. By the time I waited and then went after them, it was probably an hour or so. Then I spent almost an hour trying to talk to that asshole, but he wouldn't budge. Kept telling me to shut up, he had to think. I think the guy may be missing a few brain cells."

I was breathing hard by then and trying as hard as I could to guess what might be waiting for us up ahead. We came around a corner then and Daniels flipped on the flashlight. The road straightened out in front of us and started up an incline. I remembered the lodge was just past the top of that section of the road.

A shot rang out, and I felt a spray of gravel sting my face. Daniels shoved me hard and I dove for the ditch on the right side of the road. I hit hard on the little pile of wet dirt and rocks along the shoulder. Then I rolled further into the gulley. I splashed loudly into about six inches of water in the bottom of the ditch.

"HEY! Don't shoot. Alaska State Troopers. Stand down!" Daniels was shouting as he took cover.

More shots smacked into the mud around me, and I buried myself into the sidewall of the trench as best I could to get something between me and where the bullets seemed to be coming from.

Then everything went quiet. I strained to hear something but it was dead still. Even the bugs and bird sounds were gone. The cold water had drenched me completely and my hat was gone. I felt around for it and even though it was wet I pulled it back over my head and waited. Where was Daniels?

I was afraid to lift my head and look around, but I wanted out of there. My right side was still in the water and the cold was clutching me with an icy grip. I started to slowly crawl backwards. I figured I could backtrack until I was out of range, then I could get out of the ditch and run for the plane.

Then I heard the scuffling of feet moving fast across the gravel road toward me. Two more shots ripped through the darkness. One of them hit the water just a foot from my head and a blast of frigid mud splashed over my face and neck.

Before I could do anything else, Daniel's body landed on me hard and shoved my head into the muck. I couldn't breathe and had to wrestle off his weight to get some air.

"Stop moving," he whispered harshly into my ear. His body was half on top of me and the other side was laying in the water.

"What the f...?" I started to say, but his hand clamped over my mouth before I could finish. I could see he had his gun out but was keeping his head down below the rim of the ditch.

"Sh...h...h," he whispered again.

My eyes must have been bugged out staring at him. He stretched his neck up to peek over the edge and then quickly came back down. He let go of my mouth, his face just inches from mine.

I was looking at him in total terror then, and he grinned at me like a crazed person. "We're in it now, ain't we, Johnny?"

I was speechless and paralyzed. My lips burbled but no sound came out. I couldn't believe he was actually smiling, like he was turned on by the adrenalin.

He grabbed me by the collar and shook me a couple of times. "Hey, Wainwright, settle down. I need you here. Take a deep breath and listen up."

I looked at him. His eyes were serious then, the wildness was fading away. More like concerned. I could read it in his eyes. We were in trouble.

I blinked my eyes a few times and tried to focus. I just wanted to get away, some freaking psycho was trying to kill us.

I remembered he had a gun, but we couldn't see a damn thing in the dark. How were we going to eliminate the threat? I started crawling backwards again. Get away, get away. That's all I could think about.

He had a different idea. "Stop moving, goddamn it. He can't see us, but he can hear you every time you move." He pressed his face against mine rasping into my ear.

I wiped mud off my mouth and stammered out a whisper, "Got to get the hell out of here."

"You wanna get shot in the back? Stay put and listen to me. I know I was pretty hard on you back there in Seward, I apologize."

I gaped at him, he'd surprised me with that. "I thought maybe you just didn't like to fly."

"I don't, I hate it," he said with a tight grin. "But get over yourself, you're a good pilot. You proved that. Now I need you to help me get this guy. We gotta get busy."

He was confusing the hell out of me. First he's a hard ass, and now he's being nice?

"How?" I rasped. "What is this shit? I never should have landed. I should have turned around and taken us back to Seward."

I struggled against him and tried to crawl again but he had me pinned. His body was all bones and wiry hard.

"What? And miss all this fun? Welcome to police work, Mister Pilot. Now shut the fuck up and get your shit together."

I quit struggling and just tried to breathe. He snatched my hat off my head, turned away and fumbled with something in the water. Turning back to me he said, "Now, listen up. I gotta plan."

I started to object but a sharp hand motion stopped me cold. "I need you to stay right here and distract this motherfucker. I'm going around behind him. You stay here under cover. Stick this in the mud over there and shine the light on it for a second. Just hold this up and shake it once in a while to draw his attention."

I looked at what he was shoving in my face. It was an alder branch with my hat stuck through it.

I stared back and forth between him and the stick. My mouth was hanging open as I tried to fight off the paralysis.

"Do it now," he grunted and started crawling backwards.

"Okay, okay." I followed directions. I was beginning to understand. This was life or death and I needed to act.

Before I could say a word he low crawled down the ditch and motioned for me to start working the stick. I kept my head down and crawled forward to position the hat and stick above the edge of the ditch. Then I moved back. I looked for Daniels and saw him motioning for me to use the light.

I pushed myself against the bank as tight as I could, held the flashlight beside me and flicked it on. I trained the beam ahead of me and lit up the cap. Nothing happened. I heard a scuffle behind me as Daniels moved. Then a bullet slapped the hat in front of me and spun it backwards into the water. I snapped off the light. Holy Christ almighty, the guy was a crack shot. I looked back for Daniels but he was gone.

I could hear him scrambling through the brush on the other side of the road. Afraid he was exposed to shots, I tried to set up the stick up again, but it had been shot in half. I groped around in the water and found my hat. It had a ragged bullet hole through it, and I shuddered to think what that would look like in flesh. My flesh.

It took a couple of minutes but I finally got it set up again. I couldn't hear Daniels moving anymore, but I hoped he was okay. I also was hoping the shooter had wised up and had taken off. I put the stick and hat back in place and got in position. I turned on the flashlight and lit up the hat again, but there was no response. I flicked the light on and off a couple of times, but something had changed.

It seemed like an hour went by but it was probably only a few minutes. Then I heard shots again. They sounded just like the earlier ones but aimed in a different direction. I ducked even further down but nothing hit nearby. Then I heard other shots from the direction where Daniels had gone. They were answered by a hail of shots ripping through tree branches and echoing around the rocks and then dying in the dense undergrowth. Then silence.

I waited and listened. My heart was pounding so hard in my chest, I couldn't hear anything else. I didn't want to shout out and reveal my position, but I didn't want to stay in that damn ditch anymore either. Another guy might have crept forward to sneak up on the opposite flank. Another guy might have found a rock or a sharp stick and continued the attack. Not me. I grabbed my hat and ran.

With a burst of energy I lurched up out of the ditch and lunged into the trees expecting the hot searing impact of a bullet any second. But I made it.

I hid behind some thick bushes and tried to listen. All I could hear was my own heaving chest and breathing but I finally calmed down enough to listen. Nothing. I looked down at my wet clothes and mud covered shoes. I had no weapon, no radio, no flashlight, nothing. All I had was a real bad feeling. For all I knew the shooter could have a night vision scope or something. Somehow I'd managed to hang on to the sat phone box, but it wasn't any help.

I pushed backwards and bushwhacked through the trees and bushes toward the airstrip keeping the road off to my right. That way I could dive back into heavier brush if I needed to. The going was rough, but I didn't care. I moved as fast as I could. Branches hit me in the face knocking off my baseball cap several times. Devil's club ripped at my legs and alder roots wrapped around my ankles and pulled me down over and over.

Finally I couldn't push my way through any more. I crumpled to the ground to catch my breath. The soil around me smelled like dead earthworms and ants. After a few minutes I started getting chilled again and had to move.

Still hearing nothing I pushed out to the road and looked both ways. The darkness was dense and quiet. Not even the bugs and birds were saying a thing. I stepped into the road and looked back up toward the lodge. Maybe Daniels needed me, maybe I should have gone back up there to see what I could do to help. Maybe, maybe, maybe, but fuck it, I was scared. I turned and hurried into the darkness toward the plane. I fought off the nagging doubts by telling myself I'm no hero, I'm no soldier, and I'm not a cop, damn it. I'm a pilot, and gunfights are not part of the job.

My soggy shoes slapped on the damp dirt roadway even as I tried to move silently and once in a while I slipped but not enough to fall. I tried jogging even though I was tired as hell. The effort warmed me up which I needed desperately after spending all that time in the ditch. Finally the airstrip came into view and I made my way to the plane. It was raining again and the fog was still as thick as oatmeal.

Looking down the runway to the water erased any ideas about taking off.

I thought about getting in the plane but that would make me a sitting duck. I could picture a killer moving toward me in the dark. In the plane I wouldn't stand a chance. What could I do? Start the engine and try to hit him with the prop? Dumb idea.

I opened the cargo door and pulled out my green day pack. When I grabbed the sleeping bag from the rear luggage compartment the airplane's tow bar clanked forward against the seat back. I stared at it for a moment, then picked it up. It was a big fork kind of thing, about three feet long, made of aluminum. It was used for pulling the plane around by hand. Not very heavy but the only thing like a weapon I could think of. I took it with me, imagining swinging it like an axe and bashing somebody over the head. Yeah, right. But having it in my hand felt better than nothing. What else was I gonna do? Smother the guy with my sleeping bag. I felt myself rolling my eyes. I closed the cargo door quietly and moved off into the woods again to hide.

Before I got into thick cover I stared down the runway again wondering if I could take off. Still no way. Which would be more terrifying? Flying blind just above the water in thick fog or playing hide and seek with a crazed killer on a cold wet island in remote Alaska. I suppressed a shudder and made myself a sheltered place to hunker down and sleep. If I didn't get warm soon, I knew hypothermia could kill me in my sleep. There was no way to make a fire but my body temperature was pretty good after the fast retreat down the road. Inside the sleeping bag I could trap the heat and be alright.

As soon as the sky opened up a little I was going to get in the plane and scoot. To hell with the troopers. What could I do? Maybe their only hope was me getting to civilization and calling for help. I pulled off my wet shoes and socks and my hat and pulled the sleeping bag completely over my head to seal it tight. The air inside smelled like mud, body odor and fear.

I thought about bears for a minute, but somehow that idea didn't bother me near as much as a psycho killer with a gun. I also wondered if this could be the end. Was I going to wake up dead? The blood was racing through my eardrums with a roar, but somehow I fell asleep listening to raindrops dripping off the leaves and branches above me.

CHAPTER
7

I heard something and my eyelids fluttered open. It was still dark. No, wait. I was inside a sleeping bag. I pushed the heavy cloth away from my face and saw gray morning light. Where the hell was I? I listened but all I could hear was early morning in a forest sounds.

I pushed myself to sit up, but it was a struggle. Flashes of agony pulsed from my neck. I winced with one eye closed from the effort and tried not to moan out loud. My back was stiff and tight too. I closed my eyes again and just sat there moving carefully, stretching and groaning to myself. A rock had spent the night in the middle of my lower back, and spruce needles had worked their way inside my shirt.

When all the pains began to subside a little, I opened my eyes again and looked around. I couldn't see much through all the brush and trees around me. Then I started to remember. The troopers, the road through the woods, the lodge, a strange person with a candle, that flickering flashlight beam, gunshots in the trees. Daniels. Oh, man.

I groped around until I found my shoes and socks, then my hat. Then I fought my way out of the sleeping bag as quietly as I could, rolled it into a ball and pushed it out of my way. I pulled on the socks. They were still wet and cold, and the shoes were slimy and hard with caked mud. I could see my breath as I dressed. I shuddered and thought: *There has to be an easier way to make a living.*

What the hell was I doing out here anyway? And where in hell were those cops? Or at least Daniels? The uneasy feeling of the night before crept back into my gut like a dead whale beached on a black gravel shore. I spotted the tow bar and picked it up hefting the weight and thinking about how to use it like a club if I needed to.

I stood up carefully and looked around. I couldn't see much so I pushed through the bushes around me toward the clearing. A thousand drops of rain water leapt at me from where I'd disturbed them on the leaves.

The fog hadn't changed. If anything, the cold of the night had helped thicken the airborne mist. I looked down the runway but couldn't even see the water less than a hundred yards away.

Claustrophobia gripped me and I caught my breath for a second. I looked the other direction and saw the airplane where I'd left it. My escape. My magic carpet. My way out. Grounded.

It was six a.m. and cold. The fog was as dense as a closed mind. The thick gray cloud laying on the earth's surface barely let through any of the sunshine above it, and the light around me was dim and sullen. At my feet, the brown gravel of the airstrip sulked in wet discomfort. I could see colors now compared to the night before when everything was shades of gray. There were flashes of red along the edges of the runway, the late season remains of the summer's fireweed. And mottled greens of rye grass and sedge. Even the spruce trees were offset by splashes of yellow and orange from oak, cedar and elms.

I looked around and wondered what the hell to do. There was still no way to fly anywhere. I thought about calling Moose Pass or Willie, but then remembered the sat phone's dead battery and Daniel's look of disgust. I was busy kicking myself for that when I recalled that my boss didn't even know I'd taken his airplane and left Seward.

Would Willie call him when he realized I hadn't come back? Maybe. I thought about the ass chewing I would have to endure from Phil when I got back. I glanced at my watch and then toward the sky again. If the ceiling would lift just a little I could get out and back to Seward before Phil learned I was missing. But the fog was so thick I felt a sharp twinge of panic realizing there was no way I was going to avoid his wrath.

Then I heard something. I ducked back and down to get out of sight. It had sounded like a boot scraping on the gravel and not far away. I fumbled in my coat for my glasses case and pulled on my regular lenses. They fogged over immediately from my breath, and I couldn't see a thing. I pulled them off and used my shirt sleeve to dry off the lenses, but it didn't help much. I gradually rose back up to peek out through the branches, but low hanging mist enveloped everything.

Maybe it was Daniels coming back. I hunched my shoulders, hugged myself against the chill and waited, staring and straining my ears.

After a few moments, I heard footsteps moving toward the plane. The sound grew louder, and then I saw him. A large figure loomed out of the mist. It was a tall man by himself. No hat, but a dark hooded sweatshirt that blended so well against the trees behind him, I had to blink a few times to make sure I was really seeing him. His massive shoulders swung with an odd lurching stride. His face was in the shadow of the hood, but the rest of him came into clear view as he approached. He wore faded blue jeans and knee high fishermen's boots. In one of his beefy fists he was carrying something. When he got close enough I recognized it as a green metal thermos.

My heart started to pound, and I felt an odd mixture of terror and at the same time, nervous relief. Things were about to get a lot worse or a lot better. Who was this guy? Friend or foe? All of a sudden I thought about how vulnerable I was. Unarmed, unaware and unable to fly away. Bush pilot's hell.

As he came closer he pulled back his hood and I noticed his glasses. They had thick black frames with thick lenses that distorted the large round eyes behind them. He had a full head of dirty blond hair uncombed and wild. His forehead was buried under his hair above a scraggly blond beard and mustache. One of those half assed attempts at facial hair. It was hard to tell his age. I was guessing forty. He was looking at the airplane as he approached and craned his neck like he was trying to see if anyone was inside. When he got close enough he set down the thermos, cupped his hands and pressed them against the side window to look inside. He had a black day pack on his back.

I kept low behind the bushes and made sure I wasn't visible while I studied him. He didn't seem to be concerned about any kind of a threat. At least he wasn't sneaking up on the plane or trying to conceal his sounds. I looked toward the road to the lodge where he'd come from in case the troopers were behind him, but the road was deserted.

When he realized the plane was empty, he stepped away and looked up and down the runway. I could see a puzzled expression cross his face. Then he began to scan the tree line and looked in my direction.

I ducked down and held my breath. After a couple of minutes, he called out.

"Hey, pilot. You out there somewhere?" He had a high pitched nasal voice that surprised me from such a large person.

I didn't answer, thinking it better to wait a bit and try to pick up some idea of who this guy was.

He looked up and down the tree line again and tried again. "Where are you, man? The troopers sent me to tell you what's going on."

Say what? I wanted to speak up but something held my tongue. My feet wouldn't move either. I couldn't decide.

"Okay then, maybe you swam away," he called out to the trees with a chuckle. "But if not I've got some hot coffee here for ya."

He didn't sound like a psycho killer. I reviewed my limited experience with psycho killers and decided to wait some more.

The big man paced back and forth on the gravel for a minute and then called out again in his high pitched voice. "Okay, man, I'm heading back to the lodge. If you're interested, there'll be some hot breakfast there for ya."

He turned to go and I felt a stitch in my stomach reminding me I hadn't eaten in a long time. As he walked across the airstrip toward the road to the lodge, I stayed hidden but called after him.

"Hey, who are you?"

He stopped and turned around scanning the tree line. He seemed to focus in on my hiding place, but nothing changed about his relaxed body language. He smiled in my direction and pushed his glasses back up his nose.

"I'm Charlie Westridge, I own the lodge here. Are you alright?" he called in my direction.

I didn't answer thinking about what he'd said. I shifted my grip on the tow bar. "Where're the troopers?" I finally asked.

He keyed in on my voice and stepped in my direction.

"Stay right there, okay? I've got a weapon," I said with an edge in my voice.

He pulled up and held up his hands. "Whoa, take it easy. Everything's okay. I guess I can't blame ya for being cautious after all the excitement last night, but that's all over now. Hank's gone."

"Who's Hank?" I asked.

"He's the guy that started all the trouble. He was one of our fishing guides. He got wasted yesterday when I was out cutting wood and started some shit with Greta. She's the one who called the cops."

"Where're they?" I asked him again.

"Can you come out of there? I ain't never talked to no tree before." He grinned and chuckled.

I felt a little foolish but my only protection was the dense patch of woods behind me. My only chance against an attack would be to hide there again.

"Not until I know what's going on around here."

"Okay, okay, relax, man. The troopers took one of my skiffs to follow Hank. After all the shooting he took off in one of the other boats. They asked me to tell you about it."

I thought that over. "Anybody get hurt in the gunfire?"

"Nah, I don't think so." He was close enough then that we didn't have to raise our voices to call back and forth.

A big drip of cold water splashed down the back of my neck, and I jerked and tried to pull my collar closer around me. "So what am I supposed to do?" I asked.

"They wanted me to tell you to take me with you and fly over to Chenega. If Hank's not over there, maybe we can spot where he went from the air."

"I can't fly anywhere in this shit."

"Yeah, I figgered as much. We're pretty socked in, huh? Happens all the time out here." He shook his head and looked down the runway to the water. Then he screwed open the thermos and poured coffee into the metal cup cover. I could see steam rising from the hot liquid, and a chill ran up my lower back. My lips began to tremble and move.

"Coffee?" he invited with a smile, holding the cup out toward my hiding place behind the bushes.

I pushed forward and used the tow bar to hold branches out of my way. He walked toward me and put the cup in my outstretched hand. I watched him carefully and raised the trembling cup to my mouth. The coffee was good and strong and the aroma swept over me in a wave. I closed my eyes in spite of everything and let myself take a big sip.

"Well, hey then, good morning," he said looking me over. He stood almost a foot taller than me but he stuck out a huge hand like a politician. With the coffee cup in my left and the tow bar in my right, I looked at him awkwardly but then dropped the tow bar with a clunk and returned his handshake.

"I'm Charlie," he said again with a grin and looked down at the tow bar, then back at me. His hand swallowed mine. "Where are you from?"

"I'm Johnny Wainwright," I said. "I fly out of Seward." The coffee felt spectacular as it slid down my throat and warmed my insides.

"Huh, I don't think I've ever met you. Most of our guests come over by boat. It's been a while since a plane's come in here." He waved a hand at the airstrip. "You make it in okay?"

I thought back over the landing the night before. It seemed like a week ago. "Yeah, no problem."

Then I remembered more details from Daniels. "So what happened with the other trooper? Daniels told me that the guy jumped him and was holding him hostage?"

"Oh that. What a freaking jerk that Hank turned out to be. Yeah, he left one officer handcuffed inside his cabin. I think his name was Rankin? And Daniels was the other one? It took them a while to get their shit together and follow Hank."

"And nobody got hit? With all those bullets flying around? Unbelievable."

"Yeah, it was pretty dark."

"You got a phone at the lodge?" I asked suddenly remembering about Phil and Willie.

"Yeah, they used it to call in before they took off. You hungry? Want something to eat while we wait for this shit to lift?"

"Yeah, definitely. Thanks. It's been a long cold night." I swallowed the rest of the coffee and handed the cup back to Charlie.

Before I had a chance to reach down, he pointed down at the hunk of metal at my feet. "Is that your weapon?"

I picked it up with a sheepish grin. "Uh, yeah, it's a twelve gauge tow bar." He laughed with an odd high pitched yuck yuck sound and screwed the thermos cup back in place.

Then he said, "Come on, let's head for the lodge."

I hesitated. Should I stay or should I go? I didn't want to leave, but my stomach was winning the argument.

CHAPTER
8

It took me a few minutes to gather my stuff from the woods and open up the plane. I put the sat phone with its dead battery in my pack, closed up the plane again and joined Charlie where the road entered the forest.

"Well, what the hell, eh?" he said cheerfully when I reached him. "No point sitting out here in the fog starving to death. You'll like Greta's cooking. Then maybe the fog'll lift and we can blast out of here."

He turned and started walking to the lodge. I had to hustle to match his long strides. I settled into the pace and tried to make sense of all the new information hitting me.

"Who's Greta?"

"She's my wife. We've been running the lodge all summer, but the season's shot in the ass now. Haven't had any guests for a while and we're packing up."

"I think I talked to her last night. I walked up here to find the troopers. I knocked but she wouldn't open up. Was that somebody else?"

He laughed. "No, that was probably Greta. She gets a little freaky sometimes. And the whole thing with Hank really set her off."

"It's just the two of you?"

"Yeah, now it is. The other fishing guides left a while ago. Well, there's us and the kid, that's all."

I was starting to get winded trying to keep up with him, so I quit asking questions and just concentrated on putting one foot in front of the other.

I glanced behind me as we left the airstrip area for a last look at the plane. It looked wet and cold and worthless at the moment. The fog layer still hung over the water's edge like the end of time. Then the trees engulfed us and shadows closed in like octopus ink.

Charlie walked steadily down the road staring off into the distance. He didn't seem like a problem. Except he was so large. Like a yeti in a hoodie. But he seemed like a nice guy. Harmless probably. And I tend to like anybody that brings me coffee.

Was I doing the right thing? I guessed there wasn't any point staying with the plane. I couldn't fly over to Chenega to meet the troopers. Might as well go to the lodge and wait there. My stomach rumbled reminding me how good some hot food would taste.

What would Phil want me to do? He wouldn't want me to try to fly, no question about that. But he'd probably be so mad that I left Seward without talking to him first that he wouldn't be able to think about what I should do in the present situation. Like when you're trying to fix a flat tire and someone keeps asking you why you were driving in the first place. I blocked out any further thoughts about him.

What would Willie do? I smirked to myself. That crazy loon would probably fly. He was the only person I could think of that would try it. And then he'd say straight faced that it wasn't so bad. Even though he'd just broken every rule in the book. But he'd lecture me forever if I ever took such a chance.

Charlie was marching along in silence, lurching down the road with an awkward gait. People that live in the bush get used to not talking much, but Charlie ran a lodge, so I didn't think he would be getting bushy like that. I wanted information and my curiosity pushed me to interrupt his reserve.

"So, Charlie, how long you been living here?"

He didn't answer right away. Like he was mulling over how to respond or how much to reveal. Then he glanced sideways and down at me, pushed his glasses up his nose and cleared his throat.

"Well, I was pretty much raised out here. The old man started the place. William Westridge. Maybe you've heard of him?"

I thought about it. "Sounds familiar, but can't say as I have."

"Yeah, well, it's just as well," he said. "He was real famous out here for a while with his little empire. But those days are pretty much done now, I guess."

"You guys own the whole island?"

"Yep, Dad had a lot of money from the family business, and back in the fifties he bought this island and built the lodge. We operated every summer for more than forty years. When you see inside the lodge, you'll see. It's high end, man. At least it used to be. Luxury in Alaska. Lots of folks paid big bucks to come up here."

"Were you born here?"

"Not exactly. We operated in the summers up here and went back to upper state New York for the winters. I was born back there and spent most of my younger years bouncing back and forth. You from Seward?"

"Yeah, I'm out at the airport there."

"Okay, I know where that is. We're actually closer to Cordova. That's where we resupply. And we keep a vehicle in Whittier for trips into Anchorage once in a while."

"What about the airstrip? You a pilot?"

"Nope, that was Dad's thing. And my older brother too. They were the pilots of the family."

I was surprised to hear that. "It's a nice strip. I didn't see any other planes on it though. You have a float plane?"

"No. That's all history now." He kicked at the muddy gravel surface with one boot heel.

"How do you mean?" I asked.

"They packed it into a mountain side about three years ago."

"Oh, sorry. That happen around here?"

"Yeah, I guess they were trying to get to Anchorage through a narrow pass in bad weather."

A distant memory rattled inside. "I may have heard something about that a while back."

"They were good pilots, but I think they were trying to get through Portage Pass relying on a GPS. Probably in the clouds. Tony, that's my brother, he had waypoints programmed in for the critical spots in the pass. They'd done it several times, once with me in the back seat. Scared me bad. In the clouds, surrounded by rocks and cliffs and depending on a little black box and a prayer."

I felt a chill run down my spine at the image. I'd been tempted by that risk more than once, but had never given in.

"It was either that or a williwaw got 'em."

"Really? What time of year was that?"

"Same as now. September. But they didn't have to be out there in the first place. I'll never know what was so important about making that trip when they knew the weather was bad."

We walked on in silence. So many Alaskan airplane crashes are never explained. Dead pilots don't answer questions.

The slap-slap-crunch of our feet on the wet gravel echoed softly then faded into the wall of dark green shadows on all sides. I shuddered again thinking about williwaws. Like tiny tornadoes of turbulence they hide in high mountain valleys and then suddenly roar down to the ocean destroying everything in their paths. Small airplanes are helpless in their clutches. Willie was always warning me about them.

The road curved and then worked its way over a hill before dropping close to the water for its final stretch to the lodge. I realized it was the place where Daniels and I had been ambushed. I looked up and saw the likely place in some rocks where the shooter had probably been. Rain had erased any sign of our struggles the night before. I thought about telling Charlie about it and asking where he'd been during all the gunfire, but something inside told me to wait.

A large sign came into view that I hadn't seen the night before in the dark.

"Welcome to Westridge Lodge, Taroka Island, Prince William Sound, Alaska. Founded by William Westridge, 1953." A smaller strip of wood had been nailed across it diagonally that said Closed.

"When did you shut the place down, Charlie?"

"The crash pretty much ended it for us. Mom couldn't bring herself to come back to Alaska after that, so it was left up to my sister and me. And she wasn't interested. Never has been."

"That's too bad. I've brought people out here a few times. Everybody always said how nice it was. And great fishing."

"Yeah, I spent a lot of years on those boats hauling in halibut and salmon. These waters are full of fish. It was a good life while it lasted. We've had a few regulars come back the last two summers but not much."

I glanced down at his hands. They were working man's hands, rough, gnarled and scarred from years of pulling line and gutting fish. Tough hands that were used to handling knives, gaffes and rope. My respect for the guy was growing. Obviously a hard worker, I couldn't hold it against him that he was born into money.

"A family operation in wilderness Alaska. I guess there's worse ways to grow up, eh?"

"I guess," he shrugged and spit to the side of the road.

The opening to the circular drive in front of the lodge came into view ahead. Another sign I'd missed the night before appeared beside us nailed to a tree on the side of the narrow rutted road.

Speed Limit 80 MPH, it read.

"Funny," I said gesturing toward it with a chuckle.

"Yeah," he agreed with a snort. "I found that along a highway in Wyoming. They didn't need it as bad as we did."

It started to rain, so we broke into a trot for the last hundred yards to the lodge, water splashing from the puddles with every step. I was breathing hard and cursing to myself as I felt my feet growing steadily wetter and colder.

The skies opened up, and it began to pour without mercy. By the time we reached the porch, I was drenched. Looking around and shaking the rain off my coat, I noticed the same dreary group of buildings from the night before. But a lot more details were visible in the dim daylight. A huge moose rack hung above the entrance to the barn, and a slight trail of smoke rose from the chimney. The smell of wood smoke hung in the air.

Our footgear thumped heavily on the wooden deck and Charlie headed for the scraping post. He kicked at the band of metal a few times, then he pulled off his rubber boots and left them by the door. I did the same with my shoes, and slapped my soggy baseball cap against one leg to shake off the rain. The ragged bullet hole jerked me back to memories of the night before, and I glanced around feeling my guard rising again.

Down at the end of the front deck I spotted a large sculpture of a grizzly bear. It too must have been concealed by shadows the night before. It was a chain saw carving, the kind you see offered along the highway outside of Seward. Cheesy stuff generally, but tourists will buy anything.

Charlie pushed open the front door, and we padded our way into the lobby entrance. His feet were quiet in thick boot socks, but mine made sloppy wet sounds as I walked and left damp rings in my path. It was a large room, but the dim daylight revealed the huge space within, reeking of splendor from years gone by. A smooth wood floor flowed into the distance across the great room to where rear windows looked out over the bay. Persian carpets covered most of the wood, and a thick brown bear hide with its head attached lay on the floor at my feet. To the left an enormous stuffed polar bear stood over ten feet high. It had a massive square head with an open mouth and jagged yellow teeth. Its beady eyes stared at me and seemed to track my movements as I walked past it. I felt my knees tremble slightly.

Log walls rose to a steep slanted ceiling where a heavy black chained chandelier hung into the middle of the room. Behind that the wide staircase climbed to the second level. I could see rich red carpet covering the stairs and held in place by thin brass bars at the back of every step.

"Wait here a minute, will ya?" Charlie whispered and he walked carefully up the stairs like he was on eggshells. "I'll see if Greta's up."

I moved into the center of the lobby and looked around. On the left side of the room halfway up the log wall two huge oil paintings hung side by side in identical heavy gold frames. You had to tilt your head back to stare up at them. There were of the same man. One in a business suit with a New York City background, the other in hunting clothes kneeling beside a dead moose.

Had to be the founder. He had a founder look about him. In the New York pose he held a pipe and a commanding chairman of the board expression. The practiced look of power you see in corporate annual reports. In the Alaska pose he held the moose by its rack with the same commanding expression. The moose's expression was mostly shot-in-the-ass dead.

He was a tall man with a high forehead and close clipped hair on a large head. Bushy eyebrows and penetrating eyes spread wide above a solid jaw. You could have photo shopped the same face between both portraits. His look said, "Money, I've got it. I own all of this and you should feel privileged to stand here on my land."

I could see the family resemblance. Charlie had inherited the broad shoulders and large hands, but not the conviction, the look of the strong self made man, confident and competent. Beneath the two portraits and lower there was a large old style mirror with cracks along the edges and black flakes in the corners. I watched myself staring back and forth between the founder and his alter ego. The New York version and the Alaska version. And me in the middle.

The William Westridge on the left wore an expensive Italian suit in dark pinstripe, and William Westridge, the great white hunter, wore a massive goose down parka with a fur lined hood folded back. In contrast my soaked blue fleece jacket hung on me like a discarded wash cloth that

I'd just used to clean a bathroom. I remembered finding it on sale at the Goodwill. An old stain of red hydraulic fluid graced my right forearm. Not to mention the recent mud stains from a Taroka road side ditch.

William's gleaming forehead shone like a bright beacon of success. I looked into the mirror and noticed that I was holding my dripping cap in my hand, and my thin brown hair was matted and sticking out in all directions. My ratty dark beard looked unkempt and was adorned with a small white feather from my sleeping bag. Alaskan William wore expensive leather hunting boots with bright blue leggings laced to the knee. I had on wet black socks. The front end of the left sock was folded back under my foot, and the right sock had a hole where my little toe poked through.

I shook my head and started to grin. I looked up at the portraits and whispered, "Pleased to meet ya, Mister Westbridge. You mind if I scratch my butt?" I could sense my mother cringing. She always said I needed more respect. A proper sense of protocol, she used to say.

I walked toward the great room and left His Worship behind. Tall wooden shelves full of books covered one wall. Dozens of leather bound volumes of the classics were lined up in reverent display. Victor Hugo, Louisa May Alcott, Machiavelli, Walt Whitman, Robert Frost, Voltaire, Dostoevsky and even Theodore Dreiser and Jack London. I ran one finger along the spines of some of the larger texts and found a heavy layer of dust on the shelf that held them.

My grin widened as I thought about my life. I had books too. An image flashed in my head of the small cabinet next to my overhead bunk in the camper back at Seward. As I recalled, there was a worn out copy of a Stephen King novel from the used book exchange. Beneath that was a rumpled Playboy magazine and a stack of Victoria Secret catalogs. No dust, I might add.

Charlie came back down the stairway then and not seeing me called out.

"Hey, Johnny. You still here?"

I walked toward his voice. It sounded odd echoing through the big empty room. I found him in the kitchen.

"Oh, there you are," he said. "Greta will be down soon. In the meantime, why don't we get your clothes dried out? Follow me."

He led the way down a stairwell to another room below the main floor. We walked through a game room with an expensive looking pool table and a long bar at the far end. Ten stools with red leather seat cushions and a gleaming brass rail stood in silent attendance. There was even a shining spittoon on the floor in the corner. A chess set with tall metal pieces mutely staring at each other sat on an inlaid teak and mahogany battle field.

"Nice place you got here, Charlie."

"Thanks, I know it still looks pretty good, but there's a lot of problems now. Wood rot, cracks in the foundation, plumbing, mold, you name it. Sometimes I just want to toss a match to it."

Another great room with a lower ceiling greeted us next. Easy chairs and sofas were scattered throughout and more informal rugs in dark colors. Games and a ping pong table were set up in front of large ground level windows. Looking out I could see the back deck that I'd walked on the night before.

"Come on through here, Johnny. There's a dryer if you want to toss in your clothes, and there's a hot tub room right through there. You might want to take a soak while your stuff dries and we get some breakfast together. You hungry?"

"Oh yeah, you could say that. I really appreciate this. I can tell you're used to taking care of guests."

Charlie smiled. "You just make yourself at home and I'll come get you when it's time to eat."

I pulled off my green pack, and took out the sat phone and looked for an outlet to plug in the charging cord. I noticed Charlie had stopped to watch me. He was staring intently at the phone.

"Hey, Charlie, is it okay if I plug this in?"

The question seemed to freeze him. He looked at his feet for just a second. I tried to read his body language but came up empty.

He recovered quickly. "Here, I'll take that upstairs and get it going. The outlets down here are messed up."

"And is there any way we can get hold of the troopers to check on their progress?"

"Aw, I'm sure they're in Chenega by now. Hank ain't that smart. They're probably working him over real good," he snickered. "Anyhow, take it easy for a while."

I handed him the phone and glanced out the window. The same low fog hung just outside, as dense as ever. "I need to get in touch with my boss. He doesn't even know I'm out here."

Charlie's eyebrows shot up behind the black frames in surprise. He looked at me and then seemed to tear his gaze away to re-examine his shoes. I could see the gears grinding, but he said nothing. He examined his fingernails for a moment and chewed on a cuticle.

"Okay then," he finally broke his silence. "I'll come get you."

He closed the door behind him and left me alone in the laundry room. Suddenly the wet clothes on me felt like a hundred pounds of cold clammy quicksand. The large industrial dryer beckoned. For a guy accustomed to coin fed laundromats, free service was a luxury not to be ignored.

There was a white terrycloth robe hanging on the wall nearby, so I emptied all my pockets and stripped off my clothes. I pulled on the robe and tossed everything through the large round door in the dryer and punched the start button. I checked my cell phone but there wasn't any service signal showing and moisture lined the inside of the screen. I wondered if it even worked anymore. I left my wet cap beside my glasses and the pile of change, keys and my phone on the counter.

I thought about going upstairs to make the call, but I was shivering in the robe. A quick dip in the hot tub and a hot shower sounded better than a tongue lashing. Phil could wait.

I opened the door that Charlie had pointed out and found myself in a dark lounge. Just enough outdoor light came through the French doors at the far end to reveal a thick shag carpeted floor with wooden benches around the walls and a covered hot tub recessed into the middle of the floor. I could smell the warm chemical fragrance of treated hot water. There was another bar against the far wall with an eight foot mirror stretching its length.

I was amazed to find the hot tub all set up and ready to go. Like it was used regularly. It didn't take long to fold back the leather and foam padded cover, drop the robe on a bench and step into the steaming water. It was hot and inviting. Slipping down over the steps, I let myself sink into the sizzling liquid a few inches at a time, until I finally felt my body settle onto a contoured fiberglass bench.

Resting my head back against the rounded lip of the tub in the dark room, I felt the cares of the world sliding away and dissipating like the swirls of steam lifting off the surface of the water in front of my eyes.

I spotted the switch for the pump and after a few rumbles and gurgles from machinery under the floor, the jets began to disgorge a strong current of bubbles. The water pump settled into a steady roar blasting me with therapeutic magic. The heat took over, and everything that had been tight became loose. Everything that had been cold, wrinkled and flaccid became warm, supple and limber. Bubbles went everywhere and tickled me in places that hadn't been tickled in a long time. I closed my eyes and let the sensations take me.

I must have drifted off. The pulsating water pump covered all sound, so I didn't hear anyone enter the room. And I didn't notice the small lamp being turned on or the person moving past me carrying a tray. It may have been the smell of coffee and scrambled eggs that brought me back to the world.

My eyes opened halfway, and at first I thought I was looking at an angel with her back to me standing in front of the windows. She raised her arms and ran her fingers through her hair in a quiet ritual of self grooming. She was petite with short cropped blond hair and wore a sheer white nightgown halfway to her knees. As she stood in profile looking out to the ocean, there was enough backlighting to leave little to my imagination. I wanted my glasses, but they were in the other room. The delicate blurred vision of soft lace and silk moved her arms in slow motion as she arched her back and swayed like a glossy mist. I blinked my eyes and wondered if I was dreaming.

Just then the timer on the pump clicked off. The flow of water gurgled and stopped. The angel turned and looked at me.

"You're awake," she said. Her voice was low, husky and soft, like folds of velvet sliding over warm flesh.

CHAPTER
9

I was transfixed. I reached up and rubbed my eyes with both wet hands to make sure I was really awake. She walked toward me, sank to her knees beside a food tray on a small stool and studied her fingernails like she was waiting for me to speak. But I couldn't just yet. I couldn't believe what I was seeing.

Her bobbed blond hair held my attention. It was more than blond. It was some kind of electric super blond enhanced with chemical attentions from the next century. Darker roots added background but matched her dark thin eyebrows. It was a very modern cut, styled and sprayed to hold a casual and at the same time carefully sculpted shape that was wider at the top and then swept down to lie closely against an elegant long thin neck. Her bangs dangled just above her eyes on one side of her face but on the other side they were impossibly long and joined the other part to flow down to her chin line. Tiny diamond earring studs in petite ear lobes sparkled at me in the dim light.

I must have been staring at her like a baboon examining a fine watch. Her lips were painted bright red, and her body gleamed with the smoothest whitest skin I had ever seen. The night gown was more like a loose silk jacket buttoned up the front.

She didn't look at me. I had a feeling she made a career of that. No encouragement, no come on, no look, no link, no contact. The room had gone completely silent. She must have noticed it too. She left the tray on the stool, stood up and turned and began to move around the room looking at the pictures and things on the walls. Her chin and small trim nose inclined upward toward the objects as she walked slowly along. The night gown swished back and forth tickling her bare thighs as she moved. I couldn't help but watch her as I tried to keep my mouth closed so I wouldn't inhale any water.

"Aren't you hungry?" She finally broke the quiet, her voice sing song and warbling at least two octaves higher than earlier.

"Uh, yeah, sort of. Yeah, thanks." I started to reach for the food, then began to feel incredibly naked. Probably because I was naked. Maybe not incredibly naked, but naked just the same. I crouched deeper in the hot water and let it rise above my chin and mouth as if I could hide there in the tub. I was hoping she wasn't planning to walk over and stare down at me. My eyeballs were at the same height as her ankles. I thought of hitting the pump switch again for the cover of bubbles, but I didn't. I was paralyzed. In some kind of spell.

She continued to move around the room humming to herself and remarking on the pictures in soft tones that I couldn't really hear. I tried to reconcile the lilting voice with the harsh raspy sound from the night before. Was this the same woman?

Trying not to be obvious about it, I rose up a little and craned my neck to watch her over the top of the hot tub cover. I didn't want her to see me watching. The air chilled my bare wet shoulders.

"Didn't we talk last night?" I finally managed to ask, letting myself sink back into the warmth. "Up there in the lobby. I was at the door, asking about the troopers?"

She ignored me and stood staring at her own reflection in a mirror on the wall. After a minute she came back and knelt again by the stool on the other side of the tray from me. She continued to examine her hands and her long perfect red painted nails. Searching for tiny imperfections.

"Last night seems like a lifetime ago," she murmured in the low silky voice again. "So much can get lost in the fog." She looked over her shoulder toward the windowed door. Gray mist still hung outside like a stage curtain fully drawn.

"Yeah, really. I'm Johnny, by the way."

She didn't say anything for a moment. Almost to the point where it started to bug me.

"Yes, Charlie tells me you're the pilot." The soft and husky voice was back.

"Yup, that's right. And who are you if you don't mind me asking?"

She continued to examine her nails holding her hands out in front of her. No rings on her fingers.

"I'm Greta," she said still not looking at me.

That brought me back to reality. "Ah, yes, Mrs. Westridge, okay." I sighed and reached for the tray. "Charlie told me you were a good cook."

I turned my attention to the food. The coffee smelled terrific and my mouth began to water.

From the corner of my eye I could sense her looking me over, but I took a big slug of coffee from a delicate china cup and closed my eyes to enjoy the warm liquid rolling down my throat. Then I picked up a piece of buttered toast, shoved it in my mouth and followed it with another swig of coffee. I was starved.

I felt a waft of cool air against my head and saw her lean to one side and adjust her nightie with a sweep of her arm. She arranged herself to lie down on her side, her head toward me propped up by one hand. She said nothing but I could feel her eyes studying me as I ate. A minute went by without a word between us. I finally looked over at her and she looked away.

"You been here long, Greta?" Something about her laying there like that made me feel bold. I stared straight at her and held my look longer than strangers were supposed to. I'd never seen a woman like her in Seward. She seemed more like Las Vegas. The Vogue magazine cover girl look was a rare thing in Alaska.

"Seems like all my life," she said with a sigh. "Almost six months." Her eyes dropped to the carpet. I followed her gaze and saw her tiny white feet curled under her legs with toenails manicured and painted, the color matched to her fingernails. She slowly unbuttoned the jacket and let it fall open. There was a white half slip underneath. At least I think that's what you call it. A lacy thing with thin shoulder straps holding it on.

I struggled to think of other things to say. Small talk wasn't natural to me, but more than that I think I was having a hard time ignoring my nakedness only a couple feet away from her thin silky nightgown. I thought about what it would look like wet.

I cleared my throat and blinked my eyes to break the spell. "So, uh, what's up with those troopers? They back yet?"

Her back stiffened slightly and then she sat up on her knees and leaned on her fists directly toward me. The nightgown jacket billowed and opened. One of the little spaghetti shoulder straps dropped off one shoulder. I traced the line of her neck with my eyes where it curved down past a delicate and well defined collar bone and over the satin arc of her bare shoulder. Perky bumps and cleavage invited my eyes and welcomed them.

But then her eyes locked onto mine, and although she was about five feet away we might as well have been nose to nose.

"Johnny," she half whispered, "I don't know a thing about those men." Her look was sincere and concerned.

I don't think I'd ever seen eyes that blue. A thick liquid pale blue like a newly opened can of enamel paint. Not exactly warm, but magnetic just the same. Her eyes were so wide open they revealed everything but nothing at all. Like a mirror surface, you could stare into them for an hour and never see a thing. Maybe your own reflection peering back. Looking for something. And failing.

The silted streams and lakes around Seward carried that same mysterious blankness. It was like you could reach into the blue clouded depths with your whole arm and pull back nothing but a cold white bone of regret. A frigid emptiness that grabbed your attention but gave nothing in return.

"But they must have been here," I said, my eyes wanting to pull away but unable. As soon as the words left my mouth, I wanted to haul them back in. I felt the instant remorse of the child who drops an ice cream cone on a hot summer day.

I felt my breath catch. Her expression didn't alter, and she didn't blink. Nothing about her moved, but something changed in her eyes. Still the bluest of blue, they held me in an icy grip. Instantly I was neck deep in a half frozen glacial lake, ice crystals forming, compressing and choking me. My jaw and face began to shudder throwing my vision into a fuzzy lack of focus.

It was like a blue sky summer day that suddenly transforms when a thunderstorm flows over the horizon. The blue in Greta's eyes clouded over and began to seethe. Like a tornado wind howling with hatred, ready to shred the earth with a million shards of recrimination and spite. I saw the hidden williwaw in those eyes.

She tried to hide it behind a veil of coolness and pretense, but it was there alright. A thin line of dark mascara and lashes surrounded each of her eyes like a tangled shoreline of delicate willow branches. I watched her take a deep breath and some internal struggle began to pass. Her gaze returned to her fingernails.

I wondered how I had offended her. Had I questioned her answer? Expressed some kind of disbelief? Dared to press a suspicion? Dared to tread on fine china with a bull's lack of grace?

Scrambling I fumbled for words to repair the damage. "Sorry, I just can't get over those cops taking off without telling me anything. It's pissing me off."

She seemed to think that over for a moment. I watched as she took in another slow breath and looked at me again.

The storm had passed. As quickly as it had appeared, the disturbance was gone. Swept into a back room with a flick of a wrist. The blue waters were clear and calm again. Her eyes locked on mine once more, and I saw the hint of a smile.

She slid forward then like a cat and stretched out on the carpet beside the hot tub setting one elbow on the rim above me and resting her chin in her hand. Her eyes left mine to stare at the ceiling, and I blinked hard as an involuntary shiver took my shoulders in a spasm that sent ripples across the surface of the tub. She reached up with her other hand and stroked through her hair again, pulling the blond tresses away from her head and then letting them fall.

I began to understand how an icicle felt when the sun comes out. Overwhelmed by the sudden warmth, it thrills in ecstasy. And then slowly begins to melt, soon to disappear forever.

Snap out of it, Johnny, a voice from somewhere inside whispered. *Are you losing your mind?*

"Nice place you got h-here," I stammered and pulled myself closer to the wall of the tub in a futile effort to hide myself.

She smiled wider then, her eyes reaching for mine. Tiny lines appeared at the corners of her mouth. Past the glare of her red lipstick and slightly open moist lips, I could see perfect white teeth. A slight fragrance like crushed roses filled my nostrils. Faint but expensive.

"So you're a bush pilot, Johnny?" She picked up the fork and slowly began to toy with the pile of golden scrambled eggs on the plate between us.

I watched her and nodded fascinated by the way she moved, and the way her odd little voice formed each word. I especially liked the way she said Johnny. I could imagine hearing that sound close in the dark, those lips barely touching my ear.

"Maybe you could fly me somewhere sometime." She lifted the fork and took a small bite. I watched her mouth and felt my own moving in unison.

Wait a minute, I thought. That was my line. I used it with some success around town on Saturday nights.

But before I could figure out how to turn the tables, the fork was full of egg again and headed my way. I glanced at it determined to resist. This wasn't right. It felt weird and uncomfortable. Then I made the mistake of looking at her. Her pale blue orbs took me in, and my mouth dropped open. The taste of buttery egg filled my mouth, and the smell of warm toast made me drool. Suddenly I felt hungrier than I could ever remember. I leaned toward her and rested my head against the side of the tub to stare at her and wait for more. She took another bite for herself, slowly working the fork before bringing another for me.

Somewhere in the back of my mind I knew what was happening, but I didn't care. I let it happen. I let the moment continue and pretended I could stop it anytime. I knew it was a thin act, but it was all I had.

I reached for the coffee cup, but she intercepted my hand with her own. Her touch paralyzed me. She took my hand and stroked the back of it with her cheek and then moved it to her lips breathing warmly against my fingers. I could only stare in disbelief. For a moment our eyes met. Then she dropped her gaze to our hands, arched her back slightly and sighed. She slowly released my hand, picked up the coffee cup and moved it out of my reach.

Noticing my questioning look, she pursed her lips in apology and said, "That one's cold. I'll get you another."

I let my eyes close, took a deep breath and let my mind slip wherever it wanted. The warm water, my nakedness and the smell of eggs, coffee and her took me far away. Even the drips of water from my elbows sounded like fine music. My imagination was racing, and the feel of her warm hand and her cheek had sparked a fantasy. I conjured an image of her slipping into the tub beside me, her thin nightgown dissolving in the hot water. Our lips merged in moist perfection, tiny tongue probes sent electric shock waves down my arms and legs and out to the ends of my fingers and toes. We began to sway gently together, our hands exploring and thrilling in their discoveries. I found myself smiling in a strange wild abandon holding that amazing delicate little body against mine.

My eyes jerked open with a start to find her watching me through half open lids. She was leaning her chin on one hand again as she curled up on the carpet beside the hot tub. She had an amused look.

"Hey, dreamer boy, you gotta girlfriend?" she probed with a playful grin.

I shook my head a little more brusquely than I intended. "Nope." I felt my chin jut, and I turned my head slightly to avoid her gaze.

"Oh, I'm sorry," she said. "Did I touch a nerve?"

I looked at her thinking she was mocking me, but her look was sympathetic.

"No, it's okay. I was just daydreaming."

"Yes, the water's nice, isn't it? Hot water can cure so many things. Everything from a sore back to a broken heart." Her voice was soothing.

I looked up quickly to see her eyes studying me. I held the look as long as I could stand it. Which wasn't long. The blue pools behind her lids seemed safe and warm, no sign of the earlier ice. Her eyes seemed to know me. As though they could read my history, see the leaps and bounds, the trips and falls and the countless nights spent alone in the camper listening to the rain and wind rattling the aluminum roof. Maybe there was a chance here, a fleeting possibility of a connection, an understanding.

I thought about pulling her toward me, inviting her to take the plunge. I stared at her lips. They looked receptive. I looked for the blue pools, but her eyes were closed. The smell of her filled my senses. I started to reach for her practically tasting her and imagined rolling one of those full red lips between mine.

Then I remembered Charlie and caught myself.

"Isn't your husband upstairs?"

She opened her eyes and smiled at me as though amused by the thought. "Charlie's not my husband. We're not married."

"Really? I thought Charlie told me..."

"Don't think, Johnny. It's not good for you."

"But I, uh, he..." I glanced toward the closed door.

"He thinks it's common law or something," she interrupted, "but believe me, we're not married."

I looked deep into her eyes then and saw another door in the distance behind the pale blue mask. It was slightly ajar at the far end of a dark room. A faint blue light on the other side of the door beckoned, but my feet wouldn't move. The darkness in the room held me back. It was a one way trip. To enter meant no return.

Instincts tried to take over. I needed time to think. I needed something to break the spell. Or did I? Was there any reason to stop?

I blinked a couple of times and forced my mouth to speak. "What are you doing in Alaska?"

She gave me a sleepy look and asked, "What do you mean?"

"Oh, I don't know. I've been up here a while now, and I've never seen anyone like you around these parts."

"You like what you see?" she smiled, looked down and tucked the hair on one side of her head behind her ear.

I watched in fascination, but my thoughts were roiling. Don't do that, I wanted to tell her. Please don't do that, that thing with your hair, it reminds me too much of what's her name. And just like that I forgot all about Brandy Fontaine.

I dropped my eyes and shrugged, but she knew. I didn't have to say a word. She was reading me like a slide under a microscope.

"So, what was her name?" She was looking straight at me again. Damn it. Those eyes would not leave me alone.

"Who?"

"You know who."

"I don't remember," I lied.

"Sure, Johnny. You're a terrible liar."

"Ancient history anyway," I muttered.

"Okay, Johnny. It's alright. Don't worry about it." She reached over and lifted a strand of my hair off my forehead, smoothing it backwards. "You don't know me yet."

Her touch was like sparks. *You don't know me YET?*

Suddenly I regretted holding back. I wanted to tell her everything, the whole tale, spill my guts and let it all out. The barriers were falling, the sinner was crawling into the confessional. I wanted redemption, absolution, whatever it was the faithful seemed to prize so highly.

But I still couldn't move. I searched her eyes again. They invited me in, and I was tempted. So tempted, but I couldn't do it. It was too fast, too soon. I dreaded what was lurking in those blue pools. Please, just close them down. I know what's in there. You don't have to confirm it. Blue ice. So cold it burns. I looked away and closed my eyes.

No woman that looked like that had ever paid any attention to me. It wasn't real. It couldn't be real. This was some kind of weird dream, and I didn't want to wake up. Didn't want the wanting, the lonely craving ache in the pit of my stomach, the one I always tried to pretend wasn't really there, the one that leaves you walking down a deserted highway in the middle of the night, not knowing which way's home.

And yet those lips, her scent, the way she held my hand. And those eyes. *'Believe me, she'd said, we're not married.'* It was a signal, it had to be. I tried to fight the possibility but as if to confirm it, she reached over, cupped my face with her hand and lightly kissed my other cheek. So softly, so sweetly, I felt an electric charge fire straight to my loins.

This I had to have. It was an offer I couldn't refuse. My eyes flew open and I reached for her. It was now or never.

But just as I reached, she pulled away and stood up. Before I could say another word she turned and walked away. She swept silently across the carpet dragging the silky jacket behind her with one hand. Just before she reached the door, she looked back at me and our eyes locked again. It was more than a glance, she had me. Lost in the blue. She didn't smile, she didn't nod. I blinked once and she was gone.

I lay back in the water and flipped on the pump trying to breathe. Resting my head on the edge of the humming tub I stared at the ceiling. The roar of bubbles and the streams of hot water danced all around my bare skin erasing the electric chill that had coursed through me with her look.

I closed my eyes again. Did that all just happen or was it just a dream? The heat flowed through me. I let my hands and arms float in the agitated water, and my mind drifted away.

I was floating on my back somewhere in a warm ocean, alone, abandoned and staring at an empty sky. I was shipwrecked, wondering how long I would last. Hungry creatures cruised the depths below staring up at the tasty morsel bobbing on the sun sparkled surface.

Then I was watching from above. Looking down at the same expanse of empty ocean. Only it wasn't empty. There was something floating in the water. An orange survival suit, its arms and legs undulating with the movement of the waves, but the suit was empty. Where the face should have been, a vacant cavity in the hood gaped back at me from the blue gray sea.

I shuddered and wondered what the hell was happening to me on Taroka Island. Just then the pump cut off, the lamp went out and the door at the far end of the room banged open.

CHAPTER
10

"Damn it. The power's down again." Charlie cursed and lurched toward me.

I grabbed for the robe beside the tub and crawled out trying to cover myself. I almost tripped over the food tray in the process.

Charlie's eyes were wild, swirling back and forth behind the coke bottle lenses like ice cubes in a blender. He paced back and forth looking down at his hands. He clenched and re-clenched his fists over and over, not looking at me.

I watched him and waited, making a clumsy effort to dry my hair with the oversized arms of the robe. The only light in the room came from the windows in the door on the opposite side of the room from us.

"Your clothes are dry. Shoes too," he muttered finally. Then he turned and started to walk away into the dark interior of the laundry room. Was I being dismissed?

"The power went out?" I asked, trying to understand.

"It's the goddamn generator. It died again. This whole damn place is falling apart. I've about had it." He spat the words out and fumbled in one of his pockets. Finding a box of wooden matches he struck two and broke both before giving up. He slapped the box down on the granite counter top and pointed to a can with a candle inside it.

"You do it," he snapped and turned away.

"Let me get dressed, and maybe I can help you with the generator," I offered, but the door on the other side of the room slammed shut leaving me alone in the dark.

I found the matches and struck one. The flame sputtered and flared sending a tiny plume of acrid sulfur up my nose. I found a short piece of candle, lit it and tried to stand it back up in the can. The old container was dirty, rusted and partially filled with wax, cigarette ashes and burned out matches. I shook my head at the contrast between the soaring wooden beams, the marble floors, the porcelain fixtures and gold picture frames and the crumpled wreck of the tin can in my hand. The place must have been brilliant with wealth and success over many years. Now the dirty candle stub in my hand was the only light left in the darkness inside a massive luxury lodge in wilderness Alaska, its glory days far behind it.

I pulled open the door of the dryer and began to put on my clothes in the candlelight. Their warmth reminded me of my sleeping bag in the camper back in Seward. A sick hollow feeling washed over me, and I thought about how far I was from home. I pictured Mount Alice staring down at me in the morning light as I sipped coffee and listened to Willie bitch. I was surprised to realize that I missed hearing him rant about the city's taxes or the price of fuel or whatever else had him riled up at the moment.

I had to get the hell out of here. The place was making me nuts. I jerked on my shoes and hopped up and down on one foot trying to tie the laces in the flickering light. I finally sat down on a bench against the wall, took a deep breath and stretched. My muscles felt relaxed and warm after the long soak. At least I had that going for me.

Then one of the laces snapped in my hands. My breath rushed out with a sigh. I held up the broken lace and stared at it, shaking my head and muttering.

Ain't that the shits? Jesus Christ, what else? What the hell else could go wrong out here? Where's the glory, bush pilot? Where's the freaking glory?

As I fumbled to tie a knot I could hear Willie saying, "Quit your whining. You sound like an old woman."

He was always saying stuff like that. Real sympathetic, the damn guy. But, of course, he expected me to listen forever when he wanted to complain. But he was right, damn it. That's what really bugged me. I finished tying my shoes, wiped my nose and stood up.

I picked up the candle and made my way into the men's room. I walked carefully so the flame wouldn't go out. It was surreal moving past the gleaming white sinks and mirrors, the tiny light flickering all around me as I passed. Huge angular shadows danced in the corners like war painted savages around a bonfire.

I made my way through the dimly lit game room and started up the stairs. I could hear Charlie and Greta's voices up above me. It sounded like they were arguing about something in the kitchen. The foggy gray light filtering through the large windows made the candle unnecessary, so I blew it out and left it at the bottom of the stairs. I paused for a minute on the stairs to listen, but the voices had stopped.

As I came up to the main floor I heard an outside door open and then slam shut. The voices continued to argue outside, but they faded, and I sensed that I was alone in the huge lodge. The lobby with the double portraits loomed around me and the staircase to the second level seemed to beckon. I looked up and saw more animal heads mounted around a landing near the guest rooms.

With a glance toward the outside I turned and started up the stairs. Something drew me to explore. I needed a better feel for this place. And besides, I could always say I was just checking out the facilities, like any curious visitor would do in such a magnificent place.

Well-worn red carpet flowed up the stairs and across the landing in both directions. My footsteps were silent as I moved along. The heavy wooden beams below my feet were solid. No creaks. To the right I spotted the door that I had seen the night before. It must have been Greta shouting down to me, but I couldn't believe it was the same person from the hot tub room.

The door was partly open, and looking inside I saw an empty dark corridor with more closed doors on either side. A pile of laundry lay on the carpet next to an overflowing black plastic garbage bag. On the other side of the landing behind me there was a matching double door, but it was closed tight.

Something about those closed doors intrigued me. They pulled at me with a magnetic attraction. I sensed something behind them. Something important. I knew I should go back downstairs before they came back, but the magnet wouldn't leave me alone.

I walked carefully across the landing and tried the brass handle on the double wooden doors, but it was locked. I tried to peek through the crack between the doors, but I couldn't see a thing. I cocked my head and listened for any sounds or movement on the other side of the doors. Nothing. No smell either. Just the faint aroma of rich wood, brass and money.

I started to examine the door frame and the lock, looking for any weaknesses. It was an old habit. Locks hid secrets. Closed doors were a challenge. From the first time I had figured out how to use a knife blade to get into Mom's locked pantry, I had been obsessed with locks. Then the prize had been bubble gum and candy. Later I found all kinds of goodies and a sense of power and pride being able to bypass locks without a trace.

The bolt between the two doors didn't look like much of a problem. I pushed on one door enough to see that it moved, and that a simple piece of plastic would be able to push the bolt out of the way. Even the most expensive buildings often skimped on their interior locks. I was reaching for my wallet and a credit card when I heard something.

I wasn't alone. I heard a low growl. An animal growl. It was behind me and close. My skin felt like it was going to jump off my body. I turned my head to the right and froze.

A mean looking black dog was crouched only six feet away. It wasn't that big, but its teeth were bared and it was snarling, its lips quivering and drooling. Its ears were flat against its head, and it looked like it was ready to leap for my throat at any second. I hadn't heard it sneak up behind me on the thick carpet. It had me trapped against the locked door with nothing to defend myself.

I kept silent, stared at the beast and tried to breathe. My muscles had turned to stone. The animal was poised on the carpet, ready to spring. The hair stood up on its back, and its eyes were locked on me. Its breath rasped in and out with a low growl as it watched me. Every time I moved, its eyes twitched and followed. Slowly I tried to move my feet into position so I could land a kick when it went for me, but it didn't like that. The growling continued and grew louder. When I moved, it tensed even more and crept closer, so I stopped.

It wasn't a big animal, but that didn't give me any relief. About half the size of a German shepherd it was some kind of mutt. The square pit bull look of its head sent my heart into my throat. I saw teeth, yellow, ragged and glistening, moving back and forth under lips that stretched and strained as they anticipated sinking themselves into the warm bloody softness of my neck. Its whole body quivered with each guttural rumble.

I wondered why it hadn't barked, why it hadn't rushed me. I vaguely remembered something about certain guard dogs that were trained not to bark. They held their captives in place quietly and didn't attack unless they needed to prevent an escape. Then they clamped onto an arm or a leg and wouldn't let go for hours if necessary. It was working, I wasn't going anywhere.

Suddenly I heard the sharp sound of small hands clapping. I looked up to see a small figure of a child halfway down the hall. The dog stopped growling but held its ground eyeing me hungrily. Then a golf ball came flying and thumped its way toward on the carpet. It bounced crazily around the wooden doors and corners beside me. The noise distracted the dog, and it turned and chased the golf ball to the edge of the landing catching it in its teeth just before it bounced through the railing. Then it turned and ran toward the kid in the distance. I started to run toward the stairs, but the dog and child disappeared into a side room and slammed the door behind them.

I was alone again on the landing, but I'd had enough. I headed down the stairs and into the kitchen trying to catch my breath along the way. I settled myself onto a stool at a counter and played it cool watching as Charlie and Greta came in the door. Charlie was pissed.

"Goddamn generator. It ain't coming back this time." He threw a dirty crescent wrench on the counter. "Bearings are wore out."

Greta was dressed. She looked different in clothes but still spectacular. I realized my mouth had fallen open, and I quickly snapped it shut. She'd changed into faded blue jeans and a black leather jacket. Stylish high heeled white boots came to her knees. Her vivid blond hair stuck out around the edges of a baseball cap that matched her jeans. Her makeup and bright red lips were still perfect.

She didn't look at me. Almost as if she didn't even notice I was there. Like I was invisible.

"We have to get out of here, Charlie," she said quietly.

"And go where?" he snapped.

"It doesn't matter. Anywhere. I'm not living here like this anymore."

"Why? Cuz your hair dryer won't work now?"

I glanced at her. She didn't say a word, but she didn't need to. She stood stiffly with her hands in the pockets of the jacket facing Charlie. He seemed to wilt in the icy heat of her glare.

"I'm sorry, babe. I didn't mean that. I'm just ..." He didn't have a chance to finish. Greta turned and left the room. We listened to the sound of her heels hammering their way across the lobby floor before she started up the stairs.

Charlie looked like he was going to cry. An odd reaction for a big man, I thought. But maybe not. Who was it that said 'the bigger they are, the harder they fall?' He paced like he might follow her upstairs, but his feet couldn't make up their mind.

I felt like an intruder. Drama lay thick in the air like a burnt turkey on Thanksgiving.

I waited and pretended not to watch the big man struggle. I halfway expected him to turn on me if I played my hand wrong. Soup ladles and pans hanging from their hooks watched us with metallic indifference.

Charlie ran his hands through his hair, pulled off his thick glasses and laid them on the counter next to the wrench. With a sigh he finally sat down on a stool across from me and rubbed his eyes with his palms.

"Why, man?" he stared across the counter at me just like it was completely normal to visit with a stranger about a family conflict. Like I'd been there forever.

Without the glasses he had a handsome face, but his eyes were bloodshot and sunken into dark hollows. He looked like he'd aged twenty years in the last hour.

I didn't know what to say, so I just shrugged, looked away and shook my head slightly.

"Why does she have to be like that?" he persisted.

"How do you mean?" I asked carefully, staying neutral and hiding my relief that his frustration was with her rather than me.

"Ah, hell. We've been together for more than a year now, and she just can't settle into this place."

"Yeah, that can be rough. I guess a lot of women never get used to the way it is up here."

He looked at me with sad bloodhound eyes and took a deep breath. His shoulders shook slightly as he exhaled. "I thought it was going to work. I really did. She's everything to me, man. I mean, Christ, just look at her."

I dropped my eyes and tried to hide what I was thinking. Remembering the way she'd looked downstairs. Beauty like that can make a man weird. Talk about selling your soul.

I glanced at Charlie but looked away when he turned his head toward me. We were dangerously close to having a male bonding kind of touchy feely moment. Either that or he was going to beat me within an inch of my life.

In the nick of time we heard footsteps. A clatter in the lobby nearby interrupted the moment. The dog skittered sideways on the wooden floor and came bounding into the kitchen wagging its almost hairless tail and grinning a demented grin as it headed for Charlie. It seemed to notice me for a moment, but continued to scramble across the floor pawing at Charlie's legs.

"Oh, for shit sake," he grumbled. "Tambourine, get in here and take Tank outside before he pisses all over the floor."

A head of kinky red hair peered around the edge of the doorway but didn't enter. It was the kid I'd seen earlier upstairs in the hallway. He kept his head down and hovered near the doorway glancing toward me but never making eye contact.

"I mean it," Charlie bellowed holding off the quivering dog as it tried to climb up his leg. It was licking at his hands and slobbering with a slurpy snorting sound like a pig in a trough. "Get in here now, Tamby!"

The kid came in, grabbed the dog by the collar and dragged it away through the lobby and outside. The door slammed behind them. I looked at Charlie, but he was busy brushing at his pant legs.

"Damn mutt. So ugly its momma had to feed it with a slingshot."

"Your boy?" I asked fighting back a chuckle.

"Yeah, more or less," he muttered as he picked up the wrench and shoved it in the back pocket of his jeans. He must have noticed my puzzled expression.

"It's a long story."

"What was that you called him?"

"Oh, Tambourine? Yeah, that's his name. Like I said, it's a long story. A real long story. Dog's name's Tank."

I walked to a nearby window and looked outside. The boy and the dog were walking across the driveway toward the barn. The dog scampered from point to point lifting its leg and squirting in random directions. His tongue hung out one side of his grinning jaws, and it flapped up and down as he worked his way down the line of weeds and rocks lining the drive. A long string of spittle and drool trailed from his mouth and swung back and forth as he jumped from place to place.

The kid wandered along with his head down and his hands in the pockets of a worn gray down jacket. He stopped once in a while to wait for the dog who looked up and then dashed to catch up. The boy looked to be around ten years old and kind of scrawny. His hair was a blazing red afro, kinky and wild, bouncing and oddly shaped.

I cringed at the sight of him. He might as well have walked into any public school with a sign on his back, "Beat me up, PLEASE! "

When he looked back toward the lodge his face held a permanent frown. His eyebrows were scrunched, and his lips pressed together in a tight grimace. His eyes were tiny dark slits and he squinted as if it was painful to stare out at the dim gray world around him. Like the groundhog that gets dragged out of his hole every spring to look for the sun. He turned and walked out of sight, slipping in the mud and trying to avoid the slobber that Tank deposited on the back of his pants.

The fog looked the same. Thick as coagulated potato soup. I could see a few feet up the trunks of the trees nearby but nothing more.

A familiar sound came to me then. More of a vibration than a sound. Very faint but definitely there. I cocked my head to listen at the window trying to figure it out. It could have been a piece of machinery somewhere in the lodge. Had the generator come back to life?

No, no way. The power was still out. Charlie was still sitting on the stool drumming his fingers on the counter. Then he noticed the sound too, and his eyes went wide for a second and he stood up.

"What's that?" His voice quavered slightly. I had to look at him twice. He seemed alarmed.

"Sounds like a chopper," I said and headed for the front door. He followed me, and we stepped out from under the porch roof to stare up into the fog. The sound grew louder and louder, and the vibrations swelled until we could feel them throbbing straight above us.

"That's a big chopper, like a Coast Guard Blackhawk. They must be trying to find the ground," I said straining to see any sign of the aircraft. It sounded like it was only a hundred feet above us. I pictured the layer of fog just underneath it and thought about firing up the airplane and taking off in a steep climb. I could climb up through the clouds until I broke out into the clear blue sky above. Unless I ran into something first, of course. Bad idea.

The sound moved away gradually then, maneuvering toward the airstrip down the road. I wondered if they could see any gaps in the fog bank. Charlie was pacing in a tight circle staring up just like me. His mouth was hanging open as he squinted skyward. His large boots made a frantic pattern in the muddy driveway. I could see panic in the wild way his magnified eyeballs flicked back and forth behind the thick glasses.

"What's wrong, Charlie?"

He seemed startled at the sound of my voice. "N-nothing," he stammered.

"I wonder what's going on," I said. "Don't you have any way of calling out of here?"

"Not without power," he shrugged.

"Don't you have batteries that charge from the generator?" I asked.

"Nah, they went bad a while back. Can't afford to replace 'em."

"I've got to get back to the airplane. The fog may be lifting." I pointed upward. "And that chopper might have something to do with me being missing."

Charlie turned without a word and headed back to the lodge. I was left listening to the fading sound of the chopper blades in the distance. I needed to think. I was worried about Phil and Willie wondering where the hell I was. And I needed some distance from the odd crew of inhabitants on this island.

I started walking down the road to the airstrip as fast as I could. I needed to make contact with the real world again. Most of all I wanted to get the hell out of here. If there was even fifty feet of ceiling I was going to launch.

CHAPTER
11

Along the road I kept looking up at the fog layer. If it would just lift fifty feet or so I'd be tempted to take off and fly underneath it over to Evans Island. But it wasn't to be. I could barely see the tops of the trees on either side of me. The wet gray cloud clung to everything in sight.

I could feel sweat in my armpits and dampness on my back as I hurried down the road, but I didn't care. The exercise felt good. Even with fatigue lurking deep in my muscles, I had enough adrenaline to keep my feet moving just short of a jogging pace.

I felt free again for some reason. Walking like that helped me think. So did the distance away from those people. I thought about Charlie and Greta and the tension between them. And then the kid and the dog. Tambourine? What the hell kind of name is that for a kid? Some leftover hippie crap from the center of strange. I sucked crisp ocean air deep into my lungs and picked up my pace.

I was making good time humping down the road. My shoes scuffled across the gravel slipping once in a while on a muddy section, but at least it wasn't raining. The familiar scent of spruce surrounded me and when the road came close to the water line salt laden air wafted to me under the thick wall of trees and brush. Sounds were muffled by the thick fog that was like a blanket of insulation, and it felt like I was walking alone in a huge warehouse only able to hear my own shuffling steps.

I stopped for a minute to catch my breath and listened to the forest. I could sense all the unseen life forms around me. It was comforting and creepy at the same time.

"Focus, Johnny, focus," I mumbled under my breath. "You gotta get your ass out of here. You got one job to do. Get away. Contact Phil and get back to Seward. Put the airplane away and go get a beer. That's it." I went over each step like a mental checklist.

The pep talk was a good idea but doomed. Greta's eyes kept invading my mind. The blue depth of them. The smell of her, the touch of her hand on my forehead, the sensory overload, the taste of the eggs and coffee, the sound of her voice. And that kiss on my cheek. It was overwhelming. Her curves and the way she moved had me reeling. Something gripped me deep inside and wouldn't let go.

I'd never known a woman like that. I'd seen some, maybe across the room in the Yukon Bar when the Sunday night crowd came in to see Hobo Jim. But even then it was rare to see such blinding beauty anywhere in Seward. And never close up. And never ever talking to me. She was like a Victoria Secret model.

There was no approaching someone like that. Are you kidding me? It was one thing to get shot down by the regular ladies of Seward but a freaking cover girl? Forget about it. You want to pick your bleeding guts off the floor, go right ahead. Not me, buddy.

But then I would never dangle myself out there in front of a woman like that in the first place. They're not called bombshells by accident.

Greta had that look about her. There was nothing accidental in her appearance. No way. She was carefully engineered and premeditated. So why was she talking to me?

Maybe it was my imposing presence, and I'm sure she was overwhelmed by finding me naked in her basement. Imagine that, a soaking wet bush pilot in her hot tub on a foggy Alaskan afternoon. What woman could resist? Yeah, right.

But still, there she was. Right there in front of me and close. Very close and very friendly. At least, as friendly as a woman like her can ever be. Had I seen something in those eyes? An invitation, a chink in the armor, a hidden vulnerability that might let me in?

Her eyes didn't give anything away, but who knows? After all, she was with Charlie, and he was no cover of GQ magazine. What was that about, I wondered. He was a big guy. Protection? Maybe. Then I remembered the lodge and daddy's portraits in the lobby. Money?

Of course. I kicked at the gravel road in disgust. Damn it. I clenched my jaw and felt my teeth grind together. I walked on, realizing that I was almost to the airstrip. The woods were opening up ahead, and I tried to shift my thoughts to the airplane, the fog and the flight I needed to make.

Then I remembered the touch of her fingers on the side of my head, and I was lost again. I knew I had to concentrate, to get busy with something, but it was a struggle. Every time I let myself drift, those eyes came back to me. Hadn't I seen a softness somewhere in there behind the mask? A place that just might yield to the right words, the right tone, the right touch at the right time. A guy can always dream.

I left the trees then and spotted the airplane sitting next to the gloomy airstrip. I pushed the images away and reached into my jacket pocket for the airplane keys. Fog was still thick in the air and clung to the tree tops all around the runway.

I stopped for a minute to survey the area. A group of seagulls stood in a bunch down near the water. Silent and still, they stood as quiet witnesses staring toward something in the distance beyond my view. I hoped they would get out of my way if I managed a takeoff. They always did.

The Cessna sat quietly right where I'd left her. Damp and dreary in the dim light, she looked cold and stiff. Moisture glistened on her wings, and droplets of rain stood on the windows. The door snicked open with a turn of the key, and the familiar smell of her vinyl, cloth and metallic interior greeted me. There was also the faint comforting scent of aviation fuel and oil. I was back on familiar turf. I took a deep breath and looked down the runway. I couldn't see past the stand of trees at the end, and I could barely make out the water's edge just beyond. All thoughts of taking off faded like a raffle ticket fantasy.

I sat down on the black rubber tire and rested my hands on my knees. I had to sort things out. What was I going to do? Above and behind me, the ragged windsock flapped in a half hearted breeze. Its rusted metal ring creaked like a spook house door.

Just then Charlie's voice ten yards away startled me out of my reverie. "Hey, man. Let's fly!"

I stood up too quick and hit my head on the underside of the wing. But not that hard. Just enough to push my cap down tight over my eyes and knock my glasses half off.

I fumbled to rearrange everything and looked up to see Charlie grinning at me. "Charlie, you surprised me. No, we can't fly anywhere in this garbage." I waved my arm in disgust at the fog down on the water and reached up to rub the sore spot on top of my head.

I came out from under the wing and looked at him standing behind the tail section of the plane. He looked frustrated. He had a small pack on his back and his feet stamped back and forth as he studied the air around us.

"When do you think we can go?" he asked. "We really need to get out of here."

"Hell, I don't know. This stuff is thick as hell and it ain't moving at all."

He turned to stare down the runway and then back at me. "You don't want to try it?"

"Try it? No way. That's the shit that kills pilots around here. You know that better than I do."

My words seemed to sting him and I felt instantly sorry, but I wasn't budging. Fog was dangerous.

He turned toward me and stared. He had his hands in his jacket pockets and his shoulders hunched up toward his ears. I kept my distance and stayed by the wing. He seemed even taller than before. His eyes bored in at me, and he rocked side to side from one foot to the other as he thought about what to say.

Then I noticed his jean jacket was hanging open in front. There was a bulge under his left armpit, and I could see a leather strap of a shoulder holster crossing his chest inside the jacket.

CHAPTER
12

I froze inside. For the second time in as many days I was worrying about being forced at gunpoint to fly in bad weather. I turned and ducked under the wing to head for the other side of the plane. I wanted distance between us. I walked to the front of the plane, opened an access latch and reached in pretending to check the engine oil. I kept glancing his way out of the corner of my eye, but Charlie didn't move.

My mind ran over the things I could do. I glanced behind me to the woods where I'd spent the night. If I could get in there again...

"We really can't fly?" Charlie's voice was right behind me and I nearly jumped out of my skin banging my hand inside the cowling.

I turned and looked at him. He wasn't rocking anymore, and his hands were loose at his sides, standing between me and the wing.

I shook my head. "Seriously, Charlie, if that Coast Guard helicopter couldn't come down through that stuff there's no way I'm flying in it."

He took a deep breath and cocked his head back to stare up the fog. "Look, Johnny. I've got to get parts to fix that generator, and if we can't fly I'm going to take a boat over to Chenega. Why don't you come along?"

I thought about it. Leave the airplane behind? It was probably okay where it was, but I didn't like the idea of leaving it.

"I don't know if that's a good idea or not. This is a screwed up mess. I really need to let my boss know where I am and tell him about his plane. He'll be freaking out by now."

"You can do that over in Chenega. They got phones."

He was right. There wasn't much point sitting here staring at the fog. At least I'd be doing something. When Phil started yelling at me, I'd be able to explain the steps I had tried to get in touch. But the way things were going, I was getting a bad feeling that no one would believe me.

"Okay," I agreed. "Might as well. Hell, there ain't nothing I can do here."

We started walking back to the lodge. My mind was reeling. Phil was going to kill me. He wouldn't like me leaving his airplane behind. He would expect me to stay right there and safeguard it against squirrel bites or seagull shit or whatever. He was okay as a boss when everything was going fine, but one kink and boom, the guy came uncorked.

I was in a no win situation, but I decided it was better to try to find a way to communicate than it was to just sit there stranded on Taroka. That's what I thought anyway. Of course, Phil wouldn't see it that way. He was going to be pissed that I hadn't called or left a message. Well, you know what? To hell with him. And to hell with the troopers too. I was going to have to do what I thought was right. I was the man on the scene. No one else knew any better than me what was going on.

Who was going to help? Charlie and Greta? No way. I still hadn't figured out what was going on with those two. No, it was up to me all on my own.

Pilot in command. That's what they call it. You can be thousands of feet in the air in a small plane, or a big one for that matter, and if something goes wrong, who else is going to handle it? An equipment failure or a weather surprise or some other weirdness like a hijack, who's going to come up and rescue your ass? Nobody, that's who. Air traffic control? The FAA? Forget about it. They might talk to you, but that's it. If anything was going to get fixed or handled, the pilot had to figure it out solo. Even if you have a crew with you, the pilot's the boss. Responsible for everything. The good and the bad.

Just because I wasn't flying at the moment didn't change the reality of my world. I was on a strange voyage and everything was turned upside down. I had to solve this mess on my own, and if someone wanted to criticize my moves later, let them. The temptation to give up flickered through my head. I could always curl up in the back of the airplane in my sleeping bag and hide from it all. Wait for someone else to figure it out. After all, I was just a hired charter pilot. My passengers went off and disappeared. Wasn't my fault. I was just the pilot, waiting for them to come back.

"Ah, bullshit," I mumbled and kicked at a stone on the road in front of us.

"What?" Charlie said beside me as we left the airstrip and moved into the darker world in the forest.

"Nothing. I'm just pissed off at this whole damn deal. I was just supposed to fly out here and back. Easy money, you know? Instead I'm stuck out here when I should be back in Seward flying tourists around."

"Yeah, fucking cops. I never had much use for them myself," Charlie grumbled.

I glanced at him in surprise. He leaned over and picked up a stone. I watched as he threw it with a violent heave at the group of seagulls standing fifty feet away. His face contorted with the effort, and filled with rage. The birds turned and stared at us with inscrutable beady black eyes. Otherwise they didn't react. Not a single one jumped as the stone skipped past them with a clatter.

"Filthy bastards," he growled. "You should see what they do to my docks." The effort of his throw left his jacket hung up above his right hip exposing the sheaf of a large knife strapped on his waist. I recognized it right away.

It was a KA-BAR Marine fighting knife. One of those huge lethal looking things with a serrated edge and a dull black blade seven inches long. It even had a blood gutter like a combat bayonet. It was a brutal weapon designed for one purpose. Killing.

I felt the blood rise in my throat and fought off the urge to run. I thought about saying something. If I could just make a joke. Something to gauge his mood. But I didn't say a word. I kept walking beside him, my mind whirling. After a minute he shook himself and fixed the jacket.

I decided to speak up.

"So, uh, Charlie," I said with a forced chuckle and pointing to the bulge. "You packing heat? Got bears out here."

He didn't answer. Just gave me a sideways glance and shrugged.

Why did he need weapons like that out here? He was carrying a handgun and a huge knife? I didn't think an island this small would support a bear population. Then again Willie always carried.

I tried to tell myself it was just for looks. Dressing for the role of the wilderness big game guide. The great white hunter look. It was normal to carry a large knife for skinning game, but a lot of guys wore them just for show. A macho thing. But Charlie was a big man anyhow. I didn't get it.

We walked along for several minutes in silence. The gravel road crunched under our feet, and the thick fog shrouded the spruce trees on either side of the road wrapping us in fragrant dark shadows. I had to push myself to keep pace with Charlie's long legs. I was determined to keep my eyes on him, especially his hands and the weapons.

"So what do you think of Greta?"

"What?" The question threw me. It was the last thing I had expected to hear. There I was, walking in a dark section of woods with an enormous man armed to the teeth, and he asks me what I think of his woman?

"You know. Greta." His voice was matter of fact, but I could feel his eyes looking down at me as we walked. He was studying me, watching for my reaction.

I struggled to keep my voice controlled and void of all the jumpy impulses running through my skull.

"Oh, yeah. Well, she seems like a nice lady."

"C'mon, man. She's way more than that. You know she used to be a model?"

"Really? That's interesting," I answered wondering where this was leading. "You don't see many women like her in Alaska." I fought to keep my voice neutral.

"Boy, isn't that the truth. I couldn't believe my luck in meeting her. And then when she agreed to come up here with me, I was in heaven,"

I pictured the situation from above. Like a bizarre foreign film or a reality TV show. Mutt and Jeff wandering along a country road having some kind of a fern bar conversation. As strange as it was, I decided to let it keep going. Better than worrying about being shot and gutted on the side of the road. He seemed to need to talk, and I was more than willing to let him.

"I met her in California. I'd been living down there for a while. I was married to a great little gal, but she came down with breast cancer. Her name was Tabitha and in less than a year she was gone. Shook me up bad, man. This is gonna sound a little weird, but I met Greta at the funeral home. She was working there as a cosmetologist."

I let that image sink in for a minute. Greta in a white lab coat working on dead faces.

"You know, to fix up the bodies before burial?"

"Yeah, yeah, I get it," I said, not getting it at all. I looked into the woods searching for a way to throw myself off the side of the planet.

He went on telling me how Greta had comforted him at the side of his wife's coffin. And how she'd been so kind to Tambourine who was Tabitha's kid from a previous marriage. He'd adopted the boy before Tabitha died. Apparently there was no other family interested or willing to take him on.

I walked along listening and wondering about the twists and turns in life that throw people together. He went on and on about Greta and how great she was with the kid. We walked in silence again for a few minutes, the quiet broken only by the calling of a pair of eagles through the tops of the trees high above us.

"I told you it was a long story. Sorry," he said after a while, looking down at me trudging along beside him.

"No problem," I said. "I noticed the boy didn't look like either you or Greta."

"Yeah, the little shit's turning out kind of warped though."

"What do you mean?"

"I don't know. I think there might be something wrong with him. I don't think he's normal."

"Really? I didn't notice anything," I lied.

"Well, you will when you've been around him a little longer. He doesn't talk much. Stays in his room. Barely eats anything. Won't let hardly anybody touch him. Greta's the only one he'll let get close."

"You're kidding. How old is he?"

"Eleven, almost twelve."

I was stunned. "Wow, I was thinking much younger. Was he always kind of different?"

"Nah, not so much. Maybe a little. When we were first together, he talked more. But then his mom died, and he started to go strange. If it hadn't been for Greta, I don't know what would have happened. She found me, you know what I mean, Johnny? I was drowning. And she was like a life preserver. I was standing there at the viewing looking down at Tabitha. And this voice spoke up beside me. I turned and saw Greta there looking at me with those eyes. My heart just fell right to the floor. I looked back at Tabitha, and I swear I saw her smile. Like a Mona Lisa laying there on that silk pillow. She was giving me her blessing. She didn't want me to be alone, Johnny. She loved me that much. And Greta made me feel like the only man in the world."

I shook my head slightly trying to clear the cobwebs and struggled to listen. I pictured the two of them together. The beauty and the beast. The big rough man so vulnerable and in the care of the tiny painted blond. Such warmth and such ice. And the kid.

I tried to pretend to myself that somehow this world I'd landed in would sort itself out. Some semblance of normal would have to settle in eventually. Wouldn't it? I looked sideways at him. Tried to see into his mind. Was he losing it? And why was he sharing all this stuff with me? Why me?

I wasn't sure Charlie knew I was even there. He seemed to be talking to himself. But one thing seemed clear. He believed what he was saying. He was speaking from the heart, and he was upset and confused. Maybe even desperate.

I tried to keep one foot in the real world while I listened. Tried to keep reminding myself that the normal world was still out there waiting for me to return. My life back in Seward. At least it was my normal. If Charlie was going over the edge, I didn't want to go with him. I wasn't sure I was succeeding.

"You've had a really bad year, haven't you?" I knew that sounded lame, but Charlie didn't seem to mind.

"Yeah, no shit. I lost a wife, and my dad and brother before that. Makes me wonder what the big man's trying to tell me."

"Who?"

"The big man. You know, upstairs?" He jerked his head upward.

"Oh, yeah, right." I glanced upward in reflex, but all I saw was fog. I gave Charlie a sideways look and started to worry that a sermon or some kind of religious recruitment was about to begin.

"Yeah, I know," he said stuffing his big hands into his pockets as he walked. Almost like he was reading my mind.

"I know it's all bullshit. People pray their ass off when there's trouble. And for what?"

He took a breath and then went on. "Tabitha died, man. Where's the justice in that? I couldn't believe it."

I didn't know what to say. If he was looking to me for answers, he was dialing a disconnected number. Besides, he had a killer looking woman and he was asking me stuff?

"But Greta came along. That was a good thing, right?"

"Yeah, but I didn't pray for that, she just happened." He went quiet then, staring at his feet as we walked.

"Yeah, wow," I mumbled, wondering again where he was going with this. I still didn't know how to respond to a giant of a man with rough working hands who sounded like he was about to cry.

"You know what I think?" he asked, looking at me, but not really seeing. He was getting into some kind of a head game rant. Talking to himself mostly. He didn't wait for me to answer, but it didn't matter. I wasn't going to interrupt him. Let it roll, brother.

"I think it's all random. Who gets to live and who has to die? It's just luck. I used to be religious but no more. It's just luck, man. The roll of the dice. Random. Ran fucking dumb!"

Then he laughed. A little too loud, I thought. And a little too long. He looked at me and it seemed like he grew another foot. His chest swelled and his arms stretched out to his sides. His face contorted into a demented grin, and he leaned over me as he walked.

"You want to know the craziest part of it all, Johnny? If nobody cares, then what's the point?"

He dropped the grin and looked up at the fog choked tree line. His arms reached up, and he shouted, "What's the point?"

I looked around embarrassed for him. Embarrassed for me. The trees stared back blankly in confirmation.

Just then we topped a small hill, and Charlie spotted the road sign. "Speed Limit 80 MPH." He stopped abruptly and turned with a flourish. Reaching inside his jacket, he snatched out the handgun. His body took on a shooter's pose, and shots rang out one after another. Shell casings flew past his shoulder.

The explosions ripped through the dead quiet of the forest, each one echoing for an instant before the next one filled the air. I clamped my hands to my ears. My eyes slammed shut in an involuntary reaction, and I turned away hunched over at the waist. The noise wiped away every other sensation. Dazed by the sudden shock, I bit back on a scream.

When the roar of the bullets finally subsided, my ears were ringing, and I slowly opened my eyes wondering if I was still alive. I couldn't hear anything but the ringing. I turned to look at Charlie, panic rising in my throat. How was I going to escape this madman in the woods?

Being in a gunfight is not something you can forget. How do you deal with knowing that death is flying through the air all around you? I'd been shot at twice in the last year. A friend was murdered right beside me. I still jerked awake some nights remembering it.

And Brandy had almost blasted me with a shotgun outside the hangar at Seward's airport. That had made my ears ring too, but I'd survived. At least physically I had. In some ways the dead get the better deal.

Then the bullets the night before had come way too close. I reached up and touched the ragged hole in my hat as I remembered.

Gradually my senses came back like Novocain wearing off. My throat ached as I realized I'd been holding my breath. I inhaled deeply and smelled cordite. I looked down and did a quick inventory, but I was untouched.

I couldn't say the same for the road sign. It was filled with ragged holes. Big holes. There was a moon surface of jagged metal where the number eighty had been. The whole sign and its wooden post were still shaking and smoking slightly.

Charlie stood frozen with his back toward me. Still in his shooter's stance, he held the pistol with both hands. His arms pointed straight out from his body toward the sign. He looked like a statue. The slide on the weapon was fully retracted, and the chamber gaped open with a tiny wisp of smoke rising into the cool air.

I tried to pull myself together. I didn't want Charlie to see the panic in my eyes, but he wasn't looking at me. He was alone, in his own world. Fighting demons only he could see.

Then slowly he relaxed, straightened up, turned and tossed the weapon directly at me. It twisted and spun through the air in a high arc. I reacted automatically and caught the heavy hunk of metal before it hit me in the head. The chamber was still open and the pistol body was warm and smelled of burned gunpowder. In my shock I bobbled it but managed to get it under control before it fell to the ground.

I looked hard at Charlie but tried not to glare. I held my tongue, but I was thinking, 'What the hell?'

Charlie ignored me, busy with a handful of bullets. He was methodically feeding them into a spare magazine. When it was full, he motioned to me. I held out the pistol but he shook his head and jabbed the full magazine toward me. After I found the eject button with my thumb I pulled out the empty and traded it for the new full one. It slid into place and I slapped it home.

"Go ahead, Johnny. Fire off a few rounds."

Firing the weapon was the last thing I was interested in at the moment, but something about Charlie's manner felt like a test. I was on his turf and was being challenged to prove something. Besides, the way he was acting I needed to play along. I shrugged, aimed at the sign and squeezed off a shot.

The weapon bucked in my hand and surprised me at the light pressure required to make it fire. It was much smoother than the old Army Colt forty five I remembered from years back. I was also surprised to see a hole appear close to the spot I'd aimed at. It felt so easy I pulled off two more then relaxed the gun at my side.

"Nice group," Charlie said as he stepped forward to check the holes in the sign. I moved toward him and held out the pistol again butt first, but he grunted and poked his jaw toward something behind me. I looked back and saw his holster inside his pack laying open on the ground.

I turned back toward him but he was busy taking a leak behind the sign post. I shook my head at the oddity of it all, but then I turned and shoved the weapon back into the holster in his pack.

Charlie was still busy relieving himself, so I turned my back, unzipped and did the same. Then we started walking again, heading toward the lodge. Minutes went by without any words between us. He seemed preoccupied. After a while he must have remembered he wasn't alone, glanced down at me, shrugged his shoulders and spoke in the same tone as if it was just an extension of our earlier conversation.

"See what I mean, Johnny? Life is random."

CHAPTER

13

I stumbled along the road behind Charlie trying to keep up. Even though I wanted to run in the opposite direction, I thought it best to play it cool. I swallowed hard wondering if I could hang onto my nerve. And my sanity.

Everything about Taroka Island was taking on a strange and warped life of its own. I couldn't fly away, I couldn't contact anybody, I couldn't do squat.

I needed information, and I needed to think. More than anything I needed to figure out what to do or I knew I'd regret it.

With Charlie silence seemed like the best course. What would I say anyhow? I was only a bit player in this bizarre production, just a guy standing on the side of the road watching a car wreck happen right in front of him. And now I had an erratic man armed with deadly weapons and an attitude to use them. Should I try to take charge? Start telling Charlie what to do like I was The Man? Sometimes a little structure could settle things down.

A little voice inside told me to keep my head down. Watch and learn first. Trying to be a big shot could be asking for trouble. I thought about how to play it. How to blend into the action and mold myself into a working piece of the eccentric machine that was Taroka Island. As if my survival depended on adapting a new shape and form until I could maneuver myself to the edge and then get free.

The lodge came into view before I developed any better plan. I desperately needed to get in touch with the real world again. Willie, Phil, the troopers, some connection with planet Earth at least. It wasn't to be.

Greta was waiting for us on the porch. She was pacing back and forth but stopped when she spotted us. Her black leather jacket was zipped to her chin, and she had on matching gloves, white knee high boots with high heels and designer blue jeans. Her white face, red lipstick and styled blond hair blazed outward like a lighthouse on a stormy sea. She gazed in our direction with no expression.

"Hi, honey," Charlie called out when he spotted her. "You look terrific."

"I heard shots," she said, her eyes narrowing as she stared at him. I sensed a suspicion there probably born from experience.

"Yeah," he said with a nervous laugh. "Damn road sign tried to get the drop on us. Had to teach it a lesson."

Her face hardened. Her blue eyes could have flash frozen raw meat. Her jaw clenched as though her perfect teeth were biting back on a thousand razor blades of spite and disgust.

I tried to make myself invisible, but it didn't matter. Without another word she turned on her heel and jerked open the door. It slammed hard behind her, and Charlie and I stood there listening to her heels hammering across the wooden floor of the lobby until the sound was gone.

"Aw, shit," Charlie muttered. "Now she's pissed off again." He stared toward the lobby door, slammed one fist into the other and started to pace.

My eyes moved back and forth, watching him and looking around for an escape. I was speechless, dumbfounded and felt as out of place as a delivery man at a nudist colony. Finally, Charlie let out a big sigh, and his shoulders dropped. He clumped onto the deck and headed for the front door leaving me standing by myself.

He opened the door and leaned in. "Sweetheart?" he called out before he stepped inside and closed the door gently behind him. He moved like a bomb disposal crew feeling for trip wires.

I heard someone pull the crank on a small generator somewhere nearby and on the second tug it began to purr. I turned to look across the circular drive and saw a light come on inside the small cabin. The troopers? I walked quickly toward the sound and the light. I could feel my heart pounding with anticipation. Finally.

But before I got to the cabin I felt the vibration of music and the chunking solid rhythm of an electric guitar. It was a familiar grinding riff echoing surreally from the mossy log walls of the low structure. Low bass guitar joined in followed by drums. I was transported to the smoky confines of a thousand dark rock and roll bars and the screaming chaos of a Led Zeppelin concert. Robert Plant's impossibly raw vocal chords began to sing Whole Lotta Love, the strangely sensual lover's whisper in the dark.

The volume soared to maximum and I walked closer and stepped onto the porch listening as a high hat cymbal solo began, then joined by bongos, psychedelic soaring guitar swales and orgasmic moaning. I looked through the window in the door and saw the kid with a purple sash tied around his forehead in the middle of the room standing on a chair playing air guitar with an old broom. His body was posed in a perfect rock star imitation, one leg bouncing to the beat. He wore a black t-shirt and tattered blue jeans, and his face was lost in concentration feeling every note of the timeless teenage classic.

I waited, watching and listening. I could feel my own body beginning to react. The sound took over, and every other thought fled overwhelmed by the power of the music.

I took off my pack, put on my sunglasses and waited for the guitar solo. Then I spun my hat around backwards, threw off my coat and burst through the door in time with a crash of cymbals. I dropped to my knees and flailed my arms in an imaginary drum solo in perfect unison with the recording. I didn't look at the kid at first but from the corner of my eye I saw his jaw drop. He gaped at me for a second, but then he picked up the guitar solo and we thrashed out our parts together trading the drum and guitar riffs back and forth like we were center stage at the Hollywood Bowl.

I was pounding away and grimacing with every wild smash of the cymbals. I started to sweat, but I couldn't have cared less. I could feel the tension of the last several hours oozing out of my pores. When I looked up at him, he was grinning ear to ear and bobbing his head to the beat, his red hair whipping back and forth. As the vocals started again we belted them out together, shouting to hear ourselves over the stereo. My sunglasses slid halfway down my nose, and I didn't care.

We rocked it out to the finish and when the volume began to fade I stood up and walked over still bouncing and smiling at him. He lifted his hand and gave me a hearty high five that stung my palm. Then we gripped hands in a firm shake and laughed out loud.

Just then the door smashed open behind us. As we turned to look Charlie burst into the room, his face contorted in rage.

"Tamby, what the fuck are you doing?" he bellowed. "Turn that shit off! You're wasting the only gas we have left."

Then he noticed me and seemed to freeze in place staring at me in disbelief. I turned my hat back around and sheepishly reached down to pick up my coat.

He watched me for a moment, blinking and scrunching his eyebrows together in confusion. Then he shook his head and left the room.

A moment later I heard the generator cut off and the lights went out. The room went dim and I turned toward the kid, but he had already picked up his jacket and was running for the lodge. The broomstick and purple sash lay in the dust on the floor.

*   *   *   *   *

I went outside after a while, but no one was around. I realized that Charlie had lied about there not being any more power for a phone call. Walking around behind the cabin I found the generator, but the fuel cap was off and an empty gas can lay on its side in the leaves.

I listened for any sounds in the distance, but the fog muffled everything in its reach. Then I smelled smoke and walking toward the lodge I could hear voices coming from around the corner of the large log building.

It was Greta's voice, hard edged and clipped. "Get busy. I'm already packed."

"What are you talking about?" Charlie's voice sounded stressed and strung out.

"We need to leave and you know it. We talked about it before." She spat the words at him like ice pellets in a blizzard.

"Well, the pilot says the fog is still too thick to fly. Don't you think we should wait a while?"

"No, I don't think we should wait a while. We can take the inflatable. We need to get out of here now." She didn't add "you goddamn idiot" but I heard it clear as a bell.

I was just around the corner from them, and I thought about hiding against the wall to listen for a while. But then I thought better of it and walked around the corner.

They were standing over a fire pit. Flames and smoke were curling upward from a small pile of sticks and logs. Greta was using a long pole to push papers into the smoldering coals.

They glanced up at me as I approached, but neither one said a word. Charlie's body was slumped in defeat. He seemed shrunken and small beside Greta even though he was over a foot taller.

Before he could say another word, she snapped, "Now, Charlie." Without a word he turned and went inside but not before giving me a sideways glance. I wanted to ask him about fuel for the generator so I could charge the sat phone, but the tension in the air froze my tongue.

I walked over to the fire pit and held out my hands for warmth. After a minute I glanced at Greta. She returned my look with an unspoken challenge. Her blue eyes reached for mine, but I looked away quickly before her spell could grab me again.

I felt a sensation of having just stumbled onto a theater set without a script.

"Damn fog," I muttered, looking off into the distance.

She moved toward me then until we stood side by side staring down together at the fire. The high heeled boots made her my same height, and I felt her softening. The sleeve of her black leather jacket brushed against my arm. She let out a sigh.

"I have to get away from here, Johnny. I'll die if I stay."

I glanced over at her in surprise but just for a second. I hadn't expected her to open up so quickly.

"Is it that bad?"

"You have no idea. I'm just so messed up."

I looked at her then. Her chin was on her chest and with her eyes closed, she combed through her hair with trembling fingers. Her thoughts were all jammed together, fighting for release, but she held them back.

I caught a crazy urge to take her in my arms. I took a nervous glance toward the lodge. There weren't any windows on the wall above us, but I fought off the impulse anyhow. Instead I reached over and touched her arm.

"Where would you go?"

"It doesn't really matter. Just far away from this place. Away from Alaska. I'm done. I think I'm losing my mind."

"Huh, I know the feeling," I said looking up at the gloomy sky.

"Seriously, Johnny, the fog can hang out here for days. Sometimes I think it's going to cover me in gray and dissolve me like acid."

"What are you going to do?"

"Not sure, just get away. Can you help me, Johnny?"

Her words gripped me like a kitten's claws. Electric current ran down my spine.

"But what about...?" I glanced again toward the lodge.

"Forget him, Johnny. We're through. I've had enough."

I swallowed hard and thought about it. Was she serious? Put her in the airplane and fly away? Then what? I pictured us in the plane, her curled up on the co-pilot seat smiling at me as we soared through blue sky over snow capped peaks. At the end of every long flight there was always a motel nearby. I pictured that little nightgown again. Only this time it was laying on the motel floor...a puff of wet cold air hit the back of my neck and jerked my thoughts back to the present.

"Aren't you taking a boat with Charlie?" I asked, reminding her and myself what I'd overheard.

"I'd go with you right now, Johnny. Can we fly?"

Oh, man. My knees felt weak, but one glance at the sky answered her question. I tugged my jacket a little tighter around my neck and shook my head. "Maybe tomorrow."

She took hold of my arm. "Then I want you to come with us."

Words wouldn't come out of my mouth. I couldn't say the things I was thinking, and nothing else wanted to come forward in their place. She seemed to realize I was struggling and she knew exactly how to proceed.

She gripped my arm a little tighter. "Think about it, Johnny. Think about it," she whispered and leaned in closer until I could feel her hair brushing my cheek. I stared hard into the smoldering coals and tried to sort through my thoughts.

Leave the island and find a way to call Phil? Yes, I needed to do that. But that meant leaving the airplane behind, and that didn't feel right at all. But then again sitting out here alone in the fog and out of touch didn't make sense either. I'd probably have food and shelter but I'd be alone. Greta squeezed my arm again and warm waves swept down my back.

I blinked hard trying to ignore her touch. I needed to reconnect with the troopers. That was certain. For all I knew I was their only way back to Seward, but after all this time it seemed like they'd moved on. Made other arrangements and left me to find my own way back.

I thought about crossing the channel in an inflatable. It wasn't an idea I enjoyed. I was a fly guy, not a boat man.

"What if Charlie went over by himself? He could get fuel and parts and come back and..."

She didn't hesitate. "No, I need out now." She let go of my arm leaving a chill behind. I reached for her but she pulled away like she was headed for the lodge.

The exasperation finally got the best of me. "Greta," I rasped, my voice rising. "Why? What's going on? What are you doing out here anyway?"

That stopped her. She turned slowly toward me and studied my face. Then she sat down on the log bench beside us. I hesitated to move, so she reached up and pulled me down next to her. She tossed more logs on the fire and we watched as the wood began to smoke. As it burst into flames, ash swirled up and around us, and the heat bathed us in an aromatic mixture of wood smoke and her perfume.

"I'm losing it, Johnny. I don't belong in this place. I never should have come up here. All I can think about is how to get out."

I put my arm around her then. She didn't seem to notice and kept talking.

"I was stuck in a stupid job in California and when Charlie came along, I thought it was a way out. Things were good for a while, but not anymore. Charlie's weird and the kid's even weirder. Can you believe he's twelve?"

"What were you running from?"

She recoiled slightly and looked at me strangely. "What do you mean?"

"Well, they say people who move to Alaska are all running from something."

She looked at the burning coals. "That's what they say, huh?"

I shrugged and waited.

"Well, maybe so, I guess. I was broke and had been out of the modeling business for a while. I was too short and too old. And Charlie was so heart broken about his wife. We needed each other, ya know?"

She looked at me and frowned. "I sound like a gold digger, don't I?"

"No, no, I don't think that. I don't know a thing about you guys. People find each other in all kinds of ways."

She sighed and smiled sadly. "Well, it was a mistake. Coming here just isn't working out. And I can't handle anymore of Charlie."

She took a look around, then breathed in deeply letting it out with a sigh. "Man, I get so moody out here. I didn't used to be like this. I'm never sure what I'm saying from one minute to the next. I don't really know what happens to me. My brain just seems to have a mind of its own."

I chuckled at that, but her sadness made me bolder. I pulled her close. "Aw, you'll be all right. You could be a model again. You're a freaking knockout."

She stiffened and pushed away. "No, you don't get it. You have no idea what I've been through. Guys like you all think models have an easy life. You ought to try making a living under hot lights and a ton of makeup and hairspray, everyone from the producer to the pizza delivery guy hitting on you all day and all night."

The flash of anger surprised me, but I started to smile. Turning toward her I held out my arms with my palms up. "Yeah, well, I tried to get on the cover of GQ, but they turned me down. Can you believe that?" I cocked my head and gave her a pose.

She was trying to hold a pout but looking at me, she half choked, then laughed out loud. I laughed back.

Then I made a mistake. Damn it, I hate it when I do that. I turned my head and looked at her straight on. She looked back, and that did it.

Deep in the vivid pools of blue in her eyes I saw a beckoning hint of warmth. Like a candle burning on a tiny iceberg, floating in a glacial lake. I tried to look away but I couldn't. All common sense drained away. Like bath tub water seeping past the plug. I was a teenaged peeping Tom secretly worshipping a naked wonder through a keyhole when all of a sudden my fantasy lady turned, made eye contact with me and smiled. And just like a lonely teen I was lost and my jeans didn't fit right anymore.

I was incapable of speech and she knew it.

"C'mon, Johnny," she said taking my hand. "Look at that," she nodded toward the fire pit smoldering at our feet. The red coals glimmered and winked, the heat popped and crackled. With a half grin and a sideways glance through lowered lids, she whispered, "Don't you wanna jump in with me?"

Are you kidding? I would have followed her off a cliff. We sat like that for a while listening to the hiss of the flames. A line from an old song came to me. Why must I be a teenager in love? I knew it made no sense, but I was telling myself to hell with making sense. Go for it. Cut loose, man. What have you got to lose?

But at the same time the sane side of my shriveling brain kept hearing a faint but persistent alarm bell. Off in the distance but definitely there, it wouldn't be ignored.

"So what if I do go with you? What happens then?"

"Then we'll be free of this place." She took a deep breath and glanced back at the lodge. "And I can get away from him."

The alarm bell was still ringing but it was starting to fade. I had more questions, but before I could say anything I felt her finger press against my lips.

"Shush, Johnny. Don't think so much." She had leaned in against me and her eyes were two inches from mine. I blinked and stared helplessly into those enormous blue orbs.

"Then we'll be free to do whatever we want. We can fly away."

The smell of her rushed in like the evening tide. Lilacs, wood smoke and lust drowned out the remaining weak tones of that bell. She removed her finger and replaced it with her lips. Softly at first, then hungry, we kissed. I moved my other arm around her and pulled her in, hanging on for dear life.

The back of her hand dropped into my lap and our eyes flashed open sparkling wildly at the contact. We held the kiss and stared wide eyed at each other in thrilled surprise. Her hand rested there for a moment and then moved in a slow circle and climbed up my stomach and chest until she reached my neck. Pulling back she took my face in both hands. My eyes fell closed.

We were both breathless, but she shook me gently and made me look at her. "You know you want this, Johnny," she whispered. "Just say yes."

I nodded unable to speak. She kissed me again lightly tickling my lips with the tip of her tongue.

"Wait here a while, then come to the lodge," she murmured. Then she stood up and left me there staring into the heat of the fire.

CHAPTER

14

Two large Samsonite suitcases sat in the lobby next to one of those little makeup cases like my mother used to have. The ones with the mirror inside the lid and a tray full of various concoctions and tools.

"Could you help me get these down to the dock, Johnny? I need to make sure Tambourine's ready." She was all business. I looked around for Charlie but didn't see him anywhere.

I nodded and started picking up bags. As she turned away and headed up the stairs, a flicker of doubt skipped into my brain, but I blinked it away and headed outside. My feet clumped over loose boards as I made my way around the lodge then down the stairs to the dock. The hollow sound of my steps echoed off the water six feet below.

I found the yellow inflatable at the end of the stretch of wooden planks. It was tied at the bottom of a short ladder, about fourteen feet long with an aluminum floor. I'd seen plenty of them around the waterways in coastal Alaska.

There were benches to sit six people, but I grimaced at the idea of moving over the frigid water in the fog. I grunted and swung the bags into the boat space and climbed in to get them settled. I pulled off my own green pack and situated it in a hopefully dry corner. A fifty horsepower Evinrude was attached to the rear, and it looked well used but serviceable. I heard footsteps and turned to see Charlie coming down the dock with a back pack and Greta's make up case. I studied his face for signs of trouble, but he was busy wrestling with the bags. A seagull standing on a post nearby hopped into the air and flew away silently at the sight of him.

"You ready?" he grunted at me. He had his hood up, but even in the dim light I could see his eyeballs racking back and forth behind the coke bottle lenses.

"I guess." There was no turning back but sight of the water chilled my spine. I was not looking forward to the voyage. Usually I was the one in charge of the transportation. I was out of my element on the water. It didn't comfort me in the slightest that Charlie was apparently experienced at this kind of trip.

I looked across the bay toward Chenega. The ocean was flat with a slight breeze rippling its surface. I couldn't see our destination through the fog which hovered above the surface thirty feet high at best. The water lapped at the side of the boat with a limp misleading innocence. It looked cold. The kind of cold that would paralyze a man in minutes.

"It should be alright out there," Charlie said. "The Sound doesn't get big waves unless there's a lot of wind."

"Don't you want to use the bigger boat?" I asked glancing toward an old fishing rig with a glassed in cabin beached past the end of the dock.

"Nope, out of diesel," he muttered swinging the pack on board.

"You got life vests?" I asked.

"Oh yeah. Course, they won't help you much. This water's like lemonade laced with poison, ya know? Looks sweet, can't wait to kill ya," he laughed, but I wasn't in the mood. I was still bothered about the generator.

"You got any other generators so I could make a sat phone call?"

"No, I needed all the gas we had left for this trip. We're cutting it close as it is after the cops took the skiff."

Great, I thought to myself and started thinking how to get myself out of going along. It seemed like a journey into never never land. I wondered why the troopers had taken a skiff instead of this smaller faster Zodiac. Before I could come up with anything, Charlie asked me to help him tie down the bags with a length of yellow nylon cord. Then I heard Greta's heels on the hollow boards above us. Charlie turned and helped her down the ladder.

"Where's Tamby?" Charlie asked her.

"He's looking for Tank. Damn dog disappeared when he saw us packing."

"Aw, shit," Charlie said. "We're not taking that worthless flea bag."

He clambered up the ladder leaving us and the inflatable rocking against its ropes. The old black tires at the edge of the dock smelled of rotting seaweed and mold. Greta had moved forward and was settling in against the rubber side wall at the bow.

It started to rain heavily. I looked at Greta. She had on a bright blue plastic raincoat with a hood surrounding her head and face. Her blond hair set off the hood like one of those old renaissance paintings with the cherubs and their halos. She sat motionless in the sudden downpour and stared over the side at the water next to her. Raindrops danced on the surface like tiny ballerinas in lace.

I was puzzled by the disconnect. She seemed aloof and distant, and I started to wonder if I'd been dreaming at the fire pit less than an hour before. As if reading my mind, her eyes lifted toward me and with a tiny grin, she winked, then went blank again dropping her gaze back to the water.

I heard a shout. Charlie's voice roared above us from just outside the lodge.

"No, goddamn it. We're not taking him. Let's go!" I felt my teeth clench and looked again to Greta. She didn't move, and she didn't look back at me either. She was watching the rain drops.

I stood up when I heard heavy steps and a struggle on the dock. I looked up to see Charlie dragging the kid by his collar. The boy's legs were kicking at the loose boards trying to stop himself but it was pointless. Charlie easily hauled him like a bag of trash and practically threw him down the ladder.

I caught him on the way down. "Easy there, buddy. I've got you." He was a skinny thing and weighed less than the suitcases I'd carried for Greta. His face was pinched and red. He squeezed his eyes shut like he was expecting a punch any second. Tears streaked down both cheeks and his chest was heaving as he choked back on the sobs wracking his whole body. I tried to make eye contact to rekindle our connection but he wouldn't look at me.

I carried him forward and set him down between the bags and Greta. She didn't turn toward us. Her gaze was still fixed on the water's surface, but the rain had stopped.

"Here, Tambourine," I said, settling him against the hard rubber gunwale. His name felt odd coming out of my mouth. I couldn't help shaking my head at the pathetic sight of him as he slumped to the floor of the boat at Greta's feet. He buried his face in his arms and didn't make a sound.

I looked up to see Charlie untying the ropes. Greta held the bow line and waited as if she'd done it a thousand times. Charlie tossed me a small pink pack. It was new looking and decorated with cartoon drawings. I looked closer and recognized the character. Sponge Bob Square Pants. I set it at Tambourine's feet.

As Charlie climbed down into the boat it lurched with his weight. I grabbed for a hold and waited while he took up a position by the engine. Then I moved to the middle and found a place on top of the baggage where I hoped the balance was okay. Charlie fiddled with the gas can and pulled the engine rope. It started on the third tug coughing oily blue smoke across the water.

With a clunk the motor shifted into gear. Greta released the rope and we maneuvered away from the dock and turned to head into the channel. Charlie twisted the throttle and the boat began to move away from the lodge and across the tiny cove before entering the bigger water ahead.

I turned to look behind us. Charlie sat on a rear corner of the inflatable with his hand on the throttle staring out into the fog. His face was set and hard and he peered into the distance like a man trying to be a million miles away. I thought about the airplane and felt a pang in my stomach.

Then I spotted the dog running down the dock toward us. When he got to the water's edge he stopped and began to pace back and forth, his small body quivering. No one else noticed him at first. Then he yelped out an odd sound.

Tambourine's head jerked up as if he'd been shocked. He struggled to his knees and gaped back at his dog, his red face contorted. The scruffy animal saw him and started barking and jumping frantically. Each time he barked the effort lifted him off his front legs.

Charlie looked over his shoulder with disgust and gunned the engine. Tambourine stood up, raised his arms and reached out in a silent plea. Then he cried out, "Tank!"

I reached forward to steady him in the rocking boat, but he shook me off. I saw Greta turn then and look back at Charlie. I looked back at Charlie too and saw his eyes lock with hers just for an instant. His face hardened and his lower jaw pushed forward. He racked the throttle to its stop and yanked on the tiller. The boat tilted hard to the left, and I grabbed for a better hand hold just in time. When I was sure I wasn't going in, I glared at Charlie. I thought the boy might be thrown overboard, but he only fell to his knees and kept reaching for his dog with one hand.

"Goddamn it, Tamby," Charlie shouted. I tensed myself thinking that any moment Charlie might lurch across me to hit the kid. But instead he stayed put and kept the tight bank up until the boat was pointed at the dock again. As we approached the ladder Greta stood up and caught the edge of the dock with one hand. Then she tied the bow rope to a cleat.

Charlie shut off the engine abruptly and grabbed hold of the ladder. Tank hung his homely face over the side of the dock wagging all over and grinning at Tambourine with a drooling smile. The kid stood up and reached for him, but

Charlie grabbed the back of his coat and threw him harshly to the floor. Tank whimpered, tucked his tail and ran across the dock headed for the lodge.

Charlie screamed, "Get the hell back here." Then he grunted and pulled himself up the ladder. His heavy feet thundered across the wooden surface, and the boards rattled and shook above us like a rock slide hitting an old cabin.

Tambourine started for the ladder but Greta grabbed him and held on. He tried to fight but she held fast. His shoulders slumped and he turned and stared at her. His eyes searched her face, but I couldn't tell what he found there. She stared back at him with a warning look and then lifted her face to the sky with no expression.

A sharp yowl rang out. Tambourine looked in the direction of the sound. I stood up and saw a shadow of the big man against the water thirty yards away. He was standing at the edge of the dock holding the dog by the collar as it struggled at the end of his arm. The boy's arms reached out again. His mouth dropped open and his face went slack in anticipation.

"He bit me, he fucking bit me!" Charlie yelled.

A shot ripped through the air. The roar of the forty four sent a shock wave hurtling toward us. A dark shape fell from the dock and splashed into the water. I watched stunned as the liquid surface below the dock rose and fell. A dark shape floated there for a moment before it slipped out of sight. Ripples rushed toward us, slapping at the weather beaten posts and passing by the boat on both sides. The first one was strong. The next three were much smaller and then they were done. The water returned to its normally placid and indifferent state.

The three of us in the boat were frozen in place. Disbelief flooded through me. Before the reverberations had even settled in my ears, Charlie was climbing down the ladder and starting the engine again. Greta reached up and released the bow rope. Her face was grim.

I looked at Tambourine. He stood frozen in the same pose he'd held for the last several minutes. When Charlie racked the throttle to send us away from the dock, he collapsed face down on the floor of the boat. He made no sound, but I could see his small shoulders shaking inside his coat. The windows of the lodge high above looked like an old jack o'lantern left rotting on a forgotten porch. Their gaping panes reflected the gray fog all around us.

Charlie turned the boat and we left the shelter of the cove heading out into the foggy expanse of water that was Prince William Sound. The wind picked up with our speed and I pulled my cap down tighter on my head. Wet air hit my glasses as I squinted into the distance for the dim promise of a shoreline three miles into the gloom. The engine rumbled and the rubber contours of the inflatable vibrated and bumped across tiny waves underneath us. Small splashes of foam flew up and out from the bottom of the boat as we thumped along.

Taroka Island faded into the fog behind us and ahead lay the uncertain future of a thousand whispered wishes.

CHAPTER

15

A cold sweat soaked my armpits as the Zodiac clipped through the gray foggy air. Every now and then a bump sent light spray up and over the bow and into my face. With no land in sight we could have been in the middle of the Pacific rather than just a mile from shore in Prince William Sound. I was clutching a strap holding the bags with all my strength, and my arms and legs were cramped. I tried to relax so I could think, but it was no easy task.

On the water's not where I want to be. I belong in the sky. I don't even like flying over water unless I have to. Then I always try to stay within gliding distance to shore. What if the engine dies? Ignore that thought at your own peril. It's the curse of aviation.

At least in an airplane the water's a long way below. This water was two feet from my face. And cold.

I looked behind me. Charlie was standing in the back of the boat, one hand on the throttle staring into the distance. Water dripped from his coke bottle frames. He'd turned his cap around backwards, and his oily hair fluttered behind him in the breeze. I was careful not to get caught watching him, but I could clearly see the lethal lump under his jacket and the black sheathed knife strapped to his hip.

This was my captain. I'd put myself in Charlie's hands. I'd stepped into the boat and handed him all the control. Suddenly I could relate to the passengers that get nervous just before takeoff. At least behind the controls of an airplane I knew it was up to me. The decisions were mine, and I could talk myself through it like in a graveyard in the dark. But not in a boat. I was not in control.

What was I doing out here? None of us were wearing life jackets. Not even the kid. There were two orange lumps behind me at Charlie's feet, and I thought about what would happen if we tipped over. It would be a mad scramble for the vests and not enough to go around. A chill shook me and I looked back to the front. Tambourine looked even more miserable than I felt. His body was curled into a fetal position and he had Sponge Bob clutched to his chest.

Greta was hunkered down behind the elevated bow of the boat. Out of the wind she sat with her legs braced against a suitcase and her eyes closed. Disconnected. Removed.

I tried to reassure myself that the air compartments in the Zodiac would never rupture all at the same time. That would give us something to hang onto if we went over. Little comfort. I wanted to reach back and grab a life vest but decided not to draw Charlie's attention. I squeezed my eyes shut and tried to banish the memory of the dog's dark form hitting the water.

The rhythm of the boat's motion and the hum of the engine were starting to calm me down and I sat there on the pile of baggage holding onto a strap with each hand. I kept my head down so the wind wouldn't blow off my hat. There was nothing to see ahead besides fog anyhow.

We kept moving steadily forward and I was beginning to think we might survive the voyage after all. I let my thoughts drift to the next steps. What would Phil say to me when I finally got hold of him? I'd been out of touch for way too long, and by now he would know his airplane was missing.

I smirked to myself, bitter but realistic at the thought that he was probably more concerned about the plane than me. He could find a hundred other pilots to take my job in half an hour. But the airplane was worth a lot, and Phil was a businessman first. Alaska can be cold in more ways than one.

Those thoughts kept me distracted for a while, and I almost forgot about the deadly liquid streaming by beneath us. Almost forgot the discomfort of being out of control and clueless. I was almost relaxed right up to the moment the engine stopped.

The boat bucked like a gut shot soldier as the engine coughed twice and died. The bow dropped flat to the water, and everything went quiet.

Greta sat up in alarm. "What's wrong?"

I turned and looked at Charlie. He bent over the fuel tank and then shook his head. "Shit, we're out of gas."

I looked around as the boat bobbed up and down in the middle of nowhere. I halfway expected to see a huge oil tanker emerge out of the fog to bear down on us. Blind in the fog it would plow us under and never know it. But the channel was empty and we were alone. Behind us the wake was slowly dissipating in the calm water.

Charlie stood up. "Trade places with me," he snapped.

The boat wobbled, and I had to force myself to let go of the baggage straps to move to the back. I kept myself crouched to avoid pitching over the side and watched as Charlie stepped to the middle of the boat. He dug under the pile of stuff there and pulled out a pair of oars. Slipping them into the oar rings on top of the gunwales, he settled into position facing the stern and began to row. Then, thinking about it, he stopped, leaned toward Greta with an apologetic look and reached toward her.

"It's only another mile, babe. Won't take long."

She jerked her shoulder away from his touch and turned her back. Charlie's head dropped for a second. He stared at his hands then looked up at her again, but she was far away. Then he poked at Tambourine instead. The boy's body flinched and curled tighter into its fetal tuck.

Letting out a sigh he picked up the oars again and with a strong pull with his right arm turned the boat for Chenega. I peered into the fog in front of us trying to spot the shoreline in the distance. Since the engine quit and Charlie and I had moved around, the boat had turned. I was completely disoriented. For all I knew we could have been pointed toward China. Then I looked behind us and noticed a faint path in the silty water left from the wake we'd made earlier.

"There's usually a little current moving through here that should help us," Charlie said. "It comes off the gulf and pushes to the north."

He settled into a rhythm pulling and lifting the oars with steady effort. The boat began to move again. I sat on the back corner resting one hand on the cooling motor beside me. My other hand clutched a rubber hand hold. A little too tight probably but I was taking no chances. It was slow but we were making progress. I was thankful there was no wind.

Charlie was strong and handled the oars with ease. Every pull moved us through the water a little further. He looked over his shoulder now and then maintaining a straight track across the channel. I felt myself starting to trust him.

Minutes went by in a silence broken only by the groan of the oars and small splashes as they worked the water. Then he suddenly quit pulling and sat frozen staring over his shoulder.

"Uh oh," Charlie grunted. I looked up to follow his gaze to the right.

Something was moving through the water toward us. Thirty yards away a tall black blade rose from the surface and grew steadily as it cut through the water directly at us. A strong wave preceded it like oncoming surf. Then another appeared just behind and to its left. The second was smaller but over four feet tall in a matter of seconds.

"Orcas!" Charlie blurted. "Hold on!"

Just then an explosion of mist erupted from the sea with a guttural bellow. A dorsal fin loomed six feet high above us. A third fin appeared on the right side. They were close now. I slid to the floor of the inflatable and braced myself for the shock of going into the water.

Charlie hauled on one oar and turned us toward the whales. Then he stood up, yanked one oar out of its lock and with a wild yell swung the wood high over his head and slammed it hard on the surface of the water.

The three fins were only feet away, but then they sank out of view and passed below the boat. A strong wave hit us and I thought Charlie was going over. He grabbed for a handhold at the last second just avoiding a fall.

I swiveled my head trying to follow the whales. Gripping the handhold with both hands I waited for the expected push from below. I was sure when they rose again we'd be tipped over into the ocean. But it didn't happen. I could feel their enormous bulks sliding underneath us just inches away like buses cruising past pedestrians standing on a city curb.

Then the enormous fin rose again ten feet behind us and another roar of mist erupted from the sea. Sea water splattered us like a sudden rain squall. The stench of rotted fish gagged me.

Charlie sat back down and threw his head back in maniacal laughter. "Whoo hoo!!" he hollered. "How about that? Holy shit!"

My mouth fell open gasping for air. After a moment I struggled to my knees and took my seat again on the corner of the boat. I swung around to see if they were coming back for another pass. My hands were killing me, cramped from holding on so tight.

Charlie turned around to look me over. He was grinning ear to ear and his eyes were wild. "I don't think they even knew we were here," he laughed. "That was close."

I saw no humor in the situation. I think Charlie was laughing out of relief. When he was standing up with the oar in his hand I'd flashed on visions of Ahab, Gregory Peck and Patrick Stewart all rolled into one.

"Can-can we get moving again?" I knew my voice sounded small.

Charlie laughed and settled back into his rowing position. I noticed Tambourine was standing up and had moved to the right side of the boat. He was looking past me watching the killer whales moving swiftly away, their dorsal fins rising and falling. Our eyes met for just an instant then he went back to watching the whales until they were out of sight. I studied him but his face never changed expression. If you could call it an expression. It was more like a coma. His mouth never moved, and his eyes were fixed and steady. Like a child sleeping with his eyes open.

As I watched, his head cocked slightly and his stare moved upward. Then I heard the sound too. The faint sound of an engine growing steadily louder. I turned and looked into the distance. The whales were gone, and the fog hung less than twenty feet above the water. There were no boats nearby, but there was no mistaking the sound.

It was coming fast and straight at us. It was an airplane. Low and blurry and barely visible in the fog, its wheels couldn't have been more than five feet off the surface. It looked familiar. And sounded familiar too.

Charlie turned and his eyes widened when he saw the propeller headed our way. He ducked. I ducked too but I couldn't help grinning as the red and white plane roared over us. The prop blast would have blown my hat off, but I was holding onto it with both hands.

The pilot must have seen us at the last second. The plane pulled up abruptly and lifted into the murk. It almost disappeared in the clouds before dropping back down again just off the surface. I watched and wondered if the big tundra tires were going to touch the water. My grin grew wider. Only one plane around here sounded like that. And I only knew one bastard crazy enough to fly two feet off the water like that. It was Willie.

Charlie hauled himself back into position to start rowing again. We watched as the airplane banked sharply and circled us. Its left wing was dangerously close to the water. If it touched, the plane would cartwheel into the drink.

Willie circled closer and I saw him slide his side window open. He was close enough to see his ruddy round face and white mustache. His airplane fit his body like a glove. I knew that from the many hours in his back seat admiring the natural way he flew.

Passing by us just fifty feet away he waved his arm out the window. Somebody was in the seat behind him, but I didn't recognize him. All I could make out was a baseball cap and headphones. I waved back and pointed with both arms toward the dark edge of the shore line of Evans Island and Chenega Bay which I was just able to see under the gray cover still blanketing the whole area.

Charlie saw me wave. "You know that guy?"

"Yeah, that's my friend, Willie. From Seward. He must be looking for me."

Greta's voice piped up. "How come he can fly and you can't?"

The edge in her tone took me by surprise. It was that shrill voice from the previous night. The one at the top of the stairs that had denied knowing about the troopers. I looked at her but then remembered that Charlie was right there watching. I got a chill and had to shake it off before I answered.

"Some of us fly by the rules. Willie makes up his own."

"Maybe we should be flying with him," she said with a sniff.

I didn't say anything, but I felt my teeth clench and my face getting hot. I thought of a hundred things to say but decided against them all. Then I felt a rush of relief as I realized Willie and his SuperCub were my way out of this nightmare. I started to grin again. With all his quirks and crotchety moods I never thought I'd look to Willie as my ticket back to sanity. But there he was. Just when I needed him. The cavalry to the rescue.

Willie was like a harrier hawk hugging the trees and ridgelines around Seward. Sort of a local hero he showed me how to fly out and land on the beaches nearby to visit with surprised fishermen. Willie was everything people think about the classic Alaskan bush pilot. Rough around the edges but so skilled with an airplane, you just had to stop and watch in awe.

Charlie started pulling on the oars again heading for shore. I watched Willie make a final bank turning for Chenega, and I took a deep breath when I saw his wingtip lift from where it seemed to almost skim the surface of the frigid water.

The white fabric and red stripes on his plane disappeared from view into the fog ahead of us, and the sound of his engine faded until it was gone. I wondered what he could see. In a couple of minutes it was quiet again. The only sound around us then was Charlie splashing the oars in the water and the groan of the rubber around the oarlocks. The shoreline grew closer with his every pull.

CHAPTER
16

Evening was approaching and with it the fog above us grew thicker and dark. The smell of the sea became more intense, and I caught whiffs of rotting seaweed and dead fish. The edge of the island appeared ahead along with the outline of a large dock. I'd seen it from the air several times but never from below. Tall concrete columns loomed above us supporting a wide pier. Thin clouds of mist wrapped themselves around the bases of the columns.

I looked in the direction of the airstrip figuring it to be less than a mile away. I knew it was on top of a small plateau just up from the bay and the fog had to be sitting right on its surface. I cringed at the thought of Willie flying so close to the water and looking for a way through the trees and rocks to get to the runway. From where I sat it looked impossible. I couldn't see any way through. And Willie was moving at least forty miles an hour. I closed my eyes thankful it wasn't me in the SuperCub. In the front or the backseat.

I'd been in that kind of situation a couple of times before. Made some bad decisions and had to fly into fog next to cliffs just to escape.

Tree top flying is fun on a clear day, but in fog it's sheer terror. At airplane speed, you could hit a ground antenna or a tall tree and be gone in a flash. When you're that low, all you can do is pull up. You might miss the tree but then you're in the clouds. And blind.

A pilot should never be in that situation but sometimes stuff happens. Willie was another story. He pushed the limits time after time. He had brass.

My thoughts about Willie were interrupted when we moved past the high pier and Charlie turned into the marina behind it. His face shone with sweat, but his pace was still strong.

Greta had moved to sit on a side tube of the inflatable at the bow and was looking forward. A light breeze fluttered blond strands across her face. Her baseball cap was pulled down tight in front and her face was cast in shadow. Her collar was up and buttoned tightly around her neck. Her shoulders hunched toward her ears, and I could see her shiver once a while in the damp evening air.

The smell of land rushed my senses with relief. The shock of the gunfire and the dog hitting the water still hung in the back of my mind like a black cloak of dread but seeing Willie gave me hope.

Tambourine sat on the floor with his arms wrapped around his knees staring into space. His chin was vibrating, and I could see his lips were blue and quivering. The coat he was wearing was too big for him and the sleeves hung over his hands. Every now and then his little shoulders shook and he hugged his knees tighter. But he never looked toward Greta or Charlie. He was in another world.

I couldn't believe he was twelve years old. And something was seriously wrong. The rock and roll hero I'd seen before had left for the coast. His dead eyes made me think of caged dogs waiting in the pound for that final injection.

Watching him I felt a hard lump in my gut. It was like something was tugging below my chest making it hard to breathe.

Glancing up I saw we were approaching a dock. I was more than ready to get out of the rubber boat. Charlie hauled several more times on the oars and moved us into position to tie off against some rubber tires nailed into the wooden pier. There were several boats tied in slips around us. Fishing boats, working boats. Most of them beat up and in need of paint.

The marina was in a small cove, a divot in the side of the rocky tree covered island. Similar to the cove we'd left on Taroka, there was high ground above us with a couple of buildings and large white cylinder fuel tanks. The terrain to the right flattened and a small road led off into some trees in the direction of the airstrip.

I'd made several flights out here over the years. I'd even been down to the dock once or twice killing time while waiting for passengers to return. Concrete stairs with a heavy steel pipe hand rail climbed the hill beside us up to where fuel tanks sat in the foggy wet evening air. The railing was painted industrial gray and the bases of the stairs were a dull maroon. The embankment had been heavily reinforced to prevent mudslides in the wet climate.

I climbed out of the boat relieved to feel the solidness of the wooden dock under my feet. Charlie finished tying up the boat and started offloading the bags. I walked forward and looked down at Greta still sitting on the bow. She was closing up her makeup bag. Tambourine hadn't changed position.

"We made it," I said reaching down and taking one of the kid's arms. It felt like a twig inside the thick down coat. He didn't resist as I pulled him up and stood him on the dock. He turned his back looking at the other boats and stepped away when I let him go. I turned back around and reached down for Greta.

She was looking up the hill and then stood up somewhat reluctantly it seemed, but after a moment's hesitation she reached up to take my hand. As I pulled her upward I heard a voice call down from the top of the hill above the dock.

"Hey Johnny!"

I couldn't look over just yet since I was concentrating on lifting Greta from the boat. When she was standing beside me she suddenly pulled off her hat with her free hand and shook out her blond styled hair like she was throwing off the gloom. Long bangs dropped in front of her eyes, and then she gave me a huge smile and with her arms flung wide fell toward me. I had to drop my pack and move fast to catch her and found myself holding her like one of those old fashioned dip moves on the dance floor. She put both arms around my neck.

"Oh, Johnny," she swooned and laughed, raising the back of one hand to her cheek. I couldn't help laughing in surprise and amazement at the lightness of her and the ease with which I was able to hold her and move her around. As I pulled her back up she put her arms around my waist and moved in close smiling with a radiance that took me by so much surprise I grinned even wider and started giggling like a loon.

"Oh, thank you, sir," she crooned in a lilting exaggerated tone reaching for my face with both of her hands. Then she leaned forward and kissed me full on the mouth. Stunned by the soft warm contact of her lips my eyes closed and I stood there paralyzed. The terror I'd felt in the boat was forgotten, erased like a windshield wiper clearing off the rain. I wanted to soak in the thrill of her in my arms, but then I sensed Charlie watching and tried to break off the kiss.

Remembering the familiar sound of the voice in the distance I turned to look down the dock. It was Willie walking fast down the staircase in our direction. Greta turned her head to follow my gaze but she continued to hold me with her face close to mine. The scent of fresh perfume washed over me and I wondered for a second when she'd taken the time to do that. But my mind was whirling and my pants were feeling tight again. I almost didn't notice the person walking down the dock behind Willie.

As I regained my balance and started to breath normally again, Greta shifted away slightly and looked toward Willie. I pulled away too, and my face felt hot. Willie was gaping at us.

Then I realized he wasn't alone. The other person stepped around from behind him and stopped.

It was Brandy, Willie's daughter, the heartache I'd been trying to forget for more than a year. She was staring at Greta and me, and as I watched her face I saw her eyes narrow and her lips press tightly together. She dropped her eyes then, turned and walked back toward the stairs. The dock lost its solid feeling and seemed to sway under my feet. Probably my imagination. Or maybe from being on the water for so long. Maybe. Maybe not.

Willie kept coming. "Johnny, where the hell have you been? Don't you know you've got half the state looking for you?" He wasn't smiling.

I pulled myself away from Greta and reached down to pick up my pack.

"Hey, Willie. Man, I'm glad to see you," I said with a faked nonchalant chuckle. "It's a long story, let me tell ya."

"Why didn't you call in? Where's your plane? Alaska state troopers have been calling me non-stop."

"Calling you? What are they calling you for? They're supposed to be over here waiting for me."

"What are you talking about? I'm talking about their dispatch office calling me. And then two cops came by in a patrol car this morning looking for you or their officers. So where are they?" He took a step back, crossed his arms and frowned at me.

"You mean Rankin and Daniels? I have no idea where they are. I flew them over there to Taroka last night, so they could investigate a call they got. Remember?"

Willie stared back at me and I could see his mind struggling to recall our conversation the day before. He finally nodded.

I went on. "Well, they got into a gunfight with the guy they were after and I haven't seen them since. Then the fog came in, and my sat phone died. The power went out at the lodge and … Christ, what a mess."

I ran out of words then and looked behind Willie. Brandy was standing twenty feet away staring off into the distance with her arms wrapped across her chest.

"A gunfight? Where's the plane?" Willie asked me again shaking his head.

"Huh? Oh, it's grounded over on Taroka. There's no way to fly in this stuff," I said throwing my arm toward the sky.

"Then what are ya doing here?" he scowled at me.

I noticed then that Greta and Charlie had gathered their stuff and were moving past us down the dock toward Brandy. Charlie was weighed down with his backpack and the two large suitcases. Greta had her makeup bag tucked under one arm and was pulling Tambourine along by the back of his coat with her other hand. The Sponge Bob pack was laying on the pier by Willie's feet.

"Who are those people?" Willie asked looking more befuddled than ever.

"They're the folks that run the lodge out there. Hang on a sec."

I picked up the bright yellow pack and made sure it was closed. Then I hurried down the dock to catch up.

"Hello, Brandy," I murmured as I walked by her. "I'll be right back."

"Johnny," she said flatly with a nod. I maneuvered carefully around her on the narrow walkway.

"Hey, Charlie," I called. He stopped and looked back at me, but Greta started up the stairs pulling Tambourine behind her. "What's your plan? Where you going?"

"We know some construction guys up here," he said jerking his head toward the village just beyond the hilltop. "We're going to see them about those generator parts." He turned and continued up the stairs.

"You seen your skiff?" I asked looking around the marina.

Charlie shook his head and shrugged his shoulders, then turned and started up the stairs behind the others. I watched them for a moment trying to think of something to say. Greta had reached the top of the stairs and I looked at her for some sign, but she didn't look back.

"What the hell's going on, Johnny?" Willie's voice right behind me startled me.

I turned to answer him and then noticed the yellow back pack still in my hand. Swinging back around I saw the three of them just leaving the top of the staircase and out of view. I looked back and forth between them and the pack in my hand, my thoughts stumbling over each other like boulders in a mud slide.

"Johnny, you know Phil's about to go ballistic? You didn't tell him about this flight?" Willie's voice had climbed to a higher pitch jerking my attention back to him.

"Hell, it was late when I got the call. You remember. At the bar? I called them but their answering machine was on. I thought I'd be back before they even got the message. How was I supposed to know everything was going to get so screwed up?"

I wanted to ask him about Brandy, but she was too close to avoid hearing us, and I didn't want to whisper to him like an idiot.

"After the troopers called me, I called Phil and told him about your flight," Willie said, "but he's hot."

"Yeah, well, what's the big deal? Shit happens." I'd had enough of hearing about my boss and his short fuse.

Willie threw out his hands in frustration. "Well, you ain't heard the least of it. Your troopers haven't made contact with their base since last night. Even the Coast Guard has been trying to get out here to find you guys."

That threw me. I stared at Willie trying to understand.

"Well, they've got to be around here somewhere. Charlie said they took off in a skiff chasing the guy when the fog came in. How bad is it anyhow?"

"Aw, it's thicker than snot. No one else could get in here, so I gave it a try. It's only bad for about ten miles right around here. I had to get kind of low to get underneath it."

I looked toward the airport. It wasn't in sight but I knew it was nearby on a flat spot up between two big hills.

"How the hell could you see to land up there?" I asked.

"That's a damn good question," Brandy chimed in. She'd walked up to join us and there was an edge in her voice I remembered all too well. "Hello, Johnny. Yeah, there was no visibility on that landing. Illegal as hell."

Willie looked a little awkward. "Yup, it was pretty thick, but after I saw you guys in the boat I was able to find the dock. I knew the runway was just up that little trail over there, so I found it okay. No big deal. I used to fly stuff like that all the time when I lived out in Bristol Bay."

I looked to where we was pointing. The trail he was talking about started at water's edge, climbed the hillside and then disappeared in the fog.

"You're nuts, man, but I'm really glad to see ya. As much as I hate to admit it," I laughed and slapped his shoulder.

Willie cleared his throat. He wasn't having it.

"What the fuck is wrong with you, Johnny? You're in deep shit and you're laughing and playing around like it's nothing? And now you're chasing tail with some little blond bimbo?"

He waved his hand in Greta's direction. His words hit me like a slap. My eyes snapped in that direction in alarm but all I saw was Brandy glaring at me and waiting for an answer.

My mouth fell open and I felt my eyes bugging out. For a moment I was speechless, my eyes flicking back and forth between Willie's tight red face, Brandy's questioning look and the empty stairway in the distance.

"Wait a minute, wait a minute, it's not like that at all. What the hell are you talking about?"

"Look, Johnny, you're in trouble here. Phil was so pissed about you being gone he told the troopers that as far as he was concerned you'd stolen the airplane. So now they think you're involved in the troopers being missing."

"What? You've got to be kidding me! Didn't you tell them I filed my flight plan with you?"

"Yeah, I did, but they don't understand that. Phil told them the company policy is to file a flight plan with the FAA."

I slumped into silence. I couldn't believe what I was hearing. A wave of sickness filled my belly. Finally I choked out a question.

"The troopers are missing, and they think I know where they are? I don't have any freaking idea where they are." I could hear the strain in my own voice.

"I tried to tell them you weren't a problem, but they're real worked up about their officers being missing. That just doesn't happen."

"It's the fog, damn it." I stamped back and forth on the dock, my mind reeling from what Willie was saying. "If it wasn't so damn socked in around here, we'd be able to get some answers."

"You never should have taken that flight. I told you that last night," Willie snapped.

"Yeah, right. Tell that to my bill collectors."

"Guys, guys," Brandy broke in. "Settle down for a minute, will ya? We all just got here. Let's go up to the village and ask around. If the troopers are here someone will know about it."

I pulled my cap tighter and started for the stairs. I needed space from Willie's sharp tongue. "I can't believe this crap. And Phil threw me to the wolves? What a freaking jerk!"

I pulled myself up the staircase deep in thought. The metal framework echoed faintly underneath us as we climbed. At the top my head started to clear a little and I struggled to get things sorted out. How could anybody think I had something to do with this mess? What had I ever done to deserve this?

Reaching the top I took in a deep breath and paused to get the kinks out of my legs. Well, okay, so maybe I'd done a few things in my repo man career that were less than honorable. But hell, a repo man works in the shadows. That didn't mean I was flaky. Or did it?

Besides I thought I'd overcome all that. Proved myself so to speak during my escapades last year. So, maybe not. Especially with the cops. But I suppose they weren't the type to think the best of people like me. Cops take a dim view of private people getting involved in law enforcement. Guess I couldn't blame them for that. Pilots were the same way. Phil had a plaque hanging in his office that said, "If you ain't a pilot, you ain't shit." It's the same attitude.

Besides, everybody in Alaska looks a little flaky. Well, not everybody, but some of the nicest, most decent people I'd ever met looked like motorcycle gangsters or dumpster diving derelicts. I wasn't a bad person. Just a broke airplane driver trying to get by.

I didn't like the thoughts I was having. Feeling defensive. And I didn't like hearing that people were talking about me in connection to missing cops. It was making me question myself and wonder what I'd done wrong.

But I hadn't done anything wrong, and now I was in a corner, under attack, feeling caged. I wasn't used to scrutiny. Now all my decisions over the last two days were going to be questioned, people would be demanding explanations. If only the troopers would show up. Where the hell were those guys?

I looked toward the houses down the damp gravel road past the church with its blue metal roof. Chenega village. It looked as deserted as ever. Greta and the others were nowhere in sight. It was getting late and the thick fog just above our heads made everything darker. I was getting a sick feeling inside. The hot and cold I'd been getting from that little blond had me reeling. What was that all about?

And then Brandy has to show up at the same time? What was she doing here? She was the last person on earth I ever expected to see again. She'd popped into my life last year when Willie's airplane had been stolen. We couldn't stand each other when we first met, but she was Willie's daughter. I hadn't even known he had a daughter. She showed up for a surprise visit and finds her father in the hospital. I felt sorry for her and tried to help out. And she was pretty. And she was a Learjet pilot of all things.

So many times since then I wished I'd listened to myself. But I was an idiot and fell head over heels. Even Rainey had tried to warn me. One look at Brandy and she'd said, "Keep it zipped, Johnny." Something subtle like that.

But I didn't listen and we got involved. I'd never felt that way about anybody. Damn it, why was everybody smarter than me about that stuff?

And after the little adventure we got caught up in, she left. Boom, zap, just like that. Turned on her heel and walked away. Left Alaska and was never heard from again. Not by me anyhow. Until now.

I rubbed my eyes and looked around. There was no one in sight. One of Greta's suitcases was leaning against a concrete post. I thought about leaving the yellow pack beside it but decided against it.

We started walking through the middle of an empty lot toward the church. Our feet scuffling on the gravel. I was leading the way and Willie and Brandy were close behind. Mist clung all around the steeple above us. It was a round Russian Orthodox looking thing. Reminded me of all the history of this area and the slightly foreign flavor left over from long ago.

Down the hill past the church a line of spruce trees separated us from the concrete ferry dock. We stopped to get our bearings in front of a red building, the community center. The one street through the village was still deserted. I saw a native woman come out of one of the houses nearby, but she didn't look at us. A dog barked down the road.

Willie walked over to the community building to look at a notice posted on the wall. Brandy stood nearby expressionless.

I took a breath and screwed up my courage. "So, uh, Brandy, what are you doing here?" I finally asked.

"Oh, nothing. I just thought I'd come and see my dad for a while."

"Just passing through, eh?" I tried to keep my tone civil and neutral. Not too interested, nothing hostile. Joe Cool.

"Well, I had a charter from Cleveland up to Anchorage, so I combined it with a few days of vacation. Didn't Dad mention it to you?"

"No, he didn't mention it."

"I suppose it was a little spontaneous. I just told him about it a few days ago," she said matter of factly and walked over to a bulletin board hanging on the side of the building.

I turned and glared at Willie. He was climbing the stairs up to the main entrance of the community center. When he reached the top, he opened the door and went inside.

Damn guy, I swore under my breath. You'd think he could have told me that my old heart throb was coming to town. A little warning, you know? To give me time to hide somewhere so I could practice my 'I don't care' face. But no, the sonofabitch hadn't said a word.

Then again, Brandy was his daughter, and we'd never talked about I felt about her. He knew me too well already. We'd had a lot of bar conversations about women. Saying the stuff guys say to each other over beers when they're alone. When the alcohol brings out all the bullshit and bravado.

I'd never been sure what he'd thought about us, Brandy and me. Then when she left I was in a bad way.

How do you share that with her father? I didn't know how, so I kept it to myself. Except for Rainey. After we got past the 'I told you so' lecture.

I glanced up at the closed door at the top of the stairs. Willie was still inside. Rainey was reading something on the bulletin board.

I forced myself to take another deep breath. After a few moments I walked over and tried to break the uncomfortable silence between us.

"So, uh, well, uh, it's, uh, it's nice to see you again, Brandy," I said with the calmest façade I could manage.

"Right," she smirked at me. "Looks like you're doing just fine, Johnny."

"What do you mean?" I think my mouth fell open.

"Your little china doll back there? She seemed very … friendly, let's say."

"What? Her? That ain't nothing," I protested.

"You know you have lipstick all over your mouth?"

My hands flew to my face and I wiped frantically with my fingers and sleeves. Brandy gave a sarcastic laugh and we turned to see Willie coming down the stairs.

"A guy inside told me they found a boat washed up on the beach," he said. "Let's go check it out."

CHAPTER
17

Panic gripped me all of a sudden remembering that I still hadn't called the boss. Brandy and Willie started walking down the street, but my feet wouldn't move. I was worried about Phil. He was going to kill me.

It had been almost twenty four hours since I'd taken his plane. On what was supposed to be a three or four hour charter flight. I had to talk to him but I cringed at the thought. I stood there numbly until Willie noticed I wasn't following.

He stopped and turned around. "What's wrong?"

"I need to call Phil."

"Yeah, no shit. He's gonna kill you," he smirked.

When I didn't move, he jerked his head toward the community building. "There's a phone inside."

I still didn't move, thinking about what to say to Phil.

"Go on, man. Don't be a wuss. Just grow a pair and go call the guy. What's he gonna do? Reach through the phone and grab your scrawny little neck?"

I glared at him. Tried to fry his round little head with my death ray vision. "Alright, alright, give me a minute, will ya?"

"We'll go check out the skiff while you call," Willie said. "Just tell him the truth."

"Okay, okay."

He snorted. "Don't worry about it. You didn't do anything wrong. I would have done the same thing. If he can't accept that, screw him."

I felt my cheeks grow warm. Those were the words I'd needed to hear. He would have done the same thing. Confidence surged through me then, and with a deep breath I turned and headed for the stairs.

"And when he fires you, you can always work the slime line at the cannery," he called after me.

I spun on my heel to flip him off but he and Brandy were walking away laughing.

The door at the top of the stairs opened into a cluttered entry room. As I stepped inside I was hit by a wave of warm air reeking of salmon stew, cigarette smoke and body odor. The phone hung on the wall nearby above an assortment of snow boots, muddy shovels and a crumpled green can of Mountain Dew.

There was an old wood stove across the room with a pot of something sitting on top. Its lid rattled and wisps of steam leaked out around its edges. My stomach took a turn reminding me I hadn't eaten in hours.

Reluctantly I moved over to the phone. I zipped open my fleece trying to cool down and dialed the numbers with dread.

"This is Phil," a tired voice answered with a guarded tone that seemed to be expecting bad news.

"Hey, Phil, it's Johnny. I can explain everything."

There was a deadly nothing on the other end of the line. I gulped and pushed ahead. Just dove into it and started telling the story. Pausing once for a breath, he still didn't respond. So I went on. Told him about the gunfight, the dead sat phone, the generator, the skiff, everything.

He finally broke his silence. "Willy was able to fly out there, and you couldn't get back to Seward?"

"I could have if you want me to fly two feet over the ocean for ten miles. Is that what you want?"

I waited then. Waited for him to think it through. It felt like one of those deals where the first one to speak loses.

After a long pause I thought I might pass out from lack of oxygen. Then he finally said, "No, I've taught you better than that. Only a crazy bastard like Willie would do that."

The air returned to my lungs, but I could still feel the pounding in my throat.

"So," he continued, "if you're telling me the truth, at least the airplane's okay where it is?"

"If I'm telling....? Of course, I'm telling you the damn truth. Why the hell would I lie?"

He paused again at the sudden snarl in my voice. "Well, Johnny, there was that time when you weren't exactly straight with us about ..."

"Hey, Phil, gimme a break. I'd love to go over all my past shortcomings with you, but I need to get moving. Alright?" I almost slammed down the phone but closed my eyes instead and took another deep breath.

"Okay, okay," he grumbled. "At least the airplane's okay. It's been a long day and I was expecting the worst. What happens now?"

I told him about the skiff that the fishermen found, and that I'd keep him informed the best I could. When the fog lifted I'd get back out to Taroka and fly the plane back to Seward. He wanted to complain that we were missing flights back in Seward but I cut him off again and said I had to go. Hanging up the phone my lungs filled with air and I felt three hundred pounds lighter.

I picked up Sponge Bob and pushed my way back out into the chilly air, rambled down the stairs and headed for the beach. I'd been so preoccupied with calling Phil that I hadn't been thinking about anything else. The boat that washed up on the beach could be the one from Charlie's lodge. It never failed around Alaska's waters. People were always getting in trouble in canoes or fishing boats and bad things happened. Sometimes bodies were found, other times not. I felt that grip in my gut again and pushed on.

The smell of wood smoke floated over me as I walked away from the church and down a dirt street. My shoes crunched on the gravel, the sound echoing oddly in the darkening gloom. Lights were coming on in the small white prefab houses that lined both sides of the wide road. They sat on simple concrete footers and had small front yards with wire fences and little to no grass. A few old bicycles lay here and there. Aluminum chimneys poked through the roof tops and three or four of them were spewing thin trails of smoke.

It was quiet. I moved past a tool shed, a satellite dish and a large white propane tank with rust bleeding down its side. I didn't want to stare into people's houses, but one place I went by had an odd glow flickering through the front window. An old native couple wearing dingy coveralls and plaid shirts were sitting in white plastic chairs in their living room watching an oversized flat screen. Vanna White in a dazzling white sequined gown was turning letters and smiling beside a shiny red Cadillac convertible.

Otherwise the town was deserted except for a medium size dog standing in the middle of the road ahead. Before I could get nervous about its intentions, it turned and loped off with a baleful backward glance.

The town of Chenega Bay had always felt temporary and empty to me. There'd been a brutal earthquake in the south of Alaska back in 1964. Centered nearby in Prince William Sound it completely destroyed the original village of Chenega Bay on a different island about twenty miles north. So the whole town and its hundred residents were moved to this new place, but I'd never seen more than two or three of them at any one time. The Natives pretty much kept to themselves. They liked their privacy.

Walking past a few more empty houses I could hear water lapping against the rocky shoreline nearby. It was seriously dark and a wicked wet breeze swiped at my face like a cold washcloth on a fevered brow. I stopped to look around, thinking I was in the wrong place.

Then a light flickered up ahead. I headed for it passing two old wooden boats on blocks and a weather beaten pickup just barely visible in the dim glow. I spotted Willie and Brandy standing on a small beach. It was low tide and they were about twenty yards offshore. A native guy in orange rubber boots up to his knees stood next to them holding an old fashioned oil lantern. The light bouncing into their faces from below made them look like something out of a bad slasher film.

I walked carefully toward them across a wet surface of hard packed mud and small flat stones. They were talking in low tones and looking at an old bluish skiff that was laying at an odd angle beside them. Green strands of seaweed sparkled around our feet in the light from the lantern.

Brandy spoke up. "Johnny, this is Mike. He was telling us about the boat here."

The guy in the boots nodded at me. "Yeah, some local fishermen found this floating upside down. They pulled it over here and left it." His voice made a thick slurry sound like he was trying not to move his lips or jaw.

"When?" I asked.

"This afternoon, I think."

"Where did they find it?"

"Middle of the channel," he indicated with a thumb.

"And there wasn't anybody with it or nearby?"

"No, nobody."

"You seen any troopers today?"

He shook his head. I stepped over to the skiff and took a closer look. It was empty. It had been painted blue once, but now more scraped aluminum showed through than color. The engine was still attached but the fuel tank was gone. Mike came over and set the lantern down beside the boat. Faded letters on the side spelled out Westridge Lodge.

Willie came over and squatted beside the boat. "If they went in the water, they wouldn't last long."

We stood there quietly thinking about it. The images weren't pretty.

"Especially without life jackets," Willie added. "Bodies sink straight to the bottom in water like this."

"The sea was calm out there. I wonder what happened," I said, remembering the whales with a shudder.

"What were they doing out there?" Willie asked.

"They were chasing the guy they were supposed to arrest. He took a bunch of shots at us, then took off in a boat from the lodge. It was too foggy to fly, so they took the skiff to go after him."

"We need to notify their office," Willie said. "Is that phone up there working?"

"Yeah, it is. What do you think they'll do?"

"Probably send out a search team. They already notified the Coast Guard. I thought they'd be here already."

I had a question. "Hey, Mike, do you know the people that work over on Taroka?"

"Not really," he shrugged.

"Don't they come through here going back and forth to the lodge? Like with guests and all?"

He didn't answer right away. Like he was thinking about it. I looked at him but his blank face showed me nothing.

"Not really," he finally answered.

"Did you see any other boats or anything from over there today?"

Mike shook his head slowly and spit a stream of dark juice onto the mud.

When he didn't say anything else, I tried another angle. "Charlie from over there told me that one of his crew caused a bunch of trouble yesterday and then took off in one of his boats. I guess he shot up the place. You know who that might be?"

"Charlie? Charlie Westridge?" he asked.

"No, the guy that caused the problem. Charlie said it was one of his staff. Like a fishing guide or something. I'm not sure who he was exactly."

Mike lifted his head as if he was about to say something, then pressed his lips together and glanced away shaking his head.

I looked at him and waited for a moment. "What?" I finally asked, but he just shrugged. I waited some more and tried not to stare at him. After a few moments, Mike finally spoke up.

"Charlie Westridge is trouble," he mumbled and raised his eyebrows with wide eyes looking off into the darkness. I could tell he didn't want to talk about it.

Willie came up behind us. "What about the other guy? Didn't you say there were two boats from the lodge?"

"Yeah," I answered. "We were just talking about that. If the guide didn't come here, where would he go? There's Cordova nearby or Valdez or Whittier, but I don't think he had enough gas."

"How do we know who was in this boat?"

"Good question, we don't." I turned to ask Mike about that but he'd moved away.

"Let's go, Johnny. It's late." Willie tugged at my jacket and turned to go. "So what did Phil say?" he asked.

"He's pissed, but he's glad to hear his airplane's okay."

Willie blew air out his lips in disgust. He'd never liked Phil and always wondered how I could work for him.

We started walking back up the hill. Mike followed behind. His swinging lantern cast long shadows of the three of us on the gravel road. Like monster creatures from the deep lurching along in awkward movements from side to side. The shapes merged one with another and swayed crazily before separating again as we made our way up the slope.

When we reached the community building, Willie and Mike went inside. Brandy was about to follow, but she hesitated when she noticed that I'd stopped.

"What are you doing?" she asked.

I stood still for a moment looking at her and thinking. "I'm trying to make sense of all this," I said finally.

"That Mike guy isn't much help, is he?" she frowned after him.

I thought about that, wondering if Mike knew more than he was saying or if he was as clueless as I was. "I don't know," I said. "Maybe he doesn't know anything. It's hard to tell."

"That yours?" she asked looking down at my hand.

I followed her gaze and realized I was still holding the yellow Sponge Bob pack. I'd forgotten all about it.

I looked around wondering where Charlie and Greta had gone. They could be anywhere in the group of houses nearby. And there was a construction crew area down the road and around a corner. Separated from the village it was temporary housing and shelter for men and equipment when some kind of project was going on the island or anywhere nearby in the Sound.

"I need to take a walk," I said.

"Where to?" she asked studying me.

"This belongs to that kid," I said holding up the pack. "I need to get it back to him."

"Oh, you missing your little girlfriend?" she snapped.

"Knock it off with that stuff. Would ya?" I growled, surprising myself with the quick heat I felt in my voice. "They're married," I lied.

"That's funny, they're not wearing rings," she said coolly.

I let out a sigh. "Whatever. They're a couple, alright? And I just want to ask Charlie some questions."

"Sure, sure. I'll tell Dad." She turned her back and headed for the stairs. Just the way she'd turned her back that lonely night last year.

"Brandy." Saying her name felt strange after I'd spent so much time trying to pretend she didn't exist anymore.

"What?" she answered, looking back over her shoulder. With one hand she smoothed strands of brunette hair out of her face and back behind her ear. The overhead light left her face in shadow, but I could feel her smoky green eyes watching me.

I felt myself softening. My words wrestled each other trying to force their way out of my mouth at the same time. I stared down at my dirty shoes. The way she stood there brought back a memory. I caught a whiff of strawberry shampoo and remembered the feel of her, the bond we'd had.

"I, I didn't mean to grumble at you."

"Whatever, Johnny." She turned and climbed the stairs two at a time before I had a chance to say another word.

A deep sigh lifted my chest as I stared at the closed door. Feeling like an idiot, I turned, kicked at the dirt and walked away.

CHAPTER
18

I headed for the small boat dock again thinking I'd get the suitcase and then try to find the construction camp. I'd walked a hundred yards before I noticed the cramping in my hands and told myself to relax my clenched fists. My face muscles ached, and I forced my mouth open in an exaggerated yawn. My jaw popped with a painful jolt and then instantly felt better.

None of the houses nearby had any lights on. The area was deserted and all the doors were closed. Even the dogs were gone.

I was in the dark again. In more ways than one. The white expanse of the empty church came and went in the gloom as I walked by. The only light came from a dim bulb above the front door. The cross at the top of the steeple was lost in the fog and wasn't saying anything to me anyway.

At the top of the hill above the commercial dock I stopped to look at two small points of light across Sawmill

Bay. Hardy souls had homes out there carving a life out of the rocks and trees on a remote island. I envied them and wondered if I could ever live that way. It was an old dream to live alone in the wilderness. The lone wolf fantasy. Away from people and all their drama. Free from the demands of modern life with its bills and burdens and countless pressures to perform. It was tempting to think about a simple existence like that. Needing no one. Living off the land responsible only for yourself. A wonderful fantasy. A difficult reality.

The fuel tanks surrounded me then. A solitary light at the top of the stairway to the dock spilled a yellow glow in a small circle below it. The suitcase was gone.

Then I heard heavy footsteps clumping up the stairs toward me. I thought about stepping behind something to hide, but instead I stood my ground and waited.

It was Charlie hauling the heavy Samsonite. With four steps left to go he looked up and spotted me. He stopped and set the suitcase down. I thought that odd. Why didn't he keep climbing?

"What's up?" he asked looking me over with a guarded tone.

I could see the bulge still under his jacket. He had the hood of his sweatshirt up again warding off the cool mist in the air. The weak light left his face in a shadow but I could see the coke bottle lenses. The grim reaper with 20/400 vision. I could imagine his eyeballs clicking from side to side in the dark.

"They found your skiff."

"Who did?"

"Fishermen. It was upside down out in the channel."

"Really? Did they find the troopers?" He licked his lips and watched me carefully.

"No, and nobody's seen them."

"Bummer," he said. "I guess it really sucks to be them about now."

He moved to one side so the light filled his face. He was grinning at me, and his eyes moved around behind the glasses like fish eyes in an aquarium.

He leaned against the railing with one arm and pulled back the jacket to rest his hand on the handle of the sheath knife strapped to his right side.

"Is there gonna be a problem, Johnny?" He climbed two more steps and stopped, his head level with mine, grinning at me with a crooked smirk.

In spite of myself I took a half step back and glanced around. My feet got itchy. They wanted to leave.

"Problem? Uh, no way. Not from me, there isn't. I just want to get me and my airplane back to Seward." I looked out toward the water, feeling the heavy curtain of fog just out of reach.

He was watching me closely, but not as closely as I was studying him. Without making eye contact every fiber of my being was working on staying calm and showing him a disinterested guy who just wanted to go away.

"That water's a killer," he murmured, following my gaze. "If they went in, they're gone by now. Fish food, ya know?"

He was testing me. Like an octopus exploring a prey. I could feel the tentacles all over me, sensing my every move, reading my expression, gauging the threat level.

"Yeah, fish food is right," I forced out a little chuckle and glanced at him quickly. "Stupid cops."

His eyes narrowed and studied mine. I met his gaze and held it just for a moment.

He looked surprised for a second, then grinned wider and dropped his hand from the knife handle. He made a fist and extended it slowly toward me. I stepped forward and met his fist with my own. His knuckles felt warm and with the slight bump it was like a message passed between us. He picked up the suitcase and climbed the rest of the stairs to tower over me.

"I'm just curious though, Charlie. What's that guide's name again?"

"Hank," he said.

"Okay, yeah, Hank. Nobody's seen Hank come over here. Where do you suppose he went? Cordova?"

"Nah, he didn't have enough gas to get much of anywhere."

"And what color was the boat he took?"

"Blue. Beat up blue, you know. Hadn't been painted for a while."

"Sounds like the one they found. What about the other one? What color was it?"

"It was the same. You got a lot of questions for just being a pilot, don't ya?" He set the suitcase down and stared down at me with his arms crossed.

I felt the tentacles again. Crawling around my neck and all over my face in a slimy journey. Feeling every muscle twitch and eye blink. Probing every nook and facial cranny and weighing the results. Friend or foe?

I cleared my throat. "Ah, sorry, I'm just trying to figure out what happened. It's so confusing."

"Maybe you don't need to know, Johnny. Maybe you're better off just staying clear of all of it. You know?"

"Yeah, I know, I know," I answered, probably a little too quickly. "But I brought these guys out here, and I'm supposed to take them back. You know what I mean? I feel responsible."

"If I was you, man, I'd just fade into the woodwork. You know? Let things slide. And as soon as you can, get the hell out. Fly away and forget all about it."

"Yeah, you're probably right."

"Of course, I'm right. It ain't your fault they disappeared."

"Yeah, okay. So, what are you guys going to do now?"

"Well, they got the parts we need. So first thing in the morning we're heading back over to the lodge. I'll get the generator going and then we can get the lodge closed down for the season."

I thought about that. I knew Greta wanted to leave. Said she wanted me to take her out of all this. Was Charlie unaware of her plan? I needed to talk to her, but not with Charlie around. The fog could lift by morning. Then I'd have to figure out how to get back to Taroka for the airplane. Willy. That's it. Willy could take me over there.

"What are you going to do?" he interrupted my planning.

"Me? Hell, I don't know."

Careful, careful, a little voice whispered from the back of my head. *What does he know? How do I play this?*

Charlie was watching me closely. Waiting. I dropped my eyes and remembered the yellow pack I was carrying.

"Oh, hey, Tambourine dropped this on the dock. I was looking for you guys to give it back."

He hesitated but then took Sponge Bob and slung it over one shoulder. Then he stood there looking at me quietly.

"I'm probably going to get fired," I said, glad to have thought of a way to change the subject.

"Fired? What the hell for?"

"Well, it's complicated, but basically my boss didn't know I was coming out here with his plane. When I couldn't get hold of him, he assumed the worst and started telling people I must have stolen it."

He gawked at me in disbelief. "Are you shitting me? That's such bullshit."

"Yeah, so I just called him from the community center and he's pissed. That may be it for me."

Charlie leaned against the railing and gazed across the bay. A few mosquitoes had found us by then and he waved his hand in front of his face.

"That bites the big one, dude." He shifted his weight off the railing and then sat down on the suitcase, settling in.

I played it straight to the bone. I had to. Willing my face to remain impassive, my breath steady, my body relaxed and leaning against the rail.

"Yeah, well, what are gonna do, ya know? Screw him anyhow. Life's a bitch and then you die." I spat off to the side into the grass near our feet.

Sitting down like that his face was below mine again. He pulled his hood back, rubbed one hand through his hair and pulled off his glasses to rub his eyes. He seemed tired. Then he looked sideways at me. I was feeling a shift. Something was changing between us. He was seeing me in a different light.

"What do you think is going to happen now?" he asked, looking up at me.

"I don't know. But they're coming, you know?"

The statement hung out there like the ragged fog above us. Just vague enough to cushion the blow, but direct enough to underline the obvious.

"Yeah, I know," he finally murmured with a resigned sigh.

"Cops just don't disappear like that," I said, glancing at him out of the corner of my eye. He didn't react.

"As soon as they can get in here the place will be swarming with Coast Guard and State troopers. I'm sure they're coming by boat right now even. Then choppers when the fog lifts."

"Yeah," he grunted in agreement and worked the toe of his boot back and forth in the dirt. I could see his gears turning. Figuring the angles. Two moths swirled in the light of the lamp above us flitting in and out of the glow.

"Where you guys staying?" I ventured after a moment trying to keep my voice innocent and not too curious. He wasn't fooled. The tentacles knew the difference.

"Maybe you shouldn't know, man." His hand was resting on one knee, but then twitching with a nervous scratching motion up and down his leg.

Ease back, Johnny, I told myself. "Yeah, you're right. I don't need to know."

He snorted. "Freaking cops. Why couldn't they just mind their own business? They didn't have to come out to the lodge."

Uh oh. What was happening? Did I really want to hear any more?

I stood up to go and shifted my pack to a more comfortable position.

"Well, I better go find a place for the night," I said, but he waved me back down.

"Wait a minute, Johnny. You know, I've been trying to figure you out. Since you flew the troopers in here, I thought you were one of them."

I frowned at him in surprise. "Who, me? A cop? No way. That's funny."

"Yeah, but then you said you felt responsible and all. So I wondered..."

"No, no," I cut him off. "This is their problem. I couldn't care less." Nothing like a little false bravado to talk your way out of the hot seat.

He looked at me. "I could use a man who doesn't care."

Uh oh. I felt a window opening. And I was teetering on the sill. All my pilot instincts came alive. *Keep your back door open.*

I glanced at him. "What do you mean?"

"Well, I'm thinking this fog won't last forever, ya know? Maybe you ought to come work with me."

I just looked at him. That I hadn't expected.

"Yeah, come back to the lodge with me. We'll take a couple of days to get everything closed up and put away and then you can fly us back to Seward."

He must have picked up on my doubts. "I'll pay you, of course. How's five hundred bucks sound?"

My eyes must have gone wide. He laughed. "Cash," he added.

I swallowed and tried to think it through. "What about Greta?"

A look swept over him and I wished with the desperation of a drowning man that I could pull those words back into my mouth, but it was too late.

"What about her?"

I stammered a little, then recovered and pressed on. "I thought you said she was leaving. And with all her bags and stuff, I just thought..."

He swatted a mosquito on his face and made a sigh. "Yeah, you're right."

I breathed again and waited. He shuffled his feet in the dirt and then seemed to come to a decision.

"She wants out. Says she can't stand it another minute, living out here. And now this trouble with the cops."

I waited a bit but when he didn't say anything else I broke the silence. "What's she going to do?"

"Hell, I don't know. She says she's done with Taroka and never wants to see it again. She'll probably wait here until she can arrange some kind of transportation."

The news tingled my ears. I tried not to react. Tried to keep the sparkle out of my eyes.

"What about the kid?" I remembered, picturing the mass of red hair and blank stare.

"Ah, he's mine. No getting around that," he groaned and ground one heel in the grass.

I swallowed hard and looked across the bay. Tried to keep any excitement, any interest at all from reflecting itself in my face or body. It was a struggle.

"So you're just going to let Greta leave like that? I thought ..."

"I know, I know," he broke in. "She means the world to me, I said all that, I know. But what the hell? She's freaking miserable and the more I beg the more she hates me. It's time to just let her go. Ya know what I mean?"

I nodded and tried to keep my thoughts from racing ahead.

"And besides," he continued, "this will call her bluff. Cutting her loose will force her to make up her damn mind."

I gave him a sideway glance. He was no dummy after all. His manipulation just might work. I thought about that and realized the guy had a lot going on behind those coke bottle lens.

"So how about it? Will ya come back to the lodge with us?" He interrupted my reverie.

"I don't know. I..."

"Five hundred bucks, Johnny. Aren't ya gonna need some money now that you're unemployed?"

I snorted and shook my head thinking about Phil. "Yeah, I could use it alright," I agreed. I didn't say anything else, thinking it over.

"It'll only take us a couple days," he was persuasive.

I could see it happening, but I didn't want to tell him that I figured I could talk my way back into Phil's good graces. The old hothead would cool off when he saw his plane was alright, and he'd want me available for charters and to help him put things away for the winter.

I flashed on Greta's blue eyes, her blond hair tickling my cheek. And the smell of her.

I needed Charlie unsuspicious. Had to keep him from knowing where my mind was headed. He was working me for some reason and I needed him to think he was succeeding. I was aware of him watching me and waiting for my answer.

"Well, okay, that might work out," I finally said.

"Alright then," he stood up and stuck out his hand.

I returned his handshake and tried to not feel like a small bug standing next to the jolly green giant. I reminded myself that I was just a guy, just a pilot trying to get by in the wild wilderness world of remote Alaska. Nothing special but a pilot nevertheless. That was something. If I could just get back in an airplane, a thousand feet in the sky, soaring through a rocky mountain pass, looking down at a silent green forest filling a nameless valley. That would be something. I'd feel alive again.

Charlie busied himself with the suitcase and Sponge Bob. He dropped to one knee to tie a bootlace. Then he looked up.

"Where are you going to stay?"

"Huh, I hadn't really thought about it. There's a pilot's shack out at the airstrip. I'll probably head out there."

He nodded and straightened up. I tried to read where his mind was going. Something had shifted and changed.

"We're at the construction camp. You know where that is?"

"Yeah, but I thought you weren't going to tell me."

Charlie stood up then and so did I. "Yeah, I know, but I'm counting on you not caring." He stared at me for a moment then looked away.

He pulled the hood tighter around his head and his face disappeared again in its shadow. Looming over me he laid a hand on my shoulder. I could smell the rank odor of old sweat. The tentacles weren't on my face anymore, but I could still feel them. Wrapping around my ankles.

"We'll be down to the marina in the morning," he said. "Sleep in some. You've had a long day. Be there by ten." He didn't wait for an answer. It wasn't a question. He picked up the suitcase and turned to leave.

A breeze off the bay swept over us and damp wet air chilled my face.

"It's going to rain," I mumbled and pulled my own hood up over my cap.

Charlie repositioned the heavy bag to his other hand and looked back at me. "Yeah, no shit," he said and walked away into the dark.

When he was gone from view I stood there for a while under the solitary light bulb surrounded by the night.

There was just enough light to see tendrils of fog sliding through the grass nearby. The shadow at my feet wobbled uneasily when I finally pushed away from the railing and headed back toward the community building. Stepping out of the cone of light my shadow stretched out in front of me to lead the way.

A fog horn a long way off wailed through the gloom. After twenty steps the light faded and my shadow with it. With only the tiny light from the church ahead to guide me I walked quietly in the night wondering if I was part of the dark or if it was part of me.

CHAPTER
19

The community building was locked. The windows were dark and I heard nothing moving inside. I climbed the stairs to check anyhow, but the door was locked. My stomach rumbled at the faint odor of salmon stew leaking through the door frame. I hoped Willie had something in his plane to chew on. It had been a long time since I'd eaten anything. I pulled off my pack and ran my hand through its compartments but came up empty.

Even an old granola bar would have eased the hunger pangs but they'd been left in the plane with the emergency gear. I pulled my pack back on and went down the stairs realizing that I'd left my sleeping bag behind as well.

It was looking like a miserable night ahead. Cold and hungry I wondered what else could go wrong. When I reached the bottom of the staircase I got my answer. It started to rain.

Rain pellets ping panged on the metal light shade above me. I pulled my jacket collar as tightly as I could around my neck. I zipped it all the way to the top and hauled it up just below my nose. My beard was cold and wet. With my baseball cap pulled down hard around my skull I knew I looked like a headless mannequin. I didn't care.

I pushed out from under the light and headed for the airport. I had a long walk to think about that whole 'I don't care' thing. Was Charlie buying it? I didn't know, but it was the only act I had. All I knew was he was dangerous and strange, a hulking head case with a combat knife and a hair trigger. But I'd rather have him think of me as an ally than an enemy.

It was going to be a mile walk down a dark muddy road. Potholes and ruts filled the low spots and thick brush and trees were waiting for me on both sides. I hoped that was all that was waiting for me. I'd seen black bears out here every time I'd flown in. Either the bears or signs of them. Meaning bear poo.

You're supposed to make noise and alert the bears of your approach. Some tourist hikers buy little bells to hang on their boots. The locals call them grizzly dinner bells. Or carry pepper spray. The bears call that seasoning.

I'd been in bear country plenty of times. Still the thought of an attack never got easier. The image of powerful jaws and jagged teeth shredding my flesh made me jumpy. I had to clench my jaw just to keep moving forward. I tried to remind myself that bears rarely went out looking for trouble. If they knew a human was approaching they would leave. That's what the park rangers told you.

Drop into a fetal position, play dead and protect your neck with your hands. Good advice against grizzlies. But with black bears, you're supposed to fight back. How do you tell the difference in the dark? With a face full of snarling bear breath and teeth, you're going to ask for ID?

It probably doesn't matter since they tend to go for your head anyhow. I wondered if I would hear my skull crack before it all went dark. I pushed ahead and tried to empty my brain. They say animals can smell fear. If that's true I was a foul smelling cloud of putrid green panic.

I was walking fast as I moved into a narrow stretch of the road. Dripping foliage pressed in close from both sides when I heard a sound ahead of me. My heart leapt into my throat, and I could feel my blood pounding with an insane urgency.

I stopped. Not because I wanted to, but because my feet wouldn't move. I was frozen to the spot. The sound moved toward me. I was just about to drop into a fetal position when I saw a flicker of light. Like a flashlight.

I sucked in a breath and tried to think. The wildlife didn't generally carry flashlights, so it probably wasn't a bear. Could it be Charlie? Out here in the dark? I glanced left and right. The ditches on both sides of the road were knee deep in water. Nowhere to run, nowhere to hide.

The light came closer. I couldn't believe what I was seeing. Only fifty yards or so ahead someone was walking alone in the dark carrying a yellow umbrella with white gloved hands. A flashlight swept back and forth across the road, its beam moving from one puddle to the next. Whoever it was moved toward me weaving a path between the potholes and hopping now and then from one rut to another. With the umbrella in front I couldn't see a face, but there was something familiar about the way this thing moved.

I considered jumping off the road into the trees. I wasn't in the mood for company, but my feet couldn't decide what to do. Besides, the brush was saturated with rain and the cold wet night air was already creeping through my clothes. Not to mention the hungry predators I knew were waiting for me over there. Under the umbrella I spotted white boots.

It was Greta. I knew it even before I saw the boots. She must have sensed me too. Before my mouth decided it could speak she looked up and saw me standing there in the middle of the road. She kept coming and shone her flashlight straight into my eyes.

"Is that you, Johnny? Where have you been?" she asked.

Blinded I raised my hands to block the beam, and blinked to get a look at her. She was smiling at me and didn't seem nervous in the least. White gloves and white boots like she was just walking through a mall in Santa Monica. She directed the flashlight downward, but the light was still strong enough to reflect up into her face. Her makeup was perfect. Bright red candy lips. Smooth white skin surrounded those delicate blue eyes. Even her bullet proof mascara held dainty accents in her lashes making them look like star bursts above the blue.

I pulled my jacket down so I could talk. "Who, me? I was just wondering the same thing about you."

"I was looking for you, silly." She pursed her lips and cocked her head in a coquettish grin.

Suddenly self conscious I unzipped the front of my coat halfway and rearranged my hat. I had that sensation again of walking in on a stage not sure what part I was playing. I took a deep breath and it started to come back to me. Joe Cool. Hot shot pilot, rescuer of damsels in distress.

"Well, here we are," I said waving my arms at the dark tunnel of trees all around us. "Ready to fly away?"

She laughed and batted her eyes at me. "You know I am."

It was too easy. Like the meaningless bar chatter you hear at the Yukon. Tossing off glib give and take when under the surface desperate cravings roil.

But I knew I had to play along. Getting too real too fast wasn't going to work. "So you seen any bears?" I glanced out into the darkness.

She twirled the umbrella and giggled like I was flirting with her instead of raising the specter of imminent violent death. The flashlight dangled by a cord from her wrist.

"Bears? Oh, I don't worry about them. You know, if it's my time, then so be it." She paused and looked at me closer with a smile. "Why? You scared of bears, Johnny?" Again with the teasing tone.

"No, of course not. I've been out in the bush too many times to worry about them." I couldn't hold her gaze, and looked away while I wiped raindrops off the front of my coat.

She laughed. "Ooh, I love a man who knows his way around the bush."

I snorted a surprised laugh and tried to look anywhere but into those eyes. A magnetic pull was holding me in place. She had me in her grasp again, and I felt like I was tipping backwards in a wooden chair. My feet didn't seem to know how to get away. I turned my head and coughed.

"Geez, Johnny. Should I get out my rubber gloves?"

Then she giggled, and I couldn't help but smile and look at her. Big mistake. A flashlight reflection danced in the bottom of her eyes. I couldn't shake the sense that I was staring at the cover of a magazine. I was instantly hypnotized and lost in the allure, the promise of warmth and sensual delights beyond the imagination of a man's loneliest dreams.

We didn't speak for what seemed like the longest time. Water drops splattered in the puddles all around us.

"Don't you ever blink?" I finally managed to ask.

She laughed again, showing a line of fine white teeth. "I'm sorry. Do I make you nervous?"

"No, no, n-nothing like that."

"You're a terrible liar, Johnny Wainwright. You know that?"

"Who, me? I never lie," I winked at her doubtful expression.

"Yeah, sure," she chuckled low in her throat.

"Unless I need to, of course."

"You lying now?"

"Of course not," I grinned. "And that's the truth."

She blew air out and shook her head. "Typical man."

"Typical? No way," I feigned a hurt look. "You have no idea, sweetheart." I let my eyes drop and run slowly up and down her frame.

"Oh brother," she chortled and punched at my gut with a white gloved hand.

I caught her by the wrist and pulled her toward me. She didn't resist. I had to duck under the umbrella but then I took a deep breath and inhaled the scent of her. Even her perfume was perfect. Like she'd just stepped off the light stage of a photo shoot. My lips trembled. My eyes closed and I leaned toward her mouth.

The sound of her voice shook me out of my reverie.

"I don't think Brandy likes me." She had turned her head and her lips pushed forward in a pout.

That set me back. A splash of cold water where I least expected it. I looked at her closely to see if she was for real.

"What do you mean?"

"Oh, I don't know. She seemed very cold to me just now."

I remembered that we were standing on a muddy road a half mile from the airport. She'd just come from that direction. I dropped her hand and took a step back.

"You talked to her?"

"Yes, they're back there at the airport. I brought some food out for you guys. Hot soup and sandwiches."

I tried to picture the two of them together. Brandy, petite, slightly aloof and mysterious, brunette, no makeup. Natural good looks and a great set of round lovely eyes, smoky green and intelligent. Brandy carried herself with a professional air. After all, she was a Learjet pilot back in the real world. But around me, she'd worn unassuming black jeans and sweatshirts. I also remembered a bit of her quirky history. She'd once done some nude modeling for a college art class. Funny how people are. You just never know.

And then, there was Greta. Perfectly sculpted face and body, made up like a doll, stylish blond hair cut in pixie perfection, red carpet charisma, clothes out of designer magazines with names I could never remember.

I imagined the two of them walking into a room crowded with men. First Greta. They would all turn and gape and press in for a closer look, jaws dropping along with their IQ's. Her smile would illuminate the whole room and draw attention from every corner. She'd hear every pick up line ever invented, and she'd laugh and ignore every one of them.

Then later, Brandy's entrance would draw stares as well. But the men would step aside to make room for her to pass glancing carefully to check her out. Those who risked eye contact would be met with cool indifference and distance if anything at all. They'd hold their tongues with her, silenced by her aura.

Picturing the two of them together was a struggle. I've never understood what goes on between women.

"Cold, you say?" I asked, unable to avoid her eyes. Flat blue with sparkles like the sharp edges of glacial ice. They say only ten percent of an iceberg shows above the surface. Leaving a million possibilities in the dark depths below.

"Maybe it was just me. I can't be bothered with any of that nonsense," she said with a dismissive smirk. "I don't need the drama."

I smirked inside. Greta flicked people aside like cookie crumbs from a sleeve. I couldn't see her and Brandy having tea together in this lifetime.

She paused, then looked at me closely. "Wait a minute! Is she the one?" she blurted grabbing hold of my sleeve.

I looked away and said nothing.

"Oh my god! She is!" she marveled. "Okay, now it makes sense. No wonder she hates me. You devil, Johnny Wainwright. She's come back. What are you going to do about that now?"

I sputtered and wondered how I'd gotten into this mess. I couldn't tell her what I was thinking. Hell, I didn't know what I was thinking. Besides, I wasn't going to throw cold water on this thing between us. Whatever it was. She was asking the perfect question, but I had no answer.

I tried anyhow. "Oh, that whole thing's over. I don't even know what she's doing here."

"And that's the truth," she mocked me, imitating my voice and digging a finger in my ribs.

I stepped back blinking my eyes, grinning sheepishly and rubbing the spot where she'd jabbed me. I hate it when someone calls bullshit on me. Especially when they're right.

"Well, Johnny, this has been delightful, meeting like this out in the woods, but I really should be moving along. Little Red Riding Hood needs her beauty rest, you know?"

"Wait a minute, wait a minute. Forget Brandy. Do you still want out of here?"

That stopped her. Her eyes narrowed and she stared at me and sighed.

"More than life itself, Johnny."

"Charlie told me he's leaving in the morning. Going back to Taroka with Tamby. He said he's cutting you loose."

I watched her eyes narrow as she listened to me. She dropped her eyes and didn't say anything for a while.

"He said that, did he?" She didn't wait for an answer. "And what are you going to do?"

"If you still want me to help you, I think I know how to do it."

She looked up at me waiting for me to continue.

"If the fog lifts in the morning, Willie can take me over to get the airplane. I'll come back here and pick you up. Then we can fly to Seward."

She pressed one gloved finger to her mouth tapping her teeth with it and thinking.

"And Charlie thinks I'm going with him in the Zodiac," I said. "Back to Taroka to help him close the place down. He doesn't seem to be too worried about the troopers. You know they're still missing?"

She glanced at me then glanced quickly away. "Charlie thinks you're going with him?" she asked.

I nodded. "Yeah, he made me an offer and I let him think I agreed."

She looked at me with her lids half shut and a cunning smile. "You're good, Johnny, you're good. This could work."

It started to rain harder. Big drops splashed on my cap. I shivered and shrugged my shoulders for warmth.

She lifted the umbrella higher above our heads. With her free hand she reached forward, took a handful of my jacket and pulled me toward her.

"Come in out of the rain, Johnny. You'll catch your death."

It caught me off guard. I had to raise my hands to keep from banging into her which put my arms around her waist. She smiled again and looked into my eyes. Looking each other over, we stood there belly to belly under the yellow umbrella in the rain. In the dark. Under an Alaskan fog bank. On a tiny island in Prince William Sound. Just enough light from the flashlight to outline her face and hair.

Raindrops rumbled on the tightly stretched fabric above us. Lilacs and body heat. Her eyes sparkled.

"Hold me, Johnny, please. Just for a minute," she whispered. She leaned closer and my arms moved around her back. She looked at my mouth then and her other white gloved hand moved up and around the back of my neck pulling at me gently. Our lips came together.

Electricity seemed to flash between us. Her mouth was warm and soft. Her lips and tongue quivered under mine, and my brain turned to mush. All I could see was red satin sheets and her naked curves pulling me down on top of her. We were ready. More than ready to get lost in some slow silky moves in the dark.

Then she pulled back a little and broke off the kiss. Her eyes slowly came open and she stared up at me with a dreamy gaze. I wanted more and leaned toward her again. But she pulled back a little more and cleared her throat.

"Not yet, Johnny," she whispered. "Let's save it, okay?"

I could only stare at her, my head spinning. Speechless.

Her hand gradually let go of my jacket, and she smoothed out the wrinkles left by her grasp, her fingers dancing playfully down my chest. The mush began to clear slightly and I glanced around nervously and hoped nobody was watching. Like Willie. Or even worse, Brandy.

But I didn't need to worry. There in the dark and the rain we were as alone as two people can be.

"You want me to walk you to the airstrip?" she murmured running one finger up and down the jacket zipper at my chest. "So the bears don't get ya?" she giggled.

"N-no, that's alright. Thanks anyway. I think they already got me."

She looked up at me and winked. "Go get some food, Johnny. I know a hungry man when I see one." The teasing grin again.

I struggled to think of something to say, but she reached for me again, pulled me in close and kissed my cheek.

"I'll be waiting for you tomorrow, but now I really must be moving along, *darling*," she said with an exaggerated flair, her diva routine back in place. She smiled and stroked my cheek with one tiny white gloved hand, her fingers slightly brushing against my lips as if to silence me.

It worked. I was dumbstruck and mindless. I watched as she turned and walked away. The yellow umbrella glowed in the dark as she picked her way through the puddles, the flashlight beam swinging back and forth across the muddy road at her feet. A city girl fearless in the wilderness. Who woulda thunk it?

I waited until she went around a bend and disappeared in the dark. Then I turned my back and did the same.

CHAPTER
20

I walked the rest of the way to the airstrip ignoring all the sounds around me. To hell with a bunch of carnivores. Greta was right. If it was my time, so be it. It was raining steadily. Not a downpour but more than misting. My head was still spinning from the feel of her in my arms.

Raindrops hung from the bill of my cap and regularly dropped onto my mouth and nose. I jerked my head once in a while to shake them loose and probably looked like a Tourette's case bopping and twitching my way down the road. More rain was sliding down the back of my neck, so I pulled the fleece collar tighter and snugged it back up under my nose.

My boots made a wet slapping sound on the muddy road and I moved as fast as I could without running. I wanted to get out of the rain before hypothermia set in. I eventually settled into a rhythm of breathing and walking and swinging my arms that set my mind free. I kept going back to thoughts of Greta. The feel of her, the smell of her, I ached just thinking about it all.

It felt good to have a plan. All I could picture was the two of us taking off from the Chenega airport, soaring up and over the lush green islands and the waterways of Prince William Sound and then into the snow capped peaks nearby on the way to Seward. Then there was my camper or any number of hotel rooms. And their beds.

I wiped rain off my face and took a deep breath. The muddy road was moving fast beneath me. Wet darkness hung all around. I could see the road right in front of me but not much else. I kept leaning forward and pushing my legs until I noticed an opening up ahead. The edges of the airport came into view through the dark and the fog. One small light on a high antenna pole illuminated the area with a dim yellow glow.

The trees opened above me, and I could make out a blue metal building with a yellow backhoe parked nearby. Next to it was a smaller white box like the container off the back of a truck. Thick conduit connected it to the blue building. A radio shack, I remembered from previous visits. The dirt tarmac was deserted as usual. No line of small planes parked wing tip to wing tip like other airfields. A lonely metal tower on the far side held the rotating airport beacon that turned slowly with alternating green and white lights. Its beams were immediately swallowed by the fog.

There was also a bigger red building made of corrugated metal with tall white doors. It looked like a barn where they probably parked a truck or two. Next to that stood a heap of scrap metal with a tangle of red and white traffic cones piled along the side. Heavy rust stains streaked down the white barn doors and the propane tank next to it.

A light shone from a window in the blue building. As I headed for it I spotted Willie's SuperCub tied down in a far corner near the grass. I knew it had to be killing him to be stuck out here so far from Seward, a long way from the Yukon Bar with its smoky interior, wood stove, cracking pool balls and cold beer. Especially the cold beer. I'd bet Willie hadn't missed a happy hour in twenty years.

I paused for a minute and looked around. Nothing moved except the rain drops dripping into grooves in the dirt under the roof edges of the blue building. Even the birds were hunkered down and quiet.

I looked out to where the runway extended in both directions left and right. I couldn't really see it in the dark, but I could feel its wide expanse across the wet parking lot. That was my escape. It was solid and wide and long. A much better strip than the one I'd left on Taroka. But I needed some visibility. The rain and the fog looked like it would never leave and serious doubts flooded through me drenching the plan.

I peered through the lighted window and saw the small lounge with its two couches and an old coffee table covered with magazines. Two figures were inside but rain on the window made it impossible to see clearly. It didn't matter, I knew who it was.

I took another moment to collect myself. Suddenly I wondered how I looked. The window didn't make much of a mirror, but I wiped at my face remembering Greta's kisses. I pulled off my hat and tried to comb my hair with my fingers as well as I could.

Was I ready for this? I shook my head and put my wet hat back on. What the hell.

I knocked on the metal door and heard a grunt.

"What?" It was Willie.

I pushed my way inside and instantly smelled food. A thick meaty aroma hit my nostrils and made me smile. But the light assaulted my eyes and it took a moment to get used to the warm air and the dry tiled floor.

I shoved the door closed against the wet and lonely night and turned around to see Willie and Brandy sitting on the couches watching me. Willie had his legs stretched out with his stocking feet on the coffee table. A hole in one sock exposed a rough and calloused big toe, the nail ragged and orange. His wet sneakers lay on the floor like gutted salmon on a dock. He looked like he'd been sleeping. His thin white hair was standing straight out over his ears.

Brandy stood up and tossed me a towel. "Dry off, Johnny. You look like a drowned rat."

I pulled off my wet coat and hung it on a hook on the back of the door. Then I took my hat off and rubbed my head with the towel. My eyes were drawn to a feast spread out over a metal desk along the wall. There was a green thermos and blue tin cups. Apples and oranges and an open box of crackers lay next to the cups. There was even a round package of hard cheese in crinkly red plastic wrap. Already partially open, several hunks had been cut out and the waxy red covering lay in crumbled pieces. And beside that were a couple of chocolate bars and bottled water.

My eyes must have been bugging out. "Help yourself," she said.

I didn't need a second invitation. I sat down beside her and reached for the food. The stew was still steaming, and I shoveled it in with rapid gulps. It was spicy with a slightly gamey taste.

"Great stuff. What is this?" I finally managed to ask,

"Bear meat," Willie spoke up from the other couch.

I stopped for a second and looked at him. "Well, ain't that irony for ya?"

"What are you talking about?"

"For the last hour I've been worrying about them eating me. Now I'm eating them. Ha! Take that," I laughed and stabbed a fat chunk with my fork.

Willie watched me eat. "Wish I had a beer. Actually I wish I had several beers. This damn island doesn't have a bar or a liquor store."

I offered him a bottled water from the desk. His lips drew back in distaste.

"About time you got here. You just missed your little friend, Greta. What a piece of work, man."

"What do you mean?"

"Didn't you see her on the road out there? She only left a while ago."

I took another mouthful of stew. "Yeah, I saw her. It was nice of her to bring some food out here."

"Yeah, whatever. A gift with strings, ya ask me. She tried to get me to fly her out of here."

"Tonight?"

"Oh yeah. She'd go anytime I'd take her. I told her no way. At least not until morning. And even then, I've already got a full load," he said nodding toward Brandy.

"She wanted to leave by herself?" I was trying to make sense of the new information.

"I guess," he shrugged. "I only got the one seat. I ain't sure she's firing on all cylinders. What's a broad like her doing out here anyway?"

"That's a really good question." My voice trailed off thinking about the new information. "She asked me the same thing."

"She wants you to take her in the Cessna? With the others?"

"No, just herself. I guess they're splitting up or something." I didn't want to share my plan. I wanted to keep it close to the chest. Besides I knew Willie wouldn't approve and I didn't want to give him a chance to lecture me. It didn't matter. He was already putting two and two together.

"You need to steer clear of that one, I'm telling ya."

"No, it's okay. It would just be a charter flight from here back to Seward. I think she's got money. I mean, look at her."

"Yeah, we noticed how you've been looking at her." Willie shook his head at me.

Brandy sniffed and buried her face in a magazine. I looked at her but she ignored both of us.

"Ah, forget that. She's just a little flirty is all. Doesn't mean anything. I think she just likes to confuse people."

Willie gave me a disgusted look. "Well, let me help you with that conundrum."

"Canumb- what?" I wasn't used to Willie using words with more than two syllables.

"Never mind. A woman like that's a monkey trap."

"Huh?"

He smirked at my confused look. "Something I saw in Vietnam. They tie down a bottle with a narrow neck and put a piece of candy inside. A monkey sneaks in and reaches in for the candy. When he makes a fist he can't get his hand back out of the bottle. Greedy little fucker won't let go even when someone walks in and bags him."

I laughed but then the smile left my face when I realized what he was saying.

He chortled, "Dumb ass monkey can't resist."

I heard Brandy snicker and I felt my face glowing hot. I looked out the window at nothing for a minute. Then I took a bite of an apple and chewed. After swallowing I took a deep breath.

"Well, thanks for that story. You know what I like about you, Willie?"

"What?"

"Nothing. Absolutely nothing at all."

He laughed and threw a cracker at me. "I could tell you another about castrating cattle."

"Hey, I'm not doing anything with her. I'm a charter pilot, remember? That's how I make my money."

Willie sat up then. "I'm telling you, dumbass, you need to stay away from both of them. Two troopers are missing and they were the last ones to see them alive. You don't think they're under suspicion?"

"I know, I know," I said. "I told you that a while ago. I don't care if I fly either one of them anywhere. I just want to get back to Seward."

"They're a strange looking trio," Willie said. "What's up with them?"

"His family's had the lodge for years. They're from New York. He met Greta in California, last year I think, and brought her up here to run the lodge with him."

"Gold digger," Brandy sneered. "She's sure got your number."

Her voice surprised me. She'd been quiet for a while. I looked over to see her shaking her head while she stared at an orange she was trying to peel. I looked back at Willie. He was pretending to struggle with an imaginary bottle stuck on his fist.

"Oh, brother, you guys. Gimme a break, would ya? What would a gold digger want with me?"

I picked up a knife from the table, checked the blade with my thumb and then glared at Brandy with a mock evil leer. She watched me approach with big eyes. I saw her reaction and played it for a minute, but I wasn't mad. Brandy was probably right about her. And I was used to

Willie calling me a dumb ass. If I was going to let that bother me, I would have slit his throat a long time ago.

"Here, gimme that," I said. Taking the fruit from her hand, I slid the blade around the thick rind in three careful rotations. Then pulling off the sections of orange peel I handed her the naked interior.

"You're pretty good with that," she said quietly watching me wipe the knife on my pants. She pulled the orange apart and handed chunks to both Willie and me.

"Honey, I have talents you have no idea about," I grinned at her with all the phony bravado I could muster.

She rolled her eyes, sat back on the couch and picked up another magazine. Willie ate noisily, then got up and headed for the bathroom in the back of the building.

I chewed on a section of orange enjoying the tart juice on my tongue. Glancing at Brandy out of the corner of my eye, I watched her reading. Then she reached up and tucked a lock of brunette hair behind one ear. That simple gesture took me back and made me remember the starlit night we'd spent together about a year ago in Cordova. The images had tortured me ever since.

I watched Brandy until I felt my mouth watering. Then I heard the toilet flush and the moment passed. Willie walked back in and sat down with a heavy thump.

We ate in silence for a few minutes. Everything tasted so good, I was tempted to keep stuffing things in my mouth until it was all gone. Finally I sat back and wiped my sticky hands on the wet towel. It was getting late and after a long day the three of us were tired and ready to sack out. I could hear rain pattering on the roof.

I tried to think about everything that had happened over the last two days, but I couldn't shake the sensation that something was moving our way. That this meal, this whole night, was a prelude or maybe an interlude. Some kind of lude.

What was tomorrow going to bring? When the Coast Guard showed up. When the Alaska State trooper reinforcements showed up. I needed to think how I was going to avoid Charlie and get back to Taroka.

After a while I remembered something and broke the silence. "Hey Willie, did you get hold of the troopers' office?"

"Yeah, I told them about the boat. The troopers still haven't called in, but something else was going on south of Cordova. They got a call about something over that way, and they're sending a couple of units that way to check it out."

"Maybe the guys went that way?" I wondered out loud.

"Ain't my problem," Willie grunted. "Now that I found you, I just want to get away from this freaking island and get back to Seward."

"Can you fly me over to Taroka first?" I asked. "I really don't want another boat ride if I can help it."

Willie winced and scowled. "Jesus Christ, you're a pain in the ass, you know that?"

"Yeah, yeah, I know." I shrugged my shoulders and gave him a helpless look. "Come on, I'll buy you a beer when we get back."

"You'll buy me several beers, goddamn it," he growled.

"Alright, alright, no problem," I grinned and slapped my hands together. The plan was coming together.

"You're not flying anywhere if this fog doesn't lift," Brandy snapped. "And I'm not flying underneath it over the water like that ever again." She gave Willie a look of disapproval.

"Aw, hell, it wasn't any problem," Willie said, his jaw jutting toward her. His eyes were flashing sparks like I'd seen too many times. When I knew it was pointless to argue.

But Brandy wasn't through. "I'm serious. You're not getting me back in that death trap if we don't have blue sky tomorrow."

Willie snorted. "If you can't handle a little fog, you shouldn't be flying in Alaska."

"Well, you can kill yourself if you want, but I'm not going with you," Brandy fired back.

I cringed at her words and gave Willie a sideways glance. They were glaring at each other. It was the first time I'd noticed the family resemblance. I tried to hide the smile pulling at the corners of my mouth.

"Fog can't last forever," I offered, trying to ease the tension. "It'll probably clear up by morning."

No one responded. Brandy sat back on the couch and bit into an apple with a loud crunch. Willie stood up abruptly and jammed on his shoes dancing awkwardly and stumbling with the effort. Cursing and mumbling to himself, he pulled on his coat and hat, stomped out the door and slammed it behind him.

I looked at Brandy but she was drinking water and still pretending to look at a magazine.

"Oh well," I said.

She looked up finally. "Oh well, nothing. How is he still alive flying like that? He scared the hell out of me today."

I thought about that before answering. "Your dad is as comfortable flying a plane as most people are taking a walk. He's like a freaking eagle."

"But does he know his own limits? He's getting older, you know," she persisted.

"Who, Willie? He's not getting older. No way. He'll never get any older. He'll always just be there. You know ... until he's not."

She gave me a skeptical look. She cocked her head to one side, tucked her hair behind her ears again and looked at me, her smoky green eyes taking me in.

"You talking about him or yourself?"

I gulped and swore inside. Damn it, there I go again. I hated being so transparent. I cleared my throat.

"So, how long are you here for?" I asked, trying to keep my voice normal.

She looked away then and let the hair fall back off her ears. "My mom died last month."

I felt like an idiot. Her story came back to me. A mother with Alzheimer's, a recent divorce and trying to have a flying career all at the same time. Willie had left them years before and returned to Alaska where he belonged.

"I'm sorry, Brandy."

"It's okay. Not much of a surprise, you know, and the end to a lot of suffering."

"Is that why you're up here then?"

She nodded. "I needed a little Dad time. He's all the family I've got left now."

I was sympathetic but selfish thoughts pushed their way in instead. "You could have let me know you were coming."

She looked up at me with glistening eyes and I realized my voice had probably been a little harsh. "Look, Johnny, I know I ran out on you last summer. I couldn't help it."

The memory pulled a foul taste to the back of my throat. I sat back. "Yeah, I never did understand that."

"I know," she whispered and went quiet.

I waited and fought the temptation to say something mean. All the weeks and months of missing her and fighting off the emptiness flashed back before my eyes.

"I lied to you," she blurted.

Now it was my turn to go quiet. What? I just stared at her.

"I told you I was divorced. I wasn't."

The room suddenly felt extremely small. I started to stand up.

"Wait a minute, Johnny. Please? Let me finish. Okay?"

I hesitated and tried to calm the raging confusion in my head.

"I was really mixed up then. The marriage was dead and I knew it. When I met you and we went through that whole thing last year, it made me realize what I had to do."

I looked at her quizzically and she took a breath and went on. "I went home and ended it. The divorce was final three months ago."

Just then the door banged open. Willie invaded the little room like a garbage truck hitting a pothole. Ignoring us, he jerked off his coat and cracked it like a whip throwing water all around the room. Then he smacked his hat on a chair three or four times and jammed both soggy garments on a wall hook.

"It's still raining like hell out there," he grumbled.

"No kidding? I had no idea," I said wiping rain drops off my face.

"You don't have a sleeping bag, do you?" he smirked. "There's a pile of canvas in the barn. Go make yourself a bunk."

He jerked the door open and waited for me to move.

"Uh, we were..." My words trailed off. I glanced at Brandy. She caught my look and shrugged. Papa Grizzly was sending me packing. I sighed and reached for my coat and hat.

"Okay, whatever." I pushed past Willie glaring at him with all the heat I could manage. He met my look straight on. Like a block of granite. I knew better than to challenge him.

With my tail between my legs I stepped outside. Reluctant to leave the warm dry room I hesitated, but the door closed firmly behind me pushing me the rest of the way out into the rain.

CHAPTER
21

Damn guy, I swore to myself. Cold rain was peppering my cap and the back of my neck. I kicked at the wet gravel at my feet, looked left and right and then scampered across the soggy driveway, jumped over a wide puddle and found a door around the corner of the red barn.

The door was locked. I knocked and listened just in case but there was no one around. There was an overhang above the door but a wet breeze was swirling and I needed shelter. The idea of sleeping in Willie's plane or in the cab of the backhoe was not appealing. I pulled my collar up against the rain and bent over to examine the lock. There was a metal guard that prevented a credit card from slipping the bolt but the pin tumbler cylinder set in the doorknob was nothing special.

I got this, I smiled to myself.

To hell with Willie, I thought, remembering the deep inside pocket of my fleece. I reached in and pulled out a small black leather case.

It's funny how certain skills come in handy at the strangest times. I wasn't James Bond, but I could get through most locked doors when necessary. I'd taught myself how to do it over the years, and it often came in handy in the repo man world. Unzipping the case I selected two slim metal tools and took another look around out of habit. It was still dark and deserted.

Breaking and entering is a felony. It doesn't matter if you're on a remote island, but I wasn't going to steal anything. I wasn't going to break anything either. It was a point of professional pride for me. I liked to come and go leaving no trace. Lock picks don't leave scratches if you're careful.

Not only that but if I was discovered inside, I had a story ready. In the cold and the rain in remote Alaska survival is always a concern. I'd found the door unlocked and went inside to keep from freezing to death. As long as I didn't take or break anything I couldn't see anyone making a big deal out of it.

The darkness pressed in all around but it didn't matter. I could do this by feel. The rain dripping down my neck distracted me more than the dark anyhow. Darkness was my friend. It covered the kinds of indiscretions that don't stand up well to the light of day. In less than five minutes I felt the pins align and the cylinder slid left. I tried the knob and smiled. I was in.

The interior smelled like rubber tires and mildew but at least it was dry. The light switch didn't work, but I didn't care about that either. When my eyes adjusted to the dark I could make out a tool truck parked on a concrete floor. One wall was lined with picks, shovels and rakes. Stacks of red rubber traffic cones stood against the other wall.

I found enough tarps, cardboard and old cloth bags to make up a halfway decent place to sleep on a pile of boxes. I pulled off my wet coat, shoes and pants and laid them over the cones to dry.

It was chilly in the big rough room, but I sat down on the lumpy bunk I'd made, rolled onto my back and pulled a piece of tarp over me like a quilt. It had been a long day. A long strange day. Fatigue crept over me like a whole cast of crabs on the ocean floor. I was fading fast. The food sat heavy in my full stomach.

I tried to review the plan for the next day as was my habit. However, I had no idea what was going to happen. So much depended on the fog. Hopefully I could get Willie to fly me to Taroka, fire up the company plane and come back for Greta. Remembering that kiss out in the rain under the umbrella sent a wicked chill up the back of my neck.

My last thoughts were of Brandy. I pictured her in a sleeping bag curled up on that couch, very close by. She was listening to the same rain pattering on the roof under the same foggy sky as me. Within reach but so far away.

I shifted my weight to lay on my side and wondered how Brandy would react to a sleeping place like this pile of boxes and rags. Heck, she'd be fine. She was a pilot and could handle almost anything. We'd already shared some rough and tumble conditions together.

Then I thought of Greta being offered the same idea. I smirked to myself with a snort. There was no way. I couldn't see her with her perfect makeup, blond sprayed hairdo and white gloves bunking down in this squalor. But then again she'd surprised me out on the road in the dark. What did I know?

It was quiet in the truck barn. And dark. The only thing I could hear was raindrops gently peppering the metal roof above me, then plunking into small puddles beside the building outside. At least I didn't have to listen to Willie like Brandy did. I caught myself hoping I'd hear a knock on the door when she decided she'd rather listen to my snoring than his. But then the hollow ache of that thought slipped away and fatigue took me.

* * * *

My first sense that I wasn't alone was the feel of warm fingers tracing their way up my leg. I wasn't usually a heavy sleeper, but that took me by surprise. I hadn't heard a thing. An electric chill jolted me, but then I felt myself smile and relax. Oh yeah, I thought, this is going to be good.

The warm fingers were replaced by warm lips and they made their way up my calf and then swirled around my right knee. I groaned lightly and reached down, urging her to keep heading north. She did. With a slow wet nibbling slide up the inside of my thigh. I was painfully ready for her and then I felt the tickle of her hair dancing across my hip bone as she wriggled into position. My eyes fell shut and my legs tensed as I felt the warm wet sensation begin to caress and relieve the ache. I didn't want the party to ever end, but deep inner signals began to tell me that it wouldn't last much longer if I let her continue.

I was reaching for the sides of her head to pull her up and astride me when I felt warm wet lips against mine, a hungry tongue darting with quick stabs against mine. I couldn't believe the double ecstasy I was ...

Wait a minute. I froze. Hair covered my face and I smelled strawberry shampoo. A face was pressed firmly against mine preventing me from looking down or seeing anything. But I could feel a hot mouth working its magic. Down there.

I didn't want to be rude, but who the hell was on the other end? I tried to gently push her away and my hands settled on short cropped hair slightly stiff with hair spray. In a sudden unstoppable red hot rush all my senses roared to the surface. My eyes rolled back in my head and my back arched as I let out a throbbing groan.

When the pulses calmed and I was able to breathe again, I opened my eyes and threw off the cover. The warm and wet sensations lingered but I was alone. The tool truck headlights stared back at me unlit and blank in the darkness, and the warm and wet quickly turned to damp, sticky and cold.

CHAPTER
22

The light outside the windows was gray and dim when the sound of a slamming door woke me. My muscles didn't want to move. Even my eyelids resisted, preferring the dark state of unconsciousness. I'd spent the last several hours trying to pull back the dream. Trying to make it real. But it was out of reach.

My eyes popped open then and I struggled to remember where I was. The tool truck sat beside me on the concrete floor looking cold and tired. With a deep sense of dread I swung my feet to the cold concrete floor and sat up.

I sat there for a minute until I started to shiver. The air in the truck barn was damp and chilled, but it had stopped raining. I started remembering where I was and why. Then I wished I hadn't. The troopers, Daniels and Rankin, were apparently lost. They were people I had known and talked to and flown with. How could they be gone? I shuddered and tried not to think about the huge body of cold water just down the hill from where I sat. I didn't want the pictures that pushed themselves in front of my eyes, but I couldn't help it.

Then there was the image of the whale's enormous dorsal fin coming right at me. And the kid's terrified face and empty eyes. What was his name? Something weird, I struggled to recall. Oh, yeah, Tambourine. Lord have mercy.

The day ahead was a mystery. Any one of several things could happen. It all depended on the fog. I rolled my neck feeling and hearing crackles and crunches. The window showed nothing but gray. I was at an airport, but I didn't have an airplane. The plane was miles away and across a stretch of lethal water. I couldn't think of a worse feeling.

Sure, I was a pilot. I could slip the grip of gravity and fly high over clouds and mountains. Free as an eagle. As long as I had wings and an engine. But without them who was I? Just another earth bound plugger with dirt on my shoes and nowhere to go.

I reached for my clothes. They were cold, damp, heavy and stiff. Pulling them on was torture. The shoes were the worst. Pulling the laces tight made water run from my fingers. I glanced at the make shift bunk I'd made the night before and seriously considered climbing back in.

A bang on the door canceled that idea. "You awake in there?" Willie's voice rasped colder than the concrete floor.

"Yeah, what's it to ya?" I hollered back.

He pushed the door open and came inside. "Come on, will ya? I need your help starting the plane."

"Well, good morning to you too, sunshine," I grumbled at him. Then I looked past him to see fog wrapped trees. "You think you're going somewhere?"

"Yeah, we're going over to get your plane, so we can get the hell out of here."

I pulled on my fleece jacket and zipped it to the top. The damp fabric clenched my neck like a cold rubber glove.

"What's wrong with your plane?"

"Nothing." He said and started walking toward the tarmac. I followed tugging my cap tighter to ward off the chill.

"Then why do you need my help?"

He stopped and glared back at me. "What? You don't want to help?"

I had to pull up short to keep from running into him. "Damn it, Willie. Just tell me what's wrong with it."

He threw up his hands and started walking again. "Aw, the damn battery's acting up. It ain't got enough juice to turn the starter."

"So there IS something wrong with your plane."

He jerked to a stop again with his hands on his hips. "Look, you gonna help me or not?"

"Sure, sure, I'll help you, but seriously, Willie, you're gonna fly in this crap?"

"WE'RE gonna fly," he corrected me. "I can't fly both planes back by myself, you know."

His SuperCub sat quietly at the edge of the parking area with large stones shoved against the tires. The wings and tail surfaces were covered with large drops of cold rain water. She looked about as ready to fly as I'd felt sitting on that pile of canvas.

I looked out to the runway and downhill toward the bay. Taroka Island was out there somewhere but you'd never know it. An orange wind sock fifty yards away hung limply from a pole like last week's forgotten laundry. The hillside beyond it was a gray bank of cloud. I couldn't see the water off the far end of the strip either. All I could see was fog. A murky sky full of sullen gray mist. Brighter areas here and there in the distance glowed with the promise of sunshine somewhere above.

"Uh, Willie. I don't think this is such a good idea."

"What are you talking about?"

"Well, for one, we can't see shit. Secondly, we REALLY can't see shit."

"Aw, hell. It's not as bad as it looks. I walked down the hill to the water and there's at least thirty feet of clear air underneath the fog. The sun's even trying to break through."

"Thirty feet? Your damn wings are thirty six feet wide. And that sun glow's just another thing to blind you. There's not even a quarter mile visibility up here on the runway."

"It's not a problem, believe me. As soon as I take off I'll drop us down to the water. It won't take long to get over to Taroka. Then we get your plane and you can follow me back over here."

I folded my arms and looked back and forth from the cloud choked runway to Willie's face. I felt the hair standing up on the back of my neck. He was staring back at me, but I couldn't meet his eyes.

"So spin that prop for me, will ya? Time's a wasting."

"Look, man. I'll help you start the engine, but I'm not flying in this stuff."

"Why not?" He was pissed. His jaw was working back and forth like an agitated bear and his eyes were boring holes through me.

"Well, it's not only illegal as hell, it's just not safe. There's plenty of other reasons too, but those are the first two I could think of."

"Illegal? Christ almighty, man. If you want to be a bush pilot in Alaska, you're gonna have to fly in bad shit sometimes." He stood in front of the plane glowering at me with his hands on his hips.

"That's just it, Willie. I DO want to be a bush pilot in Alaska. And I want to be a bush pilot in Alaska tomorrow too, and the day after that. And I DON'T need to fly in any bad shit like this. I'm waiting until the fog lifts."

He turned away from me and stared down the runway, thinking. I wondered if he knew I was right, but was so anxious to get moving, he couldn't bring himself to admit it. Willie couldn't tolerate standing still when there was a chance to move.

He hadn't survived this long by being stupid. He had to know I was right. Hell, even the ravens weren't flying. A group of them were sitting on the ground nearby bitching to each other about something.

Willie was a man with strict habits and daily routines, and I knew it had to be killing him to be away from Seward this long. I knew he'd much rather be drinking coffee and reading the paper at the Breeze Inn right then.

That was his morning routine. Looking out over the small boat harbor and gossiping with local boat captains. Then he'd drive slow along the gravel beach and stop to talk to a fisherman or a cab driver parked by the outlet from the lagoon. And he'd watch the gulls flocking around the tall blue crane next to the coal ship dock. Touching base with his network. Some thought him a simple man, but I'd heard him quoting Tennyson one minute, then making a call and talking with his congressman the next.

After a few moments, I spoke to him in a softer tone. "You know, you could agree with me once in a while."

"Why would I want to do that?" he snapped.

"Well, for one thing it would make you less annoying as a person."

He blew out a puff of steamy breath and dismissed the idea with a wave of his hand. "Okay, you don't have to fly. Just ride over in the back seat. Then you can wait over there as long as you want."

It was tempting. I wanted to get moving too. I took another look down the runway and shuddered seeing the sliver of clear air between the fog and the water.

"Sorry, man. No dice. I'm waiting here."

Willie threw his arms in the air. Brandy had walked up by then and had been listening. He noticed her, pointed at her face and waved her toward his plane.

"Get in. We're going back to Seward."

"No way," she said. "I already told you I'm not flying two feet off the water."

I thought he was going to lose it. He looked around wildly with clenched fists like he wanted something to break. "Okay, goddamn it, you people. Then get the hell out of my way," he shouted at us.

He whirled around and kicked the rocks away from the big tundra tires. Brandy and I moved off to the side and watched him. We looked at each other but neither of us dared say any more. We knew Willie well enough to know he was going to do whatever he decided to do regardless of what we thought.

When he was ready he slammed open the door on his plane, climbed inside and settled into the pilot's seat. Ignoring us, he turned his hat around backward and pulled on a set of green headphones. I watched him punch the starter button, but the propeller only jerked briefly and then froze with a groan.

He glared over at me then and slashed with one arm pointing at the prop. As I hustled over to the front of the plane, I could see his face was red and flushed. I gestured with my arms like I was signaling a pilot to slow down. Calm down, please. His eyes went deadly flat, and he waited in silence for me to get into position.

"Mags off?" I called.

"Mags off," he repeated. That was good. At least there was a reasonable chance that I wouldn't lose my arms before I got ready.

I stood with one foot ahead of the other, reached up and turned the propeller until I could grip the blade with both hands at the top of its arc.

"Okay," I called again. "Mags on?"

"Mags on," he shouted. "Hurry up!"

With my knees bent I swung one leg and then pulled down with all my weight and made sure to let my arms and body swing down and out of the way. The engine caught, coughed once and then roared to life. I backed out of the way and rejoined Brandy. Willie gave it gas and began to taxi.

We stood there together watching the small red and white plane roll out to the runway. Willie stopped briefly, ran through a quick engine check and then shoved the throttle full forward. He never looked in our direction. I knew he was pissed.

Loose gravel and rain water flew from the back of the plane in a wet brown misty cloud. The throaty roar of the little four cylinder engine ripped through the soggy quiet of the foggy airport and rattled the windows behind us. The big tires rumbled forward splashing through the puddles. In less than two seconds he lifted off the muddy surface and struggled into the air.

Instead of climbing Willie kept the plane just off the surface. The fog hung right on top of him but he stayed just below it and kept going. As he made his way down the gently sloping airstrip toward the bay we began to lose sight of him through the mist. I shivered knowing he could barely see his way and his only chance was to keep the ground in sight just below his wheels. I heard Brandy suck in a breath.

Willie and his SuperCub lumbered past the lethargic wind sock and at the end of the runway we saw him sink out of sight following the hillside down to the bay and toward Taroka. The sound of his engine grew gradually quieter until we could barely hear him in the distance. I could picture him flying just a few feet above the water, and I tried not to think about his engine quitting.

"So, tell me why he's doing this?" Brandy asked.

"Hell, I don't know. Your Dad doesn't like to sit still."

"Yeah, no kidding," she muttered and shaking her head she turned to look at the red fireweed leaves spreading along the edge of the tarmac.

"Want to walk down there?" I asked.

"Why? To pick up pieces of the wreckage?"

I looked at her to see if she was joking, but she didn't look back. And she wasn't smiling.

"He'll be okay," I tried to reassure her. "The old bastard is too stubborn to kill himself."

"Hey," she elbowed me. "That old bastard is my daddy."

I was about to express my condolences when I heard a sound in the distance that replaced Willie's engine noise. It was a heavy dense tone that echoed through the stillness. It seemed to reverberate off the hillsides above us.

"What the heck is that?" Brandy strained to see out over the bay in the direction of the sound.

I'd heard that sound before. Around the docks in Seward. I wrestled my watch free of my coat sleeve and took a look. It was seven thirty.

"That sounds like the Alaska State ferry," I said, my mouth going dry. "It must be coming in to dock. I hope Willie doesn't run into it."

Brandy looked at me with alarm in her eyes.

"I'm kidding, I'm kidding. You need to lighten up."

My mind started to race. Maybe cops or the troopers were coming in on the ferry since no one was flying. Hell, maybe even Daniels and Rankin were on board. Charlie wouldn't be expecting me until ten, but I had to get down there anyway to meet him. The ferry's fog horn went off again.

"I've got to get down to the dock," I said.

"Wait, I'm going with you."

"What for? Willie should be back soon. He's probably just seeing if he can get over there and back."

"I don't want to sit around here worrying, and I could use the walk. I'll leave him a note, and if I hear the plane coming back, it doesn't take long to walk back here."

I frowned to myself but I knew better than to argue.

* * * *

It took us a half hour to get our stuff together and walk to the harbor. On the way I told Brandy about meeting Charlie and going back to Taroka. The road was muddy and slick but we made good time hiking fast along the drier edges of the ruts.

When we reached the big fuel tanks above the harbor I stopped to look around. Down the hill to the right I saw that the ferry was already settled in place. The M/V Tustamena. She was one of the older ships in the Alaska state fleet, but she was long and sleek and her topside was painted bright white. The lower half was dark blue with a stylish yellow line running from bow to stern. Thick ropes stretched diagonally and wrapped around heavy yellow cleats to hold her to the pier.

The small boat harbor was down the hill to the left. Walking to the top of the metal stairs I looked down the pier and saw Charlie's Zodiac where we'd left it, but there was no one around. I looked down toward the ferry dock and saw a few people and a couple of vehicles milling around.

My watch said it was eight o'clock. While I was thinking about what to do, Brandy tapped me on the arm.

"What's that?" she asked, pointing down the stairway.

The yellow Sponge Bob pack was sitting three stairs down jammed in a corner like it'd been dropped and maybe stepped on.

"That's weird. That's Tambourine's," I said.

"Yeah, I remember it from last night. What's it doing here?"

"I have no idea. I gave it back to Charlie last night and I watched him walk away carrying it."

"So he's around here somewhere?"

"Yeah, I guess so." I looked down the pier but his Zodiac was still tied where he'd left it and no one was around. While I bent down to pick up the pack the ferry's horn sounded three times startling me.

"Sounds like the ferry's getting ready to leave. Let's go down there and see what's up."

At the top of the hill we were almost level with the upper deck. But when we walked down and entered the dock area, the ship loomed over us, four decks higher. And on top of that, barely visible through the fog I could just make out a glass enclosed structure and various railings and masts that extended out of sight into the gloom. They called it the sun deck.

A boarding ramp from the middle of the ship sloped down to the dock. A small group of people stood at the bottom. A couple of them wore dark blue uniforms with matching caps and fluorescent red and yellow vests. A couple others looked like locals getting ready to board. I searched up and down but didn't see any troopers.

To the left of us another opening in the side of the ship held a vehicle ramp. A pickup and an older looking station wagon were in line and moving slowly onboard. Above that was an elaborate black frame of steel beams rising from the aft deck, some kind of a crane and lift system for cargo containers.

Native Mike from the beach the night before was standing at the dock entrance looking official. He wore black uniform pants, a black fleece jacket and a dark cap with the picture of a ferry and AMHS printed on it in gold letters.

I headed for him and called out. "Hey, Mike, anything new?"

He recognized me right away and shook my hand with a limp grip and solemn face. He nodded at Brandy.

"The cops are out there somewhere," he gestured toward the bay.

"The missing guys?"

"No, the searchers."

I stared at him not understanding.

"They got here a while ago in a couple of boats. They're searching now for the troopers."

"What about the Coast Guard?" I asked. "They here too?"

"Nope," he shrugged. "I heard they had a distress call from Middleton."

Middleton Island was a remote radar station more than forty miles away in the Gulf of Alaska. I'd seen it on the map many times before and had thought about flying out to its big airstrip, but the wide stretch of open water intimidated me.

"Have you seen Charlie?"

"Yeah," he mumbled and poked his jaw toward the big blue vessel.

"What? He got on the ferry?"

He gave me a wary look and nodded. "All of them," he added.

"What? Charlie and the woman and the kid?"

Mike nodded again and nervously wiped at his nose.

"Charlie got on the ferry with the little blond woman and a red headed kid?" I knew I was repeating myself and sounding like an idiot but my brain was struggling to understand the sudden change in the plan. I still had the image of Greta in the airplane beside me heading for Seward. But it was evaporating fast.

Mike nodded again shifting back and forth on his feet. He glanced down at his watch. "They leaving."

Questions were jamming together in my head like an ice dam in a spring time river. Where were they going? What happened to Charlie's plan to meet at ten o'clock and go back to the lodge? And what about Greta last night saying she'd wait for me to come for her with the plane?

I was getting a sick feeling. Like I'd been had.

"Are you sure they all got on board?" I asked again.

Mike stared at me, then looked at his watch again. "I said yeah. They're on board.

"Didn't the cops want to talk to Charlie? How could they just let him leave?"

Mike shrugged, and I knew I wasn't going to learn any more from him. Then I remembered Sponge Bob.

"Hey, I've got something that belongs to that kid. Can you get this to him?" I asked and started to pull the pack off my back.

"See her," Mike answered.

I turned the way he pointed and saw a check-in podium near the ramp with a woman in uniform standing behind it. I turned back but Mike was already walking away.

I looked up then to the higher decks and spotted three familiar figures walking in front of the glass wall of the highest level observation deck. Greta was leading the way carrying her makeup case. Charlie was loaded down with a back pack and two Samsonites. He was shuffling along wrestling with the bags with Tambourine walking ahead of him.

I didn't know if he would be able to hear me over the heavy engine noise. I waved my arm at them and was just about to shout when I saw Charlie stumble, dropping one of the Samsonites and almost falling. Even from my distance I could see the contorted scowl on his face. In a sudden move he dropped the other bag and swung forward with one arm. The blow caught Tambourine on the side of the head knocking him to the deck. Charlie leaned forward, yelling something down at the boy that I couldn't hear. Then he hauled Tambourine to his feet and threw him after Greta.

The kid landed on his knees and scrambled to avoid being kicked. When he turned to look back at Charlie, I could see his tortured face. His mouth was open wide in a silent scream.

Greta had already disappeared into a doorway. Charlie moved up on Tambourine fast then, his enormous size dwarfing the boy's tiny figure. He took a furtive glance behind him, but he didn't look down and didn't see me. Then he snatched Tambourine up again and I could see his mouth working, saying something into the boy's ear. It almost looked like he was going to sink his teeth into the kid's neck.

I'd seen that face on Charlie before. Right after he'd plugged the sign full of bullet holes and again when he'd killed the dog. A chill ran through me thinking how easily he could just toss the kid's little body over the rail. Tambourine's mouth continued its soundless shriek.

"Did you see that?" I elbowed Brandy.

"What?"

I looked back up and pointed but Charlie was just disappearing through the doorway.

"There's something going on. That guy is scary."

"I think the ferry's about to leave," she said.

Thinking fast I looked down at the yellow pack in my hand and then turned on my heel. I walked over to the podium. The young lady standing there wore a crisp white shirt with epaulets and an embroidered logo. She was closing up a booklet looking like she was about to leave.

"Can you take this bag?" I asked. "It belongs to that red headed kid that just boarded."

She looked down at the pack and frowned. "I'm sorry, sir, we're just about to cast off."

"I know that, I just need you to take this to the kid."

"I'm sorry, sir, but our policy only allows passengers to take on their own luggage."

I wasn't in the mood for bureaucracy. I turned and looked up at the railings nearby. It would be an easy thing to throw the pack up on deck and walk away. But there was a burly looking guy in a yellow vest up there and the way he was staring at me changed my mind.

My thoughts were racing. Feeling like the rug had just been yanked out from under my feet, I tried to put the pieces together. State police and the Coast Guard were all converging on this small island. The people who knew the most about the missing troopers were about to leave the area on the ferry. Charlie and Greta. Everything they'd told me was completely changed. And Charlie's rage at the kid. Something wasn't right.

I took a deep breath and turned back to the ramp agent. "How much to Seward?" I asked.

"The ferry doesn't go to Seward, sir. We're on our way to Kodiak. Ninety one dollars per person," she answered.

Kodiak? Why the hell would they be going to Kodiak?

"How long does that take?" I asked.

"We get in at ten o'clock tonight."

I turned and looked at Brandy. She was five feet behind me with her arms wrapped around her chest looking at me with a blank expression.

"I'm getting on board," I said. "Tell Willie."

"What? What? Why? What are you talking about?" She was staring at me in disbelief, her face a question mark.

"I need to go after those people."

"That's crazy, Johnny. What for? What can you do?"

"I don't know. Maybe nothing. I just know I've got to go. They both lied to me. They're up to something and somebody has to keep their eye on them."

Her mouth was hanging open. Then she must have realized how she looked and snapped her jaw shut and pressed her lips together.

The agent spoke up. "Sir, we're just about to cast off."

I reached into my wallet and handed over a credit card. The agent opened her book and start taking down the information she needed. Brandy moved up beside me.

"I'm going too," she announced pulling out a credit card.

"No, you don't. No way." I tried to block her with my elbow but she held her ground.

"Willie's going to be back soon. You're just going to disappear on him like this?" Brandy ignored me and waited for the agent to finish my paperwork.

The agent broke in again. "Sir..."

With a sharp glare I stuck my hand up in her face and cut her off.

"Brandy, give me a break. Kodiak's a long trip. Don't you have to get back to work? This is something I need to do alone."

I was still thinking about Greta. Maybe Charlie had changed the plan and was forcing her to go along. I had it in my head that she still might need my help getting away from Charlie. And then things between us might develop. Brandy was the last thing I needed around me, butting in and complicating everything.

I looked up to see the agent staring at us strangely and handing me my receipt. "Thank you, it'll just be me..."

"Sign me up, too," Brandy interrupted, stepping in front of me. She slapped her credit card on the podium with a smile, then turned and swung her pack into my gut.

"Hold this for me, won't you, sweetie?" she cooed. "Don't mind him," she winked at the agent. "He's just a nervous traveler."

I grunted and stepped back, stunned into silence.

The agent grinned back at her with a knowing look. "No problem," she said, taking Brandy's card. "We get that all the time. At least he's got Sponge Bob for comfort. He'll be fine once we get under way."

When she had her receipt Brandy took her pack back from me and taking my arm nudged me toward the boarding ramp. I resisted and felt my face glowing bright red.

"Damn it, Brandy. You're a pain, you know that? A real freaking pain," I muttered into her ear with barely controlled fury. I busied myself stuffing Tamborine's yellow pack inside my other pack.

"Folks, you need to board right now," the agent waved us up the ramp like she was shooing children out of her kitchen.

"And I'm not your sweetie," I snarled and wrenched my arm away. Brandy threw her head back with a victorious laugh as I stumbled against the loading ramp. In my haste I almost bumped into another uniformed crew member walking down toward us.

"Johnny?" A familiar voice stopped me short and I looked up.

It took a moment for my brain to register. "Rainey?"

"Johnny? What the heck are you doing here?"

CHAPTER
23

Rainey Peterson, the best friend a guy like me could ever have, was standing on the ramp gaping at me in disbelief. She was wearing dark blue slacks and a white blouse and a dark fleece zippered jacket just like Native Mike. But her baseball cap said 'SECURITY' in bold gold letters. With bright blond hair pulled back into a ponytail that stuck out the back of the cap in a bouncy curl of femininity, she looked great.

"Rainey? That can't be you." I stared at her in confusion.

She grinned back at me in her Rainey way, lighting up the gloomy sky for miles around. At least that's the way she affected me. We took each other by the hands and stood there for a moment wordlessly struggling to adjust to the shock. I almost forgot that Brandy was standing right behind me.

When I remembered I turned and awkwardly dropped Rainey's hands. "Brandy, you remember Rainey, don't you?" She hesitated and I realized with a groan under my breath that she didn't. Rainey jumped in to the rescue.

"Hey, Brandy," she piped up. "You probably weren't here long enough to remember me through all that mess last year. I'm Rainey. I used to work at the Breeze Inn in Seward."

Brandy reached forward to shake her hand. "I'm sorry, Rainey. How are you? Johnny seems a little surprised to see you."

They smiled at each other. Something passed between them. A look, a code, Hell, I don't know what it was, but something happened. Like one of those secret women things when they go to the bathroom together.

They glanced at me at the same time and then made eye contact with each other again and laughed. I stepped back and felt the blood rising in my face until my ears must have been glowing bright red.

"What? What? Is there something hanging out of my nose?"

The ticket agent walked past us up to the ferry's main deck. A handheld radio strapped to Rainey's belt started to squawk. She answered it and listened to a static filled voice asking her something about securing the ramp. After speaking a few words into the radio, she motioned for us to move up the gangway.

"Come on, we're about to cast off," she said herding us forward. "What are you doing here anyhow? Aren't you flying any more?"

"Yeah, but I got fogged in. Can't fly in this junk," I said waving my hand at the sky. "Listen, there's these people..."

She held up her hand frowning at her squealing radio. "Gotta go," she said.

"Rainey, when you get a chance I need to talk to you," I said, but she was walking away and talking into the handset again. I don't think she heard me.

I glared at Brandy. "What the hell are you doing? Why are you here?"

"Oh, lighten up, Johnny Wainwright. Somebody needed to keep their eye on you," she sparkled back at me.

I turned on my heel and headed for the deck where I could see crew members scrambling to remove the lines holding the ferry to the dock. As guys in uniforms worked to haul the ramp aboard and stow it, I looked around to orient myself on the huge craft.

I'd only been on ships like this a few times in my life. A couple times as a boy and then much later in the Seattle area around Puget Sound. I was always impressed with the solid feel of the metal decks and the rumbling vibrations that hummed through the enormous structure. The horn startled me again bellowing out three enormous blasts. Crew members scurried in all directions making final preparations. The Rusty Tusty was ready to sail.

Brandy was following me but then she stepped into a passageway and headed for a restroom. I spotted Rainey moving rapidly around the stern area checking on the vehicle deck one level below us. When she headed toward the bow I caught up and walked along beside her. The sight of her was such a welcome relief. I couldn't stay mad.

"So what the heck, girlfriend? Look at you. I remember you told me you were getting some kind of a boat gig, but I thought you were going to be a waitress or a bartender or something."

"Not any more. You gotta watch those assumptions," she winked at me. "I've been wanting something different for a while. So I'm Security now."

"I see that. I'm impressed," I said, eyeing the way she filled out her uniform. Rainey was a little taller than me which isn't saying much, and well built which is saying plenty. They say men and women can't be friends. Probably true. Straight men and women anyhow. That tension thing always get in the way.

There was no ignoring the way she looked and the way her hair flipped back and forth when she let loose a belly laugh. I always seemed to be able to make her laugh. I didn't care that she was laughing at me most of the time. Watching her wide mouth twist into a big open smile with her eyes sparkling, I'd be her clown anytime.

Rainey and I were great friends. Nothing more. She was married. Lucky bastard. So, I'm a dog, okay, I'll admit it. But not toward Rainey. Even a hound dog can have some principles. But I'd be lying if I didn't admit an idle thought once in a while.

"Hey, quit checking out my ass," she elbowed me out of my thought track.

"Who, me? Not me. I was just admiring the high tech equipment you're wearing on your belt there."

"Admiring my equipment, eh? And now you're back together with the little heart breaker, Johnny? Johnny, Johnny," she shook her head at me with a mocking sad smile. "I thought we talked about this."

"No, no, it's not like that at all. I had no idea she was going to show up out here. That damn Willie comes flying out here and he brought her with him."

"Yeah, okay. I can see there's nothing going on at all. Right." Her playful words danced like ice crystals on my warm flesh.

"Look, Johnny, I'm really busy right now, but in a little while I'll be able to visit more."

"Wait, Rainey. I've got to tell you something important. There are these people that got on in Chenega. I think they're trouble."

She looked at me puzzled. "What do you mean?"

"I don't know exactly, but I think you should know about them just in case ..."

Her radio belched again and she raised a finger while she listened.

"I've got to run. I'll come find you and we can talk some more later, okay?"

"Sure, no problem, I'll be around. I need to tell you what's been going on."

"Yeah, okay. It's very strange seeing you without your airplane." She turned to continue with her duties, but then stopped before disappearing through a hatch.

"Oh, and Johnny? Keep it in your pants this time, please?" She grinned and nodded toward Brandy who was walking toward us down the side railing.

I dropped my jaw in mock shock. "Yeah, of course. Good advice. Thanks, Rainey," I said as Brandy came within hearing range. I saw the two of them exchange winks. Then Rainey rolled her eyes at me and hustled off shaking her head again.

I knew she was remembering the long and heated discussions we'd had over the winter. Too many days of bad weather, warm beer and me whining about my bad luck with women. Even I'd grown sick of it. Now that's a friend -- someone who'll listen to all your bullshit and not suddenly need to go do their laundry.

The vibration intensified then and the ferry began to slowly move away from the dock. The heavy smell of diesel fumes swept around us as the big engines ramped up below in the belly of the beast.

The ferry felt solid. Loaded down with more than a hundred passengers and dozens of vehicles it didn't feel like a ship setting sail. It felt more like a city block had just separated from the rest of town and was drifting out to sea. No sense of floating or rolling in the waves. But that was in a calm bay. I wondered if it would change once we left the Sound.

Brandy and I stood next to each other at the railing and watched the village slide past. The few quiet houses on the hillside looked just as isolated and deserted as they had the night before. We passed the battered green skiff from Taroka lodge lying at the water's edge where it had been dragged. The tide was in and whatever secrets the old boat held were as impenetrable as the wet black mud all around it.

Wet air blew in our faces as the ship gained speed. The rumbling vibration blocked out all other sound. Waves of foamy salt water rushed past the side of the ship below us leaving a wide unsettled wake behind.

I watched the surface of the bay sliding by and thought with a shiver about the missing troopers. They could be anywhere. It was creepy thinking about it. My eyes searched the rocky coastline expecting but at the same time dreading the discovery of human remains.

The water held a gray cast that blended into the foggy airspace in the distance. My stomach cramped and I suddenly felt hungry, I turned to Brandy who was staring at the water lost in her thoughts too.

"How about some coffee?"

"Good idea," she agreed. "But what about those people?"

"I know. They're not going anywhere and I'd just as soon keep my distance for now. Besides it'll take us all day to reach Kodiak."

She nodded and we headed inside.

As we pushed our way into the interior of the ferry I cringed at the sense of so much humanity so close. I didn't like crowds. Never had. And the noise. So many different voices, some happy, some agitated, some bitching at spouses or children, others confused and asking each other questions. Like tourists everywhere. With time on their hands and money to spend.

I hunkered down into the collar of my jacket and pushed forward to the dining area. The smell of warm food pulled me ahead and helped me ignore the press of the other passengers. I looked behind me and noticed Brandy following. She looked comfortable and right at home. I shrugged my shoulders and told myself to relax.

You have to share the planet with other folks, Johnny. Get used to it.

Yeah, whatever.

I pulled off my pack and left it at a table with my coat while we loaded two trays with coffee, eggs, toast and hash browns. My mood picked up. It felt good to sit down. I shoveled food in hungrily and washed it down with several swallows of weak coffee. I looked around for any sign of Greta or Charlie but didn't see them.

People were spread out throughout the large room and the air was filled with laughter, clinking utensils and the clatter of plates. Underneath it all the metal floor vibrated steadily sending a constant ripple through the soles of my shoes. But no Charlie and no Greta. And no kid named Tambourine.

Brandy and I didn't talk much. With my hunger pangs settled I felt restless again. I wanted to ask Greta why she changed the plan. I was playing with my spoon when a bright swath of sun swept across the table. Brandy and I looked up at each other in surprise. A murmur ran through the room as others noticed it too.

Without a word we grabbed our stuff and headed outside. We had to hurry to beat the herd crushing its way out of the cafeteria.

The breeze was cool and brisk, and my eyes watered at the shock of fresh air after leaving the warm interior. We made our way to the railing and followed it forward while I fumbled through my jacket pockets and finally found my sunglasses. They were covered with dust and lint from disuse. Brandy pushed her way around me and halfway up the side of the ship she stopped and pointed into the distance.

The ferry had moved out from underneath the blanket of fog. Blue cloudless skies stretched above us. A group of seagulls flapped and squawked in the slipstream behind the ferry. Green mountains beckoned in the distance. I recognized them as the peaks of the Sergeant Icefield where I'd flown many times.

Turning around, I looked at the fog bank we were leaving astern. It lay heavily on the sea behind us like a dirty wet pile of rotting goose feathers. It was a ragged mass and unmoving, but sunbeams glowed at its edges and warmed the side of my face at the same time.

"That crap could hang there like that for days," I muttered to Brandy. She was leaning against the rail with her smiling face pointed at the sun, eyes closed behind her sunglasses.

The sunshine was hot and dazzling. I closed my eyes against the painful brilliance and let the beams bake my face. What would I give to be away from here? Alaska's beautiful but after too many rainy days, too much fog and cold damp clouds I craved to get away. To a distant beach with warm sand under my feet and the sun heating my skin, glowing bright red against my closed eyelids. With a friendly warm body laying next to mine on a beach towel and cold bottles of beer dripping beside us. Free from the pressures of daily life. Free from the dread grinding in my gut. I tried to ignore it, but it kept jabbing me from somewhere deep inside.

"I need to start looking around," I said. "Why don't you stay down here."

Turning to walk toward the stern Brandy grabbed my arm and pointed across the water. About a hundred yards away a massive chunk of ice floated in the open sea.

Even from our distance I could see the vivid blue colors of super compressed ice. It was an iceberg that must have recently dropped off the face of Chenega Glacier ten miles north. Its top edges were curling and melting in the sun forming strange pillar shapes with a cave like formation in between.

"So that's the famous ten percent?" Brandy asked.

"Huh?"

"The ten percent they say you see above the surface." She looked into the water closer to us with a frown.

"Oh, yeah, I guess so," I answered. If we'd been above it in an airplane we could have seen the murky edges of the rest of it under water and spreading in all directions.

"I'm going to look around with you," she said. "Four eyes are better than two."

I grimaced but knew better than to argue. We turned together to make our way to the bridge deck moving past other passengers in groups of two or three. At the top of the final stairway we found the highest deck with a tall blue smokestack planted in its middle. Just past that were the glass paneled walls of the solarium. The deck continued forward to an area with several antenna masts. I could see the rotating white head of a radar unit.

Above us on the side of the ferry a large orange tarp was stretched across the shape of a lifeboat. I took a careful look at it and noticed the propeller of an outboard motor sticking out under the end of the tarp. My pilot brain kicked in. I nudged Brandy. When she turned to look at me I pointed to the lifeboat.

"There's our back door."

Seeing her puzzled look, I translated. "Our escape."

"That's it?" she sounded concerned. "How many people will it hold?"

"Not sure, maybe a couple dozen. I think there's one on the other side too."

"And what's the ferry hold?"

I caught her point. "A couple hundred or so. I know, I know, not enough seats, but there are life rafts too. See those white tube things over there?"

I pointed to the next deck down. Two pods that looked like fuel tanks were perched on a small ramp hanging on the side of the railing.

"Life rafts in there are all set to launch if necessary."

"How many can they hold?"

"I'm guessing ten or twelve each." I watched her doing the math. "Hey, don't worry about it. There's life jackets for everyone."

"Great. What have I gotten myself into?"

"Hey, you get no sympathy from me, brainchild. I still don't know why you're here."

We moved into the solarium. I set my pack down on the deck and laid down beside it. I pulled off my shoes and rubbed my feet. Brandy did the same, but we didn't have a chance to continue the discussion. Rainey came up behind us.

"Hey, Johnny." She knelt down beside us. "Can you guys come with me?" There was an uncomfortable urgency in her pretty face I'd never seen before.

"Sure," I said sitting up. "What's up?"

She glanced around the room and her voice dropped. "I can't talk about it here. Follow me."

We stood up and scrambled to get back into our shoes and gathered our jackets and packs. Rainey waited, but I could tell she was working hard to be patient. She was bouncing the hand held radio against her leg.

Trying to stay calm, my mind raced through all the possibilities. Something was happening.

CHAPTER

24

We followed Rainey down the stairs to the next deck and along a long passageway toward the front of the ship. Pushing her way through a heavy door marked Crew Only we entered an office area filled with desks, filing cabinets and lockers. For some reason I flashed back on old memories of being escorted to the principal's office. And not for a Good Citizen Award either.

When the door closed behind us, Rainey turned and stood with her arms crossed over her chest. Her face was dead serious, but when she reached up to fix a strand of hair I noticed her hand shaking.

"Willie called in. Those troopers you flew out to Taroka? He found them."

My eyes bugged. "And?" But I knew the answer before she said anything else. She was looking at me closely.

"Dead. Both of them."

The news hit me like a slug in the chest. The dread I'd been trying to ignore had come true. "Willie spotted them in the water?"

"No, they were in the lodge. Shot to death."

"In the lodge? What the hell? Where in the lodge?"

Rainey shook her head. That was all she knew. I stared at the carpet trying to make sense of it.

I'd just been in that lodge. Spent several hours there as a matter of fact. That's why I'd been there. Looking for the troopers. I pictured Daniel's face and his strange wicked grin during the fire fight. And Daniels, with his blond young guy crew cut. Both dead. Had to have been behind those locked doors.

I studied Rainey's face. There was something in the way she was looking at me. Something in her eyes was completely foreign. Like she didn't know me. Like she didn't want to know me.

"Rainey, what's going on?"

"Willie said the cops are talking about you."

"Me? What about me?"

"Johnny, just look at me and tell me you're not involved in anything weird."

My mouth fell open. "Rainey, are you kidding me? I don't believe what I'm hearing. I can't believe you even have to ask me that."

She was studying me closely. Way too professionally for my tastes. I could feel my blood pressure screaming in my ears. Everything around me had gone dark and all I could see through a murky tunnel was Rainey's doubtful look. I thought Rainey was one of my closest friends. And now she was interrogating me?

Brandy chimed in. "You can't think Johnny had anything to do with this." She held onto my arm as if I needed the support. She was right. I did. Rainey just stood there with her arms folded looking at me.

"Rainey, for God's sake. I don't have any idea what happened to those guys. I flew them out there. They walked away heading for the lodge. They were supposed to be back in a couple of hours, but only one came back. Then the guy they were after started shooting at us. I got away but the troopers never returned to the plane. I went to the lodge looking for them but they'd left. You gotta believe me."

I saw Rainey take a deep breath. Her face seemed to relent. She uncrossed her arms and reached for my hands. She closed her eyes briefly and exhaled.

"Thank God, Johnny. Of course, I believe you, but I had to ask. The cops are freaking."

I breathed a sigh of relief, but it was short lived. I had to know more. This was getting out of hand.

"Tell me everything Willie said."

"Okay, okay. Somehow he figured out how to call me here on the ship. He knew I was working here now, and he asked if you two were on board."

"Where is he now?"

"He was at the lodge and he was pretty shook up. He called the cops first about what he'd found. They told him to wait there and they wanted to know why you weren't there."

"Me? What about the people running the lodge? You know they're on the ferry with us? I've been trying to tell you that."

"Wait, Johnny, wait." Rainey put her hands up to slow me down. "Then Willie said that the cops kept asking about you, the pilot that took them out there. He asked why and they said that in one of the last reports the troopers made they'd said something about not liking their pilot's attitude."

I just stared at Rainey speechless.

"And when Willie told them that you'd left Taroka and then left Chenega on the ferry, they said 'That's a problem.'"

"Oh hell, I didn't do anything. I just flew those guys out there. Nothing else."

I had to sit down. I found a chair and collapsed into it. Rainey rested a hand on my shoulder.

"Why are you on the ferry?"

"Look, the fog has had me grounded for days now. The phones were out at the lodge so I came to Chenega with a boat to call in. Those people running the lodge got on the ferry so I followed them."

"You followed them?" Rainey's voice sounded confused. I looked up to see both her and Brandy staring at me trying to understand.

"I know, I know, it's these lodge people, I'm telling you. I didn't want them to just disappear before the police talked to them."

Brandy elbowed Rainey. "One of them's a little hottie."

Rainey's eyes dropped shut. "Oh no. Johnny, you didn't..."

I jumped to my feet. "No! That's horse shit. That's got nothing to do with anything!"

Rainey put her hands up in front of me again. "Stop, Johnny. Settle down. Willie called me to warn you, but I've got to let the captain know what's happening. I can vouch for you, but I'm just a rookie out here."

"Vouch for me? I can't believe this. What about Greta and Charlie? They're the ones that need to be talked to."

Rainey headed for the door. "Just wait here. I'll see what the captain wants to do."

Brandy and I sat there looking around the small office. My mind was racing. I couldn't think. I was hot.

"What the hell is wrong with you?" I growled at her. "Why would you say something like that?"

Brandy threw up her hands. "What? About the little hottie? I saw how you looked at her. And how you just had to get on this damn boat."

"Brandy, give me a break. People were murdered. Somebody killed two cops! And you want to play little jealousy games?"

She glared at me, her eyes smoldering. Then she turned on her heel and left the room slamming the heavy metal door behind her.

I didn't care. I hadn't wanted her on board in the first place. I needed to figure this thing out by myself, and I didn't need any stupid distractions. My mind was whirling trying to come to grips with all the odd events that had happened in the last couple days.

I went back over every detail and all the events on Taroka Island, step by step, everything that had happened. If the bodies had been found in the lodge, Charlie and Greta must have known all about it. They'd lied to me about everything.

The door opened then and Brandy stepped back in. I started to tell her to stay out, but she beat me to it.

"I'm sorry, I'm sorry," she said. "You're right. This is some serious shit. I just got distracted."

I just looked at her. Then I flashed on Greta's blue eyes and realized the effect she had on people. Not just me. Everybody.

"Let's go over it again, Johnny. Tell me everything from the beginning."

I took a deep breath. The earlier sarcasm and challenge in her voice were gone. I knew I needed help, and Brandy was smart.

"Okay." I started from the beginning. From the phone call at The Yukon Bar.

She listened carefully looking for any angle that might help. After a minute she broke in.

"So why would one of the troopers report something about your attitude? What did you do?"

"Nothing. I don't know. One of them was an older guy. Kind of crotchety. Daniels. He seemed to take an instant dislike to me. So I returned the favor."

"How do you mean?"

"Not much really. Nothing that should cast any suspicion on me. He was worried about the weather and sort of challenged me. Like whether I knew what I was doing or not."

Brandy nodded. She'd dealt with nervous passengers before too.

"I think I said something about we didn't have to fly if they didn't want to. He probably didn't like being told that. But, really it was no big deal."

She didn't say anything, thinking it over.

"For Christ's sake, Brandy, these guys were murdered. No wonder everybody's freaking out."

"Okay, so let's assume you're innocent," Brandy started to ponder out loud.

I cut her off and snapped, "Assume I'm innocent? What?"

"Relax, relax," she said. "I'm kidding. Lighten up, would ya?"

"Very funny. You got a rotten sense of timing. Have I ever told you that?"

She reached over and took my arm. "I don't remember any complaints," she poked at me with a grin.

I sat back and gave up a little smile. "Okay, okay, you're right. Having a heart attack won't help anything."

"That's right." She put her hand on my back and rubbed gently. "So, if you didn't do anything, who did?"

We looked at each other. "Well, Charlie told me about some fishing guide I never saw and Greta really wouldn't say anything. They're the only possibilities, Charlie and Greta. And the kid, but …"

"We can probably eliminate him, don't you think?"

Before I could answer, the office door swung open with a bang. A big guy in the same dark uniform as Rainey looked at us in surprise. He was about twice Rainey's size with a shaved Charlie Brown head and a pink clean shaven face.

"What are you doing in here?" he snapped.

I stood up but then I wished I hadn't. He puffed up his chest and glared down at me like an exterminator eyeing a cockroach.

"We're authorized," I said.

"How? Are you crew?" He didn't wait for an answer. "Didn't you see the sign? Or can't you read?" His fat face twisted into a sneer.

That pissed me off. "Hey, back off, will ya? Rainey brought us in here and told us to stay put."

"Rainey? Who's that?"

Oh, shit. "Rainey. She's part of your security crew. Don't you even know who you're working with?"

That made him frown and pause. I jumped at the chance.

"She's new. Blond ponytail. She put us in here. I'm serious. She told us to wait here."

"Well, she's not here now, so you can't be in here." His tone was a little more civil, but not much.

We stood up, but his bulk made it impossible to get to the door. He awkwardly backed out into the corridor, and we left.

I led the way down the passageway and turned around to give Brandy an exasperated look, but the Michelin Man was still standing in the doorway staring at us.

"Let's see if we can find Charlie and Greta."

We made our way back to the Solarium. I had to get to the bottom of the mess before more fingers started pointing in my direction. I tried to think like a cop.

I could understand why they were looking at me. If you come upon a crime scene and find three or four people there, they all have to be considered suspects. I'd seen enough TV cop shows to know that much.

I just had to make sure I didn't act suspicious. So, maybe getting on the ferry hadn't been such a great idea after all. Leaving the scene of a murder.

But I didn't know there was a murder at the time. The cops wouldn't understand that, of course. I should talk to them. That was a good thought. Try to interrupt their suspicions as soon as possible. But how? Out on the water miles from civilization didn't make it easy.

Brandy tugged at my sleeve and broke into my thoughts. "Johnny, why don't we just walk around the entire ship and look in every possible spot from top to bottom?"

"Yeah, good idea. I think there's a sitting area two decks down toward the front."

"Tell me again what this Charlie looks like. I didn't get much of a look at him."

"Too focused on Greta probably. Checking out the competition?" I smirked at her.

She punched at me but I ducked away. She laughed then and agreed. "You're right, she won't be any trouble to pick out of a crowd."

"He's a big man, maybe six five or so and well over two hundred pounds. Scraggly blond beard, but the main thing is his glasses. Coke bottle types and crazy eyeballs. When I last saw him he was wearing a black hooded sweatshirt and blue jeans."

"Okay, a wild eyed Goliath. Got it. Like a regular at the Yukon?"

I chuckled and nodded in agreement. We took the stairs down to the lower deck, and walked its length on both sides passing more doors marked Crew Only. The doors leading to the bridge had windows in them and I peeked in as we walked by. Crew members inside were seated in front of instruments panels and radar screens. We didn't meet anyone in the halls on that deck, so we continued the search one level down.

The observation lounge was half filled with people. Most were sitting in the front row of easy chairs attached to the deck in rows and facing out through tall windows. Perfect for watching the scenery. We split up and walked the perimeter of the room eyeballing every person in sight. We met up again in the center of the lounge.

I looked at Brandy's face for any sign of success. She shook her head and looked to the exits.

"I think the private cabins are on this deck. Two rows of them. Here, let's check out the map." She stopped in front of a small framed diagram on the wall that showed the emergency evacuation plan. Arrows from cabins and the lounge led to the rear of the ship where the life boats were located.

"Yup, two rows of cabins alright." I looked down the narrow passageway at a long line of closed doors.

Taking our time we walked to the rear of the ferry. I listened as best as I could to any sounds that might come through the doors on our way by, but didn't pick up anything. At the end of the row of cabins the deck opened onto an open sitting area and I stopped for a moment to look around. Brandy circled the room while I moved to the other side of the ship and surveyed the people there. Seeing no one likely I waited for Brandy to rejoin me.

Listening to people's voices it seemed that the level of conversation had settled down. I reminded myself that most of the passengers had probably been on board for more than a couple of days and were settled into the routine of riding the ferry and its life aboard.

Not everybody was happy though. Seated in a corner near me, an older woman was hugging what looked like her teenage granddaughter. Grandma looked stoic, but the young girl was shaking and crying. Two suitcases were at their feet. One of them was half open, held by only one clasp. Clothes were bulging out of the opening.

I looked at the older lady and leaned over trying to make eye contact, but she wouldn't look at me. Either would the young girl. I wrote it off as a teenage mood swing. Brandy walked up and crooked her finger at me.

I stepped away from my place against the wall and followed her. "Over there," she nodded with a slight movement of her chin. "Is that him?"

A tall guy in a gray and white plaid jacket was pouring himself coffee from the beverage bar across from us. Not Charlie.

"Nope, but kind of looks him," I said. "Let's check this corridor."

We walked down the row of cabin doors in slow motion again, but no one came out and I didn't hear anything either. When we reached the observation lounge again, we stopped.

"What's below us?" Brandy asked.

"I think it's the vehicle deck. Wait, there's Rainey."

We spotted her across the room and caught her eye. She came toward us carrying a clipboard.

"Hey, you two. I'm glad I found you."

"We've been looking for those people, but no luck so far. Is the vehicle deck below us?"

"Yes, but it's locked up. No access to the public unless we're in port. What was that name of the guy from the lodge?"

"Westridge. Charlie Westridge."

She flipped through the pages on her clipboard with a concerned expression. "No one on here by that name."

"You're kidding. I saw them from the shore. Uh, maybe they're under her last name. And I have no idea what that is. What about their first names? Can't be that many Charlies and Gretas traveling together."

"Nope, I already looked."

"Weird. Can I see that?" I felt my blood pounding at my ears again. This was not good. Not good at all.

Rainey handed me the clipboard as her radio started squawking. She stepped off to the side and Brandy and I started looking at the list of names. Before we had a chance to make any sense of the pages, Rainey interrupted us.

"We need to go to the bridge. The captain needs to talk to you."

"The captain? What now?"

"I don't know, Johnny. I just work here. That's what I was told. To bring you to the bridge."

She headed for a stairway up to the level above us. I followed but looked at Brandy with a question mark on my face. Brandy looked back at me and shrugged her shoulders with a tight lipped blank face.

Again that sense of heading for the principal's office. Before I stepped through the doorway I stopped to catch the view in front of the ferry. We were making steady progress. The green mountains above Puget and Johnstone Bays were in view now to the north. Along with bright sunshine, cloudless blue skies and white snow fields on the peaks.

I scanned the horizon ahead and then to the south. Miles away but easily visible well out in the Gulf I could see another fog bank. Low and gray just like the one we'd left behind, I was glad it was far away.

When we reached the bridge Rainey had us wait in the hallway outside. She pushed through the door while I watched through its round window, but then she moved out of sight to the right. Another crew member was seated in front of slanted windows looking out at the ocean. Next to him were the engine controls and a large screen like a video game.

When Rainey came back into view, someone else was right behind her. It was the Michelin Man again. He spotted me through the window and his eyes narrowed in recognition. I pretended to be casually waiting, but I tracked his eyes and realized he was listening to a conversation that I couldn't hear. Every few seconds he looked out at me with increasing interest.

It didn't take long. The door began to open, and I stepped back and steeled myself for whatever was about to happen. I figured the captain had been called by the troopers with some questions for me, or even to put me on the phone with them. This would be my chance to clear some things up. To explain that they didn't need to waste any time wondering about me. I took a deep breath and started to feel the relief of putting the misunderstanding behind me.

A pleasant looking brunette woman in a white shirt and epaulets bearing four gold stripes came out first. Rainey was right behind her. The brunette stopped in front of me. She wore a pair of half glasses with dark frames attached to a silver chain around her neck.

"Are you Johnny Wainwright?" She didn't smile. Her voice was flat and her eyes gave me no clue what she was thinking.

"Yes. And this is Brandy Fontaine," I said. "What can I do for you?" I reached forward to shake hands.

She didn't shake. Instead she crossed her arms and straightened up. Arching her back with her nose raised, she looked me up and down. She never glanced at Brandy. I looked at Rainey behind her and saw her clenching her teeth and shaking her head at me with a strained and worried look. The kind of look you see on someone who's standing on thin ice when they hear it crack.

"I'm Captain Ferguson and I've been directed to take you into custody. Darrell?"

The big snarly guy stepped around Rainey and came up beside the captain. "Yes, m'am?"

"Would you take Mr. Wainwright here below, please?"

"Hey, wait a minute. What is this?" I felt my knees go loose like I was about to drop. I raised my hands in protest. "You can't be serious. Am I being arrested or something?"

The captain turned and nodded at the big man moving toward me. I tried to step to the side to keep talking to the captain, but a meaty hand grabbed my jacket in the chest and held me in place against the wall.

"As the captain of this vessel, Mr. Wainwright, I have the legal authority and responsibility to carry out the duties of local law enforcement in situations like this."

"Situation like what? I haven't done anything. What am I being accused of?"

Darrell turned me around to face the wall and pulled off my pack.

"Save it for the police. You can tell them your story when they get here. In the meantime, you get to wait below." The captain turned and started back to the bridge.

"Captain, wait a minute. Listen to me for a second, please. The people you really need to worry about are on your ship here somewhere."

She kept walking and opened the door. I raised my head to stare at the ceiling in frustration. I looked at Brandy trying not to scream. I thought about running but then thought better of it. Not to mention that I was pinned to the wall like a butterfly on a board.

Brandy put her hands up toward me in a calming gesture. "Take it easy, Johnny. Just go along for now. I'll find Charlie. And we'll get it cleared up. Don't worry."

Yeah, right, I thought. The captain looked like she was ready to hold a trial and hang me from the radar mast.

"Uh, captain?" Darrell spoke up. "You need to see this."

Captain Ferguson stopped and looked back. Darrell had opened up my pack and the Sponge Bob pack. Holding it up for her to see, he held a clear plastic bag with a handgun inside. It looked like a Glock.

All eyes locked on me. I gulped and stared. "That isn't mine. I swear. It belongs to that kid."

"Yeah, right," said Darrell. He was holding the bag by the corner and holding it up to the light inspecting the weapon. "Looks like it has blood and hair on it. The crime techs will love this."

I was getting pissed. And kicking myself thinking about how Charlie had tossed me the Glock back on Taroka. When I get pissed I get sarcastic.

"Gee whiz, CSI boy, you've got it all figured out, don't you?"

Darrell shoved me against the wall again with an elbow and leaned over to speak into my ear. "They'll test you for gun powder residue too. You're screwed, dude."

He smirked when he saw me cringe. "Where do I put him, Captain?"

She frowned. "That is a good question, isn't it? It's not like we have a brig on board. Never had to arrest anybody before." She looked at me like I was a dead rat. Something that the cook had just pulled out of a stew pot and held up for the crew to behold. Then she chuckled.

"We don't even have any handcuffs on board, do we?" she asked with an embarrassed laugh as if the novelty of the situation was funny somehow.

"No problem," Darrell chimed in cheerfully. He held up a pair of shining metal cuffs and smiled.

"Well, there you go. Use the forward supply room," the captain said. "A boat from Seward is on its way to meet us." With a grim nod she collected the two packs and the Glock and stepped through the doorway out of sight.

Darrell fumbled with the cuffs trying to get them open. I stood there in disbelief. Brandy and Rainey looked at each other, speechless. Needing both hands to wrestle the cuffs open, Darrell shifted his weight to hold me against the wall with a heavy forearm.

I was fed up. "Say, maybe I can help you with those, Darrell." I lifted my arms and slid my hands through the open rings while he struggled to close them. When he was satisfied that I was secure, he pulled on the front of my jacket to start me moving down the passageway.

Along the way Darrell twisted his huge shape around to take a look at Rainey and pushed me to walk in front of him.

"Good thing I used to work as a private security guard and still had my cuffs with me," he said to her.

"Yeah, Darrell," I gushed in a high voice as fake as a Chinese Timex. "You really got it going on. You got the key too?"

He didn't answer right away. I wasn't sure if he was thinking about the answer, or simply trying to walk and talk at the same time.

"Uh oh," I said to no one in particular. "The Junior G-man may be one key short of a full ring."

"You shut up," he thumped the back of my head with a flick of a finger that felt like a two by four. I took his advice.

We walked on in silence until Darrell realized he had a little parade following him. He stopped before opening a locked doorway at the top of a metal staircase.

"I can take care of this myself," he said looking at Rainey and Brandy. They didn't need any further explanation and turned on their heels. I tried to make eye contact with one or the other, but they didn't look back. Rainey had her hand at the small of Brandy's back and the two of them walked away in silence. The heavy metal door slammed shut echoing through the metal stairwell.

CHAPTER
25

On the way down the stairs, I tried to think. It wasn't easy. Mister Darrell had me by the back of the neck. I was starting to realize that he probably wasn't the brightest herring in the school. He hadn't searched me, he should have cuffed my hands behind me and he hadn't noticed how I'd rushed him along helping him forget the basics.

I was in survival mode. Helpless as a gaffed rockfish I was grasping at anything I could think of to gain an advantage.

We walked down the stairs past three decks. One of the landings had a sign that said Vehicle Deck. To keep me moving Darrell held a fistful of my collar in one hand and pushed me along in front of him. I felt like the Count of Monte Christo being taken to a dark underground dungeon.

"You going to hang me from the wall by my wrists, Darrell?"

He chuckled as we stopped in front of a doorway labeled Supply.

"Ha, that's a good ..." I turned toward him and exploded with a violent sneeze in his face before he could finish.

Bending forward with the force of the eruption I threw my hands up to wipe at my face and turned my back.

"Sorry, Darrell, sorry. I didn't mean to do that." As quick as I could I reached into my jacket with one hand and grabbed the little tool case from my inside pocket.

Darrell had me by the collar with one hand and he wiped his face with his other arm giving me a moment to stick the case under my armpit out of his view. I waited for him to unlock the door and push it open. He reached in and flipped on a light switch. Then he pushed me forward. I had to step awkwardly over a foot high bulkhead to get inside.

As I did I looked to the right, recoiled and shouted, "Oh, crap, there's rats down here!"

When I felt Darrell's head swing to the right, I tossed the case away from me to the left. Out of the corner of my eye I saw it tumble behind a cardboard box. I yelled again to cover the sound.

"You see 'em? You see 'em?"

"Where?" he asked dully.

"Over there. Oh, man, you can't leave me down here. Please, Darrell, have a heart."

He pushed me forward and forced me to sit down on a wooden crate in the center of the room. Shelves and boxes filled the space around us. I leaned back against a round support post and looked up at him with my best pitiful expression.

"Quit whining," he said. "You'll only be in here another hour or so." He reached into a box and pulled out a heavy chain and padlock. He wrapped it around the post and through the handcuffs.

"Not too tight, okay, Darrell? In case I have to stand up to fight off the rats."

He chuckled again. Then I saw him blink as if remembering procedures. He patted me down quickly but didn't find anything.

"Hey Darrell, what if I have to ... you know?" I pantomimed taking a leak.

He thought about that for a moment, frowning. "You'll just have to hold it," he said with a shrug. He checked my wallet and finding it empty, put it back in my pocket.

While he was putting the padlock in place, I changed tactics. I made nice.

"Hey, Darrell, I'm sorry I made fun of you back there. You know, I didn't have anything to do with those troopers. Ask Rainey, she'll tell ya."

He snapped the padlock shut and pocketed the key. "Whatever, dude."

He looked me over coldly for a moment and then, satisfied that I was secure, he turned to go. Spotting an empty coffee can by the door, he slid it over next to me with his foot.

He gave me a deadpan look. "Enjoy," he said. Then he turned and left. The big steel door banged shut with a hollow echo and I heard him locking the deadbolt from the outside.

The supply room was a simple place. About thirty feet across it was shaped like the bow of the ship. Its side walls were about eight feet high and sloped forward in a vee. Bare light bulbs were suspended from the ceiling every ten feet enclosed in wire mesh cages.

I could hear the hum and vibration of equipment outside the room, but otherwise it was quiet. I knew the ocean was surging past me just outside the walls. It was cool and damp in there and I sat on the crate staring into the shadows and smelling wet cardboard.

I was past being mad. I actually understood why this had happened. I didn't like it, but maybe if I stayed patient, everything would work out. I was reasonably sure of that. At least I hoped so. Whistling in the graveyard maybe, but a little false confidence right then was all I had.

But the Glock had me worried. My DNA was all over it. It had been in the Sponge Bob pack the whole time and I'd never even looked inside. What an idiot. They'd set me up perfectly. Charlie and Greta. Holy crap. What a pair. No wonder they were on the run. They probably thought they were free and clear now with me back at Chenega holding the bag.

At least I'd been able to get rid of the lock picks. When the real police arrived they were sure to search me again. If they found a set of burglary tools on me I'd be in trouble for real. No need for that. At least there was nothing on me now to further incriminate me. All I had to do was wait.

I looked down at the handcuffs and the chain holding me to the post. Then I stood up and tested the arrangement. I could move around a little, but Darrell had done his job well. I wasn't going anywhere.

I sat back down and looked down at the coffee can. It had a few cigarette butts in it and a gum wrapper. The irony struck me. Within a few feet above me tourists and travelers were enjoying a beautiful day soaking in the Alaska scenery, and here I was chained up down below.

Time dragged. I felt like a caged border collie in a field full of sheep. So much to do. The worst part was the boredom. No music, no TV, no pool table, no newspaper, no nothing. Jeez, a guy could go nuts like this. My mind wouldn't stop racing. No wonder convicts start running head first into the walls.

I tried retracing every step of the past several hours. I needed answers but all I had were questions. The troopers had been in the lodge the whole time? The story about the fishing guide was total bullshit. It had been Charlie all along. And that meant that both he and Greta had been lying to me the whole time. Even during all her flirty suggestive times with me?

I gulped when I realized that I could easily have been a victim too. Why hadn't he killed me? Why the troopers but not me? Charlie must have been thinking I could fly him out of there. Help him escape. And then I remembered him saying 'I could use a man who doesn't care.' Yeah, no kidding. And where the hell were they now? They're the ones who caused all this, and I'm the one locked up?

A sense of doom washed over me. I couldn't even imagine the hell on earth of a federal penitentiary. Or correctional facility as they called them these days. Maximum security. A six by ten foot cell. They say the lack of human contact is the worst punishment of all. But in a double cell with a sadistic sociopathic sexual pervert psychokiller? No thanks, I'll do my time in solitary.

What to do? What could I do?

Okay, enough. I was making myself crazy. Fifteen minutes of imprisonment and I was a basket case already. Good thing I wasn't in for twenty five to life.

Wait a minute. That wasn't a happy thought. Bad images started flooding in like the little room was filling with water. And snakes. Or gasoline? Did I smell something? No, my imagination was the only thing on fire, and suddenly it was a raging inferno.

Two troopers were dead. What if they never found Charlie and Greta? What if I was left holding the bag? When cops got killed the system went into high gear. The outrage demanded somebody's head. Guess whose they had?

I could just hear the news report and the police press conference. 'Yes, two officers are down, but there's a suspect in custody. A part time Seward pilot and repo man with a shady past named Johnny Wainwright was apprehended fleeing the scene. The apparent murder weapon was recovered in his possession.' I made a handy scapegoat with a slightly shady reputation and no good alibi.

What now? Sit here and wait for things to get worse?

I stood up and pushed the wooden crate away from the post. The chain dropped to the metal deck with a clang. Looking toward the boxes six feet away I stretched a leg out as far as it would reach. Kicking at the edge of the box, it moved just enough to let me spot the black leather case behind it. I looked over to the door and listened. Hearing nothing I laid down on the floor on my belly and crawled backward as far as I could go. With my arms fully extended above my head I finally reached the case with one foot and started fumbling at it.

The floor was dirty, but I didn't care. I had to do something. They say an idle mind is the devil's workshop. Apparently mine was a nightmare spook house full of panic and paranoia. Especially when locked up. Grunting and wrestling I fought for my future.

Worried that someone would come in, I calculated how long it would take to get back to sitting innocently on the box. Screw it. I'll just tell them I'd stretched out for a nap.

The minutes crept by like a Seal team in the dark. Little by little I made it happen. Working my toes and rolling back and forth, the case was finally where I could pick it up. I got up and brushed the dirt off my clothes as best I could and sat back down on the crate. If I heard someone coming I could always toss the picks away again. Now I was getting somewhere. The panic had subsided, so I zipped open the case and picked out the right tools.

I don't know how much time elapsed when I heard keys clattering against the door. I straightened up and slid the tools under a box next to my feet. The door swung open and Rainey's head appeared around the corner.

"Johnny, you in here?" she called before she spotted me.

"Hey," I called out in relief.

Rainey pushed her way into the room and walked toward me. She looked at me sitting there and shook her head at the chain and handcuffs wrapped around my wrists. Brandy stepped over the bulkhead behind her. She was holding a white Styrofoam cup and a bundle wrapped in napkins.

Rainey closed the door behind them. "Don't get excited, Johnny. I can't let you go or anything like that. They would have my ass, but I did get permission to bring you a snack."

"Oh, man. It's great to see you guys. What a freaking drag it is down here."

"How about some doughnuts and coffee, Johnny?" Brandy asked, looking at the chains and trying to sound cheerful.

"Well, I don't really like doughnuts, you know. But I'll eat some to be polite."

They laughed. "And I suppose you're prepared to be very polite, aren't you?"

"You betcha," I said and reached out to take a cup of coffee.

With my other hand I reached for the doughnuts. The handcuffs fell at my feet.

Their jaws dropped so fast, I thought the lights might blow. "My God, are you crazy? What have you done?" Rainey's eyes went wide and her face turned ghostly white.

I sat back and worked at opening the coffee. They stared at me speechless. Rainey looked back nervously at the door.

"Johnny, you're nuts. How did you do that?"

"I'm nuts? This whole situation is nuts. You find Charlie yet?"

Rainey shook her head. Her eyes couldn't quit gaping at the chains on the floor. "You can't do that. And you'll get me fired for letting you escape."

"I'm not escaping, silly. Would you like a bite?" I asked holding out a sticky glazed hunk of pastry with only one bite missing. "Gee, it sure is great to see you all."

"But you can't, you can't just unlock yourself. You're under arrest," Rainey's mouth was still hanging open. "How did you do that?"

Brandy started laughing and shaking her head. "Relax, Rainey, I've seen this routine before. Johnny has more hidden skills than you could ever imagine."

Rainey sat down on a box trying to pull herself together. "Well, can you put them back on before I get fired?"

"Yeah, yeah, no sweat, but listen. You've got to find Charlie and Greta."

They nodded their heads in unison. I took a slurp of coffee.

"Okay, look, I've been thinking about that."

I reminded Brandy about the cabins where she saw the guy she thought might be Charlie. "Rainey, I think Charlie and Greta are in one of those cabins, laying low. I don't know why they don't show up on the passenger list."

"But that's impossible, I checked and all the cabins have been occupied since Whittier."

"I've been thinking about it. Go back up there and look for a grandma and a teenager sitting together looking upset." I gave them more details. "I'll stay here and lock myself back up in case Bubba Gump comes back to check on me. Where are we anyhow?"

"Almost to the mouth of Resurrection Bay. We going to stop there to meet a boat from Seward."

"Okay, get going. If Charlie and Greta get away I'm the only one the cops have in custody for the deaths of two troopers."

"Wait a minute." Rainey looked perplexed. "So what if I find these people, then what?"

"Just keep an eye on them, so when the police get here you can point them out. I can't think of anything else."

Brandy chimed in, God love her. "Yes, that could work. Johnny tells the cops that he delivered the troopers to make an arrest. And then they disappeared. Charlie was the last person to see them alive. They'll have to listen. And they'll have to at least question him. Right?"

I tried to look hopeful. "Uh, right."

Rainey picked up on the need for some positive energy. "Okay, so they might not believe you, but I can't see them letting Charlie and Greta just leave without being questioned. They were the only others out there, right?"

"I guess," I said. "But you've got to find Charlie and Greta and keep track of them in the meantime. If they get away, I'm cooked."

"Shouldn't be a problem. How could they get away from the ship without being seen?" Rainey was heading for the door.

I looked doubtful again. So did Brandy. "The same way they got on board and disappeared," she said.

"And the same way they managed to not show up on the manifest." I added. I could hear the doubt, confusion and near despair in my own voice. "Do we even know for sure they're on board?"

They both looked at me then, sharing the same bewildered expression.

"You said you saw them boarding. Did you ever see them, Brandy?"

Brandy shook her head. "Not really."

They looked at me again. I was worrying too much. Starting to question everything I thought I'd been sure of. But the last thing I needed was for my only two allies to start wondering about me. If they got the idea that it was a wild goose chase or that I was mistaken about seeing Charlie and Greta, I was screwed.

"Hell, they have to be on board. I saw them, both of them and the kid too. Remember when I pointed them out to you?" I put all the positive energy in my voice that I could scrape together, but they didn't look convinced. "Please go check on that grandma. You've got to find Charlie."

"Okay, okay, don't worry, Johnny. We'll go find them and we'll let you know. In the meantime, lock yourself back up. Don't make it worse." Rainey squeezed my shoulder and Brandy touched my cheek. Then they left together. I listened to the big metal door bang shut again and the keys rattling in the lock.

I leaned back against the post and arranged the handcuffs and chain in my lap. I didn't relock the cuffs but I placed them so I could snap them shut if I heard someone coming.

I finished the doughnuts and washed down the sticky lump in my throat with a big slug of lukewarm coffee. Doughnuts and hot coffee were some of my favorite things in the world, but the thrill just wasn't there. I looked around the supply room again. Rows of boxes and crates stared back at me like bored children waiting for the morning school bus.

All I could do was imagine the activities above me. I grimaced at my complete lack of control. I had no way of knowing what would happen next. Would they find Charlie? What would happen when the cops showed up?

Paranoia leaked into the recesses of my mind again like wetness invading tiny cracks in an old rowboat. Of no concern at first, but then it builds and grows. Before you know it, there's more water inside the boat than outside. You don't have to be a sailor to know what that means. You're sunk.

With only my dark thoughts for company I reached for another swig of coffee, then thought better of it. Nothing like sugar and caffeine to make the motor race. I tried to relax. Breathe deep, inhale, exhale slowly. Slow the pulse. Keep your head.

I closed my eyes and tried to forget about time. Tried to just focus on my breathing and hold on. I fought the temptation to give up and give in. To roll over and wait for the end. Bad dog, chained up in the basement.

A crackling voice called out over the ship's speaker system. "Charles Westridge, please report to the bridge. Charles Westridge, to the bridge, please."

At least Rainey was trying everything. And Brandy had to know I was close to losing it. The announcement may have been more for my benefit than anything else. And it helped. At least I knew something was happening up there.

I don't know how much time went by while I tried to keep my head above water. Not long, I suppose, but then I heard a frantic banging at the door. I jumped up and listened. I was about to lock the cuffs again, but something made me wait. Darrell would have just come in. This was something else.

I heard a high pitched yelling through the thick metal and a hand slapping the door. No sound of keys. Only the slapping and yelling.

I dropped the cuffs and the chain and ran to the door. I pressed my ear tight against it and listened. It sounded like Brandy.

"What?" I shouted. The slapping and screaming stopped.

Then I heard Brandy's voice barely audible on the other side of the frame. "Johnny, let me in. Hurry."

I cranked the deadbolt and Brandy pushed her way in. Together we shoved the door closed.

"What? What's going on? Where's Rainey?" I held Brandy by the arms and stared into her face. She was gasping and gulping and coughed a few times, unable to speak. She looked scared to the point of panic. I shook her gently. "Come on, come on, talk to me."

"Okay, listen. We found the grandma you told us about. It took a while but she finally broke down crying and said a big wild eyed man had followed her and her twin granddaughters and pushed his way into their cabin. He pulled a gun and told her he needed the cabin and that if they said anything to anybody, he'd kill them. He kept one of the girls hostage."

"Where's Rainey?"

"It happened so fast I couldn't believe it, Johnny. Rainey screwed up. It's horrible."

"What happened?" I shook her again.

"She made a radio call but didn't get an answer. So she went over to listen at the cabin door. A big guy inside was watching and he grabbed her before she could even call for help."

"Then what?"

Brandy was shaking. Her jaw quivered, but she kept talking. "He twisted her arm behind her back and dragged her down the stairway with him. I think they went down to the vehicle deck. Johnny, what are we going to do?"

"We've got to get help. Who knows what this guy's going to do? It was Charlie, wasn't it?"

"Yes, as best as I could tell. Big guy, coke bottle glasses, wild eyes, dirty blond beard. Right?"

"That's him. Did you see Greta?"

"No, it all happened so fast. He looked crazed, Johnny. Desperate, you know?"

My mind was racing for real then. All I could see was Rainey in front of that maniac's gun. Just like he'd shot the dog. I'd blocked that image from my mind, but I remembered. Charlie hadn't hesitated. No reluctance whatsoever. Pull a trigger, solve a problem. I flashed on the troopers thinking that's probably what happened to them. I shook off the picture.

"Okay, Brandy, go find Security or the captain and tell them what happened. Go to the bridge."

"What are you going to do?"

"I'm going to the vehicle deck."

"Jesus, Johnny, you can't do that. Can't you wait? You'll be in deep trouble leaving this room. And this guy, Charlie ..."

I didn't let her finish. I checked to make sure I had the lock picks with me throwing the previous caution aside.

"Let's go." Pulling Brandy's hand I opened the door, looked out into the empty hallway and stepped through. As

I was pulling the door closed, I felt the floor shift. The engine noise dropped and the vibration changed.

"What was that?"

"We're stopping," she answered. She looked at me with alarm in her eyes. "They'll be coming for you."

"I know. Go now. Tell them everything."

Brandy and I locked eyes. She glanced back and forth between my face and the door trying to picture what was coming. I met her gaze and we nodded at the same time. A look passed between us. Without another word she turned and started up the staircase two at a time.

CHAPTER
26

I crouched in the stairwell and listened to Brandy's feet climbing the metal stairs above me. Then they were gone. The engine room was nearby. I could feel the vibration underneath me and I even thought I could hear the big diesel engines throbbing one floor below. I crawled up the stairs to the next level, the one I remembered as the vehicle deck. There was a round glass window in a closed door, but all I could see through it was a dimly lit area that looked like a parking garage.

I thought I was going to have to pick another lock, but as I leaned against the door I felt it give. It wasn't locked. I pushed it open just a couple of inches and got down on my knees to peek around the corner into the car deck. Nothing moved. No sound either.

Then I heard noises from behind me and above. Heavy clumping footsteps were coming down the metal grate stairs. Brandy must have gotten somebody's attention. It was too late to get up and get back to the supply room. Before I could move the footsteps came on fast.

I looked up to see who it was, but all I could see was a handgun pointed at my face. A voice called out.

"Freeze, motherfucker." It was Darrell, his round face red and puffy. He sounded like he'd watched too many Wildest Police Videos.

I was really starting to dislike the guy.

"What the hell are you doing out here? Who let you go?"

My sleeves had fallen down over my hands. I raised them in front of me and flapped the phony stumps at him. With an anguished cry, I moaned, "The rats, the rats! They chewed off my hands!"

At first he recoiled in horror. Then his eyes narrowed and he looked at me skeptically. Reaching forward with one hand he pulled one of the sleeves down.

"Okay, funny man," he said in a growl and reassumed his shooter's stance. "Put your hands behind your back. You and your psycho partner are under arrest."

"Aw, Darrell, heck, you got me, man." I slowly raised my hands but leaned slightly against the door.

"Don't do that," he ordered. "The guy said if anyone came in, he'd ..."

I shoved hard and dove through the opening missing the last part of his speech. I never was any good at taking orders. I landed hard and tumbled down a flight of five metal stairs on my belly. The door swung itself shut behind me.

In a different frame of mind, I might have regretted that decision. But I was in 'go mode'. I would not be stopped. Besides, overinflated humps like Darrell always made me want to do the exact opposite of whatever they ordered.

It's been a long standing issue for me. A child psychiatrist once called it "oppositional defiant disorder." Some shit like that. They say it's usually self destructive. And childish too. Whatever.

When I hit the bottom of the stairs, I found myself in another world. The car deck was a dimly lit underground structure with a high ceiling and rows of parking spaces filled with all kinds of vehicles. Even some campers.

Laying on my face on the concrete next to a truck, I took a moment to look around and listen. I was a little banged up but I didn't care. All I could feel was the adrenaline pumping through my veins.

I was staring underneath a red pickup with running boards and chrome exhaust pipes. In the distance I heard a loud thunk. A metal against metal sound and then an echoing boom. I got up to my knees and shuffled to the edge of the pickup to peer around the front tire. I still couldn't see anything.

Then I heard the sound again. Definitely metal on metal and not like machinery. The place smelled like most car garages do. Rubber and engine smells. Oil and gasoline, wet pavement, road dirt, exhaust fumes.

I moved to the other end of the pickup against the wall and crept in the direction of the sound. The odor of gasoline grew stronger. A lot stronger. The pavement was wet too. I reached down and touched the floor with one hand. Even before I brought my fingers to my nose, I knew what it was.

Gasoline was spreading across the deck of the parking area. I duck walked around another car and looked underneath. A stream of gas was dribbling from the fuel tank. I leaned in for a closer look. There was a punctured hole in the gas tank near the rear bumper. It looked like a stab wound.

I thought instantly about Charlie's Ka-bar. The combat knife he wore on his belt would make that kind of hole.

Holy shit. Gasoline was everywhere. Standing up enough to look over a car hood, I saw Charlie at the far wall. Toward the stern of the ferry he was walking from one vehicle to another. I watched him bend over a light green Honda four door and thrust something underneath.

Thunk. The big knife punctured another tank. Then I saw him dance backward like he was trying to avoid the rush of fuel that jumped for his feet.

I retreated for the car behind me. I was trying to stay out of the spreading pool of fuel, but my boots were soaking in it. The fumes stung my eyes.

I looked to the stairs and doorway. Ten easy leaping strides and I could be out of there. I thought about it. But then what? This mad man was building a bomb right below two hundred innocent people. Sitting up there in the sunshine, they didn't suspect a thing.

Staying with the cars didn't seem like a good idea. But running away seemed worse. Not to mention the fact that I knew the mad man by his first name. And he knew mine.

Another thunk rang out down the line of vehicles. I sneaked another look toward Charlie and watched as he pushed over a motorcycle sending gas splashing from its open tank.

The vehicle behind me was a four wheel drive Toyota pickup with a camper shell on its back. A length of rope was hanging out of the back of the shell. I wouldn't have given it a second look, but it moved. Not from wind either. There wasn't any wind in the dark cavern.

Then I heard a noise from inside the truck bed. A shuffling sound and a grunt. The rope danced at the same time.

I had to look. I worked my way around to the other side of the pickup to keep it between me and Charlie. Then I cupped my hands against a side window and looked in. It was dark inside the truck bed but enough light filtered through the darkened glass that I could see a figure tied hand and foot laying in the back of the truck. The figure had a blond pony tail that thrashed from side to side as it struggled.

It was Rainey. She didn't see me, and I wasn't about to make any noise to attract her attention. There was duct tape wrapped around her head covering her mouth, and the rest of her face was contorted in pain as I watched her straining to untie herself.

I moved to the rear of the truck and peered carefully around the corner toward Charlie. He had his back to me while he struggled to tip over another motorcycle. I lifted the rear window of the camper shell above the tailgate, crawled onto the bumper and dove in pulling the window closed behind me. The spring loaded hinge knocked me over on top of Rainey pushing my cap down over my face.

One of my elbows must have landed in the middle of her solar plexus. I heard the whoosh of air escape her lungs, and I raised up to see if she was okay. My face was only two inches from hers. Her eyes were half crossed and looked like they might roll back in her head.

"Hey, hey, Rainey," I whispered as loud as I dared. "Don't flake out on me."

Then I heard her take a breath. The oxygen must have done her some good. Her eyes began to clear. I waited for her to get her senses back.

They say that tension, panic and stress can lead to strange thoughts. It was bad timing and way out of place, but I couldn't help noticing that I was in a really interesting position. Lying on top of Rainey and feeling her warm softness beneath me made my mind go places that were definitely inappropriate.

I almost started to grin at the irony. Here we were about to be blown to pieces and I was having erotic thoughts. My close friend was bound and gagged underneath me. My very attractive and curvaceous close friend. And she was completely helpless. Unconscious and unaware of my restless thoughts.

I was shocked at myself. Absolutely shocked. Sort of. I was about to apologize for all of the above, but she didn't give me the chance.

Her eyes flashed open, her body went rigid and her knees came up in a reaction so fast, all thoughts of apology vanished. My entire manly bulk of a hundred and fifty pounds was propelled over her head and slammed into the front wall of the camper.

Then it was my turn to go cross eyed and glassy. Flames of agony sprang from the place where no man wants flames. The pain took my breath away. Stars danced drunkenly in a black sky filled with northern lights. Blue lightning flickering in wicked pulses.

Rainey was thrashing wildly at the ropes trying to get away from me. Somehow she spun herself around and was about to pulverize me again with her powerful legs. Then she stopped. In spite of my gritting teeth, closed eyes and both hands clutching my crotch, somehow she realized who

I was. She struggled to sit up and stared at me in mute astonishment.

I fought to remain conscious and slowly my eyes uncrossed and focused again. Rainey's face above the strips of duct tape made her look like some kind of a strange Egyptian belly dancer wearing a gray veil. Her blue eyes bulged huge and full of anguish, tears and fear. Strands of tangled blond hair fell all around her face. She tried to say something, but her lips couldn't move behind the tape. All she could manage was a strangling whimper.

I finally managed to get some air back in my lungs, and gradually the pain began to subside enough to where I could speak.

"Damn, Rainey, you're a fun date," I groaned, still bent over double. She hung her head in mime-like sorrow, but only for a second.

Then she kicked at my shins with her tied together feet. Still massaging my hurting place I looked at her sharply. The last thing I needed at the moment was another kick. Her eyes were on fire. She jerked her chin at me to hurry up, grumbling behind the tape.

"Okay, okay, give a guy a break, will ya?" I took a deep breath and winced at the shots of pain radiating from deep inside my crotch. I moved toward Rainey and reached for her face. "I'm sorry, I'm sorry," I mumbled at her as I pulled at the duct tape.

I saw her wince and grimace with my clumsy efforts. I knew I was pulling hair out by the roots, but it couldn't be helped. Tears ran from her eyes, but finally I got her lips free enough that she could speak. Instead she gasped and wheezed.

"We've got to get out of here, Rainey. That guy is filling the place with gasoline. Are you okay? Did he, did he … hurt you?"

"No, I'm okay," she answered panting and sucking in deep breaths of air. "I thought I was going to suffocate with that tape over my mouth," she muttered between gulps.

"Security is right outside the door. What happened?"

She told me about Charlie grabbing her and putting a gun in her back. When they got to the vehicle deck, he'd taken her keys and her radio and tied her up in the back of the pickup.

"He called up to the bridge and told them that if anyone came into the vehicle deck, he'd kill me. Where is he?"

"He's nearby. We've got to move fast."

"Wait, there's something else. I heard a woman come back on the radio. She wasn't part of the crew, I'm sure of that."

I thought about that as I worked on the ropes holding Rainey's hands. I leaned over and tried to see where Charlie was through the tinted glass, but I couldn't see him anywhere.

When Rainey's hands were free, she went to work on the ropes holding her feet.

"Hold still and let me get this tape off," I said. "Do this." I tilted my head back and stretched my neck up and away from her. The tape was still wrapped tight around her chin and neck like an ugly gray necklace tangled in strands of blond hair.

I pulled at a corner of tape where it was wrapped around her head. I tried to hold her hair with one hand while I pulled at the tape with the other. I felt her jerk with every hunk of scalp that the tape took with it.

"Sorry," I whispered over and over as I worked. She ignored me and kept pulling at the knots around her feet. When I finally yanked the last part of the tape away from the flesh of her neck, she winced and yelped.

"Ow! Damn it! That's the only face I've got," she shoved at me with an elbow.

"Oh, stifle yourself," I said. "I need some kind of revenge. You damn near killed me with your knee."

"Oh, tough titty. What the hell do we do now?" Her feet were free, and she was blinking at the gas fumes. She wanted out.

I crawled forward and jimmied the window that separated the camper shell from the cabin of the truck.

"Climb through there. He'll spot us if we open the back window."

She didn't need any further instructions. Clambering forward she stuck her head through the opening while I peeked through the windows trying to see where Charlie was. I didn't see him, so I opened the back window of the shell just an inch so I could listen. The smell of gasoline almost took my breath away.

Blinking my eyes at the irritation I couldn't see much. Then I spotted him several vehicles away. I turned and crawled to the front of the truck bed. Rainey was sitting in the driver's seat looking at me with big eyes.

Drawing close to the window between us, I pointed past her to the stairs.

"Open the door as quiet as you can, then get up those stairs and out. It's not locked."

She was moving to go, but then she turned back. "What about you?"

I paused a moment. Good question, I thought. I knew what I had to do, but I didn't think explaining it to Rainey was a good idea. Besides, there was no time for an argument.

"I'll be right behind you," I lied. "Now go."

She nodded and with tiny movements she unlatched the side door and let herself out. Leaving the door ajar for me, she crouched behind the side of the pickup and peered toward the stern of the vehicle bay. I stuck my head through the opening into the cab and looked around. I didn't see Charlie, so I turned back to Rainey.

"Go now, go!" I urged in a whisper and pretended to start crawling through the opening.

She turned and still bent over tiptoed across the wet deck to the stairs. Then she leaped two at a time and disappeared through the doorway. The heavy metal door banged shut with a loud clang.

"Hey!" I heard a loud shout behind me. Charlie ran along the wall at the front of the vehicles parked there. First he was looking toward the stairs and the door at the top of the landing. Then he stopped in front of the pickup, and he noticed its half open front door.

I ducked out of sight and tried to hide against the side wall of the truck bed making myself as small as possible. I could feel him inches away from me with on the other side of the camper shell moving slowly past. I squeezed my eyes shut in traditional ostrich fashion.

Several moments went by, and I dared to open my eyes again thinking he had moved away. I shifted myself to crawl through the cab window again, but then a big shadow darkened the window at the back corner of the shell. Charlie's face pressed against the glass as he tried to see inside. His bulk blocked out the light, but I could see his glasses reflecting what little light there was. Behind the thick lenses his eyeballs were rattling back and forth like crickets on a hot plate.

I think I stopped breathing at the sight of him. I tried to make myself invisible but it didn't work.

The rear window swung up with a whoosh and I was staring into Charlie's face. His teeth were bared and he hissed as he breathed through clenched teeth glaring down at me. Sweat and tears ran down his face and dripped from his mustache.

Gasoline fumes swirled around him and filled the camper. I thought I might throw up. Charlie held the Ka-bar in his right hand wrapped in a red bandana. It was dripping with fuel. His left hand held a handgun pointed straight into my face.

CHAPTER
27

"Oh, hi, Charlie," I swallowed hard and raised my hands beside my head. I knew it sounded lame, but what else could I say?

His eyes went wide as he recognized me and tried to make sense of seeing me instead of Rainey in the truck. Then his eyeballs settled and focused on me with a deadly steadiness.

"Where's the bitch?" He was not happy.

"Who? Rainey? Uh, she had other things to do. I traded places with her. Hope you don't mind." I tried a friendly smile. It didn't work.

"GET OUT OF THERE!" he roared at me, stepping backward and straightening his arm. The gun pointed directly between my eyes.

I scrambled to crawl over the tailgate. Cooperation seemed like a good idea. I stood there and tried hard not to look like a road sign. Like the one we'd shot full of holes back on Taroka. I glanced at his face once but thought better of making eye contact.

I could feel his mind working. He wasn't sure what to do. His breath hissed and rattled and his weight shifted from side to side. He'd been breathing gas fumes for a long time. With one sleeve he wiped at the tears running from his red irritated eyes.

He wanted to shoot me. I could feel it. He was picturing me dead on the floor with a bullet hole in my forehead. I was too. But he was also thinking that the gun discharge would probably set off the gasoline.

Better to stab me in the belly with the Ka-bar or just hammer me to the deck with the gun butt. I stood there in front of him with my hands up trying to get a breath of untainted air, but there wasn't any. My eyes were watering too, and I felt like gagging.

Finally he reached across his body with the knife and slid it back in the sheath on his hip. He stepped forward, turned me around and pushed me against the back of the pickup. He kicked my feet apart. I knew what to do. I hadn't watched four hundred reruns of Hawaii Five-Oh without learning how to "spread 'em." He was better at this than Darrell.

Towering over me with almost a foot height advantage, he put the end of the gun barrel against the back of my head and ran his hand around my body. He found the lock picks.

"What the hell are these for?" he demanded.

"Uh, I'm a repo man, Charlie. Just a part time thing, you understand. A guy's got to make ..."

"Shut up!" he cut me off. "Christ, you sure can run your mouth with some ridiculous bullshit. I thought you were a pilot."

"Yeah, I'm that too. It's complicated, ya know?"

I'd had some self defense training a long time ago. They'd taught me how to get out of situations like this. I racked my brain to remember. If the bad guy made the mistake of touching you with a gun from behind, you could make a nifty spin move and knock it away with one arm while you attacked his face with your other hand. Then kick him in the groin.

Man, that seemed like a bad idea.

I actually considered it for at least half a millisecond. But then I imagined myself hanging from the end of his arm with his fist around my throat and decided against it.

Before I had a chance to contemplate any further insanity he spun me around and shoved me back against the pickup. Just then the floor began to vibrate strongly and engine noise resumed at full force. I felt the ferry shift into motion again.

Holding the gun six inches from my face, Charlie reached for the radio he'd taken from Rainey. He had it tied it around his chest.

"Hey, Greta," he called into the mike. Watching me closely, he waited. In a few seconds a scratchy burst of static came back. Then it cleared and I heard her voice.

"Yeah?"

"Everything okay up there?" His eyes were flicking back and forth again. He wiped at his red eyes and then grabbed the back of my collar. Marching me in front of him we headed for the other side of the vehicle bay.

"Yes, we're underway, heading south like we talked about. How about you?" Greta's voice was high pitched and shaking.

"I'm fine. Can they hear all this?"

"Yes, Charlie, I've got the captain right here."

I blinked in complete disbelief. Greta on the radio? I looked around the vehicle bay. What had they done?

"Okay," Charlie went on. "Then he needs to know that the vehicle deck down here is covered with gasoline and I've got a lighter right here in my hand. If any one tries to stop us, I'll flick my Bic and the whole ship blows. Does he understand that?"

There was a pause. "He's a she, Charlie. And she understands. She wants to know what we want."

He licked his lips and stared at his feet for a moment. "I'll get back to you on that."

"What's that mean?"

"It means there's been a change down here. The woman got away. I got Johnny down here now, and I need to think."

There was a pause.

"Johnny the pilot? Where'd he come from? What the hell happened?" Greta's scratchy voice asked finally. She sounded pissed.

"Never mind," he snapped as a dark cloud flashed across his face. Then he glanced at me and smirked. "It don't matter. Having Johnny Boy here will do just fine."

"I don't know, Charlie," she sounded doubtful. "Hang on. They're telling me something here."

I took the chance to chime in. "Charlie, what have you done? That's Greta on the radio?" I couldn't make sense of it.

"Yeah, didn't you hear her? We took the ship, man."

"What do you mean, you took the ship?" It was starting to dawn on me.

"She's got a forty four Magnum, and she knows how to use it. When I came down here she went to the bridge. It's funny how people start cooperating with a gun in their face."

I thought about the gasoline that Charlie had spread throughout the garage. A lot of it would evaporate, but there had to be a drainage system built into the ferry designed to collect spills in the bilge. That meant that the long lines of pipes and holding tanks throughout the lower area of the ship were filling with gasoline. Any spark would result in a massive explosion first in the vehicle bay. The ferry's own fuel tanks would go next. It would be one of those fireballs visible from outer space.

I knew I had to think of something quick. If the gas didn't explode on its own, the fumes could get us any minute. The only weapons I had were my voice and my brain, and they were both fading fast.

"Charlie, listen to me. I'm on your side. We need to work together."

"Bullshit. You came in here and let the bitch go. You're with them." The coke bottle orbs examined me like a mad scientist behind a microscope.

"Charlie, gimme a break. I'm not with them."

"Then why'd you let the bitch go?"

"Who?" I was stalling.

"The security bitch!" he roared at me and punched the back of my head with the fist at my collar.

"Okay, okay, yeah, Rainey, the security bitch. She's a friend of mine. From Seward. You don't need her now. You got me."

He thought about it. After a pause, his mind came back to his plan. "It would have been better with both of you. That way I could knife one of you and still have one left."

I gulped and stared at my shoes.

"To hurry them along, ya know? If they stop cooperating. Know what I mean?" he growled.

"I get it, I get it," I mumbled shaking my head and waving one hand trying to erase the idea.

"Now I only got you. And you're trying to help them find out what happened to those troopers."

He jerked the gun indicating where he wanted me to walk. The fumes were getting to both of us. He pushed me in front of him over to a dry part of the deck in the direction of the bow. Fresh air flooded in through a big vent above us in the ceiling.

We stopped by a low slung sports car. Charlie shoved me to the deck and sat on the hood above me. I thought about our conversation the night before. When I'd thought I was working him.

"You gotta believe me, Charlie. I'm on your side. Those troopers are not my problem. I don't care about them."

He stared at me and his eyes settled again into steady focus. "The man who doesn't care," he said slowly, studying me up and down. His arm relaxed slightly. I could see him remembering.

"That's right. I don't care about those troopers. They had me locked up until a little while ago. They think I killed them. I used those picks to escape. That's why I came in here."

We looked at each other. He was staring and trying to read me through half closed eyes. I met his gaze and tried to give him my best impression of a partner in crime. A guy he could trust to help him through a difficult time. What did they call that? A collaborator. Yeah, whatever that was. I tried to look like that. The fumes were making me loopy.

He keyed the mike. "Hey, babe. Johnny says they had him locked up. Check on that, would ya?"

"What do you mean, locked up?" Greta didn't get it.

"Just ask," he barked with an impatient edge in his voice.

A few minutes went by. The fresh air pocket was doing its job. My eyes quit stinging, but I could still smell the fumes nearby, and the air around the light bulbs in the ceiling had a strange color.

"Charlie?" Her voice came over the radio again.

"Go ahead," he keyed the mike.

"It's true. They had him chained in a supply room. That's why we stopped a while ago. The cops were almost here to pick him up. They know he shot those troopers."

My eyes went wide at the way she said it, and my mouth dropped open. She was obviously talking to an audience.

Charlie looked puzzled. Then he understood and he threw back his head and laughed. "Well, how about that shit?" He threw a mocking smile in my direction. "We'll be fine," he said into the mike and dropped it back to his chest.

Charlie laughed at me then. "Oh, that sweet Greta. Ain't she something?" More laughter. "You're screwed, dude. They're after you now, not us!"

"Not so fast, man. I didn't do anything to those troopers. Remember?" I glared at him in defiance.

"Yeah? What about Sponge Bob? Did they find the gun?" he asked.

I didn't answer but my eyes dropped. His face lit up and he howled. "Ha. Bingo. You are totally screwed, blued and tattooed."

"So then why did you do all this?" I snapped and waved my arm out at the pool of gasoline behind us.

That wiped the smile off his lips. His face went dark and he kicked at the deck.

"Damn it!" He stomped a few paces away, then stopped and studied the gun in his hands. "We shoulda waited."

"Waited for what?" I was stalling for time, anything to keep him talking, so I could think.

He whirled back toward me. "When they made that announcement telling me to go to the bridge, I thought I was finished. So I grabbed that security chick and came down here. I'd been planning to hijack the ferry all along. After you couldn't fly us out, it was our only way. If I'd just waited..." He kicked at the car beside us leaving a dent in the driver side door.

I watched Charlie and felt my head getting light. He was right. If they'd waited, I'd be in custody and on my way to Seward as the only suspect in a double cop murder. And Charlie and Greta could have hidden in that cabin all the way to Kodiak. And then disappeared.

I looked around in a nervous search. I pictured the door bursting open any moment and men with guns charging in and blasting away. My mind was racing to figure out what to do. Somehow I had to reason with him. He was acting like an animal backed into a corner, and as much as he tried to delude himself, he was no fool. We both knew it was only a matter of time.

"What are you going to do now, Charlie? The cops are coming, you know? The Coast Guard too probably. Maybe even the whole damned Navy. They'll be here any minute now."

"They don't dare try to stop us. I'll blow this place sky high." He grinned at me then. I didn't like the look on his face.

"So, then where are we going?"

"Hawaii," he said grinning at my expression. "She made the captain turn the ship for Hawaii," he laughed.

"You hijacked the Alaska State ferry? To Hawaii? What the hell, Charlie? That's over two thousand miles. This ferry can't make it that far. Over all that open ocean? With all these people on board?"

He chuckled shaking his head. "Yeah, I know, I know. So geography ain't Greta's best subject. What can I tell ya?"

"What about Tambourine?" I asked. I couldn't imagine what the kid was going through in the middle of this nightmare.

Charlie shrugged. "He's with Greta." He shook his head but didn't say anything else.

There was a Subaru nearby that had two yellow kayaks strapped to its roof. He was staring at them, studying them and trying to think.

I interrupted. "Charlie, what's to keep the cops from sneaking in here? You know they're going to try."

He tore his gaze away from the kayaks and looked at me. "There's only four doors into this garage," he said. "I've got them all tied off and barricaded except the one back there. We need to take care of that right now."

He pulled his jacket up over his nose and motioned for me to do the same. Then he took me by the collar again and marched me toward the door I'd come in. The same one Rainey had left through. The gas fumes instantly attacked our eyes and we were both squinting and wiping tears as we made our way in a blurry rush.

Still holding the handgun, he approached the door carefully and dug in a pocket for a ring of keys. I noticed he was keeping me in a position where he could fire either at me or the door. He kept me at arm's length in case I got brave. Or stupid, depending on your point of view.

When he had it locked he directed me to stack some nearby gas cans in front of the door. When he was satisfied he pushed me back to the fresh air bubble by the Subaru. We were both coughing and gasping for air. The back of my throat was on fire.

"Greta," Charlie rasped into the microphone and then dropped it back on his chest to wait for her answer.

It didn't take long. "What?" She sounded tense. Her voice echoed through the dim garage.

"Where are we now? There's no windows down here."

"We're in a fog bank, Charlie, straight south of Seward."

"What can you see?"

"Nothing, Charlie. It's just as thick as it was back on Taroka. And low too. I can't see anything outside."

"Okay, good. Shut her down. And the bilge pumps too. Like we talked about."

Two minutes later I almost fell over when I felt the rumble and vibration drop off below us again. Instead of plowing steadily through the ocean the ferry lurched and then gradually slowed. The engines were still running but at idle. Then they shut down too. The deck shuddered and everything got quiet.

"See?" he gloated. "I can make 'em do anything I want."

I waited for a minute, but then I had to ask. "Charlie, what's the plan? How are we going to get out of here?"

He didn't answer. I glanced sideways and saw his eyes working back and forth. Like he was searching for an idea. Then his eyes stopped and his head cocked toward me.

"I got demands," he said brightly.

CHAPTER
28

I closed my eyes and tried to hide my cringe. I was inside a ticking time bomb with a guy that was making it up as he went.

"Demands? Like what? You think they're going to just let you go?" I stared at him in wonder.

"Oh yeah. They got no choice. I could blow up the state ferry with hundreds of people on board. Imagine that headline." He grinned at me again. "And I got you."

I couldn't help but snort. "Me? That's not going to help you. Are you kidding? They'd like nothing better than to blow me away. Thanks to Greta they think I'm their cop killer."

He frowned and stared at me. His forehead wrinkled.

"Not only that, Charlie. Now they think we're working together. In their eyes, I'm not your hostage. I'm your partner. Threatening me won't bother them at all."

He glared at me and wiped at his nose with his gun arm. The pistol whipped through the air pointing in all directions. "Well, hell then, you're so smart, you figure it out."

Oh, Lord, I thought. This was getting more pathetic by the minute. "Why don't you just give up, Charlie?"

"NO!" he shouted standing up and waving his arms. "I can't." Then he slumped back against the car. "I promised Greta I'd get us out of this mess. She's counting on me, man. And I can't go to jail. I, I can't. I'd rather..."

"Okay, okay, take it easy. You said you had demands. What are your demands?" I was grasping at anything. Trying to keep him from going off the rails.

Another pause. The eyeballs were working again.

"Well, either they let us go or I blow this up and kill everybody."

I stared at him to see if he was serious. His eyes were steadier behind the thick lenses, but he was bouncing the gun up and down in his hand. Stillness was not Charlie's thing.

"And then what? If they let you leave, where are you gonna go?"

The gun stopped bouncing, but his eyes were still oscillating like ping pong balls in a bingo machine.

"I'm still working on that part," he said.

"That's your whole plan?"

He sniffed. "So far anyhow. I'm still thinking about it." He sounded a little pissy.

I looked down the row of vehicles toward the stern. I let Charlie think while I peered through the dim light toward the other exits.

"Okay, I got it," he said after a few minutes. "We'll get some more hostages, like women and children, and I'll make them bring out a chopper and pick us all up. Then the chopper takes us to Seward and we transfer to a jet. And then the jet takes us to some place far away. Like Brazil or Cuba. Yeah, Cuba, man, they take anybody."

He looked at me with a proud smile. The man had a plan.

"Charlie," I said as calmly as I could manage.

"What?"

"That's a really bad plan."

He glanced sideways at me and slumped. He looked hurt. "You got a better one?"

I twisted my mouth to the side, chewed on the inside of my cheek and thought about it. I didn't want to offend or upset him, but I needed some way to avoid a fiery death in an explosion. Not to mention being shot, stabbed, bludgeoned or drowned.

"Why don't you call upstairs and tell them you want to give up? Then you can plead insanity or something."

He snorted. "You saying I'm nuts?"

"No, no, of course not. It's just a strategy. You know, so a fancy lawyer could get you off with that. Not guilty by reason of insanity. I mean, look at this. Hijacking a ferry from Alaska to Hawaii? I think that could qualify."

He glared at me. "You're starting to piss me off, you know that?" He pointed the gun in my face and I could see him thinking about pulling the trigger.

I raised my hands in alarm staring into the open barrel. "Wait, Charlie, wait. Come on, think this through."

"I am thinking, and maybe you're right about something."

"About what?"

"About them not caring about you. So what do I need you for?"

Uh oh. I didn't want him thinking along those lines. My tongue was dancing back and forth trying to keep my teeth wet. Two desperate guys playing fools' gold poker.

"Well, uh, well, maybe I was exaggerating a little."

"About what?"

"Well, if they think I killed the troopers they want me real bad. Ya know?"

"Hmm, yeah, but if I killed you they might appreciate it. Saving them a lot of time and paperwork and stuff. Might give me a better deal."

"No, Charlie, that's not a good plan either. I'm pretty sure they want me alive." A ball of sweat ran down the middle of my back.

He smirked at me. "You're tap dancing pretty fast, aren't you?"

I ignored that. He was having too much fun at my expense. "C'mon, Charlie. We're in this together now. You'll have a better chance getting out of this mess with me. You need me."

"Oh really? What for?"

"For the jet, Charlie," I blurted. "You need a pilot to get us from Seward down to Cuba."

His eyes narrowed, looking at me and thinking about it. He folded his arms but kept the gun pointed in my general direction. I relaxed my hands from shielding myself into a more natural pose like I was explaining selling points to an interested buyer.

Before he could consider too many questions, I plunged ahead. "You don't want to trust whoever they send. You know the jet pilot will be a cop just waiting to get the drop on you. You need somebody you know. Somebody you can trust," I added hopefully, giving him my best 'Gee, I really want to help you' face.

Charlie's eyes steadied slightly, watching me closely. "And, and I speak a little Spanish too. That'll come in handy down there. You habla any Español, Charlie?"

"Una cerveza, por favor," he grinned.

I grinned back and started to breathe a little easier. I was about to continue when he cut me off with a wave of the gun. "Alright, I won't kill ya. Not yet anyway. Now shut up. I need to think."

I sat down on the hood of the car and looked around the vehicle bay. Nothing moved except my shaking knees. I could only imagine what was going on above us. A few minutes went by.

"What about Greta?" Charlie asked finally.

I glanced at him. His face had taken on a different look. The same expression he'd had when he was telling me about her the first time back on the island.

"What do you mean?"

"How is she going to explain her part in all of this?" he asked waving the gun toward the pool of gasoline shimmering nearby.

"Uh, well, she can say you forced her. Battered wife syndrome or something like that. They'd feel sorry for her."

"Oh, shut up, idiot. Greta pulling a gun on the captain and taking over the ferry? They don't like that kind of shit. Besides, she's been in the joint."

He saw my jaw drop and laughed. "Yeah, how about that? Looks can be so deceiving, eh? Let's just say she's had a colorful past."

I was floored. I thought back over the last two days. That face, those eyes, she'd had me in the palm of her hand. I would have done almost anything for another taste of those lips. This new picture was too strange to handle.

"Greta was in prison?" My mind was slipping into neutral. I couldn't make sense of it.

"Yeah, manslaughter, they called it. But she was framed. Or so she says."

Oh, brother, I thought to myself but didn't share. I closed my eyes. What next? I'd been thinking about getting cozy with her, and the whole time she'd been playing me like a hillbilly hick at the carnival.

I struggled to pull myself together. Now I was the one that needed a plan. I had to save myself. These two were way out there. I was seriously out of my league and I knew it.

"Okay, Charlie, maybe you can use her history to save yourself."

He knew where I was heading immediately. "NO! I'm no rat. Now shut the fuck up and let me think."

"Okay, okay, sorry. I'm just brain storming here."

So he wasn't totally out of his mind. I was going to have to be smarter than that. And I could tell he didn't like me being smart.

"This is a big mess," he muttered.

"Yeah, you're right about that," I agreed. I was trying to be as agreeable as possible. But not smart. Nobody like's a smart ass. Especially cornered guys with guns.

We sat in silence for a few minutes. He studied his fingernails. After a while he slid the handgun back into the shoulder holster inside his jacket. I was about to breathe easier until he pulled out the Ka-bar. I watched him from the corner of my eye, but he seemed to have forgotten me. He went to work with the tip of the giant blade digging grease from under his nails.

Time slipped by and I could feel the huge vessel bobbing gently in what must have been calm seas. I thought about all the people above us. Did they know what was happening? Were they panicking? And what was happening in the rest of the world?

I had no way of knowing who was talking to who, in spite of what I'd said to Charlie. I had to assume everybody was on alert. At least I hoped so. If Greta controlled the bridge, did that mean all communication from the ferry was cut off and nobody knew about it? I doubted that. This was major. A lot of people were going to be involved and soon.

I thought about telling Charlie that the Coast Guard had a station in Seward and I'd seen one of their cutters in port the last few days. I figured it was on the way toward us, and it wouldn't be long before we were surrounded by big burly men with weapons and bad tempers. But I decided to keep that idea to myself. Even if he wasn't already thinking about the same stuff, there was no need to fan the flames of his paranoia.

The sudden sound of his voice startled me. He was on the radio. "Greta, tell 'em we want a chopper."

A few moments went by. Then the handset crackled with static. "What?" Greta's scratchy voice came through barely recognizable, but I was able to picture her up in the bridge.

Everything I'd learned in the last few minutes had changed my image of her completely. What I saw now in my memory of those eyes wasn't the blue warmth or the sparkle. It was the ice. And bitter cold has a way of calming brainless lust.

"A helicopter, babe," Charlie explained. "You know, a whirlybird. To get us away from here."

There was a delay. "Did you hear me?" he prompted.

"Yeah, I heard you," she answered. "Hang on."

We waited. Then, she was back. "They say that's a problem, Charlie. All the choppers are away on missions.

And besides, they couldn't come into this fog anyhow, it's too thick."

I remembered the helicopter we'd heard trying to get into Taroka. They wouldn't try an approach without at least some visibility.

"They're feeding you a bunch of shit, Greta. Tell them they got thirty minutes."

After a pause, she came back on. "They say they'll work on it, but they can't promise thirty minutes. And they want to know, then what?"

"Then the chopper takes us to Seward to get on a jet. Tell 'em we want a jet too."

I could picture the law enforcement people listening to this and rolling their eyes. But what could they do? Charlie was holding all the best cards at the moment. Was he bluffing about lighting off the gas? There were a lot of kids on board. No one was going to gamble two hundred innocent lives to find out if a crazy guy was serious.

I didn't know what he would do either. I stood up and started to walk to the rear of the TransAm.

"Hey, where do you think you're going?" He reached for the gun inside his jacket.

I raised my hands. "Easy, man, easy. I need to take a leak." The beginnings of an idea was starting to blossom in my head.

"'You try to run for it, I'll kill you."

"Okay, okay, relax, Charlie. You want me to wet my pants?"

"Stay where I can see you."

He called Greta again. "What are they saying about the jet?"

With my back to him I relieved myself but at the same I reached inside my coat, found my pen and an old gas station receipt. Glancing over my shoulder I saw he wasn't watching. I scribbled quickly, then zipped up and walked back.

He looked up from listening to the stream of static from the handset. He eyed me over suspiciously, but I played it cool. "You getting hungry, Charlie?"

"I don't know. Yeah, I guess. Why?"

"I'm starved and I could use something to drink. These fumes are leaving a bad taste in my mouth." The fresh air bubble was keeping us alive but every now and then waves of the toxic vapors came through with sickening force.

He turned his head and spat. "Me too. I guess we could get them to bring something down." He patted the lump under his jacket with a grin. "I got the best credit card in the world right here."

I chuckled along with him. "Yeah, how about some sandwiches and beer? Call 'em, man. We gotta keep our energy up, you know?"

He picked up the mike and told Greta what we wanted.

"Tell them to leave the food on a tray outside that door," I suggested.

He looked me over carefully before making the call. "No funny stuff."

I raised my hands again and shook my head. "Don't worry about that. I'm the bad guy, remember? That's what the cops all think anyhow. Thanks to Greta."

He laughed and made the call. Talking about the food I saw him licking his lips. When he was finished talking to Greta he lay back on the hood of the car and put his hands behind his head. A strange calm seemed to come over him. Almost like he was kicking back and relaxing. A sense of being in control.

"Can you believe this shit?" he asked.

"What do you mean?"

"A couple of days ago I was fishing in Prince William Sound hauling in a huge halibut over by Montague Island. And now look at me. Life is weird. Randomly weird."

I nodded. "No kidding. This isn't the way I thought my weekend was going to turn out either."

"Is it the weekend already?" he asked. "Guess I lost track of time."

"Yeah, I think it's Saturday."

"Saturday night, eh? Did you have plans for a big night in Seward?" he snickered.

"Oh, you know, there's still lots of tourists around."

"Tourist chicks, huh? You do pretty good in town there, Mister Hot Shot Bush Pilot?"

"Who me?" I blew a puff of air. "Yeah, right."

Charlie was looking me over like he was trying to picture me in normal times. Then his gaze shifted toward the door. Then back to me.

"You know they're going to try something, don't you?" His voice took on a different tone. A resigned sounding tone filled with reality.

"What do you mean?" I asked realizing Charlie was thinking ahead. It was strange how his mind worked. Distracted and confused one minute, then right on the money the next.

"Greta and I just hijacked the Alaska State Ferry, man. That's never been done before."

I had to agree. "Yeah, okay. Especially if you take it to Hawaii. That would definitely be a first."

He laughed. A little too loudly, I thought. His eyes were rattling around, but at the same time he was leaning back on one elbow enjoying himself. We were keeping our eyes on each other like a man and a rattlesnake at the bottom of a dry well. He had to know I was looking for a way out.

A few minutes went by. Then he broke the silence. "You know, I was just like Tambourine when I was a kid."

"You're kidding. I can't see that."

"Oh yeah, it's true. I was puny and skinny and I always had these stupid glasses. Since I was five years old." He pulled them off and rubbed his eyes. "Kids were always picking on me. And my older brother was the football star, you know? He enjoyed pushing me around too."

"Well, a lot of us had shitty childhoods. What can you do?"

He nodded and put the glasses back on. "When I turned thirteen I started to grow. I got tall and gained weight. That changed everything. I think I got mean too. Settled a few scores, you know?"

I glanced over at him. He seemed in a world of his own, thinking back. Almost forgetting I was there and talking to himself.

"But my dad and my brother never quit treating me like a loser. They were the hot shot pilots with the airplane and all. I couldn't fly because of my eyes." He uncrossed and recrossed his ankles and looked at his watch.

"And now they're gone." He paused, his voice catching. "And so is my chance to show them they were wrong." He pushed the words out in a whisper and wiped his mouth with his sleeve. Then he fell silent.

I didn't know what to say. I could feel the ferry rolling slightly. Without being able to look outside all I could do was imagine the huge ship idle in the water surrounded by thick fog. I could sense the people upstairs above us and the dozens of law enforcement types that must be getting close.

"What about Tambourine, Charlie?"

"What about him?" His voice went cold.

"He needs a dad, you know?"

He sniffed loudly and spat off to the side. "Hell, I never had one. Mister Westridge was always too busy off somewhere being the big man. Tambourine'll have to figure it out for himself. Just like the rest of us." He wiped at his mouth again.

I thought about the little guy and his wide eyed empty stare. I wondered what he was doing.

Just then Charlie jumped to his feet and drew the gun. In a crouch he pointed the weapon at the door.

"I saw something."

"Where?" My pulse cranked to triple its previous rate.

"Through the window at the door. Someone's out there," he snapped. He grabbed the back of my collar and forced me to get in front of him.

I stared in the direction he was looking, and I saw it too. Through the round window in the door a shadow moved.

CHAPTER
29

We watched the door and saw a movement. Somebody was trying to get a look. I could see the rounded shape of a man's head.

"Greta!" Charlie screamed into the mike. When she didn't answer immediately, he shouted louder.

"GRETA!!"

"What?"

"They're at the door! Tell them to back off or I'm lighting this place up. Tell them!"

The shape disappeared.

"It's the food, Charlie," Greta called over the radio.

I started breathing again and turned to hold up my hands at Charlie. "It's okay, it's okay. Let's go get the groceries. We gotta move fast before the gas fumes get us."

He stayed in his crouch and motioned for me to go ahead of him. When we got to the landing at the top of the stairs, he took hold of my belt with one hand and pointed the gun at my head.

"Hey," I objected. "Don't you trust me?"

"Not an inch." He shoved me forward. "Okay, real slow. Move the gas cans."

While I worked to clear the doorway, Charlie kept hold of me and pointed the gun at the window.

"Okay, now open the door and get the food. And if you try anything or if anybody else tries anything, I'll blow your head off. You understand that?"

I nodded, bobbing my head up and down and holding my hands up. He shoved me against the wall and leaned over me to unlock the door. Even with smell of fuel around us he reeked of rancid sweat and bad breath.

When he moved back behind me again I moved up to look through the window. I peeked through, but just for a second, then Charlie pulled me back. I felt like a Chihuahua on a short leash.

"What did you see?"

"Nothing. Let me look again."

He let me move forward again. I stretched my neck to the glass and looked all around. Charlie pulled me back after a couple seconds.

"Who's out there?"

"Nobody, I couldn't see anybody, but there's a food tray down there."

"Okay, open the door real slow and look again. No funny stuff."

I dropped to my knees and pulled the door open a few inches. Fresh air rushed in, a welcome burst of relief. I tried to peek around the corner, but I couldn't move. I looked back at Charlie. The gun was only inches from my temple. His eyes were bouncing again. I wondered how he could focus with his pupils doing that frantic dance.

"C'mon, Charlie, give me a little slack."

Slowly, he relaxed his grip enough to let me move ahead. I peeked around the corner. The hall was filled with guys in dark clothes, baseball caps and weapons all pointed right at me. One of the hats said SWAT in gold letters on the front.

I tried to keep from reacting, but my head recoiled from instinct, ducking the bullet I was sure was coming my way. Charlie jerked me back through the door. Everything went quiet. No bullets, no noise, no nothing. The door still stood partially open and the crowd out there was still as death.

"Who's out there?" he demanded.

My collar was choking me and cutting off my breath. I had to gasp in some air before I could answer. "Let up, damn it! I can't breathe. It's just one guy from the kitchen," I lied in a loud voice. "And he's ten feet back."

"Why did you jump like that?" He had the gun in my face and I could see his trigger finger trembling. The gas fumes were bad.

"No reason, no reason. I'm just a little nervous, ya know?"

I could see his suspicious eyes working, worrying over the danger. But his mouth was moving too.

"There's huge sandwiches, Charlie. And beer. It's okay, alright? Can you take the gun out of my ear and let me move?" He thought about it, then licked his lips and nodded.

"Okay, out there," I announced. "I'm going to reach out for the food now. Stay back and be cool."

I heard some shuffling in the hallway. And a high pitched male voice said, "Okay, okay, I'm back."

I moved forward again and Charlie shifted his grip to my ankle. He held on tight and glancing back I could see the gun still pointed at my head. Leaning forward the metal edges on the bulkhead cut into my arms, but I pushed ahead and extended them through the door toward the tray.

Around the corner where Charlie couldn't see, I pulled the scrap of paper out of my sleeve and dropped it toward the group of men five feet away. Six serious faces and six gun barrels stared back at me. I gulped but managed to give them a thumbs up, then grasped the edge of the tray and pulled the food through the door slow and careful. There were two big sandwiches wrapped in white paper, two beer bottles laying on their sides and a bottle opener. I set it all down on the landing.

I nudged the heavy door shut with my shoulder. Charlie leaned over me again and relocked the door. He motioned with the gun for me to pick up the tray. While I took the food down the stairs he replaced the gas cans in front of the door and followed me.

When he rejoined me he kept his gun pointed at the door and waited several moments listening before he checked out the food. The group outside the door didn't make a sound. When Charlie was satisfied he held me in front of him again and walked us backwards back to the TransAm. He kept the handgun resting on my shoulder and pointed at the door. As we shuffled awkwardly together the fumes swirled around us. I had to concentrate with all my strength to balance the food tray with my coat up around my face and my eyes streaming.

When we finally got back into the better air, Charlie let go of my collar and sat down. It took us both a couple of minutes before we were breathing normal again. We stared at the door in silence. I halfway expected it to fly open for the Swat team to charge in, but it stayed shut and nothing moved.

I wanted to distract Charlie in case something moved over there. I could feel the mental gears grinding out in the passageway as they read my note and discussed their plan.

"This is going to taste great," I said picking up a sandwich. It was sliced turkey with lettuce and tomato in a thick roll. I took a huge bite wishing I had some mustard. Geez, listen to me, I thought. Probably eating my last supper and I'm craving condiments.

Charlie unwrapped the other sandwich and sniffed at it suspiciously. He opened the roll and examined the contents.

"You don't suppose they put anything in these, do you? Like poison or sleeping pills or something?"

I stopped chewing and thought about it. A possibility, I supposed. Screw it. I was beyond caring. I took another bite.

"Nah, I ain't worried about it. Tastes okay to me," I mumbled through a mouthful of bread and meat.

Charlie stared at me for a minute probably waiting to see if I fell over dead. Then he took a bite and swallowed. He was quiet, chewing and thinking.

"They're coming, aren't they?" he asked after a few more bites.

"Whattaya mean?" I looked at him and wiped mayonnaise off my beard with my sleeve.

"The cops. You saw something out there."

I focused on the food and tried to act normal. "Nothing special. Just a cook."

I could tell he didn't believe me. "But he had a gun. That's why I jumped," I added hoping it made a better story.

"Well, I know they're coming."

I stopped eating and set down the sandwich. "Yeah, I'm sure you're right. Shooting cops draws attention. No way around that."

I glanced at him. He was looking straight at me. "You know, don't ya?"

"Know what?" I wasn't sure where he was going.

"About the troopers." His eyes bored into me, and I looked away and shrugged but he didn't let up.

"You ever been in trouble?"

"No," I shook my head. "Nothing like this. You guys set me up really good."

Charlie let out a big sigh and waved one hand. "Yeah, but they'll figure it out. I know that. Greta and me both got records."

We sat in silence for a moment feeling the forces in space and time. Moving. Putting the pieces in place.

"Well, we both know I didn't shoot them," I said finally.

"Yeah, I know. I wonder if they'll believe me about what really happened."

I waited and glanced sideways at him. Something was changing.

"Greta did it," he finally muttered and took a big bite of sandwich.

I stared at him in disbelief. He was chewing slowly. Strands of lettuce hung out of his mouth until he noticed them and stuffed them back in with one dirty finger. He swallowed and reached for one of the beer bottles. First he inspected it for signs of tampering, but it looked normal. Ripping the cap off with the opener, he handed it to me and motioned for me to drink. He watched while I took a big swallow, then he shrugged and opened the other bottle.

"Drink up, man," he said. "Heinekens. This is the good stuff."

While he tilted the bottle back for a long pull I looked down to see where he'd left the bottle opener. It was one of the old style with a pointed can opener on one end and a flat bottle cap opener on the other.

"Greta? Greta did what?" It seemed like he wanted to talk and I wanted to let him.

"Yeah, I know. It surprised me too," he said shaking his head.

I waited again. Possibilities were flickering through my mind. I was starting to see a way out, but Charlie's voice was taking on a hopeless tone. With nothing to lose, what would keep him from setting off the bomb? And why was he telling me all this? Why now?

"Yeah, she kind of lost it that afternoon," he said finally. "We got in a big argument and I shoved her. That's when she called the cops. She was so pissed, she wanted me locked up. She cooled off later, but goddamnit, she'd already set the whole mess into motion."

"So there wasn't any fishing guide?" I asked.

"Nah," he chuckled. "I couldn't believe you all fell for that story."

I didn't tell him that I'd been doubtful about it for a while. "So the troopers didn't leave in a boat?"

"Nah, that was bullshit too. Greta plugged the first one as soon as we got them separated. I couldn't believe it. As soon as he turned his back she pulled a gun and nailed him in the back of the head."

I was thinking back trying to remember the sequence of events that first night. It didn't sound right. Different from what Daniels told me. Charlie was watching me again, a smile tugging at the corners of his mouth. I wasn't going to call him a liar.

"That other guy ran like crazy, so we went after him. We were set up on the hill waiting. After a while he came back running around down below us like Rambo or something. We couldn't see much in the dark but then he turned on a flashlight. You were there too, right? Wasn't that you flopping around in the ditch?"

"You know it was. You damn near shot me." I wasn't seeing the humor.

"Hey, no offense, Johnny. Don't take it personal. We didn't know they had a pilot waiting for them. We thought one of the troopers was the pilot."

"So what happened to Daniels?"

"The other trooper? Ah, he was trying to sneak around on us, but we could hear him coming a mile away. He wasn't much of a woodsman, ya know?"

I didn't say anything. I watched him and waited. As long as he was spilling all the details, I wasn't going to slow him down.

"The funny thing is, I wasn't trying to shoot you guys. I figured we could tie him up and have you fly us out of there. But Greta had a different idea. She hid behind a rock and when Daniels came crawling by, she plugged him."

I was trying my best to picture that scene in the woods. It fit with what I remembered, but Greta? I hadn't seen her handle a gun so the story didn't work for me.

"You think they'll believe me, Johnny? All the killing wasn't my idea. Greta did it all."

"Greta? Really? She doesn't seem the type."

"Yeah, I know. But there's a lot about her you don't know."

I let that idea hang there between us for a while. I was busy thinking about how to get out of there alive. I needed Charlie to keep thinking they had a chance. If he lost hope it could get real ugly. And I needed him thinking I was trying to help.

After a few moments I said, "Well, you won't need to explain anything if we get out of here and fly down to Cuba." I tried to keep my voice neutral and upbeat.

He looked sideways at me and chuckled. "I know. I'm just working on my backup plan, ya know? Just in case."

I took a deep breath. And another swig of beer. Then another. I checked the bottle and it was already over half empty. I wished we'd ordered a whole case. I could feel my heart tapping against my rib cage, reminding me how close

I'd come to joining those dead troopers. I flashed on an image of their two dead bodies. Rankin with his round blond head bloodied. And Daniels, mud covered, with a bullet hole in his forehead. I could picture my own face right beside them. Our open lifeless eyes unfocused and blank. My body shook with a sudden chill and I drained the rest of the bottle.

The sandwiches were gone. Charlie crumpled the wrappers into a ball and tossed it to the middle of the vehicle lane. It landed in a thin wet layer of gasoline. Then he leaned back against the hood of the TransAm again looking toward the doorway.

I did the same and tried to relax. The beer on an empty stomach was giving me a slight buzz. I've always been a lightweight. If only I had five or ten more I could put some real distance between me and all this reality. I wondered about Brandy and hoped she was somewhere safe. Rainey too.

Mostly I thought about the group of men outside the door. Something was going to happen and soon. There was only the one way in and Charlie had it covered. Besides, his threat to light off the gasoline had everyone paralyzed. I knew that wouldn't last. The beer was having another effect as well. The fear was subsiding. I could feel myself getting ready to make a move.

Charlie keyed the radio mike. "Greta, where's the chopper?"

"I'm checking on it, Charlie. Relax."

"Don't tell me to relax," he snarled at her. "How long do ya think I can sit down here like this?"

"Don't yell at me," she snapped. "It's no picnic up here either."

Charlie jumped to his feet. "Oh, get real. They're stringing you along, you know that, don't ya?"

I glanced sideways at the food tray and while Charlie and Greta were squabbling I reached over, palmed the can opener and slipped it in my side pocket.

Greta changed the subject. "They're saying the chopper is almost here, Charlie, but when it comes, how are we going to do this? It's getting dark now."

"Uh, from the top deck, I guess. Yeah, when it gets here, have it land up there."

There was silence from her end. I figured that idea was going to be a problem. I looked toward the small openings where outside light had leaked in before. No light now. Only a few overhead fluorescents were keeping us out of the dark.

Her voice came back in a couple of minutes. "No can do, Charlie. They say the chopper can't land up there. Too many antennae in the way."

"Well, screw it. It's the Coast Guard, right? They can haul us up with their rescue cables then. In that basket thing they use. I seen it on TV."

"Hang on a minute, Charlie." A man's deep voice broke in over the radio's scratchy speaker.

Charlie's forehead wrinkled in confusion. "Who's this?" he demanded.

"My name's Larry, Charlie. I'm over here at the doorway and I'm not armed."

CHAPTER
30

Charlie's head spun toward the door in alarm. Then he scrambled to the rear of the TransAm leaving me at the front. He leaned across its trunk and pointed the gun at me.

"Get back here," he barked.

I joined him at the rear of the car. "Put your hands up, damn it!" he ordered. I obeyed.

When I got there he grabbed my jacket and held me in front of him. Then he pointed the gun at the door.

"Stay out! I swear I'll set off the gas!" he shouted into the microphone.

We looked and saw a hand at the round window where we'd picked up the food. It waved at us, then a face appeared. It was a clean shaven guy with a wide forehead and no hat. He had a head of thick brown hair, heavy eyebrows over intelligent eyes and a serious expression. He was holding both hands up beside his head. He held a radio in one hand. The other one was empty. I wasn't sure, but I thought it looked like one of the six faces I'd seen earlier.

"Where'd you come from?" Charlie growled at him on the radio.

"I was on the ferry as a passenger. But I work for the state. I'm a state trooper."

Charlie's face went stiff. His jaw clenched and unclenched. "Where's my chopper?" he demanded.

"It's on the way," came the answer. "How many of you are in there?" he asked.

Charlie ignored the question. "How about the jet?"

"They're working on it, Charlie. But it's going to take more time. You have to understand. We're getting one from Anchorage, but getting the crew and fuel and everything. It's taking a while to arrange."

He had a calm clear voice like a radio announcer. I was guessing he was a negotiator of some kind. He seemed to know what he was doing. That reassured me and worried me at the same time. I doubted he'd been a passenger.

How did he get on board? Probably along with the other guys loaded for bear out in the hallway. They must have come from another boat. Like a special ops team boarding a hijacked oil tanker.

"Then listen up, cop." Charlie's voice took on a tone of authority. "I've got this place flooded with gasoline and I can add more anytime I want. You screw with us and I'll flick my Bic and send us all to hell. You got it?"

Larry nodded rapidly and held up one hand in acknowledgement. "Take it easy, Charlie. Let's talk about this. Why are you doing this?"

Charlie hesitated. I could almost hear the inner debate in his head. He couldn't talk about the real reasons without admitting things he didn't want to reveal. But he hadn't thought of a better explanation either.

"It doesn't matter why. Just do what we tell ya," he said. "And I got a pilot in here with me too. Right here in front of me." He shook me by the collar in case Larry couldn't see me standing there. "He'll be the first one to get it if you don't do what I say."

"C'mon, Charlie. We know you two are working together in there."

"We? What do you mean we? Who else you got out there?" Charlie's voice took on a tremor.

"I meant all the folks on the way. You're going to be surrounded here pretty soon. The Coast Guard and the Navy and every trooper in the state are on the way. You're not going to get away with this."

My eyes squeezed shut hearing the negotiator's assessment of me. Did he really think that? Or was it a ploy? I glanced back at Charlie. He looked confused and scared thinking about the approaching armada. His eyes were rattling. He looked tired too.

I looked back at the negotiator. I knew what his job was. He was a cop. The gasoline was the main problem. He needed to keep a boat full of people from exploding like a bomb. He was looking us over and calculating. He wanted us face down and in handcuffs. With no one hurt if possible. But if that couldn't happen, he wanted us dead. Whatever it took to defuse the bomb.

They couldn't just charge in blasting away. Couldn't toss in a flash bang grenade either. And they needed to keep Charlie from taking a shot. Any of those things would set off the gas. Then there was me. What did they really think about me? Good guy or bad guy? Had my performance at the doorway changed any minds? And what about the note?

"So what have we got here, Charlie?" The cop's voice came over the radio.

Charlie scowled and keyed the mike. "Go away. I don't want to talk to you. Talk to Greta. She's in charge of this."

"I'd rather talk to you, Charlie. How are you guys breathing in there? You need anything?"

"We're fine. Get lost. Just get the chopper out here."

"Looks like a lot of gas in there, Charlie."

"You're damn right there's a lot of gas. So back off, or I'll set it off."

"Okay, okay, Charlie. You don't want to do that. I'm just worried that the fumes are going to kill you in there."

"Yeah, right. You're so concerned about us. Quit stalling. We got air," he said waving his gun at the vent above us.

"There's a problem with the chopper, Charlie. The fog's so thick it can't get to us. Can't we work something out here?"

"Like what?"

"Well, I don't know. We're trying to understand why you're doing this, Charlie. What is it you want?"

"You know what we want. We want out of here."

"All of you?"

"Yeah, all of us. Me and Greta and my kid. And the pilot here too."

Charlie jerked me by the collar. "What's he up to?"

I shook my head and thought about it. Maybe they were evacuating all the passengers and crew to lifeboats. We couldn't tell from where we were. I wondered if Greta was still in control up top.

"Can I talk to him?" I asked Charlie.

"No. Shut up," Charlie snapped at me. "I gotta think." From his position he could smash my head with the pistol any time he wanted.

I gulped and studied my shoes. We needed more information. The cops were up to something. They were setting the stage, and we didn't have a clue what was going on.

Charlie must have been thinking the same thing. He was no dummy.

"Greta, what's happening up there?" There was a long pause. The more time went by, the faster Charlie's eyeballs clicked back and forth.

"GRETA!" he screamed into the mike.

Then she came on. "It's okay, Charlie. I was just away from the radio for a second."

"What's happening up there?"

"Nothing, Charlie. The captain and I are doing fine. We got some food too," she said in a sing song high pitched voice.

"What about Tamby?"

"He's sleeping under the counter here."

I saw Charlie take a deep breath and let it out in a sad sigh. "You got everything under control then?"

"Yes, we're good up here. How about you?" Her voice sounded oddly unconcerned to me. I could feel my eyebrows squeezing together trying to make sense of it. I suddenly felt a cold chill like ice worms creeping all over my neck and back.

"I don't like it. It's too quiet," Charlie continued. "Something's happening. Are there any boats around you?"

"No, I'm watching on the radar here," Greta answered. "There's nothing close by. I told them to keep everything away."

"You been listening to this guy talking to us? He's up to something. Watch your ass up there."

"Charlie," Larry broke in again. "Honestly, I'm by myself out here. You're holding all the cards. You got all the control. All I'm trying to do is get this all straightened out. Then we can all have a glass of brandy ... and relax."

Charlie didn't like being interrupted. "Sure you are. Like you're just going to let us go. The only answer is to get that chopper out here. Where is it?"

"Hang on, I'll check."

A glass of brandy? That was a weird thing to say. I glanced back at Charlie but it didn't look like he'd heard it. Was that a message to me?

"Charlie, I got an idea," I said over my shoulder.

"What?"

"Did Greta sound alright to you?"

He thought about it. "I guess. Why?"

I took a breath and plunged in. "She sounded different to me, Charlie. I think she was lying to you."

He pulled tight on my collar hauling me back against him. "What do you mean?" he growled in my ear. His breath seared my nostrils. A rank combination of gasoline, beer, sourdough bread and fear.

"I don't know, man. She sounded different to me. Do you think she could be making her own deal up there?"

That stopped him. He relaxed his grip on my collar and pushed me away as if he was repelling both the idea and anybody close to him. But I could tell he was thinking about it. Was he on his own now? Had she pulled a fast one?

It was a gamble, but I was hoping he'd start thinking she'd abandoned him. Then maybe he'd let me be more of a partner. Giving me a chance to make a move.

I turned to face him. "Look, Charlie. If she's ratting you out, you and I can still get out of here. You've got the control down here. Use me as your hostage and get us to Seward. I'll fly you to Cuba, no problem."

He stared at me with his mouth hanging open, breathing heavily. His eyes ran over me like a swarm of red ants.

"Greta?" he called on the handset. His voice was a question mark, dripping with a nervous tremor.

She didn't answer.

The negotiator's voice broke in. "Chopper just left Seward. It won't be long now, Charlie."

"WHERE'S GRETA?" he snarled into the mike.

"Uh, I don't know, Charlie. She's up on the bridge, I guess."

"WHAT HAVE YOU DONE WITH HER?" he thundered.

"Take it easy, Charlie, I don't know. Maybe the battery went dead on her handset. I'll find out. Stand by."

"Get her back on here or I'm blowing it. THIS IS NO BULLSHIT!"

Charlie dropped the mike and gawked at me. His gears were whirling trying to figure out what was going on. I shrugged my shoulders at him. I only had the one card. I took a breath and played it.

"That's what I was afraid of, man. I think she's given us up." I kept my voice calm.

In a flash he lunged forward and grabbed me by the front of the jacket. "SHUT UP!" he screamed in my face. Then he spun me around and slammed me against the car.

"You think I'm some kind of IDIOT?" He pressed the handgun into the back of my head forcing me against the car and using his other hand he reached into my jacket pocket and pulled out the can opener.

He held it in front of my face, the sharp end of the tool just an inch from my eye. "You think I missed that little trick, asshole? And now you're trying to be all buddy buddy?" He leaned his body weight against me forcing the gun hard against my skull.

"Thought you'd get the drop on me and then open up my neck like a BEER CAN? I oughta..." Spittle sprayed the back of my neck. Then he clubbed me on the side of the head with the gun sending me to the deck in a heap. Charlie towered over me shaking with adrenalin and reached for the Ka-bar with his free hand.

"Message from Greta, Charlie," Larry's voice interrupted.

Charlie grabbed up the microphone. "Put her on," he demanded.

"Uh, she says there's been a change in plans. She doesn't want to talk to you."

Charlie froze in place. My head was ringing with the shock and I could barely see his face wondering how I knew what Greta was up to. Looming over me his breath was ragged, and his eyes flicked back and forth between me and the handset. It seemed like minutes before he could speak again but it was probably only a moment or two. Then he keyed the mike.

"Greta?" he called plaintively, his voice a pitiful empty echo. There was no answer.

After a long moment, Larry came back on. "Charlie, it's over. Why don't you give it up?"

"You're lying to me, aren't you, cop? She wouldn't bail on me."

"It's no bull, Charlie. Look, I'd like to work this out with you. It's just us now. Greta's cooperating with us now, but we need to defuse the situation and get everybody safe again. Okay?"

Charlie's face was full of doubt. Betrayal and defeat sat heavily on his shoulders. The one ally he'd been counting on had split. Surrounded and running out of options, his feet moved first one way, then the other. He stared at the microphone like it was a handful of dog shit.

He dropped the handset in disgust and pulled off his glasses. He laid them on the roof of the car and rubbed his eyes squeezing the bridge of his nose and taking deep breaths. Without the heavy glasses on his face he looked smaller and vulnerable. Like a nearsighted giraffe blinking and squinting in a high wind.

I was laying on my belly with my face on the deck. The metal under me was cold and damp, and the side of my head and neck throbbed with shooting pains. I struggled to keep my eyes open and looked around to see if I could crawl under the car but it was too low.

Charlie noticed my movements and put his glasses back on. Then he put his foot on my back pinning me in place. He wiped his nose with his sleeve and picked up the mike. He started talking, his voice calm and deadly. Something had changed.

"Now listen up, cop. I'm in charge here and this whole freaking tub will go off like a Roman candle if you screw up. Bring that blond security bitch back down here now."

My scalp went cold and the ice worms started down my back again. "You don't need her, Charlie," I said to him.

"Yes, I do. When the chopper gets here, we're going to go up to the top deck. She's going to be my hostage, so I can get to the chopper. You think they're going to let me just walk up there after I leave the gasoline down here?"

He had a point. The whole reason they were talking to him was the threat of an explosion. Once he walked away from it they'd overpower him in an instant.

"But you've got me, Charlie. You can use me for that."

"Ha, you must be kidding. They don't give a shit about you. They think you're with me. They'll pop you with their first shot." He smirked at me. "You had to go play hero, didn't you?"

His words knifed into me like a cold steel blade. He was right. I felt a tunnel of darkness close in around my face. My heart started to pound. I could feel it hammering in my chest.

"I didn't understand that last part, Charlie. Who do you mean?" Larry's voice came over the radio.

"That blond security woman. I had her down here with me at first. Her name's Rainey. Get her down here now."

There was a pause.

"NOW!" he screamed into the mike.

Larry held his hands up at the window again. "Okay, okay, take it easy, we're working on it."

Then Charlie leaned down to me and said, "The stakes are climbing, man. If things don't start happening soon, it's gonna get ugly fast. And you know what else, Johnny? You just became expendable. What do I need you for?"

I started panting. My teeth were clacking together, and my mind was racing. I caught an image of Rainey with duct tape around her face. I couldn't let that happen again. I took a deep breath, twisted to the side and shoved Charlie's foot off my back. The sudden move caught him off guard and he stumbled backwards. I rose to my feet as he regained his balance and leveled the gun at me.

"Hold it right there, jerkoff," Charlie snarled at me like a pit bull with spittle dripping from its jaws.

I looked straight at him with all the resolve I could muster. Rolling my shoulders and shaking my legs I ignored him and tried to loosen up my stiff muscles and knees. Charlie straightened his arm extending the barrel at my face but just out of reach. I gave him a look of contempt and without a word I turned and headed for the doorway.

"Hey, stop. Where the hell you going?" Charlie pointed the gun at my head.

I kept walking. "You're not going to shoot me, Charlie. You'll set this whole place off." I was surprised to hear the calm in my own voice. Calm was the last thing I was feeling.

"Stop right there, asshole," Charlie hissed at me, glancing over at Larry.

I stopped out where the negotiator could see me easily from his place in the window and turned to face Charlie with my arms held high.

He was tracking me across the floor, his arm straightened. I imagined his finger tightening and going white on the trigger.

I thought he might fire at any second, but I didn't care. I was beyond caring. I had slipped into a different zone. A place where my own safety didn't matter anymore. The only thing I could think about was how to stop this animal. I couldn't let him hurt people that I cared about.

On every battlefield on the planet, soldiers fight to the death. They do it for country, they do it for religion. Some even do it for money. But more than anything, soldiers fight for each other.

Fight for me, I'll fight for you. We're in this together. All for one and one for all. Warriors.

I knew if I let him pull Rainey back into this, I'd never be able to live with myself. It was clear as a bell. And if she got hurt or killed, life wouldn't mean a damn thing to me ever again.

I'd gotten her into this mess in the first place. The whole thing was my own stupid fault. If I'd just let the ferry sail away from Chenega without me, none of this would have happened.

I could have stayed with the airplane on Taroka and let it all play out without me. But no, not me. Not Johnny Wainwright, self appointed local hero. What was wrong with me anyhow? Why couldn't I leave well enough alone? Playing the hero and putting Rainey at risk? It sent me right over the edge. Thanks, Charlie.

But, to hell with it, this wasn't therapy hour. I had a maniac on my hands. It was him or me. And the time was now. If I survived I could make an appointment with Doctor Phil.

I glanced toward the door and saw it open slightly. They were going to do something. Something needed to happen, and it was up to me. There wasn't going to be a lot of time.

I stared hard at Charlie. He waved the gun at me to come back to him. "No, Charlie! Give it up, you freaking LOSER!" I shouted as loud as I could glancing toward the door.

I started backing away, but Charlie moved fast then, running at me. His eyes were crazy. I jumped away and dodged his clutches, and I saw his left hand go in a jacket pocket. It came out holding a light green plastic lighter.

Out of the corner of my eye I saw movement. Two dark shapes bent over low came through the doorway scattering gas cans in all directions. They rushed down the stairs and disappeared behind the big red pickup.

Charlie saw them too. His lips curled into a snarl and he turned to aim in their direction. I took another step backward but smacked into a camper shell with a loud clunk. Charlie turned and lunged at me again swinging the handgun at my head. I leapt to the side and ducked my head, twisting wildly to avoid the impact.

He missed me, hitting the camper wall instead. He cursed and dropped the gun. It clattered loudly on the metal deck and disappeared under a car, and Charlie fell to his knees in front of me grabbing after it. I kicked hard at his hand and saw the lighter go flying. He looked stunned, but I didn't wait. I groped at his face with both hands and caught hold of the heavy glasses. Ripping them from his eyes I turned and ran.

He screamed and scrambled to his feet, but I didn't look back. I grabbed the front corner of the car parked beside me and hurled myself around the corner. I slammed his glasses to the deck and stomped them as hard as I could. Pieces of glass flew in all directions.

I could feel him coming. Past the front of the car by then, I threw myself to the deck and crawled under a blue Ford Expedition in the next row. I heard Charlie's rasping breath and footsteps slapping the wet floor on the other side of the car. They were coming my way.

I was splashing on my belly in a shallow pool of gasoline. The fumes and the foul liquid assaulted my eyes, but I kept scratching and crawling to get under the car. My fleece jacket caught on something and held me in place.

I saw Charlie's feet about to turn the corner above me when suddenly the lights went out. In an instant we were swallowed by total darkness.

CHAPTER
31

An inky black blanket dropped all around us. It was pitch dark, but I could hear Charlie's shoes just three feet away shuffling around the corner. I scuttled sideways and rolled on my side to get my body completely under the Expedition before he stepped on me.

His feet stopped just inches away splashing gasoline into my face. Whatever my jacket was snagged on wouldn't give, but I didn't dare move anyhow. Any rip or tear or any other sound would give me away. My eyes were on fire. I held my breath and squeezed my eyelids shut trying to force some tears out before the burning made me scream.

I could hear Charlie's ragged breathing. The gas had to be killing him too. His feet couldn't stay still as he peered around blindly in the dark and tried to figure out where I'd gone. Without the gun or the lighter he needed me in his hands as his last defense. We were both sensing the same thing. Dangerous men moving through the dark. Closing in on us.

Charlie moved toward the back of the vehicle and stopped again to lean against the fender. From under the Expedition I could hear the scurrying sounds of boots on the wet deck across the open garage. Then the quiet was shattered by another gas can tumbling down the metal stairs at the exit.

The Expedition rocked as Charlie pushed off and his footsteps splish splashed away from me into the void. I reached around to get my jacket untangled and let myself breathe again blinking hard and fast.

Rolling onto my back I finally pulled loose and lay still to listen. Everything had gone quiet. I'd lost my hat and my head was spinning with a woozy tilt. The gasoline was getting to me. My coat and pants were soaked in it, and I could feel the cold irritation as it ate at my skin.

I thought about crawling toward the exit, but that meant crossing the open lane between the vehicles. Without being able to see I'd have to feel my way and there were three killers in the dark waiting for me to move.

Charlie was nearby somewhere, probably only a car or two away. I was hoping the darkness and smashing his glasses would give the cavalry a chance to move in. His lenses were so thick, I didn't think he could see much without them. But my eyes weren't doing any better, the fumes and the tears made everything a painful dark blur.

I cocked my head to one side trying to locate Charlie. I was keenly aware of the other people as well. The newcomers. These guys were trained professionals. The one glimpse I'd had of the SWAT team in the hallway told me all I'd needed to know. They wore black. A couple of them had on black ski masks. Only their eyes had been visible. Intense and sharply focused. They were trained to overpower armed men with their bare hands, and if necessary, to kill.

I heard the crunch of glass underneath a shoe. Had to be Charlie stepping on his own glasses. Maybe twenty feet away. I took the opportunity to move. I was hoping to find an unlocked door or window in a nearby vehicle. Some place to hide. Now that I was away from Charlie's gun in my face,

I was hoping to squirrel myself away somewhere until it was over. One way or another.

I crawled out from under the Expedition, stood up slowly and moved two cars down where I remembered a pickup camper was parked. I was moving toward the door where the negotiator was standing, but I kept crouched down in case a sniper with night vision goggles was looking for me. When I reached the camper I felt my way around to its back door. It was locked. I reached for my picks, then I remembered that Charlie had taken them.

I heard a distant burst of static in the dark. It came from Charlie's radio sounding like he'd moved to the far corner of the vehicle bay. My hand brushed against a vertical object next to the camper's door handle. I felt it over and realized it was the access ladder for the roof of the camper. My own camper back in Seward had one just like it. Without a moment's hesitation, I climbed.

When I reached the top I spread out and crawled forward making myself as flat as possible. There was an air conditioning unit on top, a vent and some kind of antenna folded over for travel. I settled in on my belly beside the air conditioner to wait. Cupping my hands around my face I tried to block out the gasoline fumes.

After a few moments I rolled slightly and peeked out over the edge of the roof top. The darkness was gradually lightening as my eyes adjusted. At least it wasn't pitch black anymore. I could see the vague shapes of the vehicles below me. And something moved.

I froze. The crouched shape slid with smooth movements from behind one vehicle to another, moving toward me. It had to be a cop. He was working his way in front of the vehicles parked face in against the wall. I was guessing his partner was doing the same thing along the other side of the garage.

I pulled myself back to the center of the camper roof and lay as still as I could. No more peeking over. If I could see them, they could see me. But up where I was, over eight feet above the floor I was hoping I was out of sight.

I tried to play it all out in my head. What was going to happen next? Were the cops going to hold fire? Surely they knew that bullets flying around in here would set off the gas. Did Charlie have another lighter? Did he find the one I'd kicked away?

The cops were being cautious, but I could sense them in the dark. Moving through the black ink, feeling their way. Nerve endings tensed to detect any motion, any sound.

The one nearby me moved closer. I could hear a faint rustling of cloth rubbing together and rubber soled shoes carefully padding one after another on the wet metal deck. And I heard the leather on his equipment belt squeak just like I'd heard the troopers squeaking when they'd climbed in my plane.

The camper moved slightly as if the cop was resting against it and peering around the corner. If I'd leaned over the side of the camper I could have reached down and touched him. That's what my ears told me anyhow, but I wasn't moving for anything.

I squeezed my eyes shut again and felt hot tears trying to wash out traces of gasoline. The acrid vapors tore at my throat and the inside of my nose. I fought off the urge to sneeze.

I'd lost track of Charlie. Did he find the gun? He had to know the cops were almost on him. And he must have known that firing at them would be his last act. Unless he was ready to kill himself and Greta too, I couldn't see him firing any shots. But when he was finally cornered, who knows what he might do? I tried not to think about burning alive in a metal dungeon.

Several seconds passed in total silence before I heard movement again. Across the garage back where I'd heard the static, there was a thrashing sound, like feet kicking and a grunt and a muffled yelp. My imagination went wild trying to make sense of the sounds.

The camper rocked again slightly as I felt the creeper below me move away into the dark. Footsteps and squeaks faded into the distance and minutes went by. Lying there on the camper roof exhaustion pulled at my eyelids. Above the battle and hidden from view I was close to passing out from the fumes. Only two things were keeping me awake. Pain and terror. I tried to move my head slowly, carefully stretching the tortured tendons in my neck while listening to tiny clumps of calcium crunching inside and echoing inside my skull.

"Charlie, are you there? We need to talk," Larry's voice called out into the black cavern. His voice sounded different in person instead of over the radio handset. And he sounded worried.

Charlie didn't answer.

"What about you, Wainwright?" he called again. "You in here?"

I didn't answer either. I didn't trust anybody. Silence in the dark was my only friend.

"Charlie?" Larry tried again louder this time. His voice was coming from the same corner where I'd last seen him in the doorway. Still no answer.

"Team, check in," Larry said then. As much as he was trying to send out the command in a calm voice, I thought I heard it quaver.

"Johnson's over here, Sergeant," called a new voice low and in the distance by the far vehicle door. It sounded like a person crouched behind a vehicle near the floor. No one else spoke.

"Miller?" Larry called in the dark. No answer.

A few moments went by. "Miller?" Larry called out again.

Then a rasping sarcastic snarl broke through the stillness. "Miller's not going to be checking in."

It was Charlie's voice and it sounded like he was somewhere between me and Johnson. I rolled to my side and looked in that direction.

Suddenly the lights came back on. Charlie was standing in the middle of the garage in the open lane between two rows of cars. He was facing in my direction. His bloody t-shirt was pulled up over his nose and face and a pool of gasoline all around him shimmered in the dull glow of the overhead lights. He raised his arms and held them out in a strange posture like he was beckoning a large audience. I could see his chest heaving and the t-shirt slipped down to reveal his raggedy beard and open mouth panting.

There was a dark shape crumpled on the deck at his feet. Charlie was holding the blood soaked Ka-bar knife out from his body in his right hand. His left arm extended from his side, his hand clenched in a fist. Charlie's chest was covered with blood. So was his right arm. The huge knife dripped heavy red drops to the deck.

I tore my gaze from Charlie's odd pose to the body at his feet. It had to be Miller. Thick red fluid spread slowly in the puddle of fuel at Charlie's feet.

Behind him in the far corner I could see Larry on the metal stairs in front of the door where we'd picked up the food. Closer to me Johnson was leaning over a car hood twenty feet from Charlie with a handgun leveled straight at Charlie's chest. He was dressed in black and had a ski mask covering his head and neck. Even his hands were covered in tight black gloves.

I squinted and tried to see what was in Charlie's hand, but if there was a lighter in there it was concealed.

"Nobody move," Charlie warned. "I swear to God I'll light this place up."

He shuffled backwards and turned trying to look toward both policemen at the same time. I could tell his eyeballs were rattling wildly back and forth but without his glasses he was only guessing at the shapes around him. His head whipped back and forth as he tried to keep track of both adversaries.

"Let me take him, Sarge," called Johnson. "I got the shot." His voice sounded like heavy sheets of sandpaper scraping together in a barely controlled rage. He moved out from behind the car and crept in a deadly crouch toward Charlie, his dark lethal shape moving steadily like a snake through the weeds. The handgun was pointed straight at Charlie's chest.

"Stop right there, goddamn it!" Charlie's voice raised in a tight shriek. "I'll do it, I swear." He thrust his closed fist toward the dark crouched man only ten feet away.

"Hold up, Johnson," came Larry's voice, his calm shredded. "Any shot could set this off."

"What are we going to do here, Charlie?"

"You're going to get me a goddamn helicopter, that's what you're going to do, or I set this place off."

"Are you really ready to die, Charlie?" Larry's voice was back in control. He was standing on the landing in

front of the closed door. Through the round window I could
see two other faces crowded in and trying to watch. Their
expressions were tense and focused on the standoff in front
of them.

"If that's what it takes, you bet I am. Are you?" Charlie
asked. His knife hand was shaking, and he wiped at his
face with his other hand trying to fight off the fumes. When
that didn't work he pulled his t-shirt up to cover his mouth
and nose again.

"You'd take two hundred people with you, including
Greta and Tambourine? Don't you care about them?" Larry
called.

I crawled to the edge of the camper roof. I couldn't keep
quiet any longer.

"Yeah, what about that, Charlie?" My voice startled
him. His head jerked in my direction, but he didn't want to
take his eyes off Johnson and quickly snapped back. He
slapped one foot on the deck and splashed gasoline toward
the cop.

"Get away from me, I swear I'll do it," he hissed.

Johnson had stopped his advance but he didn't retreat.

"I thought you said Greta meant everything to you,
Charlie," I called out.

"You shut up!" he screamed, glancing over his right
shoulder trying to see me. His t-shirt slipped off his nose,
and his scraggly hair flipped across his face, tangling in his
beard wet with sweat, gasoline and blood.

The cops looked toward me too, and I felt their eyes
lock on me. Johnson stared at me over his shoulder just for
a moment like I was a bull's eye at the target range, but his
weapon stayed pointed at Charlie's chest. I raised my hands
in surrender and swung my legs over the side of the
camper.

"Come on, Charlie. You know this is over," I said. I
wasn't sure what to say or do, but I knew I had to do
something. This was it. I had to act.

"I said shut up, Johnny. You ready to die too?" His feet
were shuffling in small steps and his head swung back and
forth between me and the cops.

"Give me a break, Charlie. You think you're impressing
anybody with that weak horseshit. Look at you. You're a

pathetic mess. And we both know you don't have a lighter anymore. I kicked it away."

He bristled and shook his fist at me. "Yes, I do!" he shrieked again in a high pitched screech. I was far enough away that his myopic vision had no clue where I was. But then with a wicked grin he opened his left hand and held up the green plastic lighter.

Johnson charged and flew through the air hitting Charlie right above the knees. Both men collapsed to the deck.

My eyes went crazy. I rolled away and covered my head expecting flames and a huge blast. My head smacked into the air conditioner and I saw stars, but I scrambled backwards anyhow, crossed the camper roof and found the ladder with my feet.

It was a clumsy struggle but somehow I made my way down the ladder and around the corner of the camper in time to see Johnson on top of Charlie. He had Charlie flat on his back. One of his hands held Charlie by the throat and his other fist was slamming into the big man's face over and over. Charlie's arms were flopping, trying to ward off the assault, but it was useless. He'd dropped the knife and the lighter too was gone.

Charlie was finished. His limp body and bloodied face took the attack without resistance. His body bounced with the impact of each blow.

I stopped where I was and watched as Larry came flying toward them. On his way he pointed a finger at my face and yelled, "Don't you move."

I put my hands in the air and stared at the rampage in front of me.

Larry grabbed Johnson's arm and shouted in his ear. "Enough, enough," he yelled. "He's done, he's done."

Johnson stopped then with one fist still in mid-air, his chest heaving and his whole body shaking. He raised up from his knees and tore off his ski mask but he kept staring down at Charlie ready to attack again at the slightest movement.

Larry stepped in front of him and rolled Charlie over on his face. He pulled his arms behind him and fastened handcuffs on his wrists. Then he dragged Charlie's still form out of the pool of gasoline and looking back toward the door, he waved.

The door burst open and dark shapes poured through. A stream of men in white uniform shirts and yellow fluorescent vests ran down the steps. Larry stepped over Charlie and moved over to kneel over the dark blue shape lying face down in the gas.

"Miller?" he shouted turning the man over. But he immediately recoiled seeing the open unfocused eyes and the open bloody neck wound.

Johnson was watching but then he too pulled himself away. He picked up the pistol he'd dropped and pointed it at me.

"Turn around," he barked.

I did as I was told. I spun and spread my arms and legs. He pushed me against the hood of the camper and forced my head against the cool metal while he kicked my feet in opposite directions. I endured the body search in silence. I could see yellow vested crew members unrolling red hoses and spraying water in every direction washing gasoline into drains. The main loading doors were opened and fresh air poured through. I felt handcuffs snap onto my wrists.

When Johnson was through searching me, Larry came over. I stayed against the hood but turned my head to look at them. The two men towered over me.

"Help them with Jimmy," Larry nodded toward Miller's still form. Johnson's head and eyes dropped, and he slowly turned away.

Larry tapped me on the back. "Turn around," he said softly.

I straightened up and turned around. The vehicle deck was buzzing with activity. It was strange to see so many people moving around the space that had been my dark and deadly dungeon only minutes earlier. Cold air off the ocean felt like a million bucks.

I leaned back against the camper and looked at Larry. The SWAT sergeant was almost as tall as Charlie who was still laying on his belly coughing and spitting nearby as a stream of water from a red hose sprayed up and down his body. I took a deep breath of relief seeing Charlie's hands cuffed behind him.

Larry's eyes drooped and his jaw slowly worked back and forth as he inhaled deeply and looked me over. My gasoline soaked clothes were reeking with the fumes. He stood in front of me with his arms crossed, holding himself together. Then he ran one head through his thick hair, his nostrils flaring with each breath.

I waited. My knees were shaking, and I was glad for the support of the vehicle behind me. I moved my head around to work the kinks out of my neck. The hose guys were throwing heavy streams of water in all directions. I watched as small waves of foamy clear liquid washed across the deck and disappeared into drainage slots.

"You Wainwright?" Larry finally asked.

I nodded. "Yes, I am."

He studied me closely, his gray eyes looking into mine. I knew enough to hold his eye contact without overdoing it. He uncrossed his arms and rested his wrists on his equipment belt. The leather squeaked from the weight of his arms.

"Sorry about Miller," I said in a low voice.

His lips pressed together, and he looked down at his shoes. He nodded, but then shook his head slightly and turned his head away from the sight of Johnson helping two crew members with a stretcher beside us.

"What were you doing in here? They told me you were locked in a supply room."

"I came in to help my friend, Rainey. And I thought I might be able to talk Charlie into giving up. You got my note, right?"

He reached into a pocket and pulled out the soggy receipt. He opened it up to reveal an illegible smear of blue ink on the torn paper.

"You mean this? What did it say?"

I closed my eyes and shook my head. "It said '30 mins cut lights.' I thought you knew I was going to jump him."

He listened with sad tired eyes. His breathing was slowing. "That was either very brave or very stupid."

I nodded and shrugged. "Stupid probably."

He didn't agree or disagree. "Look, Mr. Wainwright, I don't know what your story is. Some people are saying you're flaky. I don't know, but you did help us in here. I saw that."

I felt faint. My knees wanted to let go. I closed my eyes and leaned an elbow against the camper behind me so I wouldn't slip to the deck. I was taking deep gulps of air into my lungs. I couldn't believe it was over. I'd been operating on adrenaline for so long, I just wanted to lie down and sleep for days.

"Thanks for saving my ass," I finally managed to say.

He just looked at me. "Don't get relaxed," he said. "We're not done."

"What do you mean?" I felt my throat tighten again, and my heart began to pound.

"Greta," was all he said.

My mouth must have dropped open. I was about to ask him to explain when a cold stream of water from a red hose hit me in the chest washing away the gasoline, dirt and whatever peace of mind I had left.

CHAPTER

32

The shock of cold water made it impossible to hear. After I was thoroughly soaked the police sergeant waved the hose guys back and raised his voice to give me the bad news.

"We still have a situation. The woman, Greta, still has the captain and the bridge at gunpoint." He bit off his words through a clenched jaw and a grim stare.

My temples were throbbing. "Crap," was the only thing I could think to say.

I tried to picture Greta on the bridge with a gun in her hand. And the captain sitting there helpless in front of her. I realized that we were still floating in the open ocean powerless. Instead of relief, the fear and dread returned. We still had a "situation," and I was on the hook. Again.

I looked at the sergeant. "You said, 'We're not done?'"

He nodded and returned my stare. "That's right."

"What do you mean, we?"

"She's demanding we bring you up there." He turned me around and unlocked the handcuffs.

I must have really bad karma. I wanted to ask why me, but when I turned around the hoses hit me full force again. There was gasoline on every part of me, and the sadistic bastards knew it. Two crewmen in yellow rubber suits and brown knee high boots swarmed around me. They seemed to enjoy their work. With smug expressions and efficient movements they aimed water down my neck, down my pants and even up my sleeves.

When the initial shock from the cold water started to pass, it felt good to flush away the itchy irritant of gasoline on my skin. The air tasted pure again and the heavy stench that ate at my eyeballs was gone. I let water run over my face and blinked my eyes to clean them out. But it was salt water, ocean water, and the relief was short lived.

Then the cold took over, and I started shivering violently. I waved off the hose guys and looked up to see Rainey rushing toward me. She was unfolding a large orange blanket and before I could say hello she wrapped it around me and started walking me to the door. I couldn't have spoken anyhow. My lips felt like those big rubber erasers from grade school and they were vibrating in time to the chattering of my teeth. My whole face felt like a drunken production of Smurfs On Ice.

I stumbled up the stairs at Rainey's urging. Past the round windowed door we entered the hallway and things started going fuzzy. Maybe it was the cold water or maybe the long dance with death. I don't know. Maybe both, but my knees must have decided they'd had enough, because I noticed we had stopped and Rainey was mumbling in my ear. My feet had quit listening to my brain.

"C'mon, Johnny, c'mon. We'll get you in a hot shower. Just a few more steps."

She held me tighter and tried to hold me up. I was shaking too hard to enjoy the contact. Someone else came up behind us and took hold of my other arm. She leaned over and looked into my sodden face. It was Brandy.

As we stumbled together down the hallway and up the stairs, she stared at my face wrapped in swaddling orange, my hat long gone, my hair matted and plastered against my forehead.

"Is that really you, Johnny? I heard a drowned rat was loose on board, but I didn't know it was so big."

"Berry fundy," I gurgled. I couldn't say anything else. Many clever lines were available, but my brain had turned into a thirty two ounce Slurpee from the 7-Eleven. It was all I could do to keep one foot following the other. They were carrying more of my weight than I was.

We pushed our way through a door marked Crew Only. Warm air hit me in the face with a blurry mist. Rainey and Brandy escorted me into a locker room and sat me on a wooden bench. Rainey pulled away the blanket and Brandy dropped to her knees and started pulling off my shoes. I was even too woozy to enjoy that. My mind thought of a great wise crack, but it wouldn't come out of my mouth.

She glanced up at me as she worked on my socks. "I know, I know," she said. "You've been wanting me on my knees in front of you since the moment we met. Hold that thought, hot shot."

She winked up at Rainey who laughed while she toweled my head. I tried but I was too cold and tired to smile or even reply.

I sat there feeling uncomfortably numb. The wall in front of me had a long counter with four sinks and a long mirror. Urinals lined the wall to our left. I was going groggy fast but I could see in the mirror what looked like a half drowned mongrel that firemen had just pulled out of a frozen pond.

I stared at the reflection's eyes. Is there anybody in there?

Rainey unzipped and pulled off my fleece, but I managed to stop her before she started on my shirt. She turned to grab a dry towel, her blond pony tail flipping as she went, and I heard the shower behind us come on. Brandy had my shoes and socks off. She stood up and helped me struggle out of the shirt. Rainey set down a stack of towels on the bench beside me.

"Okay, mister. You gonna make it now? Or do we need to take you into the shower too?"

"Wh-wuzza hurry? I could use a nap."

They grabbed me under the armpits and pulled me to my feet.

"Okay, okay," I protested. "I can do this. Lemme lone."

I stood up and undid the belt on my jeans and they turned for the door.

"We'll leave you now, Mister Hypothermia, before you totally embarrass yourself," said Rainey. "You got five minutes." They turned their backs and headed for the door. My mouth and jaw were beginning to thaw.

"Hey, I could use some company. How about the cute one stays behind?"

Their heads turned back to me. In perfect unison they waved together with wide grins and middle finger salutes. The door slammed and left me alone.

"But what if I drop the soap?" I hollered to no one in particular.

Steam was pouring out of the shower stall. I kicked off the jeans and soggy boxers and glanced in the mirror again. I was instantly glad the ladies had left.

I limped under the hot water. Needles of heat burned me at first, but after a few dance moves and some frantic knob twirling I was in heaven. My stiff muscles began to thaw, and I could feel blood moving back into my extremities like refugees coming home from the war.

I stood there gathering strength in the rushing hot flow until I heard a pounding on the door outside. Rainey's voice rang out over the roar of the water.

"Hurry up, Johnny. We need you now! There's dry clothes for you on the bench."

I thought about complaining, or whining, or flat out refusing. I even considered passing out, but the urgency in her voice was too tense to ignore.

"Okay, okay," I called. My voice felt stronger. I turned off the shower and grabbed a towel. I avoided looking in the mirror this time and after rubbing myself down, I pulled on the underwear, dark slacks and the white shirt laying there in a neat pile. There were shoes and socks too. Only about three sizes too big. Whatever.

I tried to focus on dressing, but questions were eating at me like mosquitoes on a summer's night. What was waiting for me on the bridge? Greta with a gun? She'd sold out Charlie, and now she was making her own deal? So what did she want with me? I couldn't do anything. I had nothing. I was nothing. No clout, no pull, nothing.

And the cops. What were they going to do? Greta was just a tiny little blond standing next to them. A party girl, a socialite, a snowflake in the breeze. But she had hostages, the captain and the kid at least. And a gun. And a history. Charlie said she was a stone killer.

Then I made a mistake. I looked in the mirror. Thin brown hair hung in my face like wet seaweed. With water dripping in front of my eyes the soaked hair made me look small and almost bald. There were dark circles under my eyes, and my scraggly beard clung to my tired face like a dirty bathtub ring. I'd seen better looking men in Salvation Army homeless ads. Or on a street corner in Anchorage holding a handwritten cardboard sign. Will work for beer.

I buried my face in a towel and closed my eyes. Enough. Spare me the self pity. Then I rubbed at my head and beard with the towel and took a deep breath.

I heard the door open. Pulling the towel off my face, I looked over to see Brandy step in wearing a white baseball cap. Her eyes bulged and her mouth fell open at the sight of me.

"Whoa, I didn't know the bride of Frankenstein was in here," she said staring at my head.

I looked in the mirror again. Sure enough, my hair was standing out straight in all directions. I buried my face again.

"Very funny," I grumbled from behind the towel. I combed my hair with my fingers and glanced at Brandy in the mirror. Her green eyes held a half smile, but I could see tension tugging at the corners of her mouth.

I didn't want to look at her. It brought back the image of the blood and the crumpled blue horror of Miller's dead face in the vehicle bay down below. I needed the wisecracks and the false bravado to get me through. I imagined a whiff of gasoline fumes then and realized how close we'd all been to a fiery hell. Brandy's face was filled with way too much reality.

"You okay?" she asked.

"Oh, yeah, I'm great," I mumbled without looking at her. I reached over and pulled the white cap off her head and put it on mine.

"Hey," she protested but stopped when I raised my hand to block her.

"I need it more than you do," I explained. "I'm having a really bad hair day. Terrible split ends. You understand."

She backed off and looked at me in the mirror. "You ready for this?"

I took a deep breath. "That's an excellent question."

I'd had this feeling before. It was like walking across the tarmac toward the airplane on a cold morning. With wind whipping at my clothes trying to tear off my cap. Glancing at the mountains nearby and cringing inside, knowing that the turbulence after takeoff was going to kick my ass.

I stared at my face in the mirror again and tried to remember the pep talk I relied on when things got tense in the airplane. Slowly it came back to me.

I'm Johnny Wainwright, Alaskan bush pilot repo man. I'm a tough guy. I can do this.

Corny, I know, I know. But it was better than whimpering in fear.

I took another deep breath and pulled my shoulders back. Brandy saw the change in my eyes. She stepped over, took my head in her hands and planted her lips against the side of my face. The surprise stopped me for a moment but an electric charge ran through me all the way to my toes. Then without a word she broke it off, stepped back and led the way to the door.

I followed her into the hallway. Larry was waiting for me there looking twenty years older than when I first saw him.

"You ready for this?" he asked looking at me doubtfully.

"That's such a good question," I shrugged. "I guess. What do I need to do?"

He motioned for me to follow and led us up the stairs to the main deck. Rainey joined us there. I could see the sadness and worry in her eyes too as she pulled at a strand of hair and tried to smile. She handed me a candy bar, and

I gobbled it hungrily. Looking around I noticed there weren't any passengers or crew nearby.

It was dark outside. Thick fog still surrounded the ship. I looked at my watch. Ten o'clock. I tried to remember all those hours going by, but it was a blur and took too much effort.

Another passageway and another staircase right in the center of the ship and then we were approaching the bridge. The sergeant stopped before we entered the corridor just ahead.

"Okay, listen. The bridge is one long narrow room all the way across the front of the ferry. There's two doors, one on each end. She's down there with the captain and the kid."

He pointed down the corridor to the left. "We've been talking to her through that port side door. She has the other one barricaded, and there's no other way in."

"What am I supposed to do? What does she want?"

"I'm not really sure. She won't talk to us anymore. We told her Charlie gave up, and that he blamed everything on her."

"He did?" I blurted.

"No, he didn't. He's still passed out, but that's what we told her. It really pissed her off, but we didn't want them getting together again. She says she'll only talk to you now."

"Why me?" I was struggling to understand.

"I don't know. It's like she's written him off or something. She wants you. Look, just play along. Try to talk her down. Convince her to give herself up. If that doesn't work, try to get her to move the ferry out of the fog so a chopper can come in. We've got a Coast Guard chopper nearby with a sniper on board. If he can get a head shot, he'll take it."

"On her or me?" I gaped at him in disbelief.

"Don't worry, these guys are good. We've got men on the roof and across the hall too."

"You're kidding me, right? What if I can get her to give up?"

"Well, sure, that'd be swell, but we're tired of screwing around with this. She's got two hundred people out here playing this stupid game. We need to get the captain safe and there's a kid in there too. Either she ends it fast, or we will."

"That's not even her kid," I said. "Can't you just rush her?"

"Not while she's holding a gun on the captain, we can't risk it. With her history I'm sure she'll use it if we try anything."

"Jesus," I looked at my feet and shook my head.

"Oh, and the way you distracted Charlie to get us in the vehicle bay? That was clever," he said. "But don't try anything like that on her. We have no position on her and she'd probably kill the captain just for the hell of it."

I shook my head. "Greta? I can't believe that."

"Trust me. I've seen it many times before. She's a serious psycho. Have you ever heard of suicide by cop?"

I nodded, staring at my shoes.

"I think she's there or very close to it. You don't know what you're dealing with there."

I thought about it. He was probably right. What did I know about her? I didn't know jack.

"How do I know she's not going to shoot me?"

He shrugged. "You don't know. You want out?"

I stared at him, thinking. I glanced at Brandy and Rainey.

"We can't force you to do this. You're strictly volunteer," he added.

"Swell. How about a plastic Junior G-man badge?"

He looked at me dead pan. "Okay, but you're not sitting on my knee at the awards dinner."

We stared at each other, half smiles flickering in our tired eyes.

"Okay, I'll just see what she wants and I'll let you know."

He nodded. "That's right. No freelancing. Leave all the moves to us. Double check everything you do with me. In the meantime we're going to see if there's a way we can gain access through the other door. Try to keep her from looking down this way."

I closed my eyes and took a breath. Could I do this? What choice did I have? No freelancing, he'd said. Great.

Just what I didn't like. Close supervision fit me about as well as a tuxedo on a wooly mammoth.

I started down the hallway and noticed that no one followed me. I stopped halfway there and turned around to see Brandy, Rainey and Larry watching me, peering around the edge of the doorway. He motioned for me to continue, moving his hand impatiently like he was brushing lint off his coat sleeve. Behind them another figure had moved in to sit by the other door to the bridge. The one Larry said was blocked. It was that overblown security guy, The Michelin Man. What was his name? Oh, yeah, Darrell.

The end of the corridor had three doors. The door to the left was probably a crew cabin, maybe the captain's. The one straight ahead went outside to a small landing that extended out over the side of the ship. Like a little balcony.

The door to the right had a round window that looked in on the bridge. It was the same door where good old Darrell had brought me up to meet the captain. As I got closer I noticed the door to the left was partially open and a man in dark clothes and a ski mask was lying on its floor on his stomach. He held a handgun pointed across the hall at the door to the bridge. He never looked at me as I approached and kept his position aimed straight and true.

I stepped up to the round window and looked in. The bridge looked deserted. The dark fog bank loomed just outside the large front windows. Over the counter with its scopes and engine controls I could barely see the surface of the ocean way below undulating with gentle rhythmic swells. The water was dark but I could see there were no white caps disturbing the surface.

The door opened slightly and a hand reached out and grabbed the front of my shirt. It pulled me in and shoved the door shut behind me. I found myself belly to belly with Greta. She was smiling up at me.

"Hello, Johnny," she said, her blue eyes twinkling.

CHAPTER
33

I tried to avoid looking at her eyes, but it was no use. She had me. I remembered to breathe then and caught a whiff of lilacs. There was a hardness in my pants which was odd considering my state of exhaustion. Then I realized it wasn't me. It was a gun Greta was holding.

I must have looked uncomfortable. "Oh, relax, Johnny," Greta said with a pouty smile. "I'm not going to hurt you."

Said the spider to the fly, I thought to myself.

I tried to move the weapon aside with one hand, but instead she pushed me down to sit on the floor with my back against the door. She took a quick glance out the window in the door then sat on the floor below the counter beside me. She rearranged her hair with one hand and made herself comfortable. Her other hand held a shiny chrome semi-automatic handgun pointed at my heart. At least it wasn't in my crotch anymore.

With her ankles crossed she looked at me for a moment, then waved the gun toward the rest of the compartment. "Welcome to my world."

I glanced around for the first time and took it in. Tambourine was laying beside her under the counter. He looked like he'd been sleeping, but as Greta settled into place, he laid his head on her leg. She stroked his pile of red hair with one hand. The hand that wasn't full of firepower.

Five feet away the captain was sitting on the floor with her back against a cabinet door. She looked tired and scared and not all that pleased to see me. It was a stark change from the proud confidence and command she'd displayed when she'd ordered me locked up just hours earlier.

"Have you and Captain Ferguson met?" Greta asked me.

I nodded and glanced at the captain, but she dropped her eyes and looked away with a bitter frown. There was a food tray beside her on the floor stacked high with empty plates and cups and trash.

Greta tilted her head in the captain's direction. "Her name's Betty. Captain Betty to you, Johnny. And Captain Betty isn't very happy right now, are you, Captain Betty?"

That's when I noticed a yellow rope tied around the captain's neck. Greta watched me as my eyes traced the rope from the captain's neck down and around her wrists then across the floor to a support leg beside us under the counter. The rest of the bridge was empty. Radios and equipment screens stared blankly back at us.

"Thanks for coming," Greta grinned and nudged me with her foot. "I've been needing someone to protect me from the carpet hugger out there." She nodded toward the hallway behind me. She meant the guy in the ski mask with the gun. Less than ten feet away and patiently waiting for a shot. I glanced back at Greta. She must have seen the alarm in my eyes.

"Yeah, I know. They're on the roof too. I know, I know. There's men all over the place. And they all want me," she chuckled low in her throat.

I gaped at her like a dope. Speechless.

"It's about time you got up here. So, how's it going, Johnny? You've got new clothes. And a shower? What have you been doing?" she asked looking at my ensemble.

I looked back at her and tried to think of what to say. She was back from the door enough to stay out of the line of fire. She had reduced her whole world, and mine too, to this small space.

Her defenses were intact. She had my complete attention and that of many others. So close and yet completely out of reach. Untouchable. It dawned on me, that's how she ran her life. It was what she'd created, what she required. All the players were in place. She'd set it all up like a play. Adding characters as she needed them. Cutting them loose when they were through.

I had been summoned to center stage. I was now sitting at drama central.

I tried to avoid her eyes but it was impossible. She looked perfect. Her face was smooth and white. Her lips were painted bright red like she'd just touched up her lipstick. The long blond bangs she draped over the side of her face hung down to her chin framing her jaw line in an artistic curve. She had on a light weight black leather jacket over a red silk turtleneck and designer blue jeans with sequin swirls. Instead of the knee high white boots she was wearing sparkling slip on sandals with thick platform soles. She didn't look like a major felon. She looked like a Christmas season shopper having tea at the food court.

She brushed the hair back from her face and turned her head straight toward me. I couldn't believe it, but it started to happen again. The magnetic pull of her eyes reached for mine and locked me in their embrace. Something deep in their blue brilliance beckoned me from afar and set a table for two between us too inviting to resist. I felt that sensation again like I was looking at the cover of a high fashion magazine.

She was a strange wonder to behold and clearly dangerous at the same time. It would have been easy to let myself sink into the fantasy and forget everything I'd learned about her, but the handgun in her lap was impossible to ignore.

Her eyes were working on me. Without a word I felt myself slipping. I could forgive a face like that for anything. I knew I was being a fool, but it didn't seem to matter. Why was every fresh look at her like falling in love?

"Talk to me, Johnny."

I swallowed the lump in my throat and tried to look away. It was no use. Her voice was intimate, soft, vulnerable, warm and inviting. Then I remembered that I was supposed to be doing the talking instead of vice versa.

"What's happening here, Greta?"

She sighed. "I don't know, Johnny. You tell me." There was a sadness in her voice.

"The police told me …" I started to say, but she cut me off.

"I'm tired, Johnny. This whole thing is getting old."

I could relate to that. Fatigue was wearing me down as well. But this ball was rolling. She'd set it in motion and she was holding all the cards. I remembered what Larry had told me about her mental state. I started to think he was right about her.

"And what did you summon me for?"

"Summon? How formal, Johnny. You make me sound like the queen from Alice in Wonderland."

Interesting image, I thought. Wasn't she the crazy one who screamed 'off with her head?' I kept that thought to myself.

"I like you, Johnny. You make me smile. Besides, I need a man like you."

"You like me? How do you mean?"

"Well, Charlie's gone and I don't like being alone."

"Come on, Greta. You've been playing me all along. What happened to our plan? You were going to wait for me on Chenega. To come get you with the plane. Remember?"

Her face went into a pout. She tried to look hurt, but I saw a flash of fire behind it. She recovered quickly.

"Yes, I remember. You're sweet, Johnny. But when I saw the fog this morning, I knew you couldn't fly. And when we found out about the ferry it seemed like the better way to go."

"But Charlie was going back to Taroka. Why didn't you just let him go?"

She sniffed and looked away. "He wasn't going back to Taroka. That was a big lie. Are you kidding? He's lost without me. That's why he told you ten o'clock. To keep you out of the way. You surprised us, Johnny boy, coming on board here."

"You know, he told me everything that happened."

I expected her to explain, to blame everything on him, but she stayed quiet. She looked at me again, studying my face. The mask was crumbling.

"Whatever, Johnny," she finally said.

I knew I was pushing it, but I had to know. "Why did you cut him loose?"

"He was losing it. And I've had enough of his weird anger routine. I'm better off alone."

That said a lot. She really was alone. With the act she was running she could never really let anyone get too close.

"But why this? Why not just give up, Greta? You can blame it all on him. You know, like the battered wife thing or something?"

She chuckled again and examined her nails. She looked so small and fragile, I fought off an overwhelming urge to take her in my arms and hold her close.

"You suppose they'd overlook this whole hijacking at gunpoint thing, Johnny?" She looked up at me half smiling through her eyelashes, her eyes half open.

I couldn't believe how calm she seemed. I knew it was an act, and she was a pro. Façade was her thing. Never mind the turmoil within.

"You can beat this, Greta. Get a good lawyer. Tell them it was a lapse of judgment. A blond moment. Well, maybe it's a little late for that. But if you give up now, you might be able to get a better deal."

"You're sweet, Johnny, but no. Can you really see me in a jail cell? Little moi?" She arched her back and held her hands out like a cabaret dancer taking a bow. "And those prison jumpsuits are so tacky. And bright orange? Or stripes? Puh-lease. I've never worn stripes, Johnny," she said with feigned disgust.

I shook my head with a smile and looked at her closely. She was enjoying herself. In some strange way even this kind of attention suited her. The belle of the ball. Making history. Infamous history maybe, but pretty spectacular all the same.

I looked down at Tambourine. He seemed awake even though his eyes were closed.

"Hey, tiger. You doing alright?"

He opened his eyes then and looked at me. I searched for a sign. Any glimpse of something for a connection. I even wiggled my eyebrows at him like a prompt, but he just shrugged, rolled over with his back to me and gripped Greta's leg even tighter. I thought he might even put his thumb in his mouth.

I looked back at Greta. She sighed out loud.

"C'mon, Johnny. I need you to get me out of this."

"Me? Why me? What the hell can I do? You've got the captain there. She can do a lot more than I can."

Greta glanced at Captain Ferguson who was looking the other way with her arms crossed. She had the expression of a long suffering airline passenger whose flight had been cancelled. Forced to spend the night on a hard bench in the terminal.

"No, she's not into it. She's just not fun like you are, Johnny. And besides, I need a man. I need a man to take care of me. Charlie tried. He really did. But in the end he didn't have it. It's too bad. I had hope for him, but he wanted to keep me out on that island. All to himself, you know? That wasn't going to work. Help me, Johnny. Take charge of this. Get me out of here. I'll make it worth your while." She put her hand on my knee.

Her little girl voice was talking to me. She was reaching deep into my heart. Looking up at me and pleading for every protective instinct I'd ever had to rescue a damsel in distress.

Be the big brother, Johnny. Be the knight in shining armor. Save me from the harshness of life in this cruel world. I'm weak and small but you're big and strong. Do this for me and I'll be yours forever.

She didn't have to say any of those words. I heard them anyhow, whispering to me from some place far away. From deep in the blue of her eyes the dream beckoned.

I tore my eyes away from hers and tried to conjure up a clear thought. What had the sergeant told me? The helicopter was nearby. If I could get her off the ship, that would help. Something had to break the standoff.

She must have noticed my effort to detach. She reached over and took hold of one of my hands. Her touch was warm and almost took my breath away.

"Johnny, please."

I squeezed my eyes shut and fought it. I couldn't look at her. I knew if I looked at her, I'd be lost.

"Why don't you give me the gun, Greta? That would make everything easier."

She pulled her hand back with a jerk. That did it. I couldn't help myself. I looked at her.

The blue in her eyes was changing. Transforming. The warmth was cooling fast. Tendrils of ice began to spread in from the edges. I was instantly sorry I'd pushed my luck.

"You're not going to help me, are you?" The little girl voice had left town, replaced by a different tone, cold and accusing.

Then she gave me her pouty look again and pushed out her bottom lip. Even now on the edge of this cliff, she was playing it to the hilt. Playfully, mockingly. In case I might give in to her ploy. The door was still open.

She wasn't going to give up. Maybe she didn't know how. I strained to think of something to say, something to do that could turn this around.

Could I grab the gun before she shot the captain? Or shot me? I glanced at it. The hammer was back, ready to go. I looked up to see Greta watching me and shaking her head slowly from one side to the other with a sad smile.

"Don't even think about it, Johnny. I know what I'm doing with one of these."

Then a sharp crack rang out. The sound of something breaking at the other end of the bridge. It startled both of us and our heads snapped to look that way. Something was happening at the other door.

CHAPTER
34

"What's going on?" Greta pointed the gun at me with a hostile glare. Her eyes shifted to the captain and down the bridge, then back to me. Captain Ferguson looked up in alarm as well.

"I don't know, I don't know," I said. "Let me look out the door."

She pressed herself against the wall under the counter, motioned with the gun and nodded.

"Opening the door!" I called out. "Be cool!"

I pulled the door open two inches and peeked through. No one was on the other side, so I stuck my head out into the hallway to take a look. Darrell was lying on the deck on his belly in front of the other door into the bridge at the far end of the corridor. Larry was standing above him and motioning for me to hurry up. Great advice, I thought. Who's got the gun in their face anyhow?

I looked to the right and one eye of the SWAT guy in the ski mask was peeking through the cracked door across the hall and pointing his gun at me. I was really getting sick of being everybody's target. I pointed at him and frowned and he closed the door and disappeared.

Knowing Greta couldn't see my face, I shook my head slightly at Larry. I hoped he would get the message. No dice. She ain't giving up.

I called out to him. "Bring the chopper in and stay away from that door," I yelled. I pointed at Darrell and used my thumb to motion him away from the door. I don't know what he was doing down there, but I didn't like it.

I closed the door again and turned to Greta.

"It's okay. Let's get that helicopter out here so it can pick us up. Isn't that what you wanted?"

Greta's look softened slightly. "Yes, Johnny. Make it happen, won't you? I'm so tired of all this."

I got to my knees, looked around and then stood up. It was totally dark outside the ferry. We were still inside the fog bank, and there were no lights to be seen outside the windows. No stars either.

I looked at the captain. "Captain, can you move us out of the fog? I don't think the chopper can get in here, it's so thick."

"Johnny?"

I turned back to Greta again. The silver pistol was pointed at my face. Her blue eyes were positioned behind it, perfectly centered and perfectly deadly.

"Don't try anything tricky. I swear I'll use this."

I gulped and swallowed hard. "Greta, we've got to get out of the fog, so the chopper can move in."

She looked at me thinking about it. She shifted her eyes to the captain and motioned at her with the pistol.

"Okay, Betty, you're on," she said. "Move us out where the helicopter can pick us up. You, me, Johnny and Tambourine."

I noticed how she didn't mention Charlie but I didn't say anything. This was her show now and she was selecting her cast with care.

"I need to use the radio," Betty said, getting to her knees. Greta nodded.

I watched Greta watching the captain. Betty stood up, the yellow rope drawing taut as she moved in front of the controls. She went through the steps required to start the engines. Picking up a microphone she asked for information and was told the edge of the fog bank was about two miles south of our position.

After a few minutes she moved the engine throttles forward. The vibration in the ship picked up. Gradually I felt the sense of forward motion.

The ferry pushed forward, but the picture through the front windows didn't change. I couldn't see anything but fog and the ocean right around us. The captain was checking the scopes beside her on the counter.

After a few minutes, the captain raised one arm and pointed to her right. I spotted flashing lights. An orange and white Coast Guard helicopter was hovering about a hundred yards away and at the same level as the bridge. A spotlight underneath the chopper cut through the fog, and a red light above the spinning tail rotor blinked like a cop car in the night.

I was standing above Greta with my back to her. She put the muzzle of the handgun against the inside of my thigh and moved it up and down. A chill ran through me but not the pleasant kind. I tried to move away but she grabbed an ankle and held me in place.

"Don't try anything, Johnny," she reminded me with a giggle. I couldn't believe she was playing around. My adrenaline was pumping hard.

The chopper moved across our bow from right to left. The ferry broke free of the fog, and I could see lights marking rocks and islands at the mouth of Resurrection Bay. Way in the distance I could barely see the lights of Seward Dry Dock.

I watched the helicopter and tried to keep my breathing slow and regular. Greta was watching me and motioned for me to move back against the door where she could see me better.

The radio crackled. It sounded like garbled static to me, but the captain seemed to understand.

"The helicopter pilot is telling us to shut down, so they can approach for the pickup," she said.

"Then do it," Greta snapped. Her jaw was set now and a frown pinched her brow together replacing the fragile little girl face of just a few minutes before.

She was thinking of the next steps. She was no fool. I could see the hard side of Greta now as plain as day. The same face that had ordered Charlie around back on Taroka.

The captain chopped the throttles and I felt the ferry slow. The helicopter moved closer and maneuvered toward us. We could hear it easily now, the big blades throbbing with a heavy beat.

Greta stayed down under the counter but she was watching my eyes to keep track of the situation through me. She was covering both me and the door with the pistol.

Our eyes met. She softened then, smiled slightly and something passed between us. I would think about that look for a long time afterwards trying to make sense of it. But right then I didn't have the time to ponder.

"How are we going to do this, Greta?"

She obviously had been thinking about it. "We'll go out the side door here. They can send their basket down to the balcony. Tell the rug rat out there to get lost."

I looked through the window behind me. The SWAT guy in the ski mask looked up, and I gave him a hand signal to go down the corridor. He hesitated and spoke into a radio. After a minute he got up and walked backwards down the hall until he was out of sight.

"See the door to the outside there?" Greta asked. "Open it. We're going out that way. Tamby and I'll go up first."

I looked over at Captain Ferguson. She was on the radio with the helicopter relaying Greta's instructions to the pilot.

I reached over and opened the door on the side of the ship. The smell of sea salt and wet air burst into my face. The sound of the helicopter washed over us like a wave. The turbine engines howled and the blades knifed through the night sky with a roar. I blinked back the moisture flooding into my face and pulled my jacket tighter around my neck. I could feel the quiet mass of the cold ocean below us moving with an eerie roll. Small waves slapped against the side of the ship where we wallowed in the swell.

I watched as the chopper edged slowly into position above us. Its side door was open and a crew member in a white helmet, orange jumpsuit and black gloves was standing there beside a pile of duffel bags and gear. He was looking toward us and had a lift basket hanging by a cable from a pulley by his feet ready to let down toward us.

Greta stood up pulling Tamby along with her and moved to the doorway making sure that my body was between her and the men at the other end of the bridge. We pushed out into the turbulent air on the landing. The chopper moved in directly above us and the basket started down.

The noise and the wind from the chopper blades threw mist in our faces and made conversation impossible. Our collars flapped like crazy and I had to hold my hat on with one hand while I held onto Greta with the other and watched the basket approaching. Greta had one arm around Tamby's neck and her other hand held the gleaming chrome handgun pressed against the side of his head. Her hair was whipping in the turbulence. The basket was spinning in the wind as it came into range. Just before it got close enough to hit us Greta stuffed the gun under her jacket and reached her hand out to grab the basket.

Just then I spotted an erratic blinking light next to the helicopter crewman. But it wasn't a light. It was a reflection in the lens of a rifle scope. There was another person in the chopper. Inside the pile of duffel bags and gear a sniper was set up with a rifle aimed directly at us.

It dawned on me in a flash. They had no intention of letting Greta get on board the helicopter. In an instinctive reflex I threw my arms around Greta and Tamby and lunged back into the bridge just as a bullet smacked into the door frame inches from my head. Before diving through the door I saw Larry and Darrell at the end of the hall with weapons and angry faces pointed our way.

We hit the floor together and Greta scrambled to free herself from my arms kicking violently and crawling backwards under the counter. I covered my head with my arms expecting more gun shots at any second. Greta jerked me up by my collar and pointed the handgun back in my face.

"Go close that damn door!" she screamed pointing down the bridge behind me.

The yellow rope lay on the floor. The captain was gone. I looked down the bridge in alarm and saw the other door standing open. The throttles were full forward and the ferry was moving.

Outside, the pounding helicopter blades changed pitch and we heard it turn and move away, the whopping sound growing gradually softer.

I got up and moved down the bridge. Darrell and Larry were standing outside the open door in the hallway. I raised my arms to wave off their guns and reached to close the door between us. But before I could get it shut the door jammed against something. I looked down to see Darrell's boot in the way. As I looked up in irritation his arm reached in, grabbed me by the front of my coat and jerked me into the hall like a bag of laundry.

I was pushed face down onto the tile floor. Darrell's heavy knee pinned me in place. Larry went to the door and leaned in just an inch to look down the bridge.

"Give it up, Greta. Last chance!" he barked.

"Screw you!" she screamed back and a shot rang out. The window beside Larry shattered and sprayed glass out into the night as he jumped out of the way.

Larry threw his arms up and said, "Nobody move. She's got a gun to the kid's head."

I realized then he was talking to his team. There were several other men in black in the corners and the stairwell halfway down the hall.

"Send Johnny back in here or the kid gets it," Greta shrieked.

"Take it easy, Greta. Calm down," he called out to her.

"I mean it," she screamed back.

"Get the grenade," Larry murmured to someone behind us.

Darrell shifted his weight off me to make room for someone else who moved up beside Larry at the door. They whispered together with rapid fire instructions that I couldn't hear.

I pushed myself to my knees and jammed my head between them to look into the bridge. Greta was at the far end but she didn't look scared. She looked lethal. She was on her knees glaring at us with one arm around Tambourine's neck. His little face was contorted and grimacing, and his eyes bulged with the chrome handgun pressed into the mass of red hair on the side of his head.

Darrell tried to block me with his knee, but I twisted around him, squirmed between them and lunged through the doorway. I landed on the side of my face just in time to see a small metal canister spitting sparks fly through the air. It clattered to a stop on the counter beside the throttles.

"NO!" I shouted and covered my face with my arms. The blast rocked my world. Glass shattered and flew in all directions and papers and debris sprayed across me like a hailstorm.

Stunned and reeling from a fiery pain in my back I struggled to my feet and looked for Greta and the kid. The bridge was filled with smoke and dust. The acrid smell of cordite assaulted my nostrils, and my ears rang with a hollow roar. I rushed toward her in a panic.

Waving my arms to clear the smoke and shouting, "Don't shoot, don't shoot!" I crossed the space in seconds, but then I stopped in confusion. Greta was gone.

Tambourine lay shaking under the counter curled in a fetal ball. He was clutching one of Greta's sparkling sandals. The door was open and so was the outside door to the balcony. I felt the rush of chilled ocean air hit me full in the face again. The other sandal twinkled at me from the wet deck just below the railing.

I turned around to see Larry and Darrell approaching with their guns drawn trying to see around me. They were shouting something at me but I couldn't hear a thing.

They moved to push their way past when I saw their eyes react to a movement behind me. I whirled just in time to see a wild blur of red hair moving through the outer door, up and over the railing and into the dark.

A hard wind blew through the ship then and slammed the doors behind us like shots in the back. I should have stopped like Larry and Darrell, but I charged forward like a man possessed. It only took me three giant steps to reach the landing. There was no stopping me. Autopilot took over and I launched.

CHAPTER
35

I was over the rail and into space before my rattled brain could conjure a rational thought. It was as if time stood still. It never occurred to me to think, "Ya know, this might not be such a good idea."

A rational man would have seen that the ferry was surging back under the fog bank. He would also have considered that a human being could only survive about fifteen minutes in the fifty six degree water off the southern coast of Alaska in September.

A reasonable man might also have considered looking around for a life jacket. But no, not me. Not Johnny Wainwright, local bush pilot hero. Self appointed savior of strange women and children.

I was a man on a mission. I was a superhero in flight. I was an idiot.

You hear about the fight or flight response. This was both. It was a reflex. A knee jerk to the rubber hammer.

Born from the deep Cro-Magnon realm of instinctual responses from the brain stem's central core. The primitive beast part of me. My inner hairy man had taken over.

Animal urges looking for trouble would not be restrained. Not by fear, not by common sense, not even by sanity. Nothing could have stopped that human cannonball rush.

In short, it was one of the dumbest things I've ever done in my entire life.

I think I started to realize that just before I hit the water. Then it was too late. The forty foot leap plunged me under the surface and knocked all the air from my lungs. The water was so cold, my diaphragm was instantly paralyzed.

The dark ocean swallowed me and the cold attacked like a punch in the gut from a fist full of frozen knuckles. I thought I might never stop the downward dive, and I began to fight with everything I had. Thrashing my arms and legs, panic seized me by the throat as I felt the first signs of suffocation. I was about to drown even before I could kick my way back to the surface.

I was only vaguely aware of the huge hull of the ferry surging past me in the dark sea. And the eight foot propeller blades churning through the foam just yards away. On the verge of blacking out I felt a wave of current pushing me and carrying me upward. When my head broke the surface my bursting lungs fought for air. Salt spray burned my eyes.

Coughing and choking, I never heard the hammering alarm bell and the three blasts of an air horn signaling man overboard. My eyes opened just in time to see the white shape of the stern above me. Moving away into the dark.

Blinded, gasping and hacking there was no way I could have seen the emergency raft system release its load or Rainey and other crew members throwing life jackets and life rings over the railing. The only thing I could see was heavy white foam surging into my face and over my head as I bobbed in the wake.

Finally with a little air back in my lungs and my face above water, I had a thought.

What the hell have I done?

I twisted back and forth blinking and trying to see around me. I was treading water and staying afloat, but I could feel my eyes bulging wider than a road kill bullfrog. Panic was taking over.

The shock and the cold held me in a cruel grip and my muscles threatened to cramp completely at any second. Horrible images flashed in front of me as I pictured my body sinking below the surface with my arms and legs paralyzed and useless. Adrift in the sea I knew I only had minutes to live.

Then something bumped into the back of my head. I spun around and grabbed hold. It was a white life ring with black letters that said M/V Tustamena. I hugged it to my chest and pulled my legs up to make myself into a ball.

I took in deep breaths and blinked rapidly trying to clear my eyes. My hearing was starting to come back along with the rest of my senses, but the news wasn't good. The ferry had disappeared into the fog and visibility was less than a hundred yards. I could faintly hear the alarm bell, and it was a long way away.

I've been in lonely situations over the years, but floating by myself in the middle of a dark fog bank in the Gulf of Alaska was the worst. They say despair can kill a man as sure as a gunshot. I could relate.

Bobbing in the frigid water I waited. What else could I do? Surely the ferry would turn around and come back for me. Wouldn't it? Then I remembered why I was there. I looked around me but there was no sign of Greta or the kid.

I knew the big ship took time to maneuver, but I was in no mood to be patient. My lips were shivering and my teeth were chattering in a rapid fire staccato. I could feel the blood leaving my arms and legs as they gradually turned to stone. Even my brain was going numb. Dark fog flowed over me inside and out. I swallowed hard against the raw salty fire in my throat and tried to keep air moving into my lungs.

The cold was killing me, sucking away all of my heat. It was just a matter of time until my body temperature matched the icy ocean. The chilled water encased me and assaulted every part of me except my head and shoulders as I clutched the life preserver underneath me.

I lost track of time, but I knew it was running out. I couldn't feel my legs anymore and my arms hugged the life ring with the only strength I had left. It was all I could do to keep my head up. Even so my eyelids were getting heavy and I wanted to sleep. Every minute that went by my grip weakened. When I couldn't hold on any more it would be all over.

Then I noticed a dark shape. Something large was floating nearby. With my face just above the surface, I couldn't make out any details. It was two or three feet high and had a dull glimmer. My thoughts had become as lethargic and frozen as my muscles. Hypothermia can make a person loopy. I was thinking whale.

Terrific. Johnny Wainwright's brilliant career is cut short when he's eaten by one of Alaska's top tourist attractions.

But it wasn't a whale. It was a rubber raft. Jettisoned by the ferry's emergency system from the side of the main deck, it moved toward me in the dark. Propelled by the white foam of the wake it collided with my head and threatened to push me under.

With the last strength I had I threw one arm up to grab a rope along its top edge. Hanging there like a minnow frozen to the side of a bait bucket, a glimmer of hope sparked inside. If I could get out of the water I might extend my life a few precious minutes.

Hope is a funny thing. I clung to the idea of crew members on the ferry resuscitating my waterlogged corpse. But only if they found me in time. I couldn't hear the ferry's bell anymore.

Like a laptop on low battery, my less important functions were shutting down one by one. Memory and hearing must have been low on the list, not to mention common sense. I didn't know what I was doing out there anymore. I only knew I needed to get out of the water. I needed to, but I couldn't. I had no strength left.

I hung there by one arm like a drunken subway rider. My legs were dead weight and my jeans sagged in the water like bags of lead shot. I thought about kicking off the heavy pants and shoes but my muscles wouldn't move.

I was powerless to pull myself up. Like rats jumping ship, my strength and even my will to survive was draining away. My energy was gone.

Then something grabbed my hand. That made no sense to me. I hadn't heard a rescue boat approach. Hadn't seen anybody nearby either. Had I passed out and missed the search team's arrival? Then something pulled at me. Weakly at first, then with more force. It felt like hands pulling at me. Small hands.

I blinked to clear my eyes and looked around. Pressed into the side of the raft I stared out at the fog and darkness that stretched into the silent gloom. Still no rescue boat anywhere in sight and it was too foggy for the helicopter. I was lucid enough to know that. I knew I was losing my mind along with the rest of my senses, but this was too bizarre. The tugging at my numb arm continued.

Spurred by desperation and my last scrap of hope, I threw my other arm up and grabbed the rope. Pulling myself up about a foot I came face to face with Tambourine. He was on his knees inside the raft. His eyes were wide with fear and his whole face was vibrating. Cold sea water dripped from the red strands of hair on his forehead, and his lips were purple. His little hands were pulling frantically at my sleeve.

I tried to kick my feet but they wouldn't move. I was like a beached whale laying across a sea wall, half in and half out. Sea water sucked at my legs. It felt like quicksand threatening to pull me back in.

I couldn't let that happen. If I slipped back in the water I was a goner. I took a deep breath and struggled to speak.

"Pull, kid. Pull!"

I don't know how we did it, but he braced his little legs against the inside wall of the raft and grabbed the neck of my jacket. Hauling backward he pulled, and I grunted and heaved and clawed and finally got my chest above the side of the raft. Tambourine fell back in exhaustion as I rolled stiffly into the bottom of the raft retching salt water.

We lay there in silence for a long time, the raft rocking gently in the calm water. Small waves lapped against the rubber walls reminding me of early morning fishing trips from my youth. It would have been a fun outing if we weren't mere minutes from death. Cold and wet, hypothermia spared no one.

I lifted my head and looked around. The raft was at least ten feet across and round. It smelled like old tires and glue. I wanted to shout and cheer but my face was shaking too much to do either. We were out of the water but not out of the woods. The kid beside me was vibrating at high speed too.

I tried to speak, but nothing came out. I wanted to ask him what the hell he was doing out here. It was no place for a kid. Then I remembered my first sight of him on Taroka Island and his tortured stares. And the dog. And the way Charlie had pushed him around and Greta's cold indifference and her hypnotic blue eyes.

I pressed my hands against my face and managed to push myself up on one elbow to look at him. He had his knees pulled up to his chest and he was starting to shiver violently. He looked back at me for a moment, then his eyes drooped and he looked down.

When my mouth warmed slightly, I tried to speak. "Where's your mom?"

"She's n-n-not my m-m-mom."

"Okay, okay, we're freezing to death here, and you want to get technical? Where's Greta?"

He shook his head, shrugged and closed his eyes.

"Hey kid," somehow I pushed the words out. "If we're gonna be stuck out here together, you gotta have a different name. I can't call you ... Tambourine."

His eyes opened sluggishly and stared at me, but his teeth were chattering too hard to answer.

My whole body was shaking too. I thought my guts were coming loose. I wrapped my arms around my knees and held on tight trying to keep my parts from separating.

The kid's eyes started to roll back into his head.

"Hey!" I sat up, grabbed the front of his coat and shook him. I forgot all about Greta. Shoved her memory out of my head. She'd made her bed. The kid needed me now.

His lids barely opened and he looked at me through glazed eyes. His lips were shaking so hard I could hear his teeth rattling. I shook him again, harder this time.

"You gotta stay awake."

"W-what?"

"You gotta stay…"

"M-m-m-Mad Dog," he blurted through trembling lips.

"M-m-m-Mad Dog?" I repeated in confusion.

"Yeah, call me Mad Dog, you got a problem with that?"

My eyes widened in surprise. That was the most I'd ever heard him say. I wrapped my arms around him and pulled him tight against my chest. We shook and vibrated together for several seconds before I looked around and saw a pile of rubber laying behind him.

I don't know why I hadn't noticed it before. It was a thick rubberized survival suit lying in the bottom of the raft with us. It was reddish orange and it was buckled to the side of the raft next to some kind of a pouch. It looked like a pair of pajamas with the feet sewed in for a kid. A large kid. A huge Baby Huey kid. There were gloves and a hood attached as well.

I crawled over to it dragging my useless legs. Peering over the side of the raft I still couldn't see any lights anywhere. Only endless fog and flat ocean. I managed to unfasten the suit and looked it over. The tag inside said XXL. I tried to look through the other things attached nearby but my hands were shaking too hard. Every movement of my fingers sent waves of pain down my arms. I pressed my hands to my lips again and tried to warm them with my breath, but they looked and felt like a pair of useless meat hooks.

"Hey, Mad Dog. C'mere."

He didn't move so I reached over, grabbed his coat and dragged him to me. He weighed next to nothing. His little hands looked as cramped and frozen as mine. I pulled him in close and we blew on our hands together over and over until he could move his fingers. We needed to get warm before anything else.

"If I'm gonna rescue you, you gotta help. Can you get this zipper open?" I pushed the survival suit toward him and he went to work on it. Tears streamed down his face from the pain, but he kept at it forcing his fingers to function while I held onto the wobbly rubber suit trying to keep it still.

As he worked I looked out over the walls of the raft again. Way in the distance I spotted a beam of light. It was moving back and forth close to the surface of the water. It had to be a rescue boat like a Zodiac or maybe one of the lifeboats that had been hanging on the side of the ferry. It was so far away and moving so slowly I didn't know if we would still be alive if it ever found us.

The kid finally got the suit open, and I started fumbling with it trying to get my wooden legs inside. He watched me with his hands to his face trying to breathe them warm. Then he rolled onto his back and turned away.

"Hey, where you going, man? Help me here, Mad Dog. When I'm in, you're getting in with me." My lips were thick and shivering but he heard me.

"Both of us? In there?" he looked at me with a dubious stare.

"Hell, yeah, both of us. Fourteen clowns and a fat man could live in this thing."

I saw a faint twinkle in his eyes that on a normal day might have been a smile. He crawled to me then and helped me sit up and pull the suit up over my back. Getting my arms inside was easier than the legs since they still had a little movement in them.

"Okay, now the hood," I nodded at him and he flopped the top part of the suit over my face. "Now you, Mad Dog," I grunted at him. "You thought I was going to leave you out in the cold? Get in here."

He was hesitant at first, but I pulled at him with my Gumby arms and before long his skinny frame lay on top of me inside the suit.

"Now help me pull the zipper up. Maybe we can trap some heat in here."

Between the two of us we got the zipper up to the middle of my chest. He was shaking so hard I thought his boney little elbows and knees might perforate the rubber suit. Every part of me was trembling too. My insides ached from the strain.

I struggled to lift my head to look for the rescue boat, but I couldn't see it any more, and my strength gave out. I collapsed back to the floor of the raft. I held the kid in position with my arms and tried to seal the neck of the hood to trap in all the heat possible.

His head was nestled in my left armpit and he started to fight my efforts to cover him up. "I c-can't b-breathe," he stuttered in protest.

"We need to get warm, Mad Dog. You can breathe later."

He twisted his neck around and looked up at me. "Are w-we gonna d-die?"

I met his stare and wondered if he cared. "No, but why did you do that, man? Why did you go over the side?"

I felt him shrug, but he didn't answer. I didn't push it.

A couple of minutes went by. Then he shrugged again. "Gotta go somewhere."

I thought about that for a while. The silence around us deepened and the fog seemed to close in like a coffin lid.

I spoke up just to break the gloom. "We need to get warm, Mad Dog, so shut up now, will ya? You're talking me to death. Think warm thoughts."

It started to rain. Wet drops of cold misery splashed into my eyes. I grappled with the collar and pulled it closed over his face and held it as tight as I could around my own head. We were quiet for a while. My brain was a blur, trying to will up some heat from deep inside.

"Johnny," his muffled voice came up from the depths of the heavy rubber suit.

"What, Mad Dog? What's on your mind?"

"Don't fart," he said.

Then it was my turn to twinkle an eye. I couldn't do anything else. Absolutely every shred of energy I had was gone. I could feel the darkness coming down. My eyes wouldn't stay open.

Laying there holding the kid against me, I thought I was feeling warmth in my legs, but it didn't feel good. Little by little it built in intensity until I wanted to kick off the suit. My skin was on fire.

I'd heard about hypothermic victims being found dead in the snow. And naked. I fought the sensation and tried to send my mind somewhere else. All we could do now was wait.

I knew I was going to pass out. So, this is what it's like, I thought. Dying. Off to sleep. Forever. I didn't care anymore. Maybe the kid had a chance, but not me. I had nothing left.

With my last thoughts I tried to beam a message to the rescuers.

Hurry.

CHAPTER
36

My mind did go somewhere else. I sailed away to a place that was warm and quiet. The swaying motion of the raft on the ocean took me to a hammock gently rocking in a tropical breeze. A sunset sky spread out in front of me, and a sweating cool bottle stood nearby with a slice of lime poking from its spout. The scent of warm salty sand and lilacs wafted past on the air.

Laying on my back in a hammock in paradise. What could be better than that? Then I noticed a bare knee on either side of me. Matching knees actually. I wasn't alone. A tender hand was stroking my hair, smoothing my face, touching my eyes.

I wanted to turn to see who was there, but I didn't dare. If it was the wrong eyes, if it was those eyes, I knew I'd never wake up. Instead I tried to soak up all the pleasure I could while ignoring the nagging sense of danger. Like we do in life. But a distant buzzing from the far reaches of my mind wouldn't be ignored.

The sound grew louder. Then something landed on my face and started to walk across one eyelid. I wanted to swipe it away, but my arms wouldn't move. Like an evil blue fly it took off again with a loud buzz but relanded two seconds later. My eyes fluttered and fought but the strange droning grew louder and louder. It was relentless and came at me again and again.

Go away. Can't you leave a man in peace? This is no time for reality.

Then a cold blast of wet wind slapped my face and a thundering roar swept over me. My eyes snapped open to see an airplane flying away from us in the dark less than ten feet above the water. Streams of mist flowed over its wings and the prop blast rocked the big raft.

The kid woke up too and was struggling weakly against me. I strained to lift my head enough to see over the side of the raft and watched as the seaplane turned, slowed and flew back directly toward us. Double beamed landing lights in its wings glowed against the fog during the turn and burned into my eyes as it came back.

I heard the engine change pitch and it slowed and landed. Ocean water sprayed up and into the swirling propeller as the airplane's big floats cut into the surface of the calm sea. The pilot cut the engine and the big prop stuttered to a halt. The plane continued to drift toward us, clicking and snapping as its hot metal cooled. I watched as a dark stocky figure clambered out of the cockpit to stand on one float.

"Anybody still alive in there?" a voice called out. It was Willie.

I tried to speak, but no words would come out. When one of his floats bumped into us, Willie tied a rope and then stepped from the plane into the raft. The rubber floor under us convulsed and heaved with his weight like a honeymoon water bed. He fought for balance, his arms and legs bouncing wildly until he finally fell to his knees beside us.

The kid woke up then and fought to get his head clear of the survival suit. The mass of curly red hair thrashed in my face. He blinked and gawked at Willie, and Willie stared back in disbelief. His stubby white mustache twitched up and down as he sat back and gaped at us.

"What the hell ...?" He must have thought he was watching an alien hatch from my chest.

I finally got my mouth to work. "Hi, Willie. Anything dangerous to do around here?"

Willie was speechless, his eyes flicked back and forth between me and the kid trying to make sense of us.

"Oh, meet Mad Dog," I said realizing his confusion. Willie pulled off his cap and rubbed his head and eyes with both hands. When he got his hat back on and rearranged again, he quit staring, closed his mouth and got down to business.

"Uh, say fellas, I hate to interrupt your little picnic out here, but I need to get this plane back before the owner finds it missing. Let's go, okay?"

I couldn't move, but the kid started scrambling to get free of the suit. Willie realized then that I needed help. He hauled on the big zipper and pulled my arms and legs free.

He stood up unsteadily and helped the kid climb up into the airplane. When he was bundled in a blanket and belted into a seat, Willie came back for me. He pulled me to a sitting position in the bottom of the raft and looked into my face.

"Here, take some of this." He held a metal flask to my lips. The liquid burned its way down my throat. I would have thrown it back up in his face if I'd had any strength. Licking the bitter liquor off my lips, I choked and spit.

"Damn, Willie, that's foul. What are you doing out here anyway? Where's the ferry?"

"Aw, they had engine problems or something. I've been monitoring the Coast Guard radio transmissions. When I heard what happened and the chopper couldn't get under the fog, I thought I'd come out and take a look."

"Holy crap, man, you are crazy." The liquor was starting to glow warm in my belly.

"C'mon, get in the plane. It's past my bedtime."

I struggled to get up. As he helped me to the float for a short climb up a small ladder into the plane, I stopped and looked around. Darkness and thick fog still spread in all directions.

"What's the matter? Keep going," he grunted pushing at me.

I pulled away from him. "I don't know about this. I'm not sure you're a safe pilot."

He threw his head back in a silent laugh and pushed me toward the ladder. I managed to get into the plane and checked on the kid. He was wrapped in a blanket staring into space.

I ruffled his hair. "Hey Mad Dog! Whattaya know? We're not dead."

He gave me a sad smile and laid his head on my leg when I sat down beside him. I combed red hair out of his eyes with my fingers and leaned over to whisper.

"Hey, Mad Dog, whatever happens, just remember one thing. Okay?"

"What?"

"You saved our butts out there, and I'll never forget it."

Willie fired up the engine and pointed us for Seward.

CHAPTER
37

I must have slept for twelve hours. I wasn't keeping track. When I finally woke up I lay there for a while until I realized I didn't know where I was.

Under several blankets and a sleeping bag I was warm and safe but everything I had ached. The bitter taste of panic rose in the back of my throat again when I felt the floor under me moving. It was like I was still in the raft. I fought my way out from under the pile of blankets and sat up. The walls of the little room around me were swaying slightly. I took some deep breaths and planted my feet more firmly on the floor.

That helped. The floors and the walls settled back into their proper positions, and I realized I was on the living room couch in Willie's trailer. At the end of a dirt road on the outskirts of Seward, his modest home sat on the bank of Salmon Creek. I could see blue sky through the dirty window.

I stood up slowly and tried to remember how I got there. Nothing came to mind. I shuddered and looked down the hall, but I could tell I was alone. Wrapping a blanket around myself and trying to shake off creepy thoughts, I walked to the bathroom and after that out to the front door. When I opened it the rusty hinges creaked, but fresh air swept in and so did the sound of the creek.

I stuck my head outside to see the sun glinting off the peak of Mount Alice. My watch was gone, but I guessed it was late afternoon. A fresh dusting of powder on the mountain's high ridges was just starting to glow alpine pink. I leaned against the door post and drew in deep breaths of crisp air scented with alders and damp earth.

My knees started to tremble as memories of the night before began to seep back in. I sat down on the top step and wrapped the blanket tighter around my knees and neck. Through the thick stand of aspen lining the creek just forty yards away I could see the water rushing by where the final stragglers of silver salmon were still making their way upstream to spawn. The leaves were turning yellow and orange. Seagulls swooped in from time to time to grab a snack.

The thought of fish in the water sent a chill down my spine. Anything under water was the last thing I wanted to think about. Gradually I remembered the raft and Willie's arrival with the seaplane. I grimaced at the image and remembered the sound of gunshots on the ferry's bridge. I closed my eyes trying to erase the memory of blood on the vehicle deck and Greta's red lipstick. And of dead troopers, the huge helicopter flashing in the fog and cold water.

I wanted to wipe my brain clean, but I knew that every time I saw blue skies, blue water or blue ice, Greta's eyes would come back to haunt me. Had it all just been a terrible dream? None of it made any sense.

I pulled the blanket tighter around my shoulders, closed my eyes and told myself I didn't care. I leaned my head against the door post and listened to the gurgle of the creek. The quiet rustle of leaves in the breeze above me carried me to a better place, and I almost didn't hear the car pull up and stop in front of me.

It was Brandy driving Willie's car. She got out and walked toward me carrying an armload of my clothes fresh out of the dryer. She set them down on the step beside me and brushed the hair off my forehead.

"You alive?" She stared into my face with a frown.

"I think so," I said looking into the smoky green of her eyes. The touch of her hand gave me a warm thrill. I was so thankful that her eyes weren't blue.

"You okay to go into town?"

"I guess so. Why? What's up? Did they find Greta?"

I was instantly sorry I'd asked but I couldn't pull the words back into my mouth. She turned like she might drive away but then she stopped and turned back toward me.

"No," she finally mumbled, then paused. "Johnny, can I ask you something in all seriousness?"

I gulped. "I, I guess so."

"What was going on between you and her?"

I knew that question had to come. There was no avoiding it.

I sat back and sighed. "I don't know exactly how to explain it."

"Try," she said.

I thought for a minute to collect my thoughts. "I guess the way she looked at me and the way she talked to me and touched me ... it got to me. The whole cover girl, beautiful people thing, and she was coming onto me. I know now it was all a con."

"You were thinking with the wrong head?" she asked softly.

I nodded. "I guess so. I don't really know what I was thinking," I said. "I've been lost for a while."

She put her hand on the side of my head and just left it there cupping my ear. Staring at her shoes and saying nothing. I loved her then. Not for what she said or what she did so much. More for what she didn't say.

She didn't say a word about how Greta had manipulated me. Using her looks and my loneliness to play me like a carp hooked on a line.

And she didn't make me look at her either. She spared me the agony of having to look her in the eye before I was ready. She knew when to let a weasel off the hook.

I turned my head and gave her hand a quick kiss, then struggled to collect myself and turned away to pull on the warm clothes.

"Some people want to see you," she said.

"Am I in trouble?" I felt a twinge of dread as more memories came back like leftovers moldering in the back of the fridge.

"No, you're in the clear with all that."

My chest swelled with a sigh. "Where's Willie?"

"It's after five, you know where he is."

"Right," I nodded and smiled. The man had a deadline. It was called Happy Hour.

I looked at her, but she turned toward the creek. I stepped inside and finished pulling on the clothes. They were still warm from the dryer and felt great. I glanced back at her as she went to wait in the car.

When I walked outside Brandy started the engine as soon as she saw me and before long we were rolling down the highway for the ten minute drive to the bar. We passed the airport on our left. I could see the Cessna parked in front of my office right where it was supposed to be. The wings were tied down and everything looked normal.

"How did that happen?" I pointed in surprise.

"Phil went out and got it this morning. He understood you were ... indisposed. The fog was finally gone. He said it was clear as a bell all the way over and back."

After a long silence my curiosity wouldn't stay quiet. "So, what happens to those people?" I asked her as we drove.

"Well, that guy, Charlie, he's in big trouble, of course. Murder, hijacking, destruction of private property, resisting arrest, conspiracy, you name it. He'll never see the light of day again."

I nodded and looked out to see a scraggly hitchhiker on the other side of the road. He was skinny and bearded and loaded down with a full backpack. He looked like he'd been living in the same clothes for months. He held a ragged cardboard sign that read "Anywhere south." He reminded me of a smaller version of Charlie.

"What about the kid?"

"Social Services has him. There's a grandma from somewhere coming for him."

I looked out the window again and felt an ache grip my stomach. What would happen to him? I wondered. What kind of future would the little guy have? I shook my head remembering.

Then I noticed how quiet Brandy was. She'd answered my questions but offered nothing more. I looked at her from the corner of my eye. She was staring straight ahead. Suddenly aware of my stare, she lifted her right hand off the wheel and tucked a lock of brunette hair behind her ear.

"Something wrong?" I finally worked up the nerve to ask.

"Nope," she said much too quickly.

Uh oh. The deadly Nope response.

I braced myself and waited. It didn't take long. Suddenly she braked hard and pulled the car to the side of the road. We were beside the lagoon across from the Breeze Motel. There wasn't a turnout there, but she didn't care.

She shut off the engine and turned toward me. "Johnny, what the hell were you thinking, going in the water like that?" Her voice was loud and it almost cracked. I could see her chin shaking while she waited for me to answer.

"Uh, I don't know. It was just automatic." I couldn't meet her eyes. "That kid ..."

She interrupted me. "When I saw the kid go over the railing, my heart almost stopped. And then when I saw you go after him... I was sure I'd never see you again."

I reached for her hand, but she pulled away. I sucked in a breath and tried to stay calm. She wasn't through. Her lips were trembling and a tear slid down each cheek. She shook her head and wiped at her face with the back of her hand.

"That was either the bravest thing or the most idiotic damn thing I have ever seen in my life." She spit out the words.

"I know." I didn't know what else to say. She was right, of course. I'd taken chances without much thought. It was only luck that had pulled me through. I was going to have to think about that sometime. Not now, but sometime.

I stared out across the lagoon. A seagull and a bald eagle took turns swooping low over the water to eyeball a fish swirling just below the surface. Ahead of the car a weather beaten raven stood over a salmon carcass on the edge of the road, picking at it between passing cars.

"I'm sorry I scared you," I finally said quietly.

Brandy wiped her cheeks again and reached over to take my hand.

"And now you're going to buy me a drink."

"Yes, m'am."

"Several drinks."

"Sounds good to me."

When we walked into the Yukon Bar, the place was about half full. Television screens in the corners flashed an odd light across the room. A football game was on with the volume muted, but no one was watching. A low drum beat shook the floor under our feet followed by a soulful saxophone solo echoing around the walls.

The Revenue Corner was full, but I didn't see any familiar faces and no one looked our way. Then I heard a chorus of laughs and glasses clinking from across the room.

I moved further into the bar and spotted Rainey and Willie drinking with a group of guys in Coast Guard uniforms. Coasties. She waved us over, but Brandy veered off and headed for the restroom.

"Well, if it isn't the Seward Splash!" Rainey said, raising her voice over the stereo and waving at the bartender for drinks.

"Very funny," I mumbled, smiling shyly at the group. "Why aren't you with the ferry?"

"They gave me a couple days off to decompress," she grinned.

She came closer and spoke into my ear. "So, how goes it with you and the lovely Learjet pilot?"

I pulled back and looked at Rainey for a moment. Why would she ask me that question when she probably knew the answer better than I did? She was a gossip junkie. Like some guys are news junkies. Seward's a small town and sometimes gossip's the only news that matters.

So I filled her in with a complete run down, bush pilot style. "We're fine."

She glared at me. "Yeah, right. Liar." She sipped her drink through a tiny red straw. I watched her lick her lips and remembered the feel of them against my ear.

"Well, she thinks I'm an idiot."

Rainey laughed, her eyes sparkling in the television light. "She's right, of course." She winked at me and nodded at Willie who had come over.

It was well after five and Willie was well on his way. His eyes sparkled at me and his cheeks were bright red.

"Hey, did they ever find Greta?" I asked.

"Who? That little blond? She's fish food by now."

My eyes dropped to the floor. Willie noticed.

"No, they didn't find her and they searched all day. Last I heard they were going to check the ferry again. Did you ever see her go over the side?"

"No. Did anyone else?"

He shook his head. "Didn't I tell you not to take that flight in the first place? Didn't I tell you everything was going to go to shit out there? When are you going to start listening to me?"

"Wait a minute. You didn't tell me nothing about that flight. You just said take a gun and watch out for bears."

"And you didn't do either one, did ya, dumbass?" he snorted.

I shook my head and looked for the bartender. I was thirsty and hunger pangs were cramping my gut. A pretty blond tourist across the bar laughed at something, her voice trilling high off the crystal wine glasses hanging upside down above the bar.

Hank, the bartender, walked up and handed us cold beers. He was a big guy that always greeted us by our first names. We didn't even have to order. He knew what we wanted. Willie loved that about Hank.

Willie pointed at my bottle. "You sure you want to drink that? Your cell phone might ring any minute."

My hand went to the zippered pocket where I carried the phone. It was still there, but when I flipped it open the screen was only half visible and soaked with water. Damn phones anyway. Just holding it reminded me of the strange forces swirling out there, conspiring before connecting.

"I think I'll take the night off," I said, took a long pull on the bottle and tossed the phone in a trash can nearby. The cold brew felt like a million bucks sliding down my throat that was still raw from swallowing too much sea water. Willie tilted his with me.

Brandy rejoined us and she and Rainey hugged. I rolled my eyes as they looked at me and laughed.

Willie's phone rang, and he moved away from the group straining to hear. Rainey pointed me toward a huge pizza box from Christo's down the street. The smell of tangy tomato sauce and garlic assaulted my nostrils and I wasted no time wrestling a huge slice into my mouth. Grinning at Brandy and Rainey I danced the happy tongue dance with the hot cheese and closed my eyes at the waterfall of flavors cascading down my throat.

The bartender came back and I leaned toward him and spoke into his ear.

"Hey, Hank, put Willie's beers on my tab tonight, okay?"

Then I remembered my bank account. The one where the fees were about to surpass the balance.

Willie had come back over and overheard. Slamming his empty down with a big grin, he announced, "I'm ready, my friend."

"But only for the cheapest domestic stuff," I said to Hank. He laughed and nodded.

I moved over to the counter by myself and looked outside. Lights were starting to come on along the street. The sky had turned a deep blue and the final rays of the setting sun streaked golden and warm through the valley west of town.

Brandy came over and sat beside me. She stared out the window with me for a few minutes not saying a word. Our arms were touching and words didn't seem necessary.

Then she leaned over, wrapped one hand in mine and spoke into my ear. I inhaled the faint scent of strawberry shampoo.

"So you're Johnny Wainwright, right?"

I looked at her in surprise.

"Let's go," she said.

I moved to get up, my knees unsteady. "Where to?"

"Who knows?" she giggled and pulled me behind her out the door.

I don't think I'll ever learn.